# STEP BY BLOODY STEP™

## A WORDLESS FANTASY

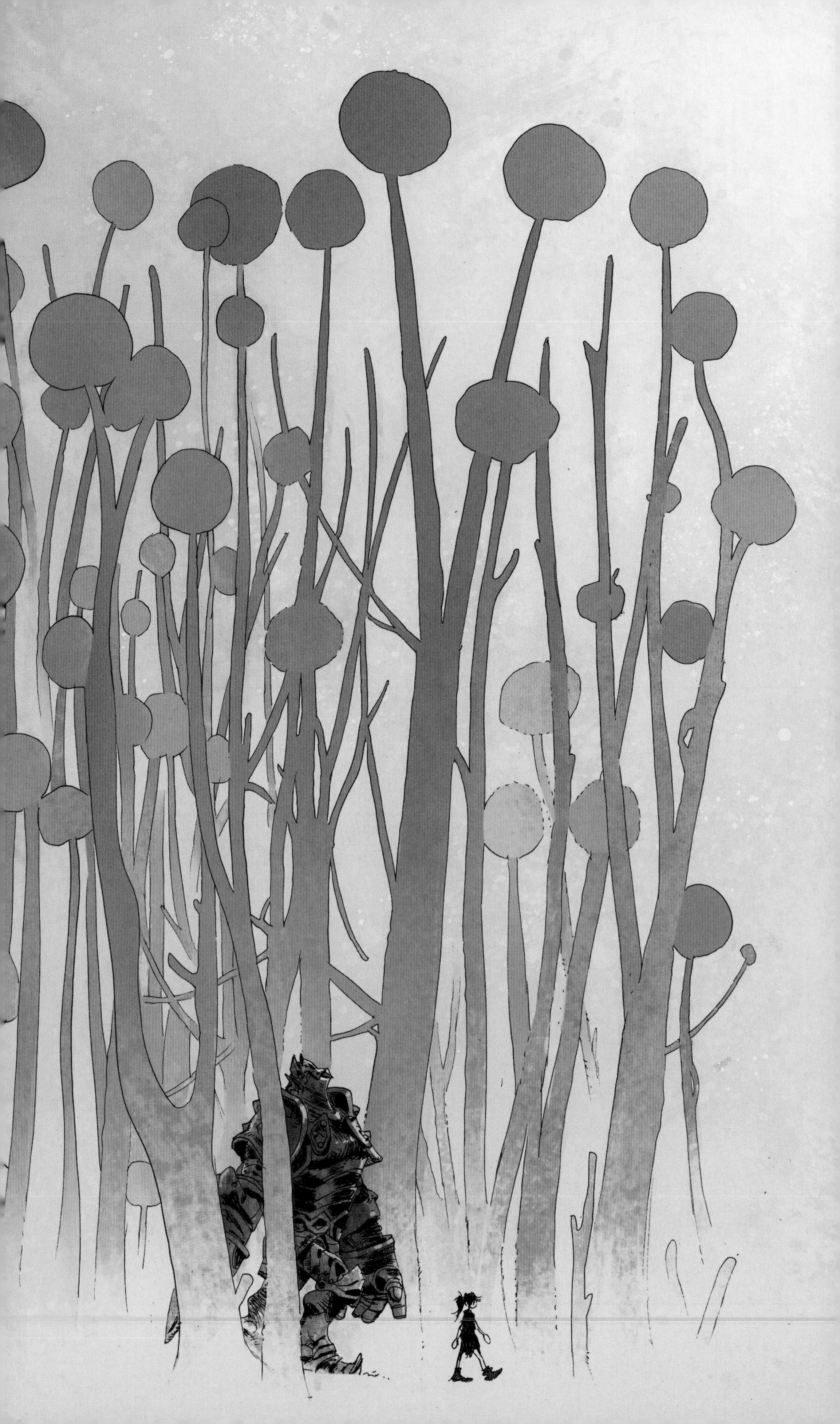

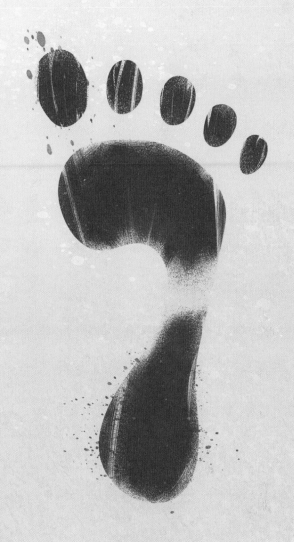

**STORY** Si Spurrier

**ART** Matías Bergara

**COLORS** Matheus Lopes

**GRAPHIC DESIGN** Emma Price

**GLYPHOLOGY** Jim Campbell

**IMAGE COMICS, INC.** • **Robert Kirkman:** Chief Operating Officer • **Erik Larsen:** Chief Financial Officer • **Todd McFarlane:** President • **Marc Silvestri:** Chief Executive Officer • **Jim Valentino:** Vice President • **Eric Stephenson:** Publisher / Chief Creative Officer • **Nicole Lapalme:** Vice President of Finance • **Leanna Caunter:** Accounting Analyst • **Sue Korpela:** Accounting & HR Manager • **Matt Parkinson:** Vice President of Sales & Publishing Planning • **Lorelei Bunjes:** Vice President of Digital Strategy • **Dirk Wood:** Vice President of International Sales & Licensing • **Alex Cox:** Director of Direct Market Sales • **Chloe Ramos:** Book Market & Library Sales Manager • **Emilio Bautista:** Digital Sales Coordinator • **Jon Schlaffman:** Specialty Sales Coordinator • **Kat Salazar:** Vice President of PR & Marketing • **Deanna Phelps:** Marketing Design Manager • **Drew Fitzgerald:** Marketing Content Associate • **Heather Doornink:** Vice President of Production • **Drew Gill:** Art Director • **Hilary DiLoreto:** Print Manager • **Tricia Ramos:** Traffic Manager • **Melissa Gifford:** Content Manager • **Erika Schnatz:** Senior Production Artist • **Ryan Brewer:** Production Artist • **IMAGECOMICS.COM**

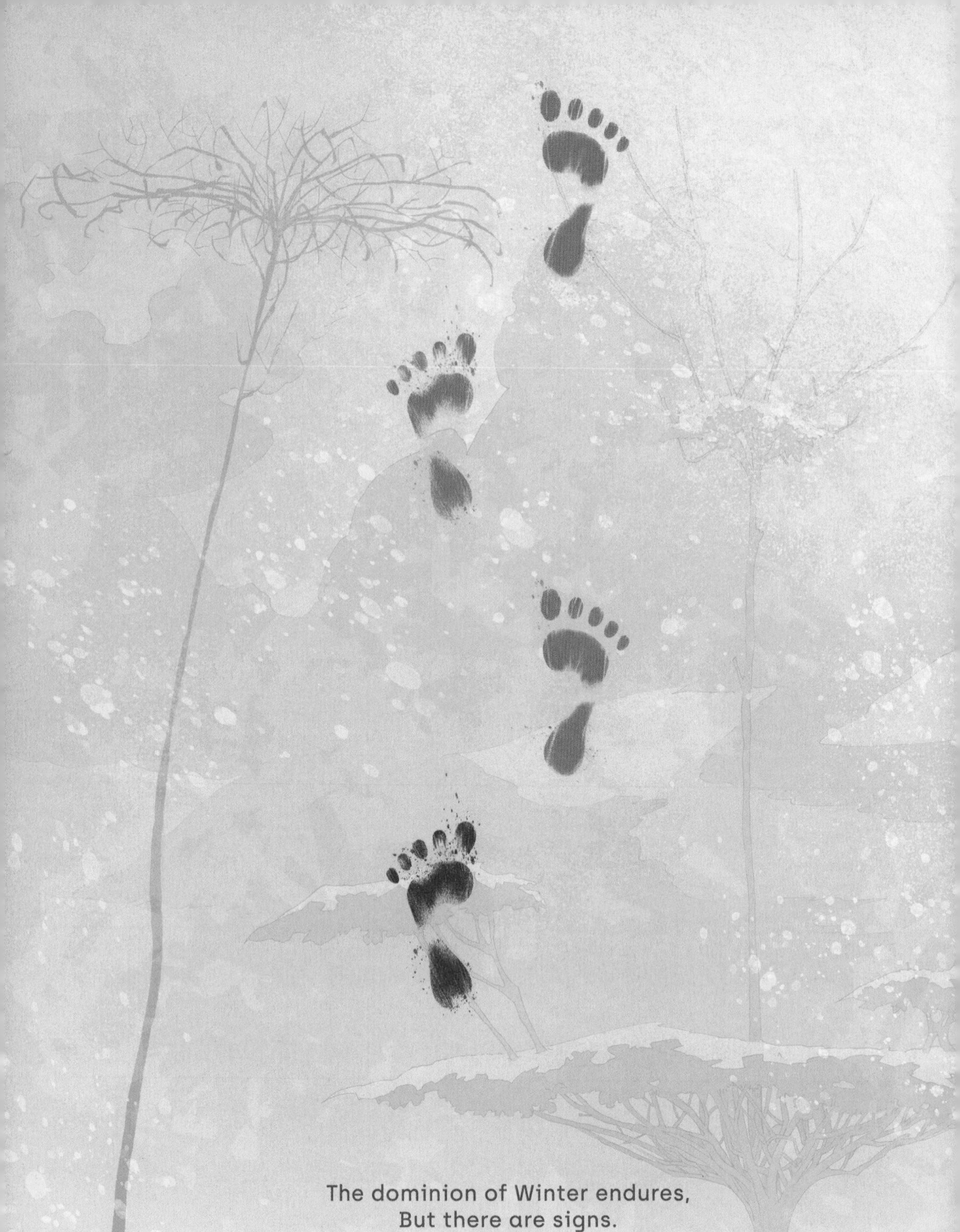

The dominion of Winter endures,
But there are signs.

A particle of pollen in the teeth of the blizzard.
The sun's ghost, bashful behind thinning clouds.
A distant warmth in the West.

Faint.
Faint promises of Spring.
But promises still.

A girl wakes.

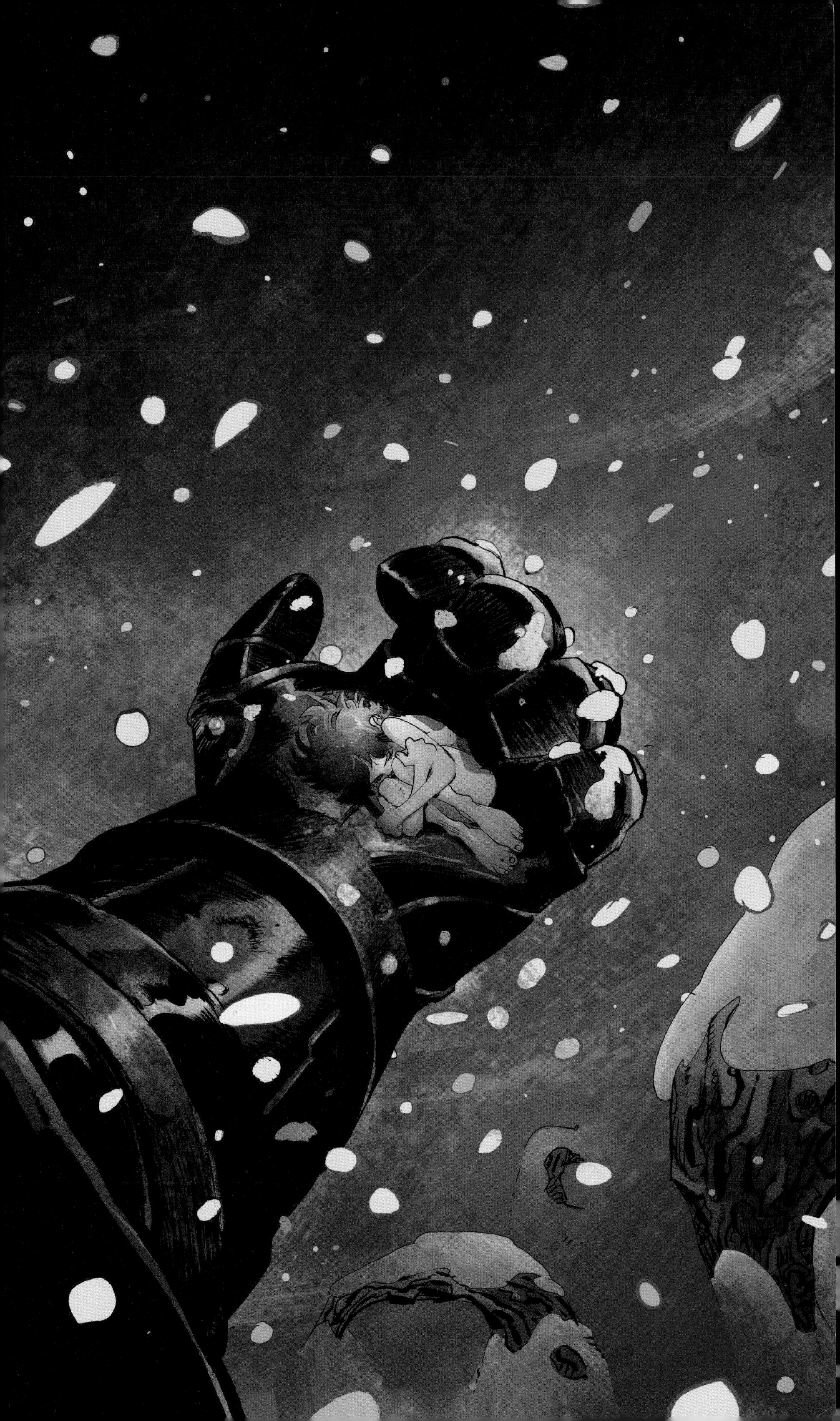

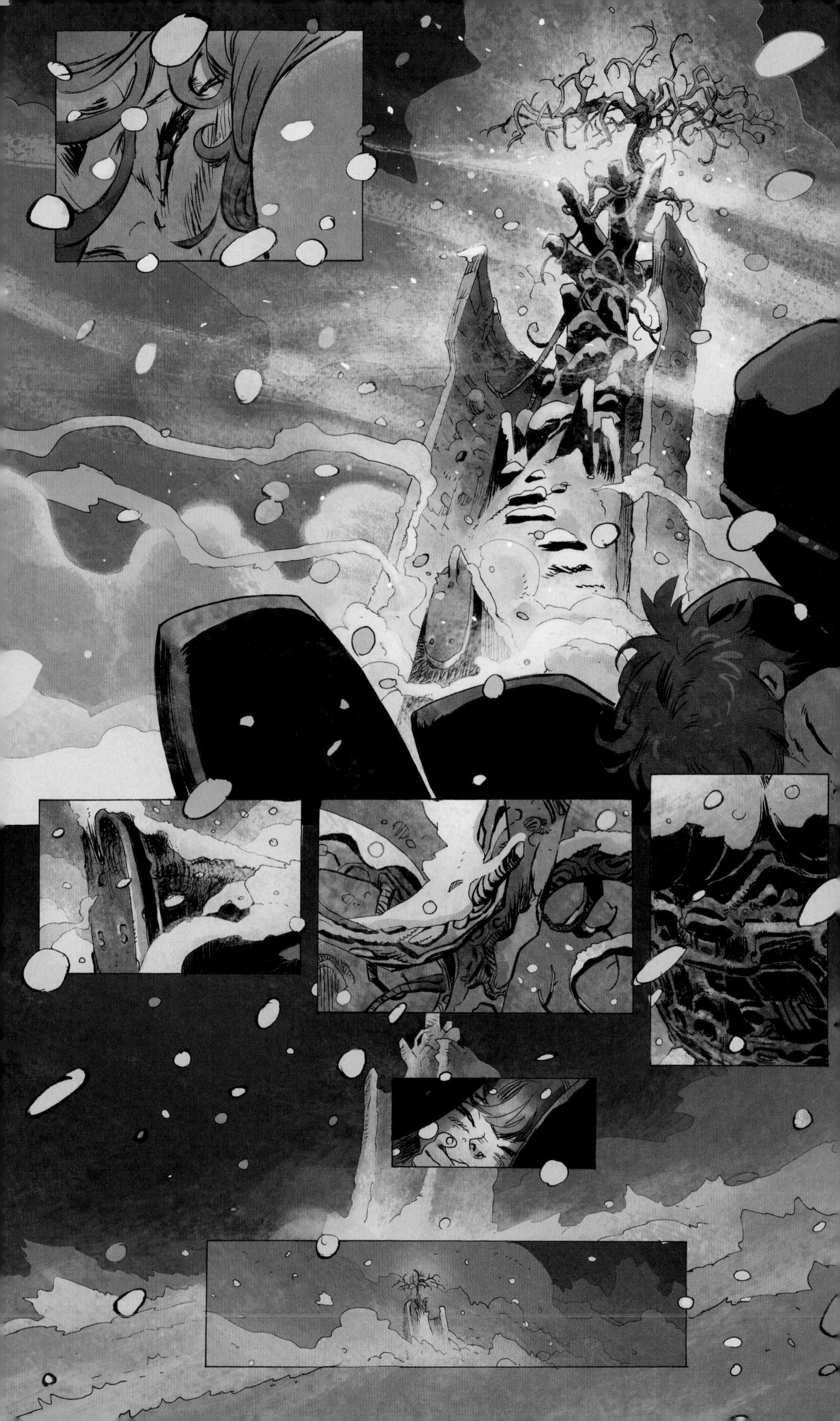

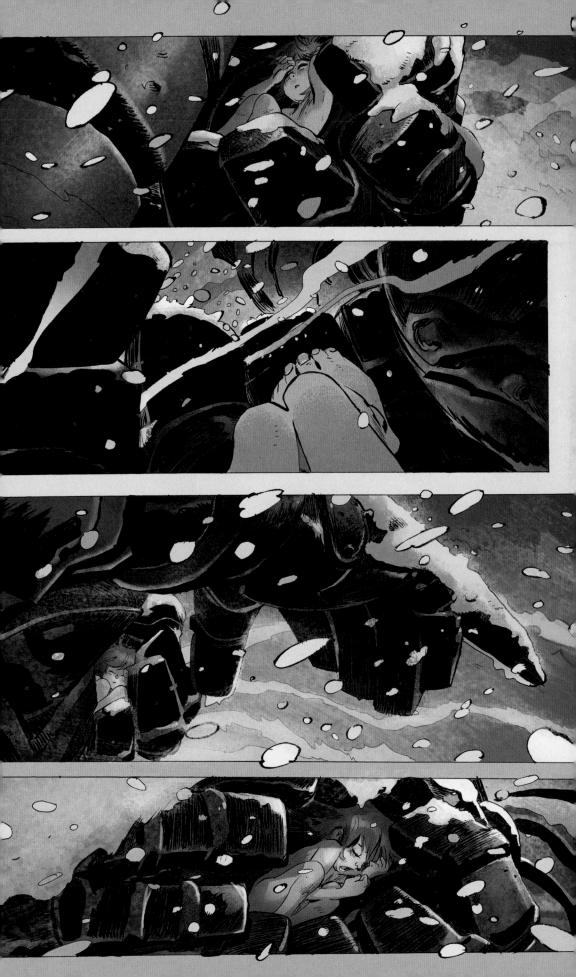

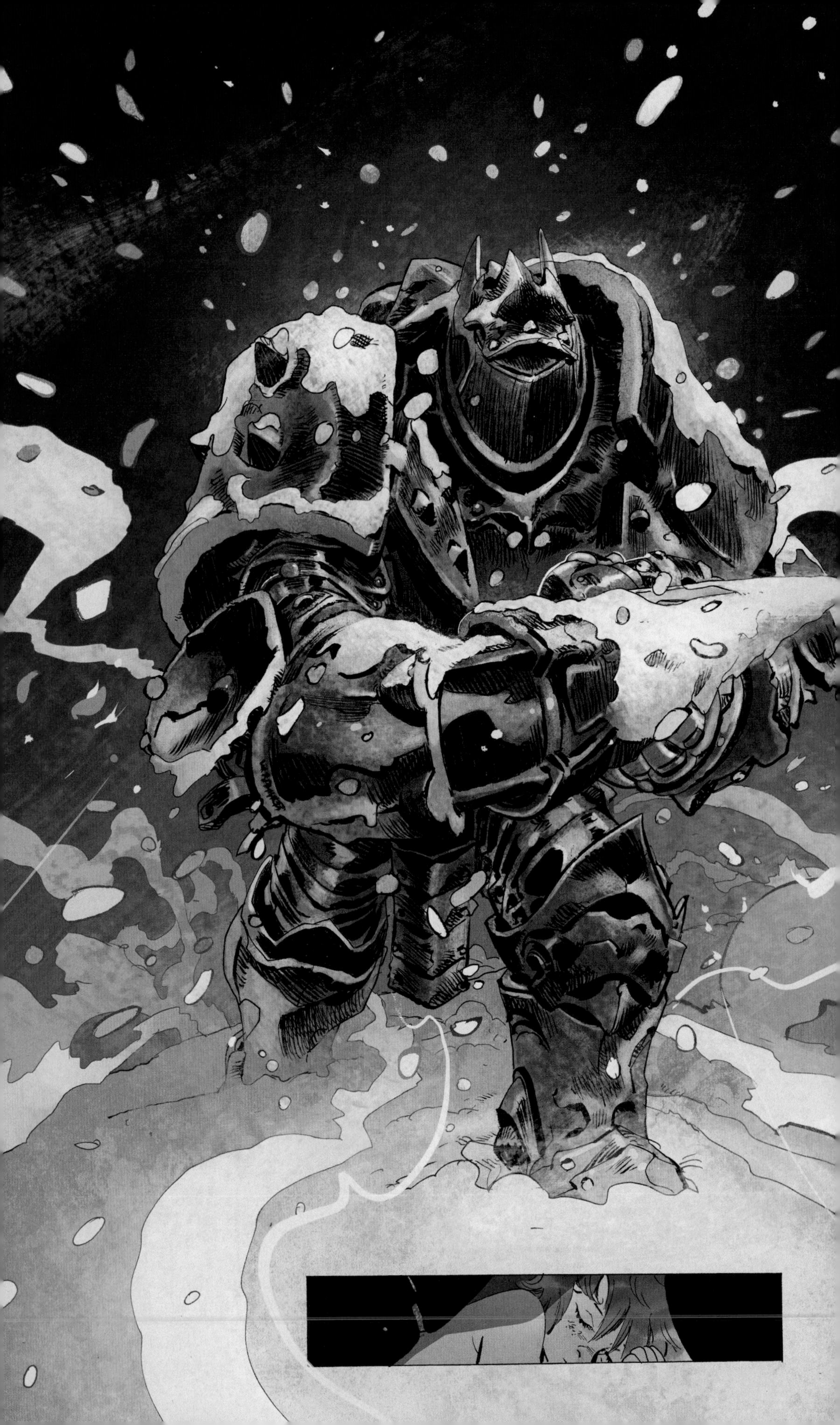

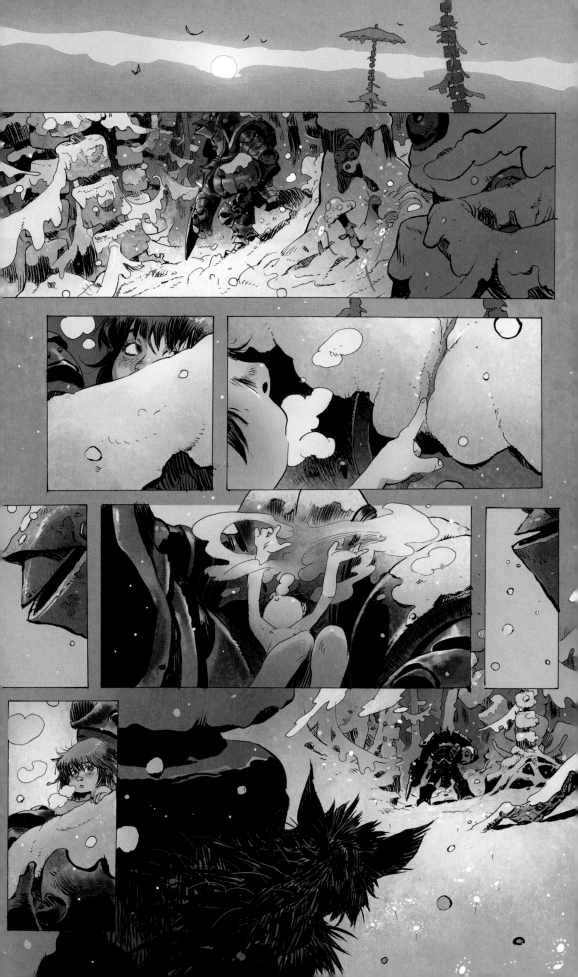

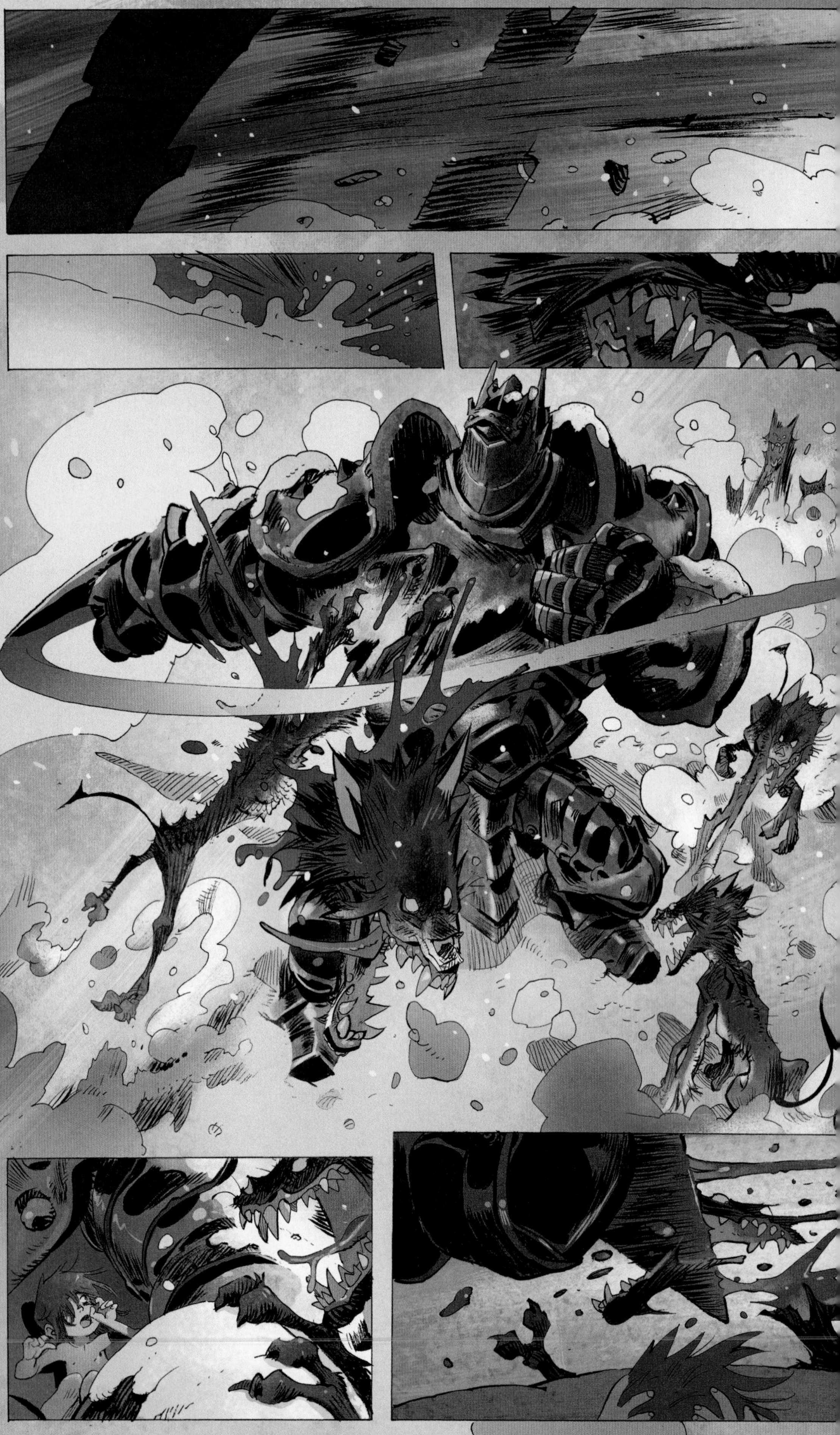

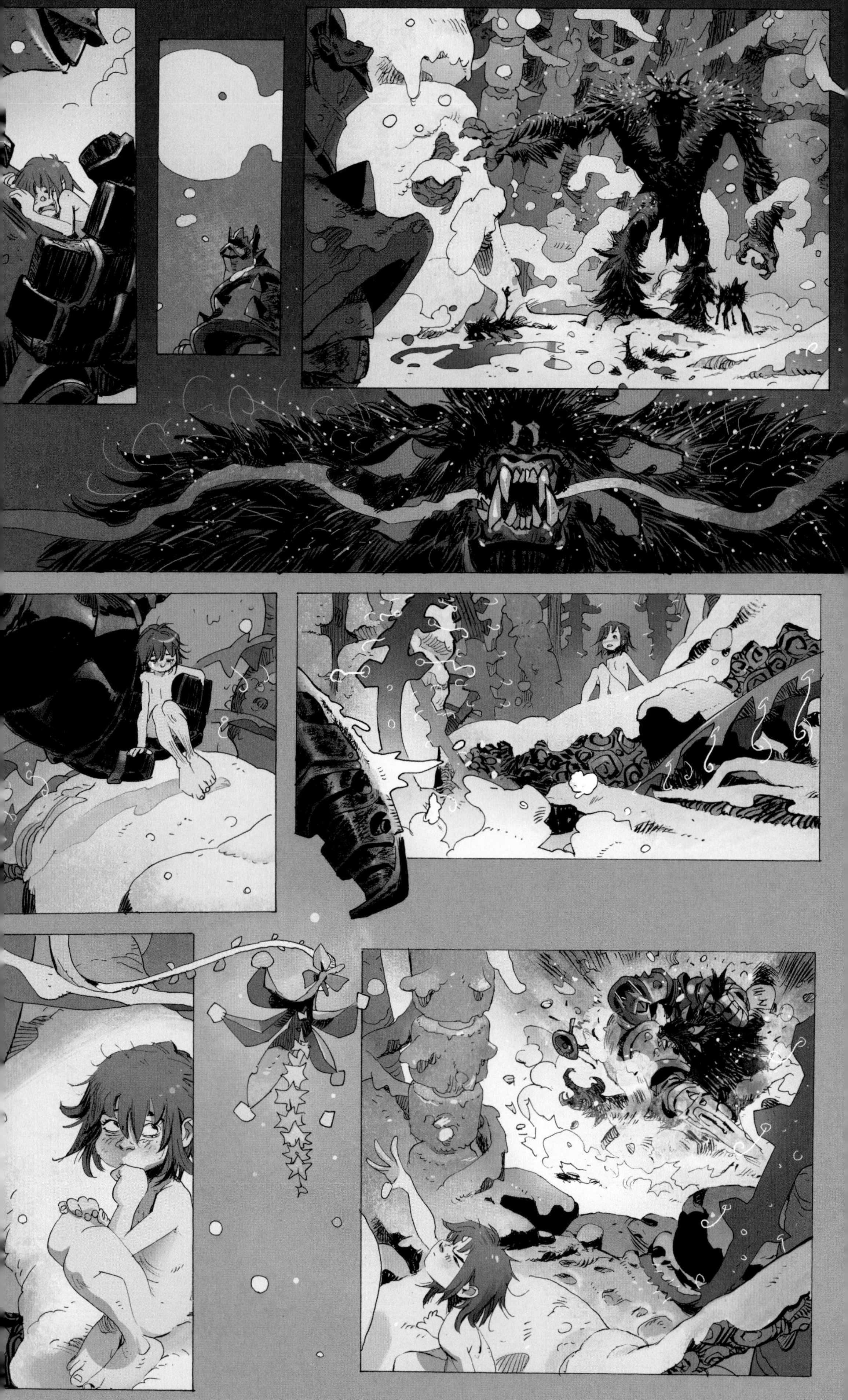

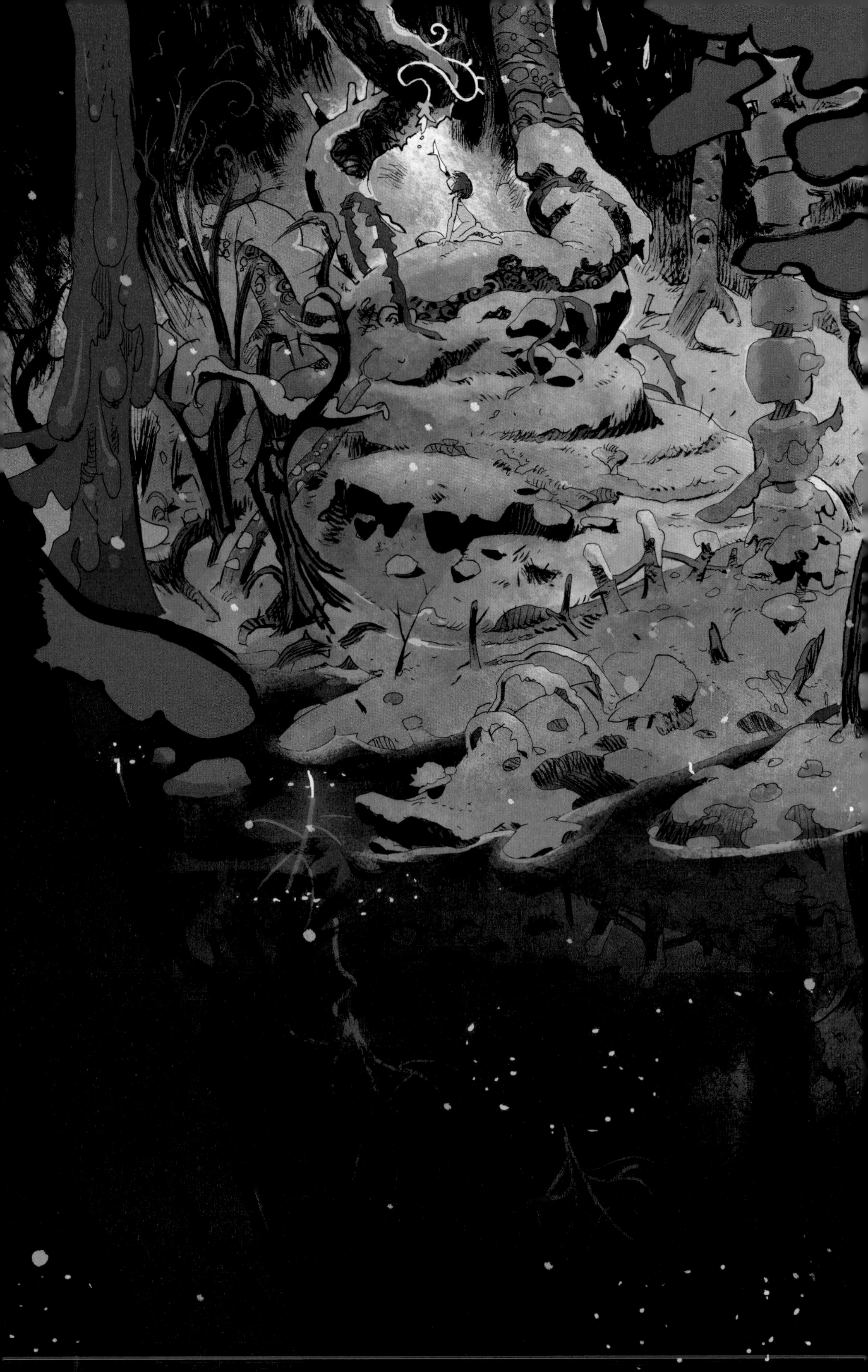

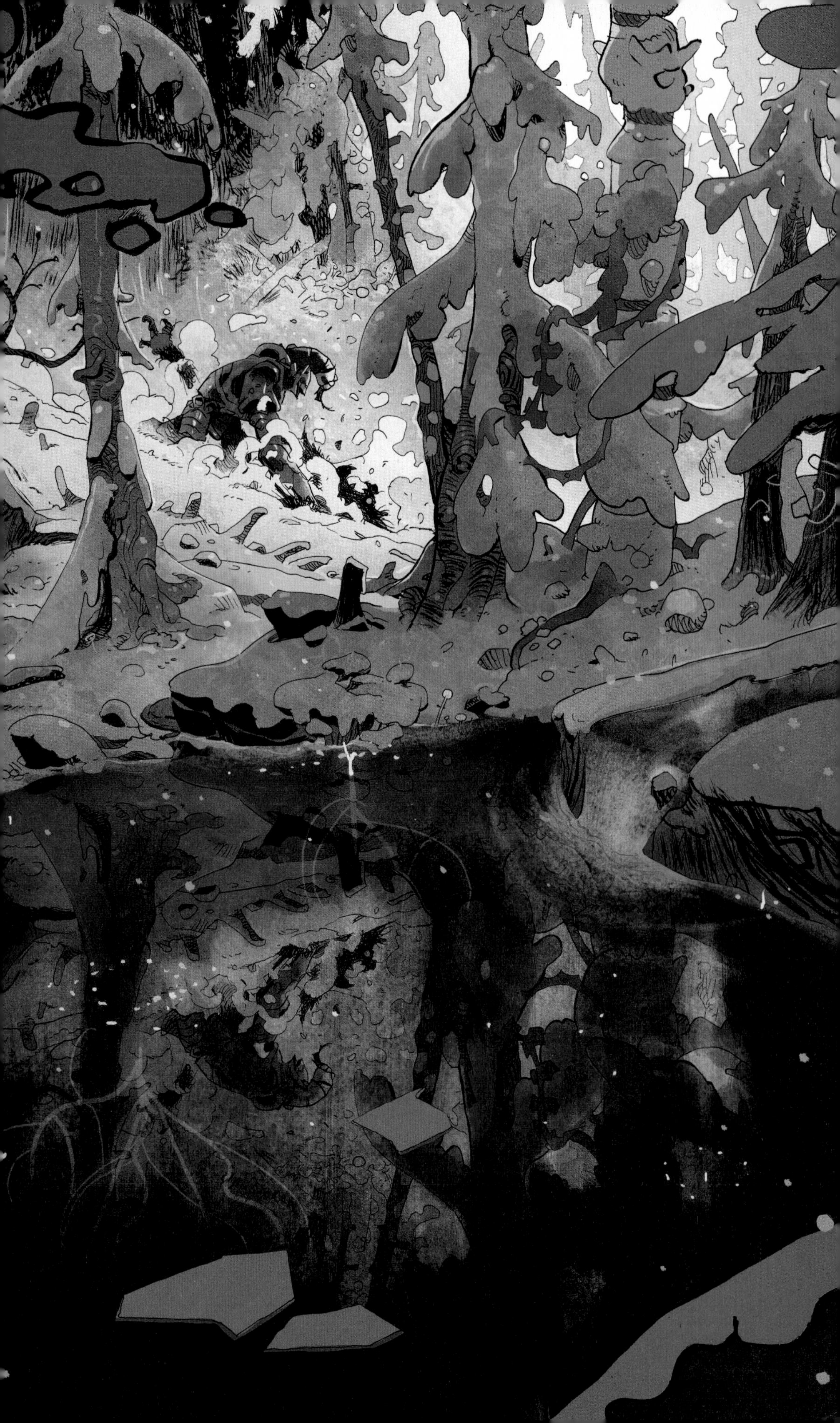

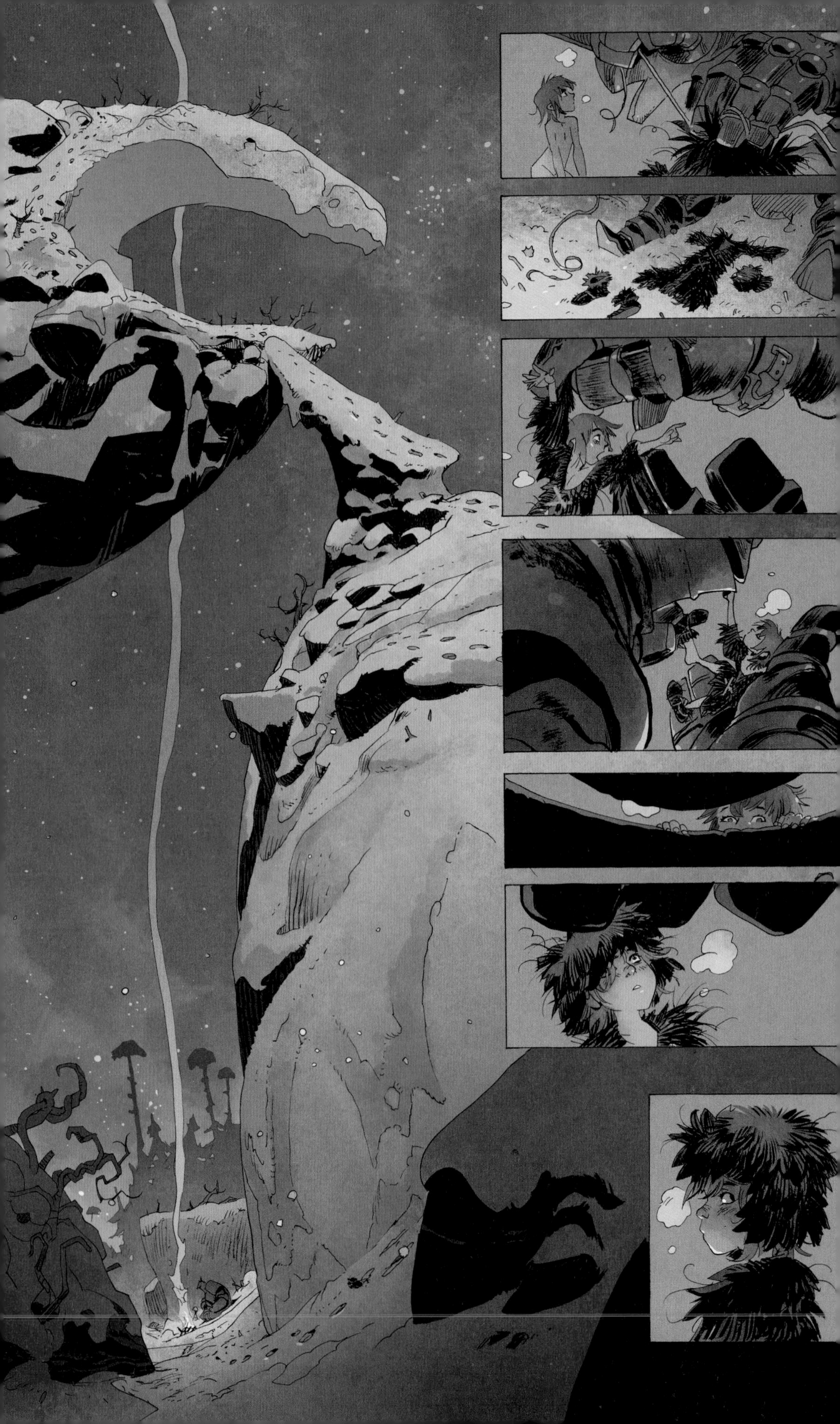

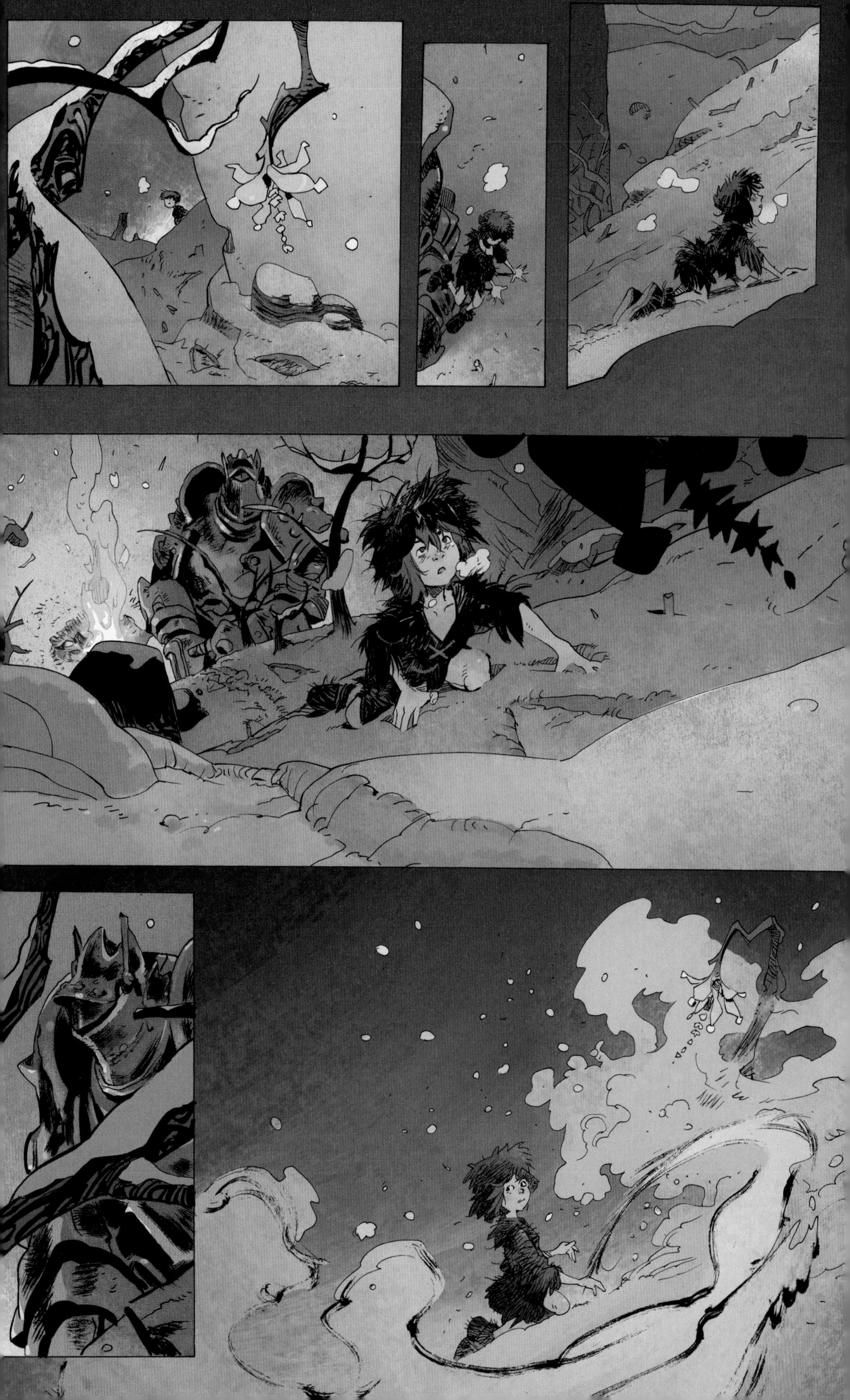

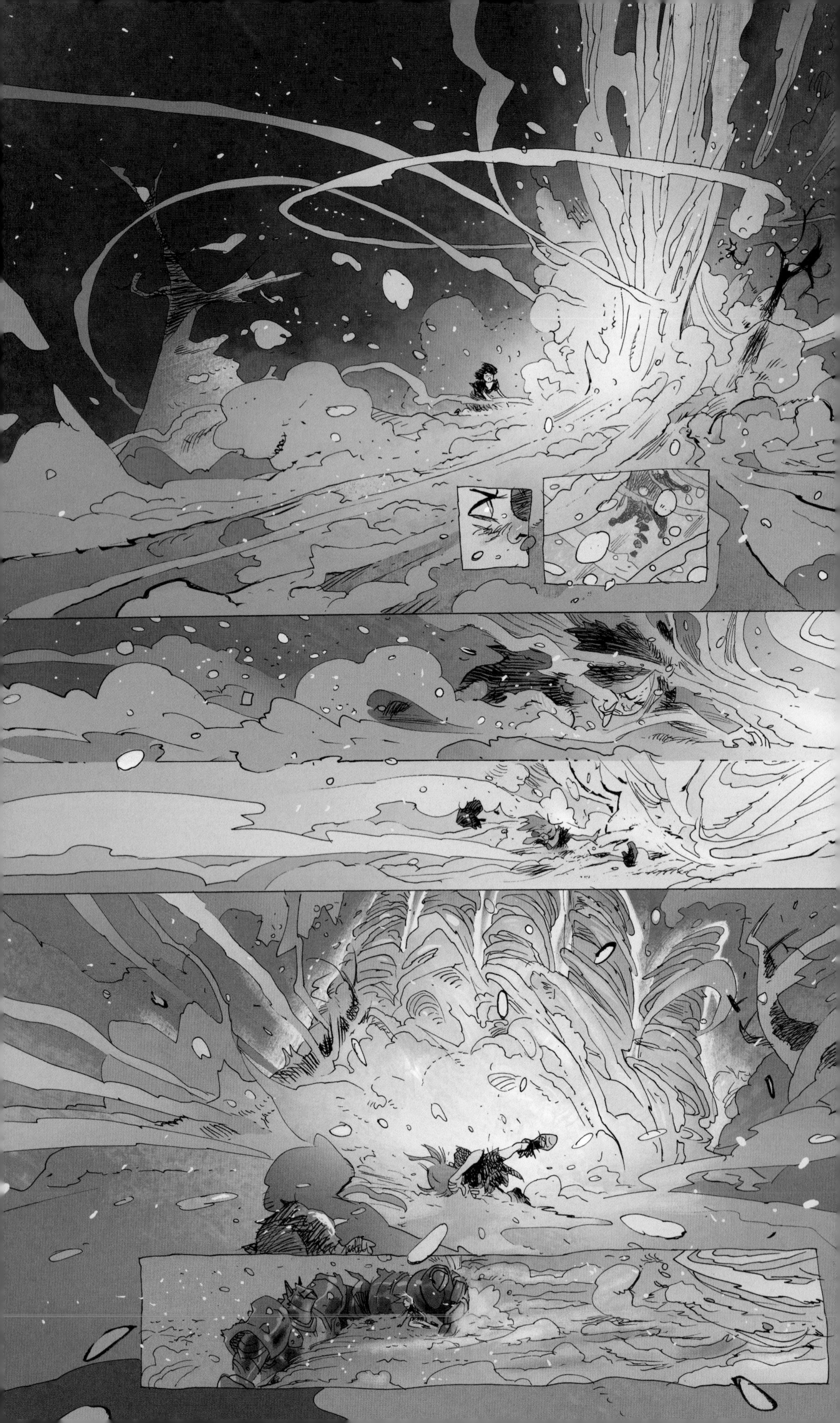

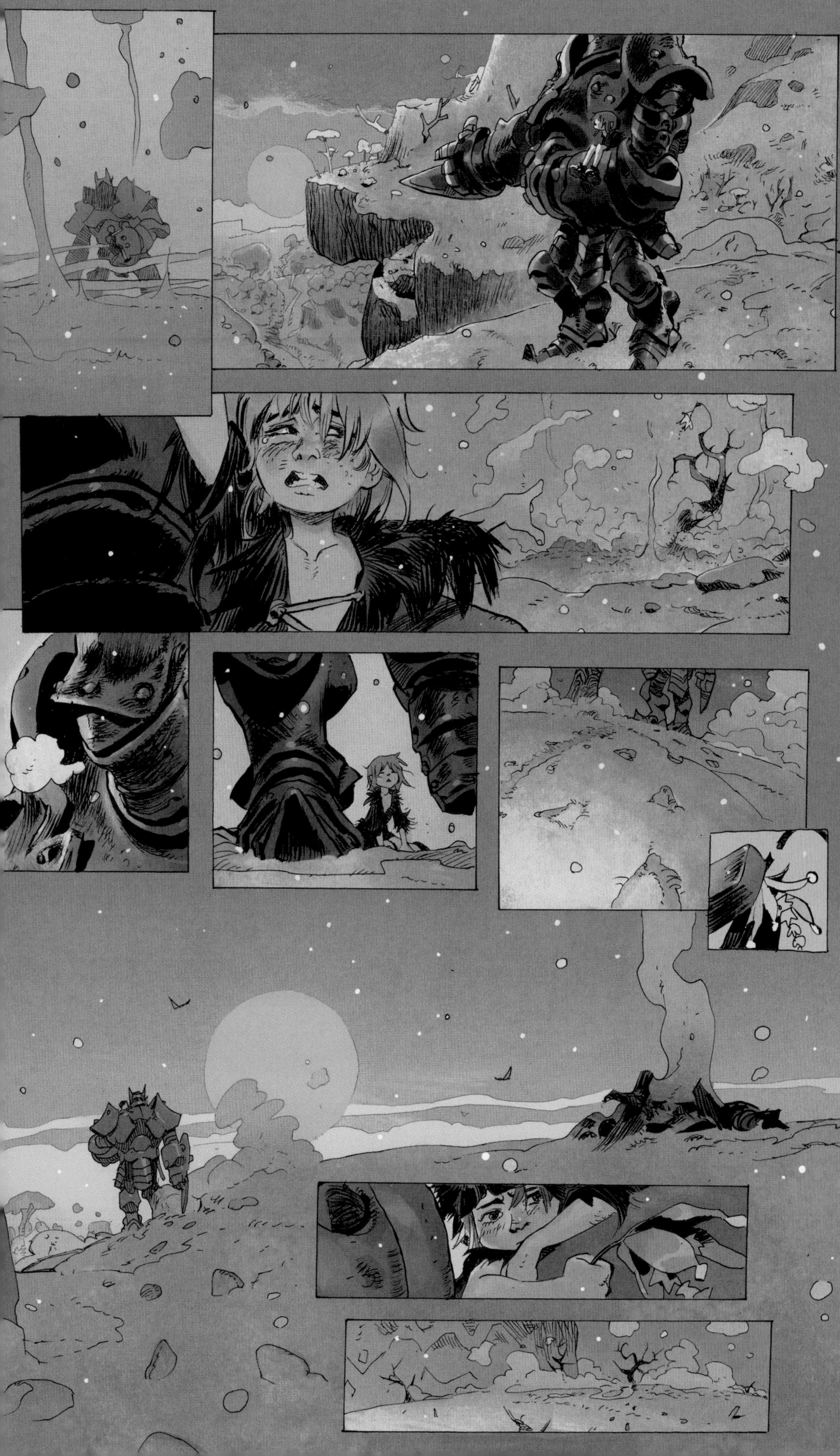

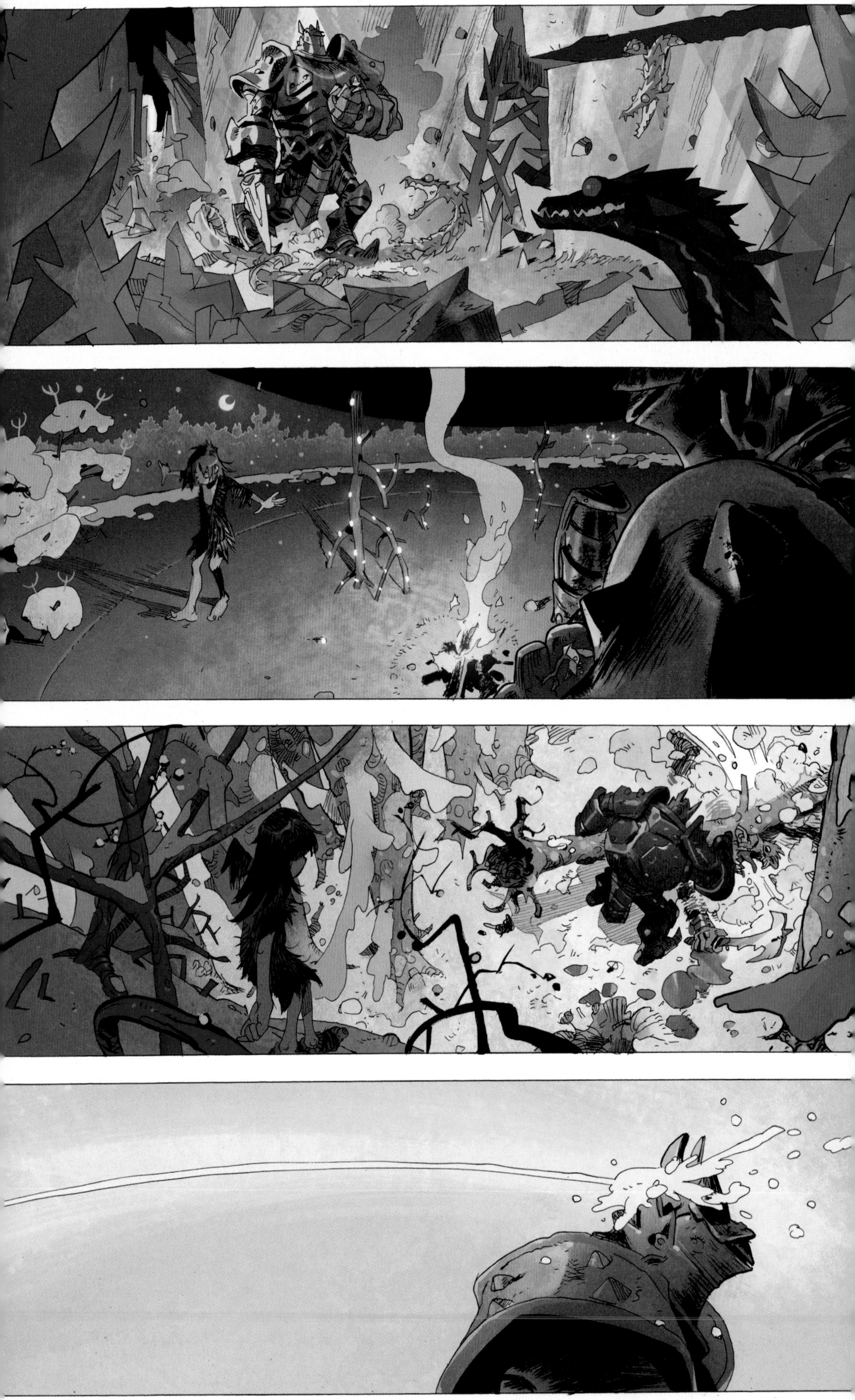

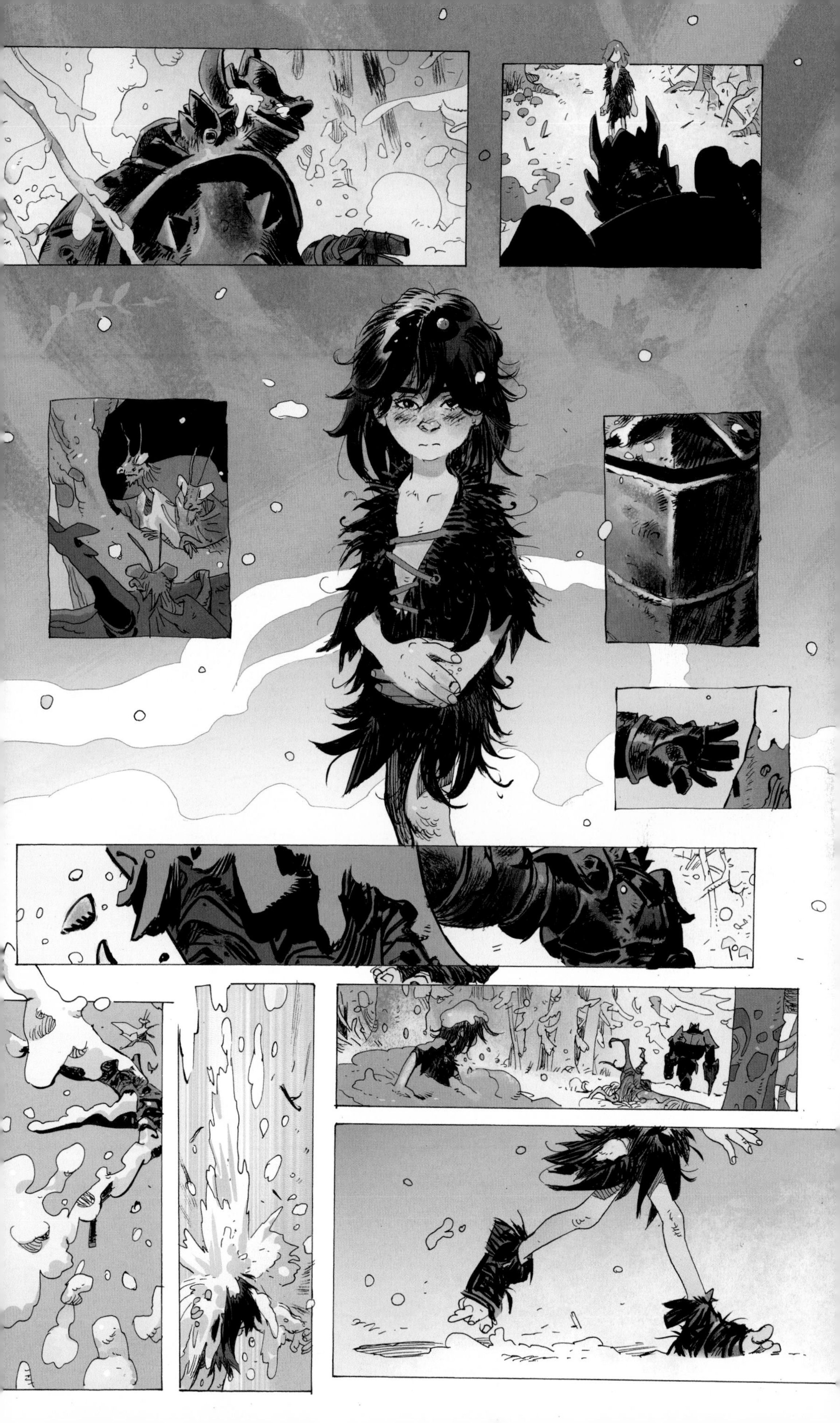

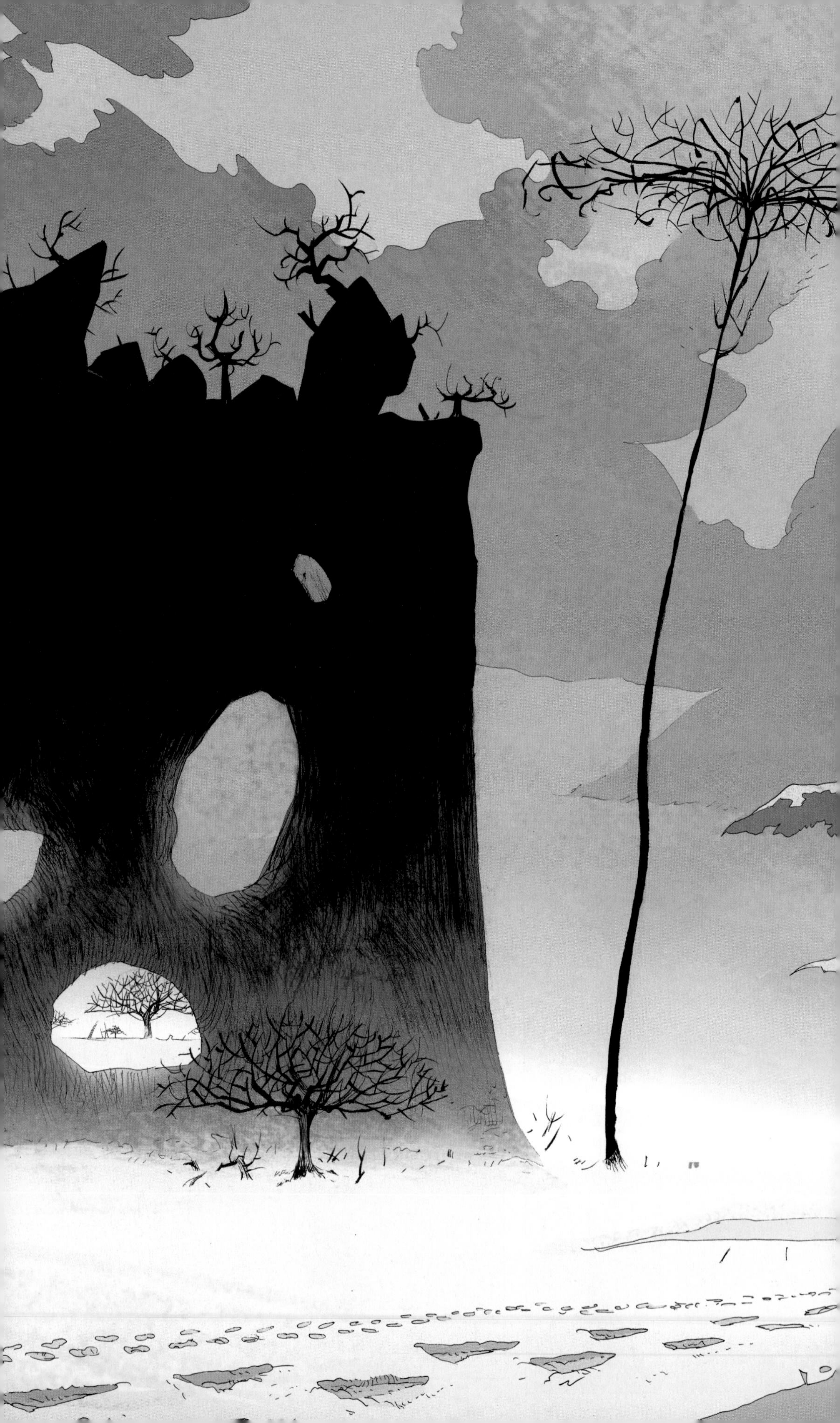

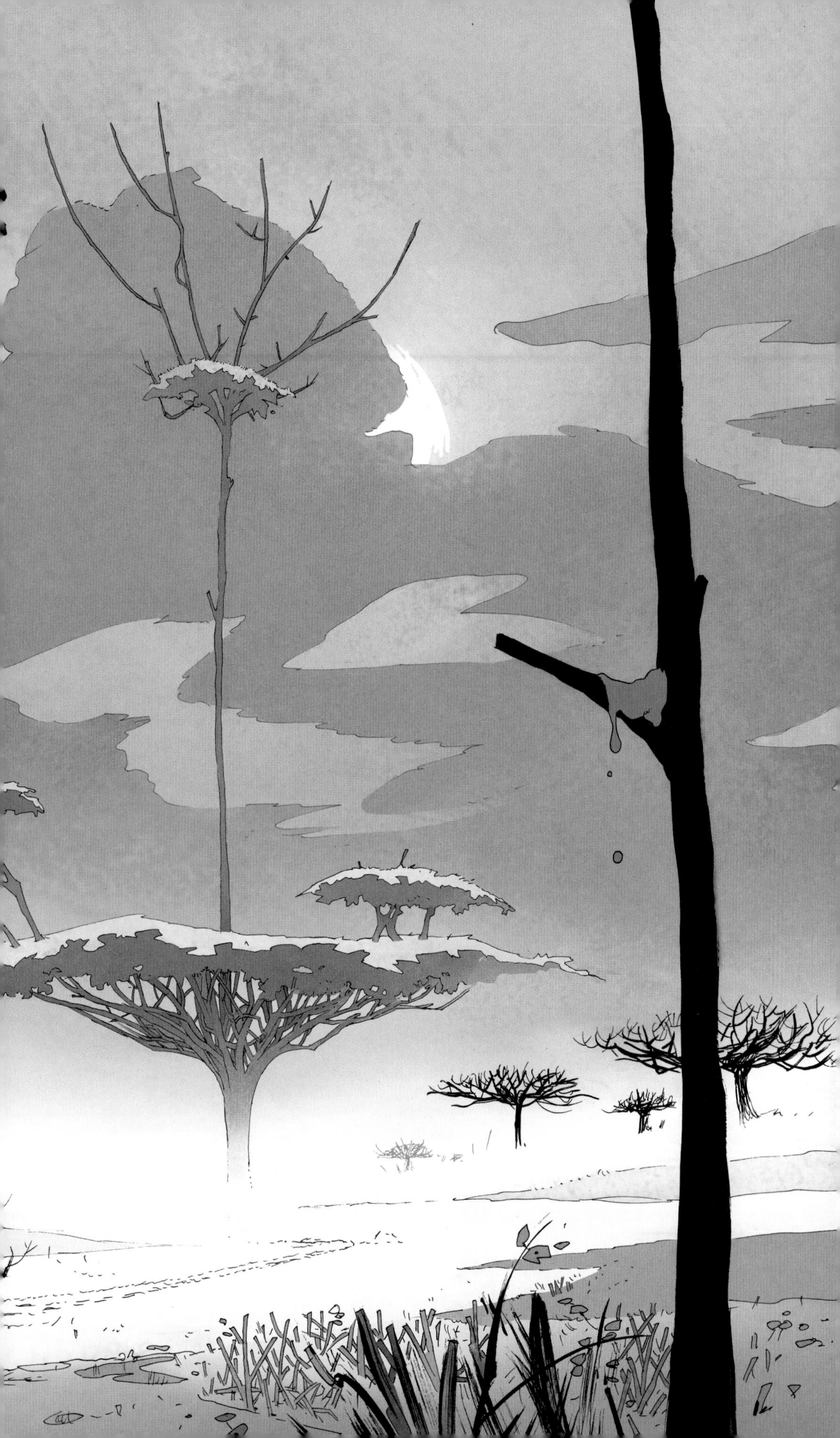

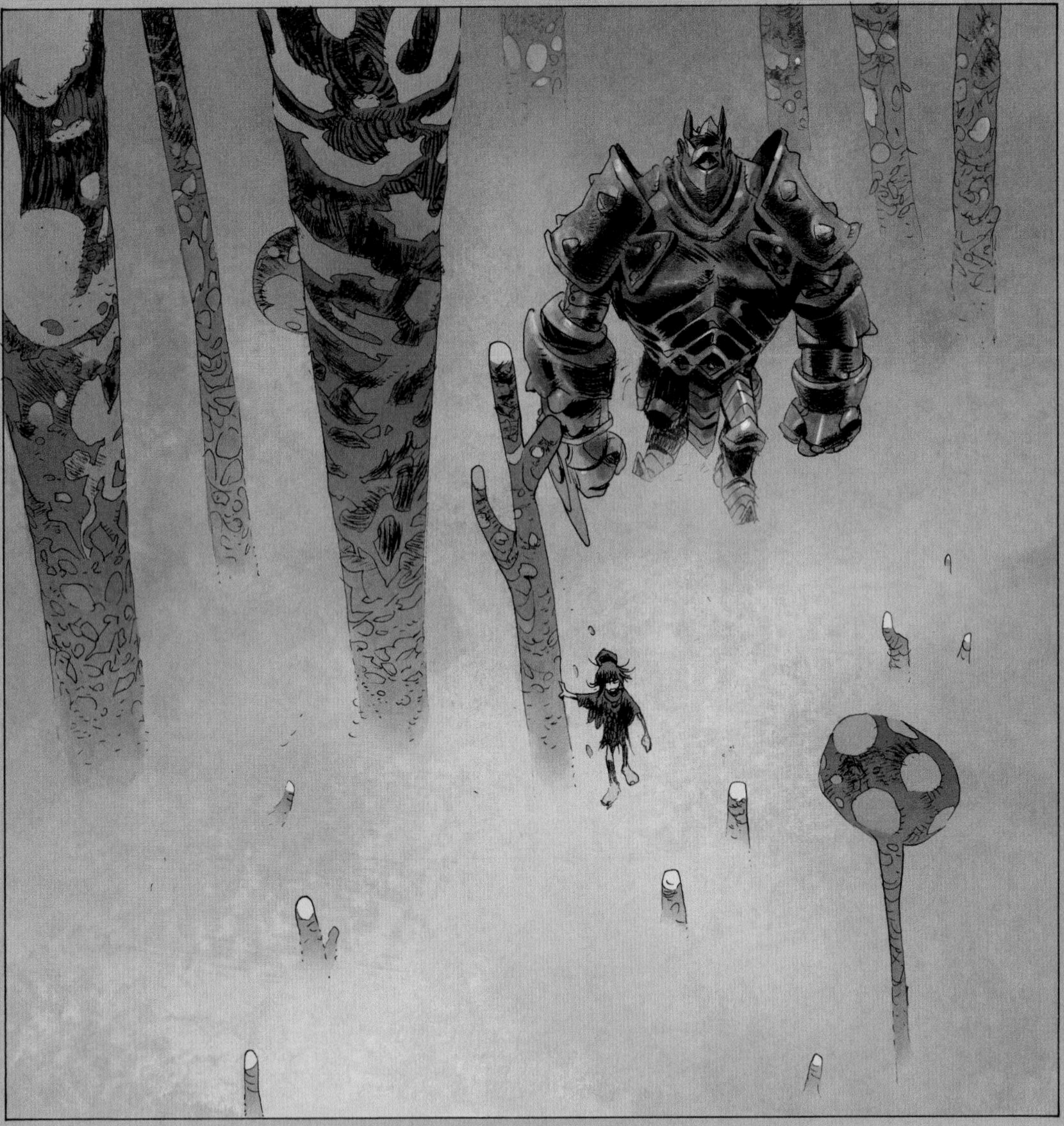

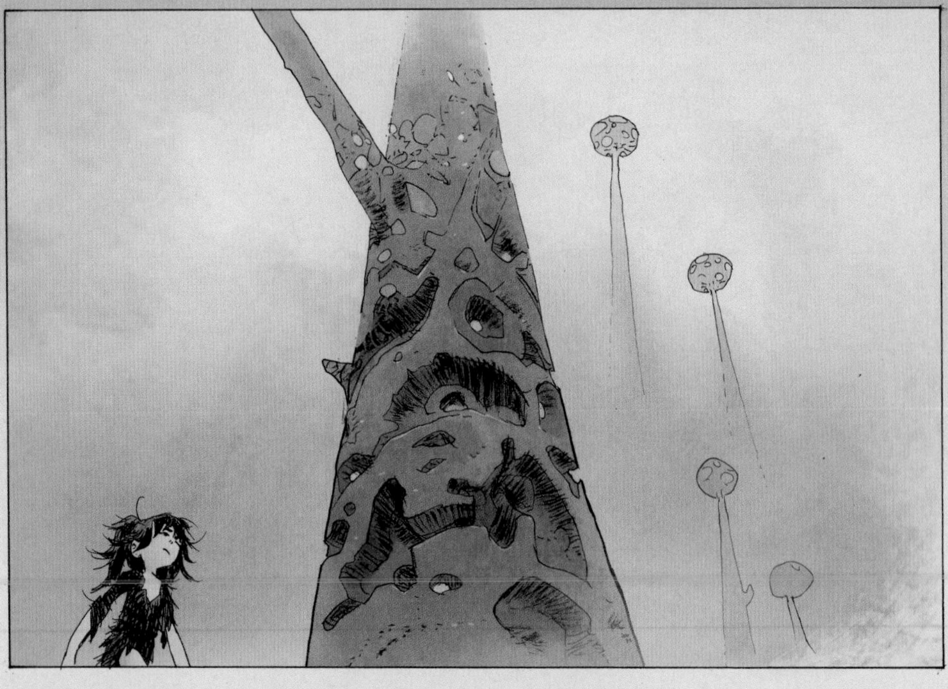

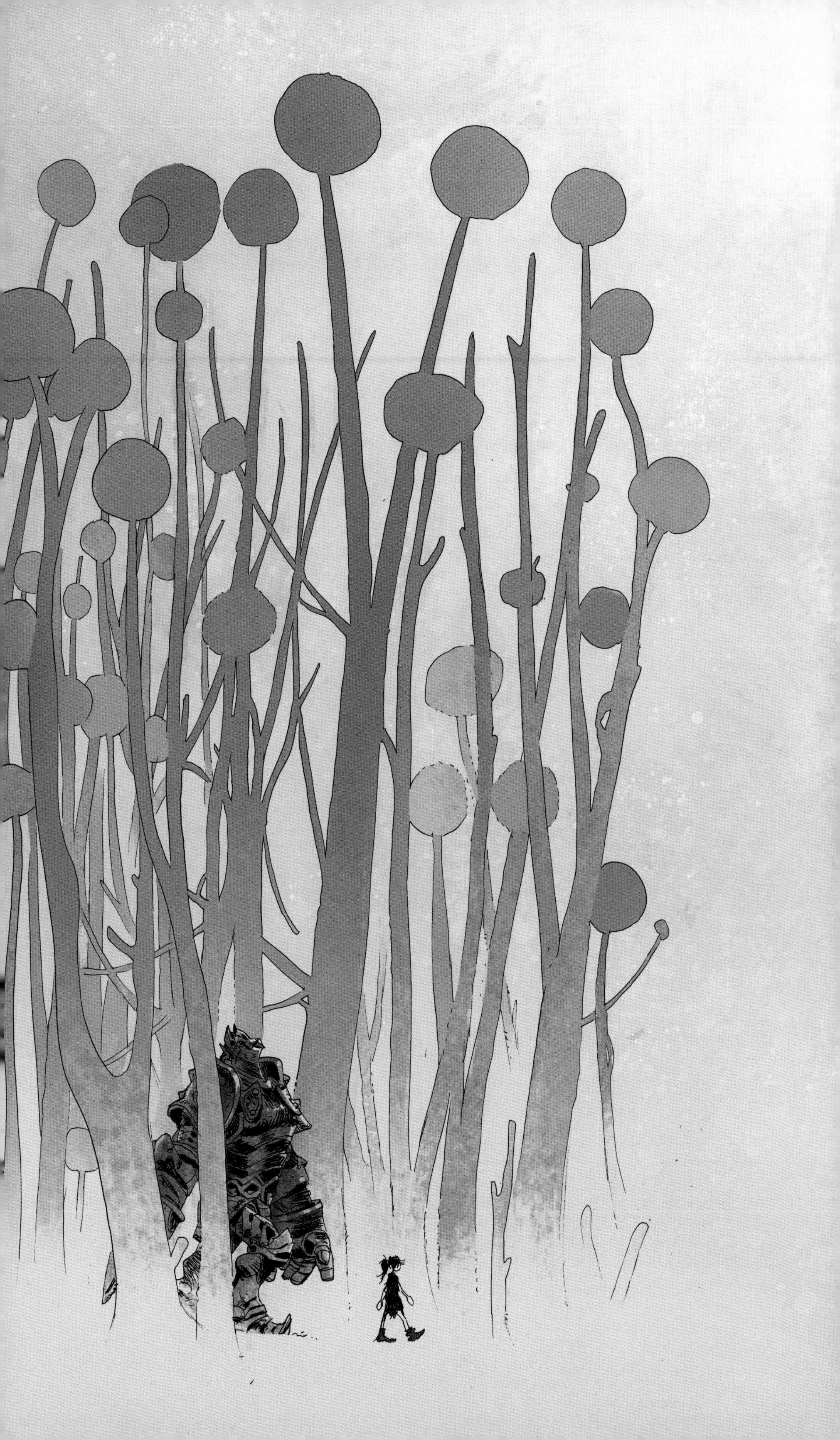

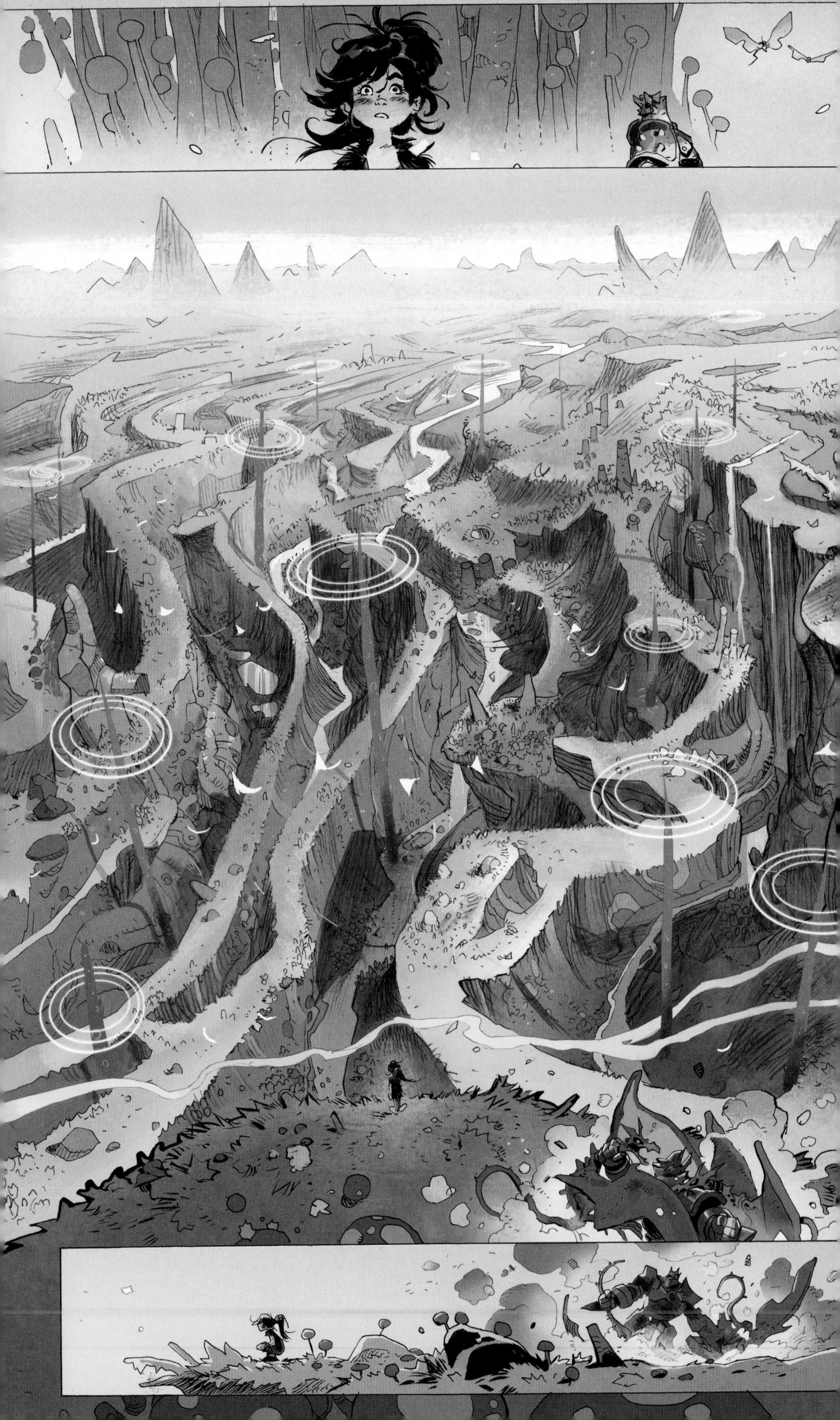

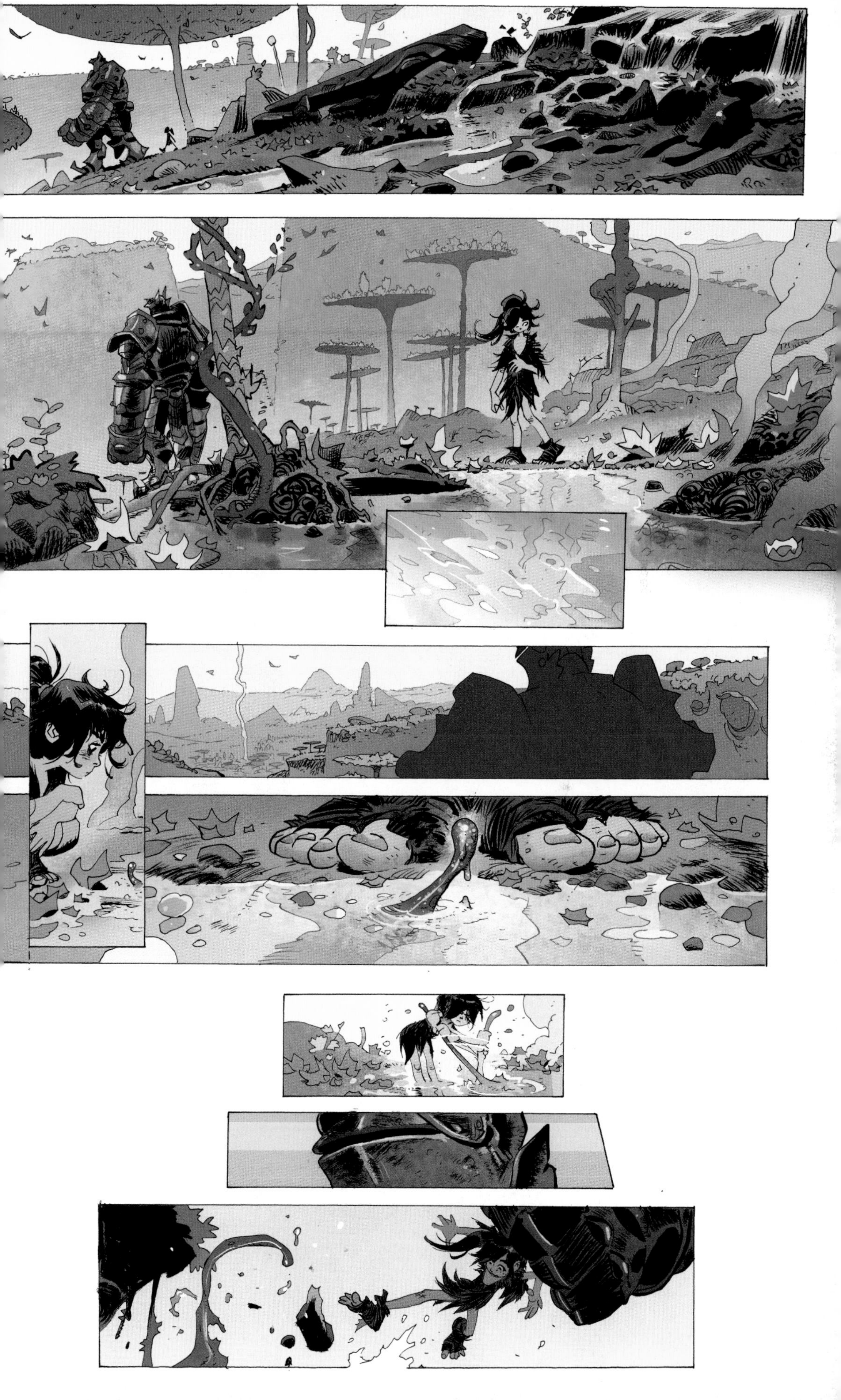

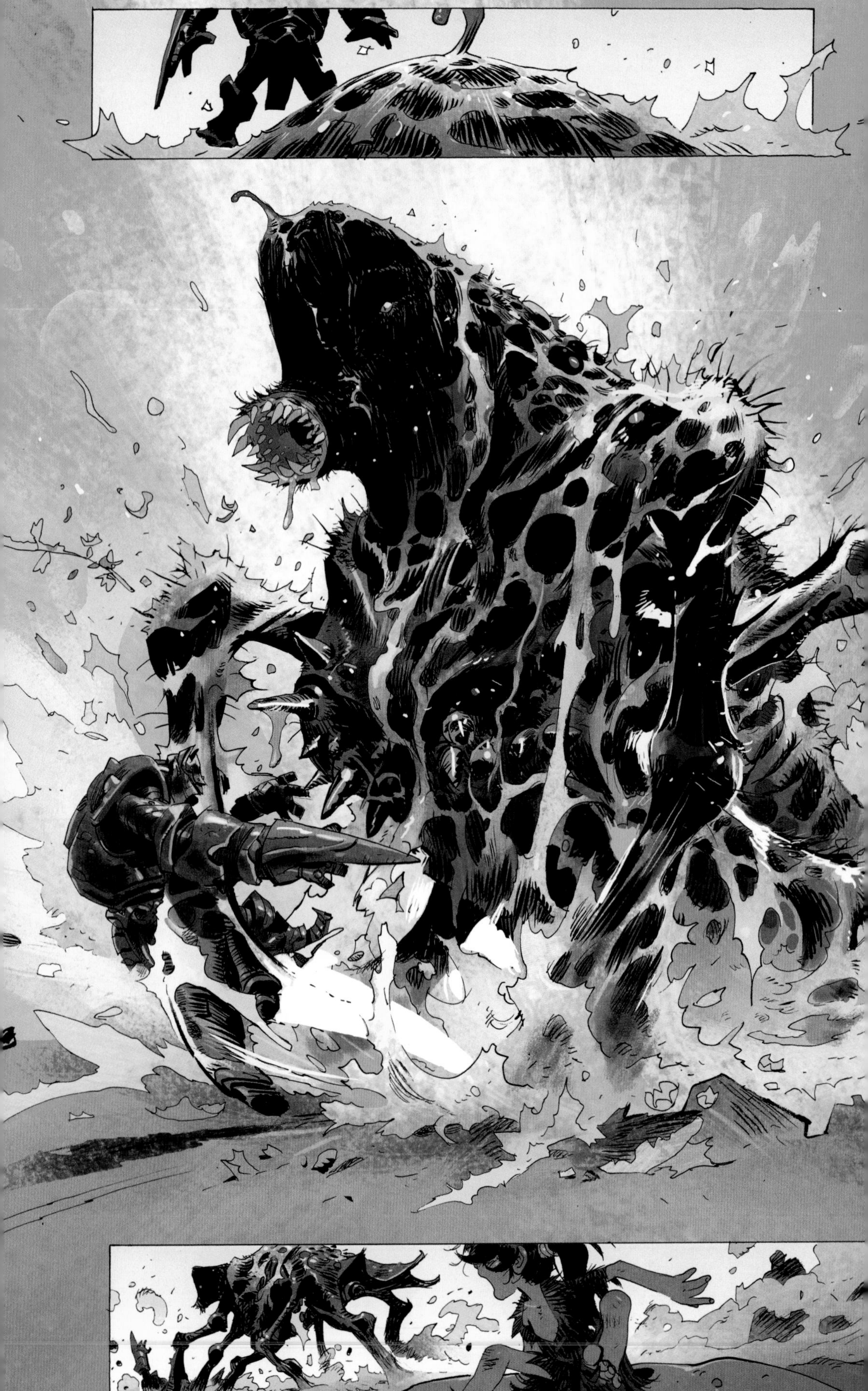

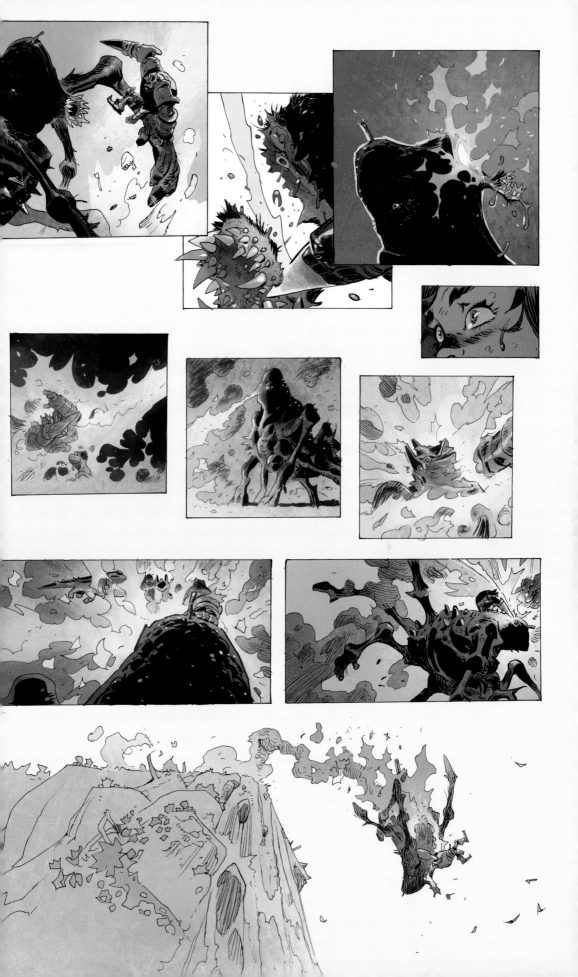

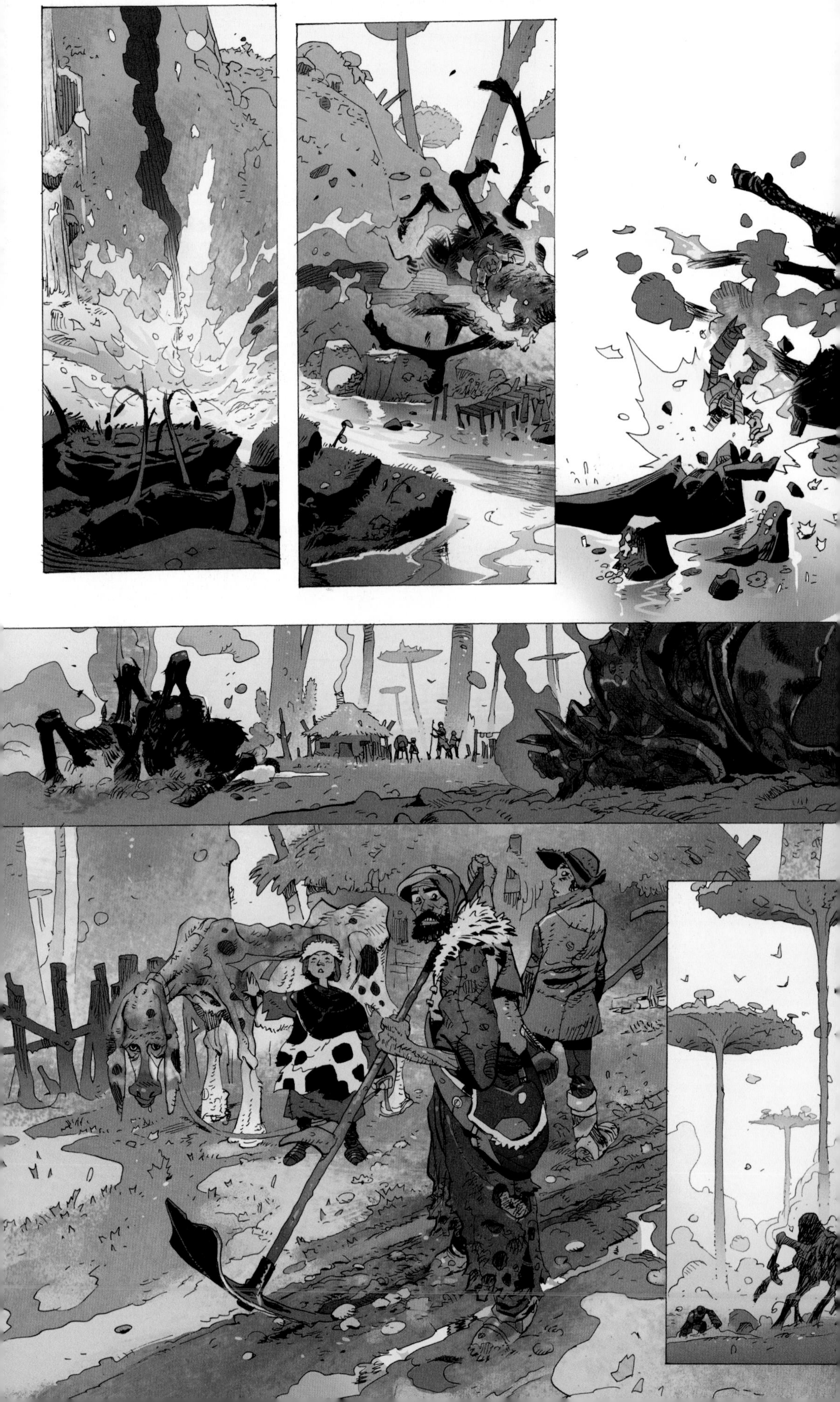

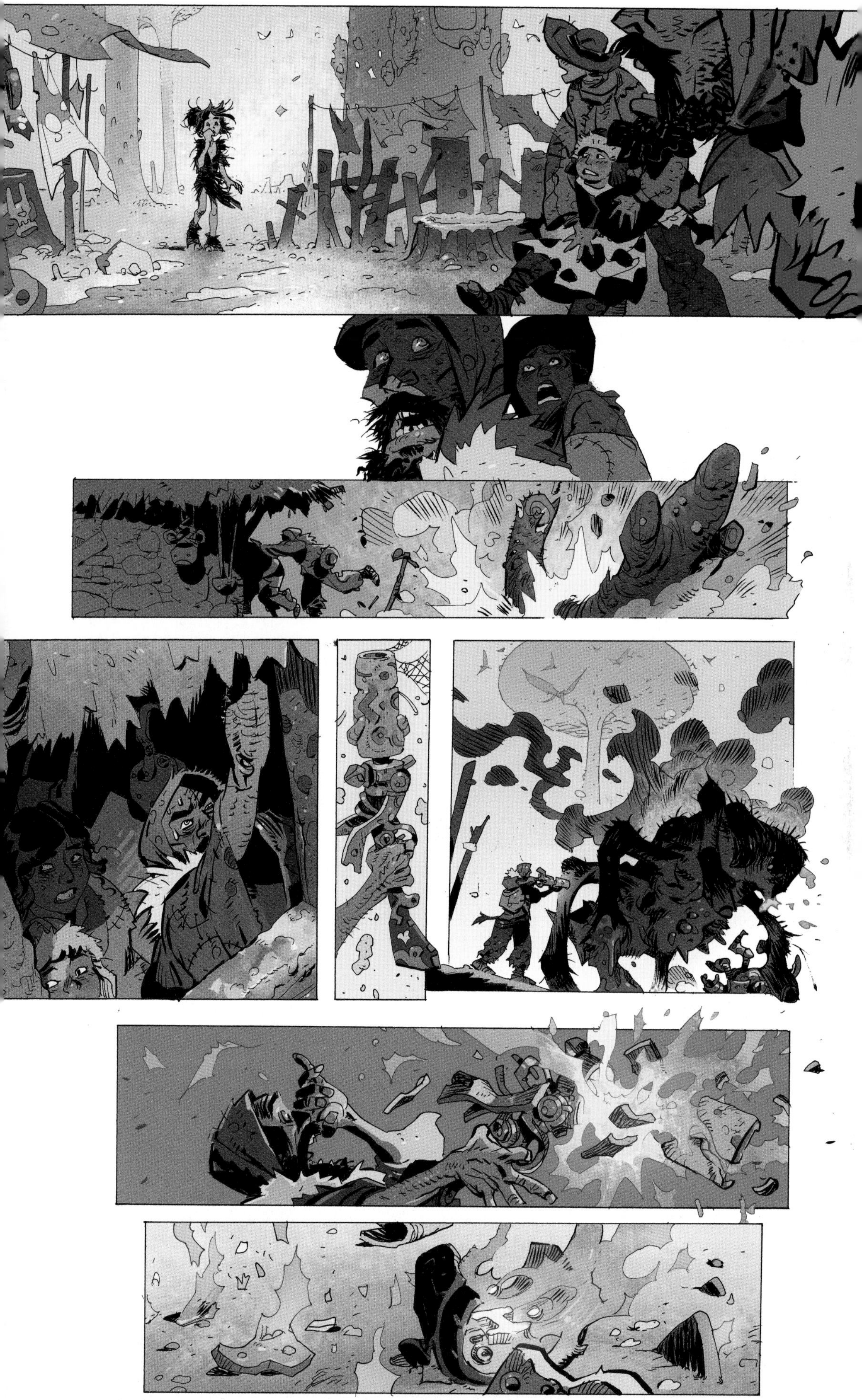

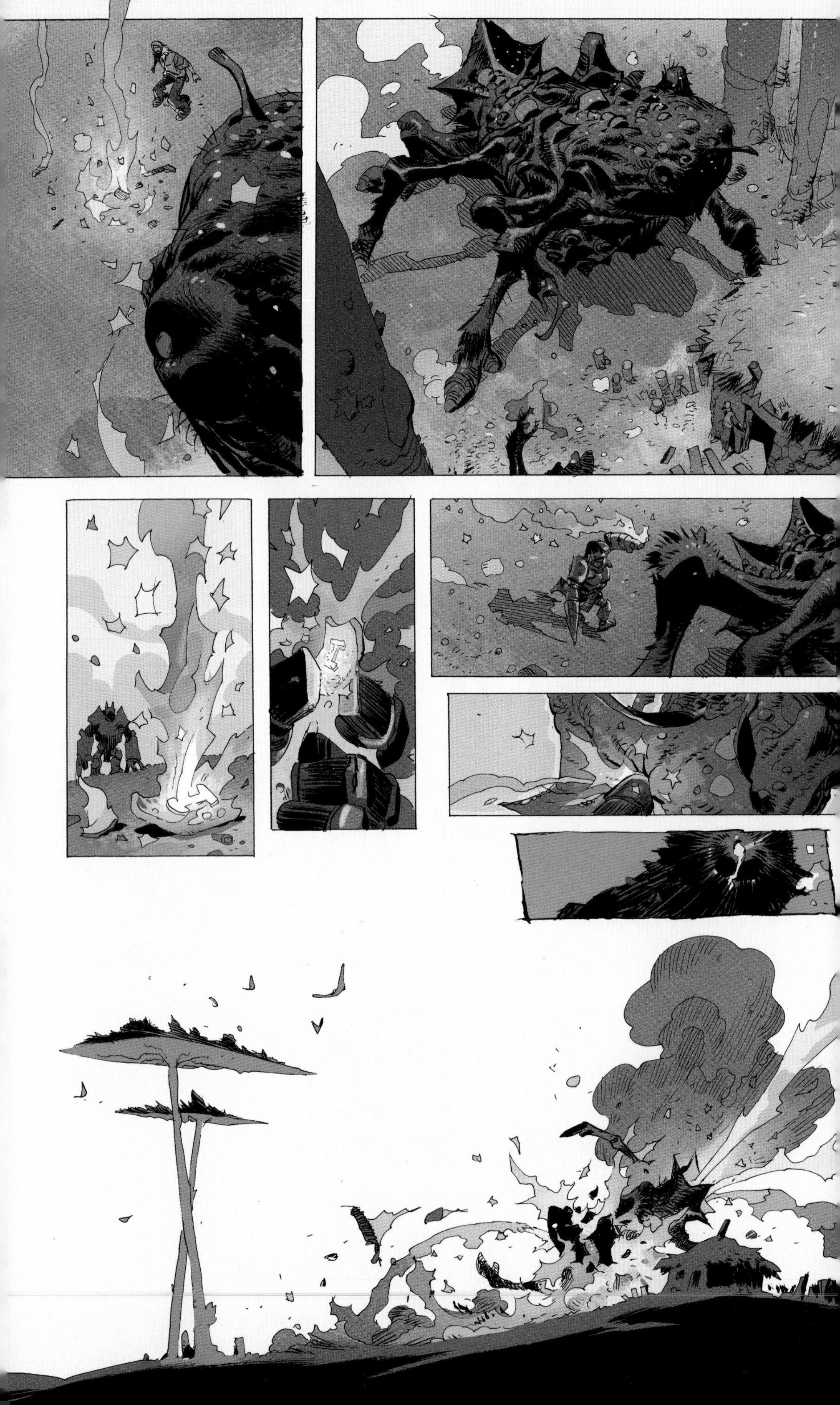

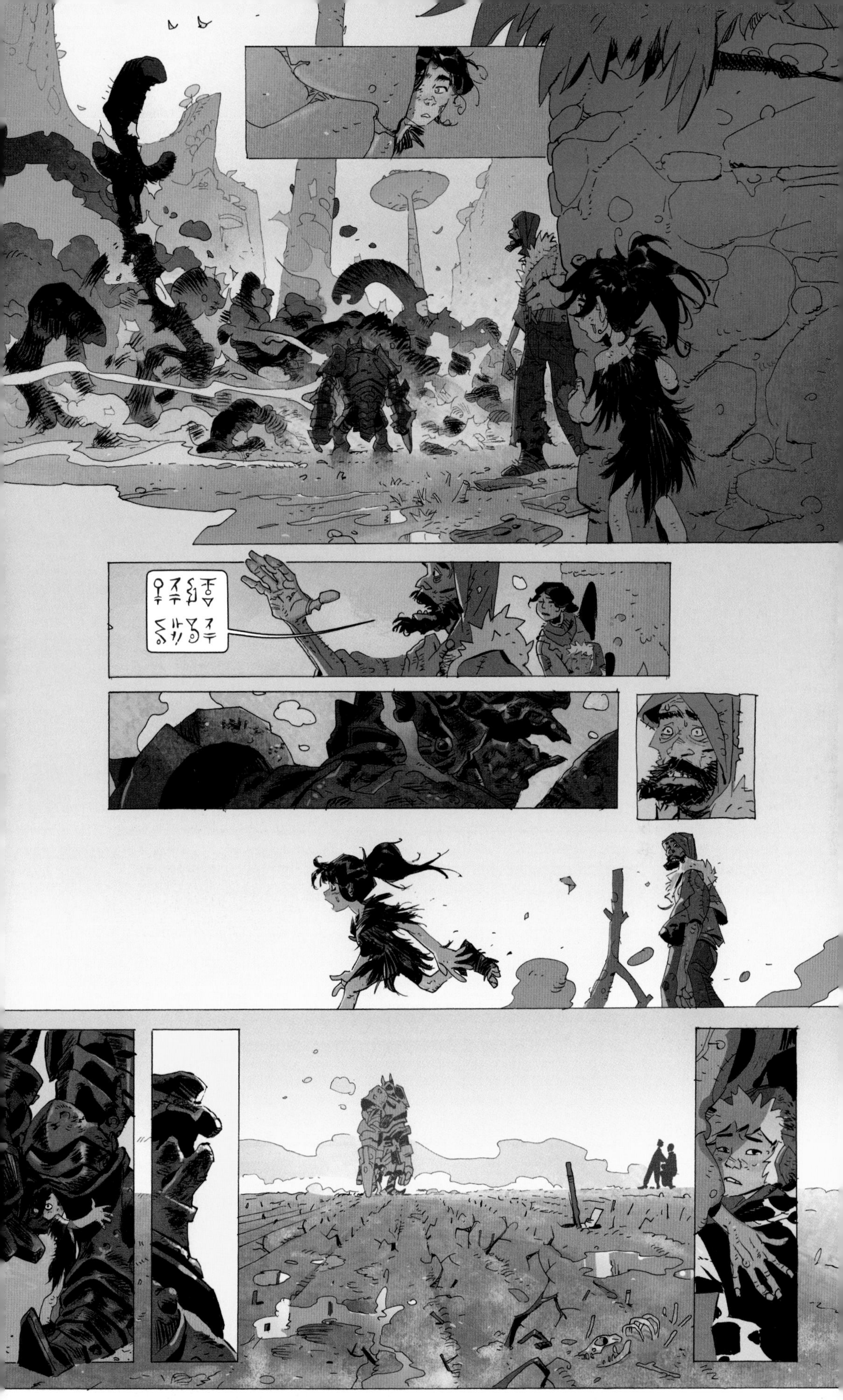

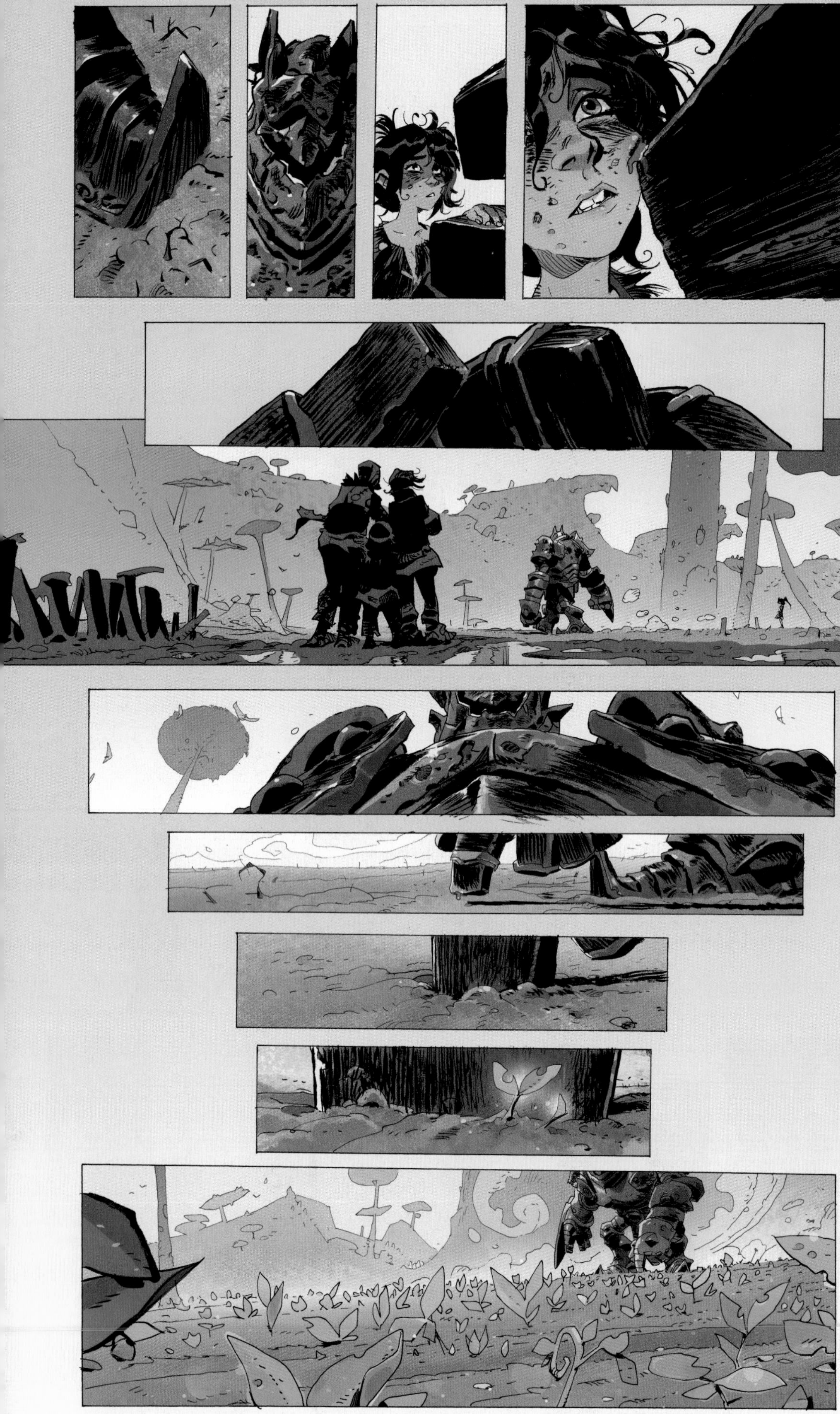

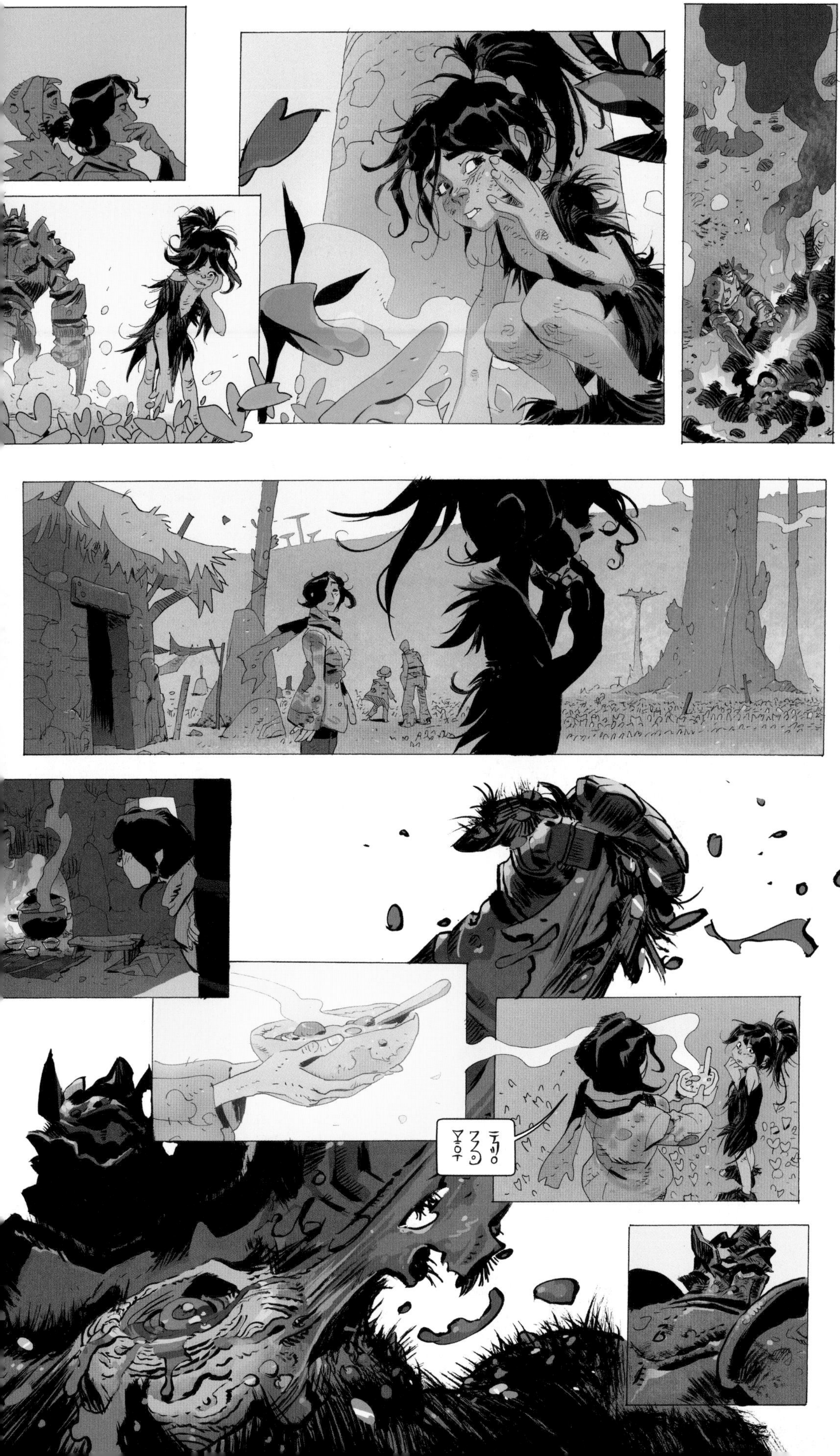

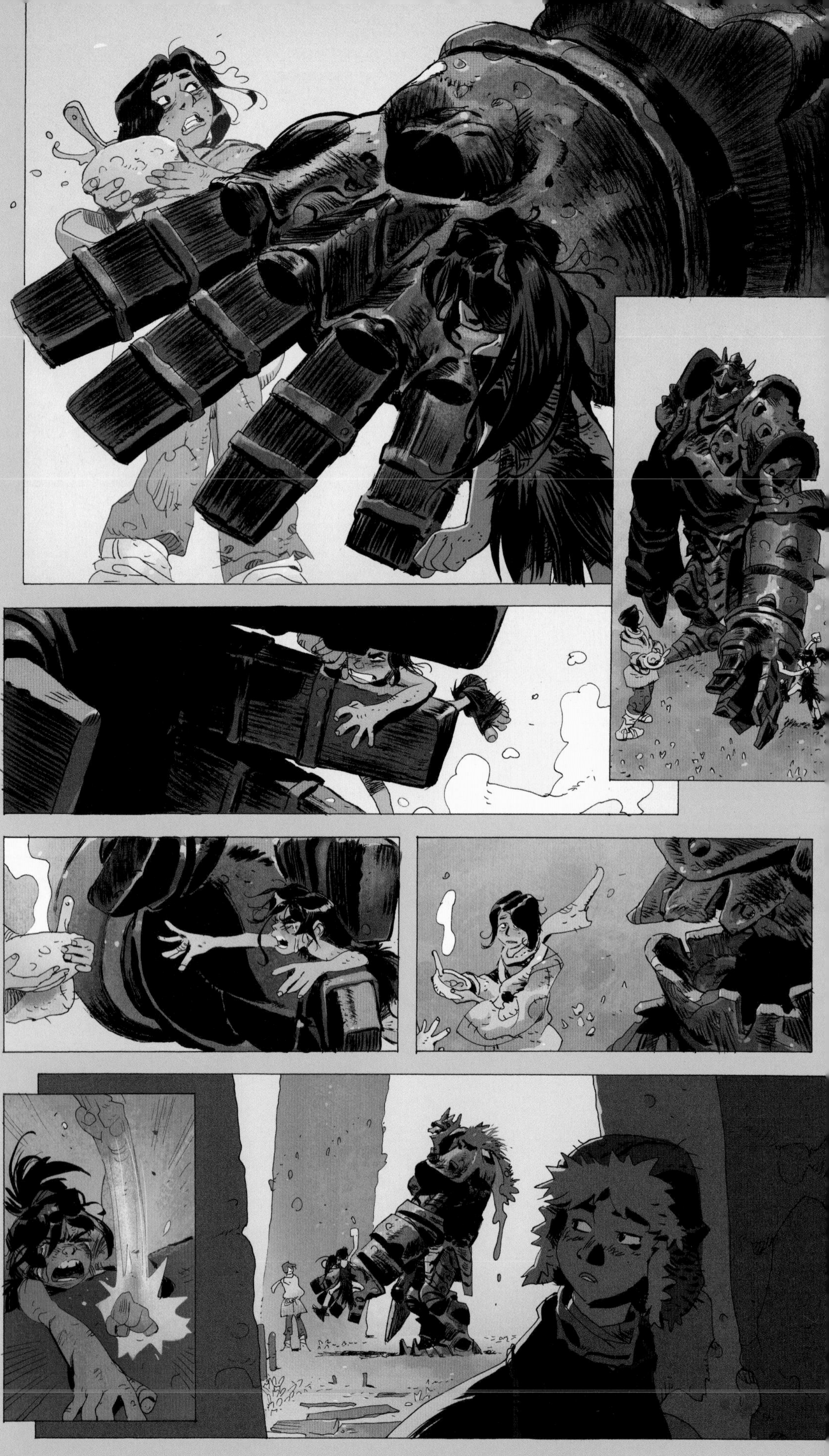

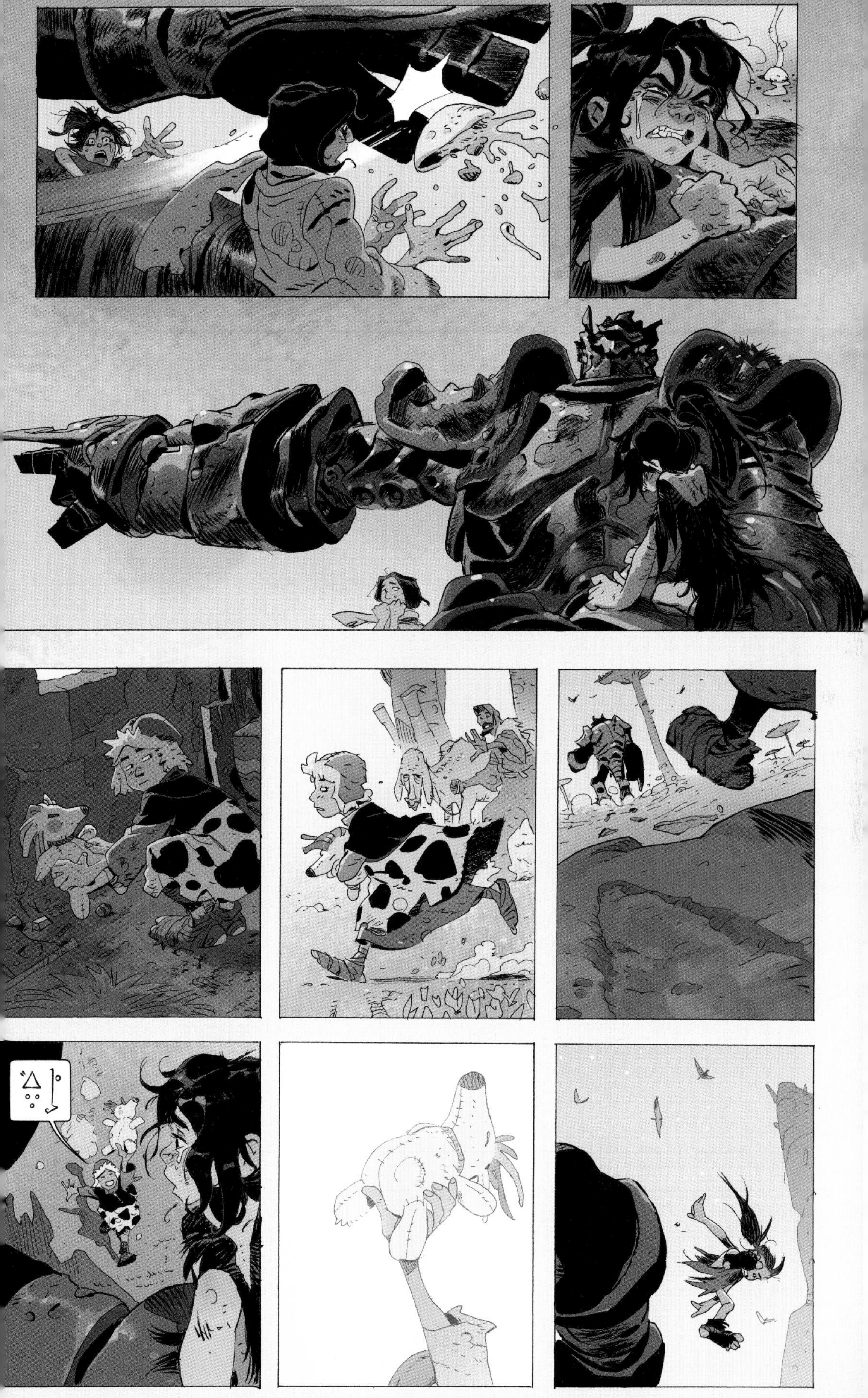

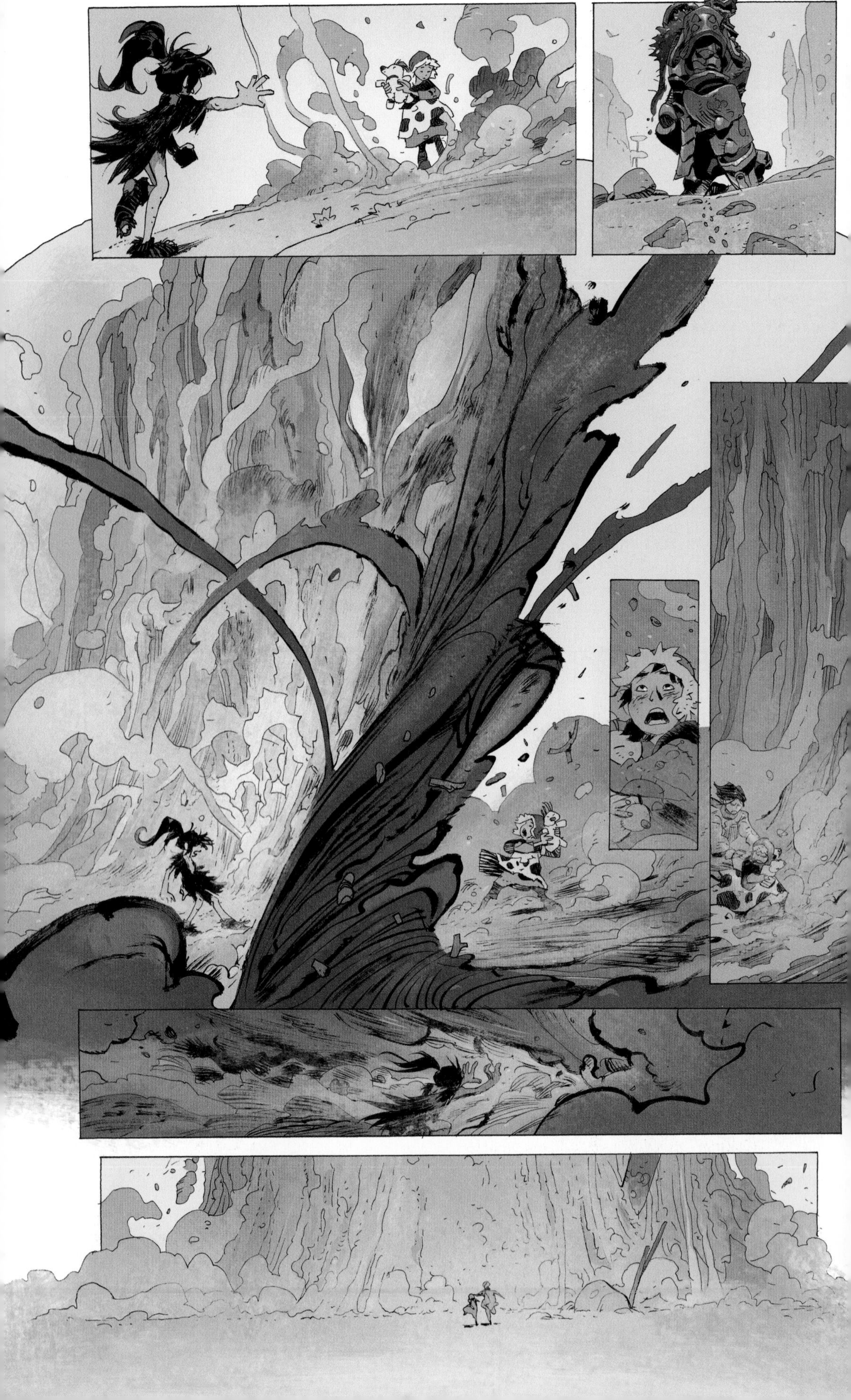

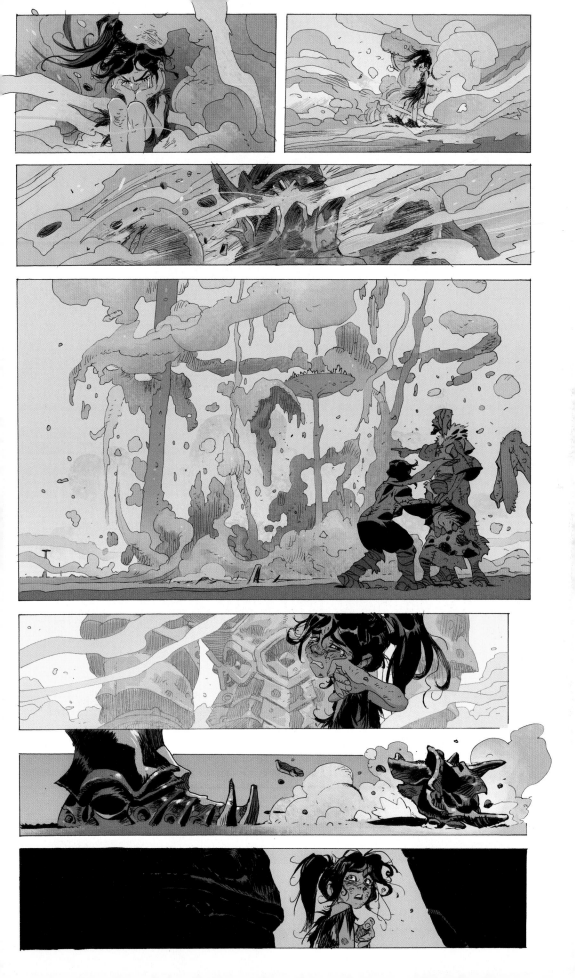

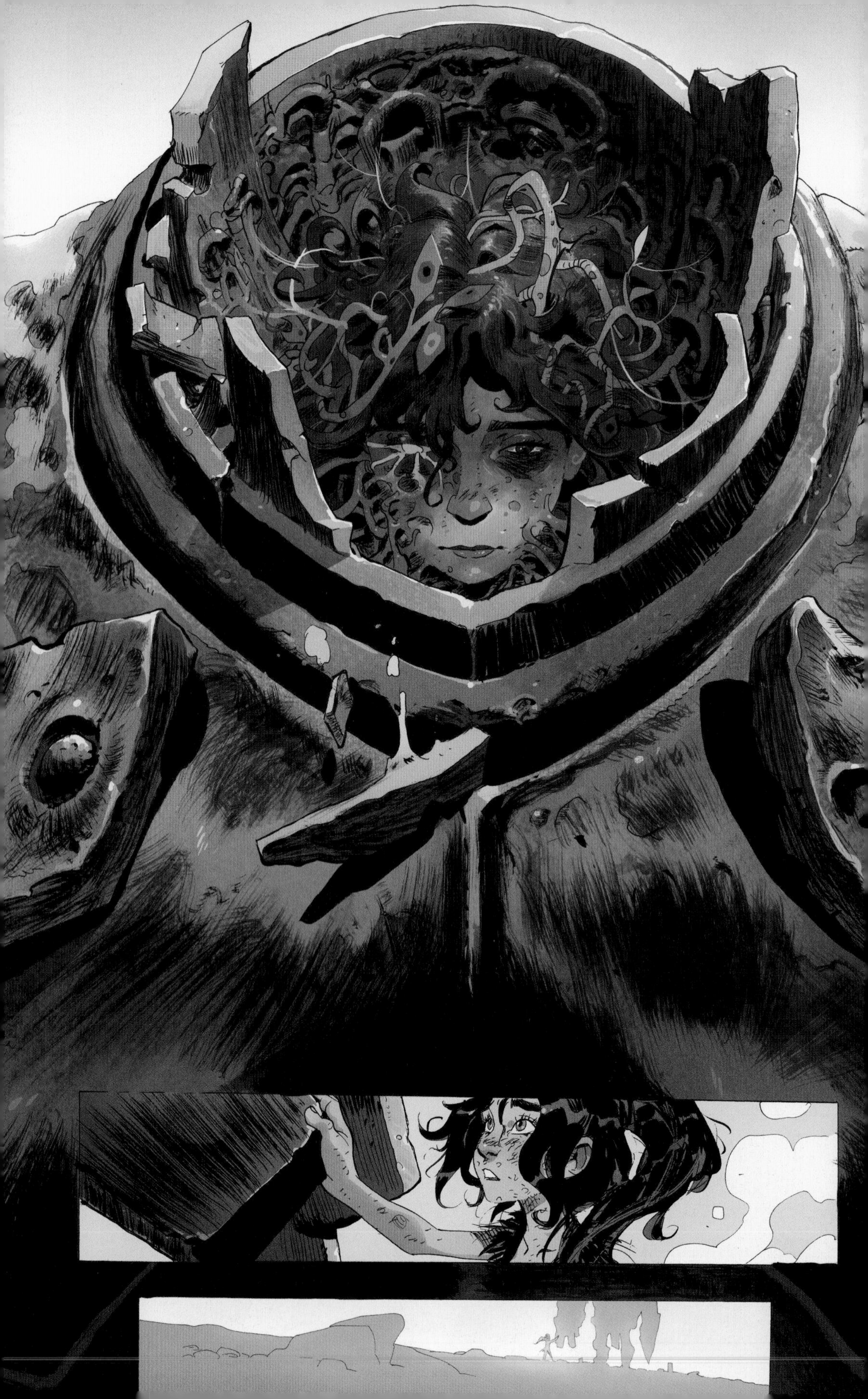

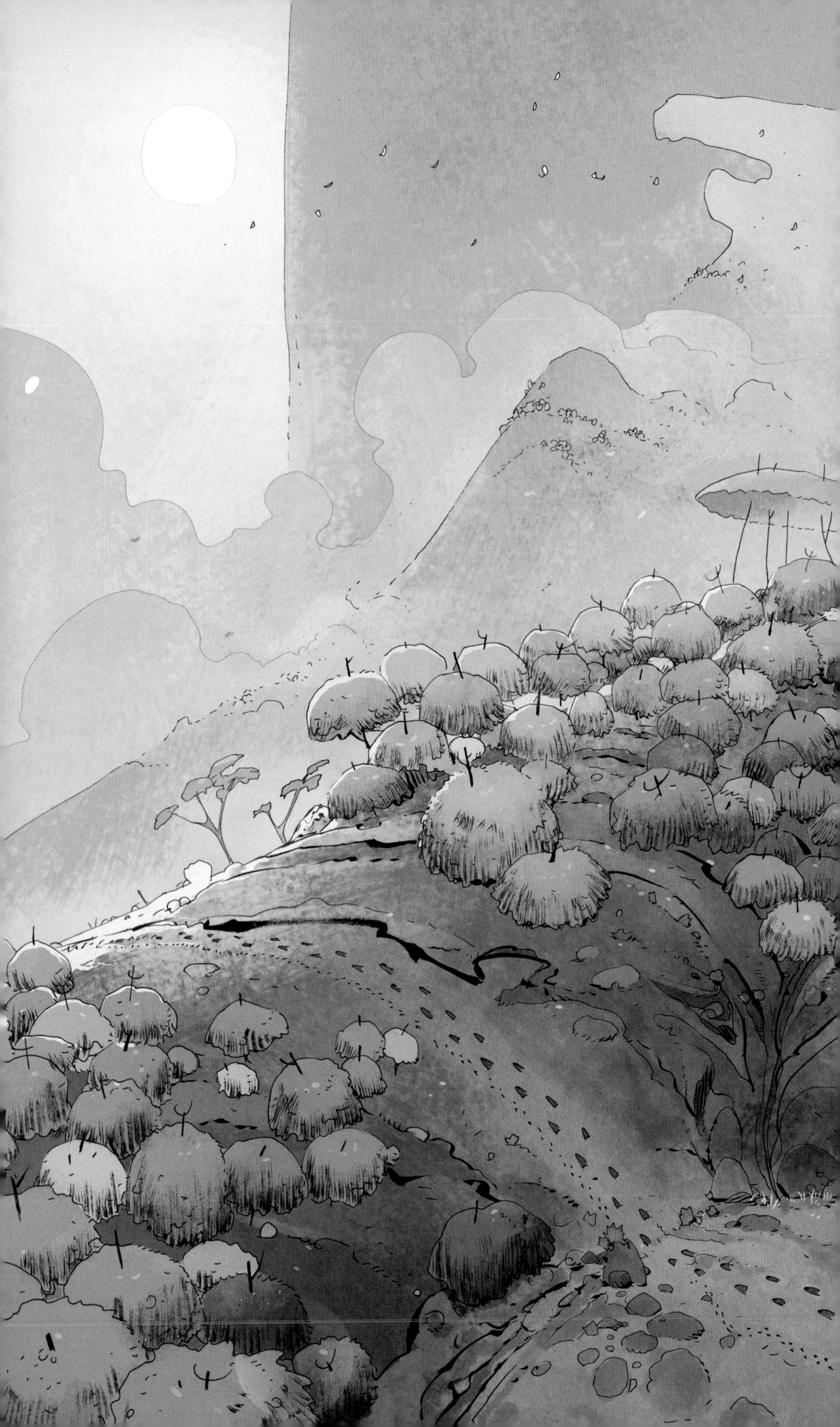

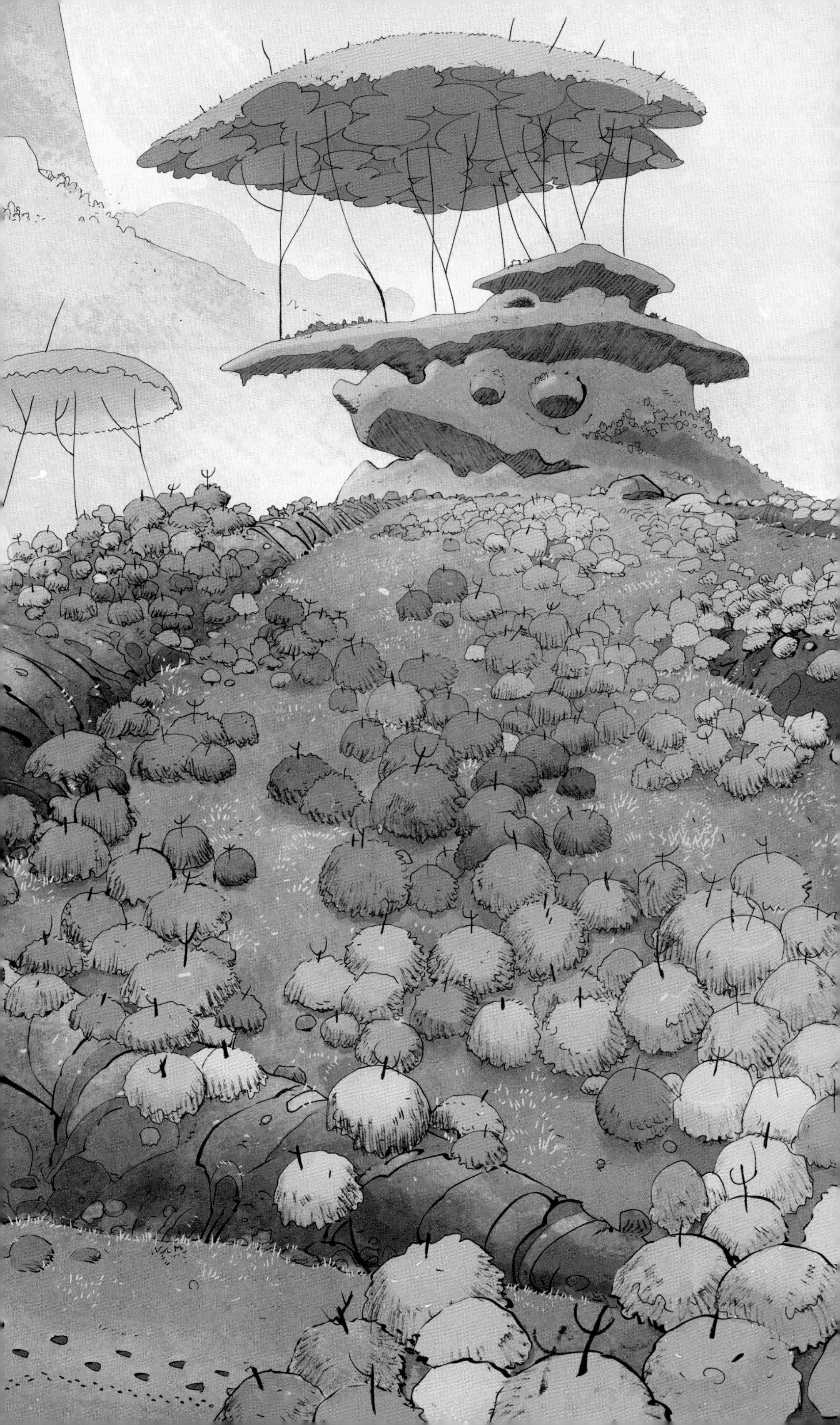

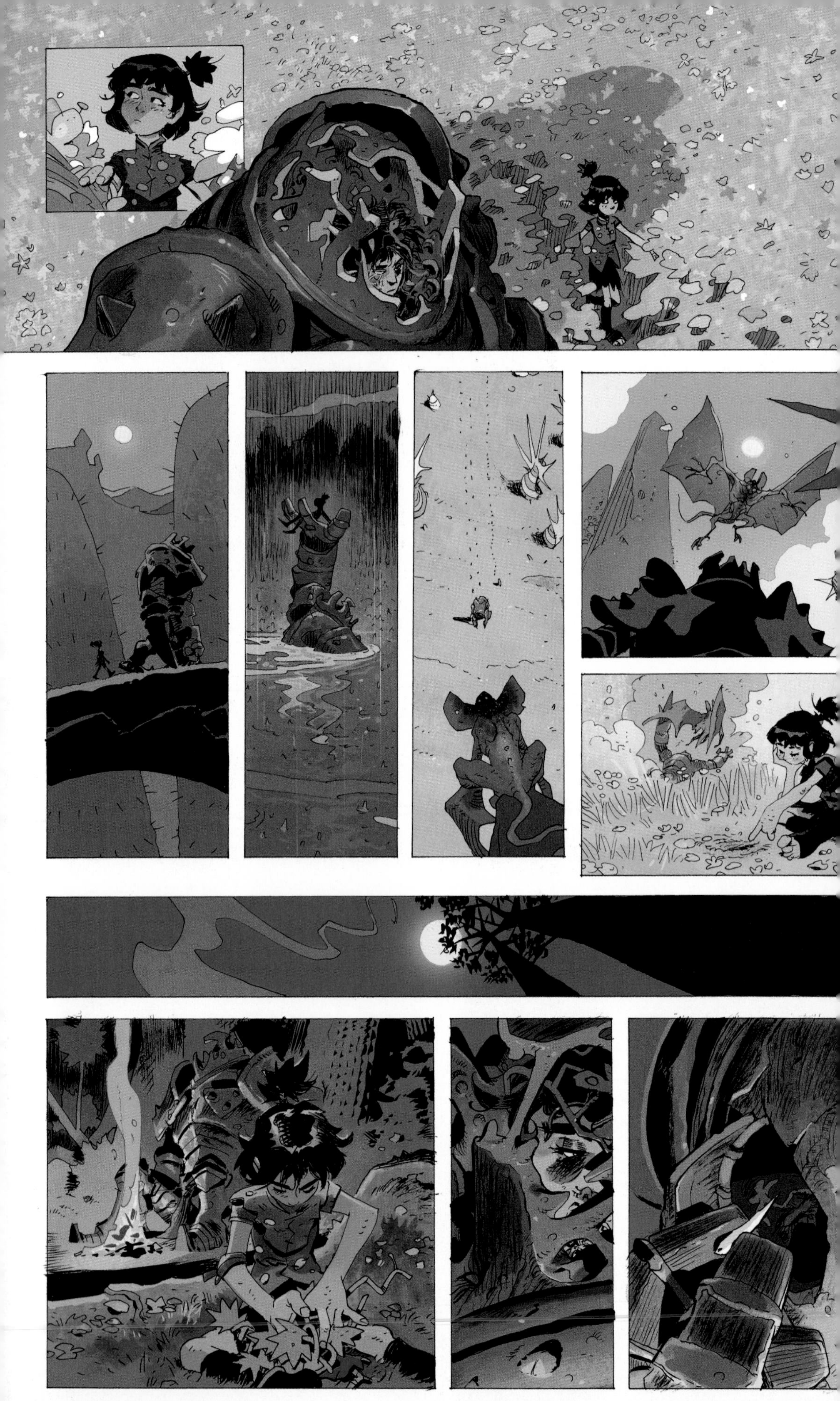

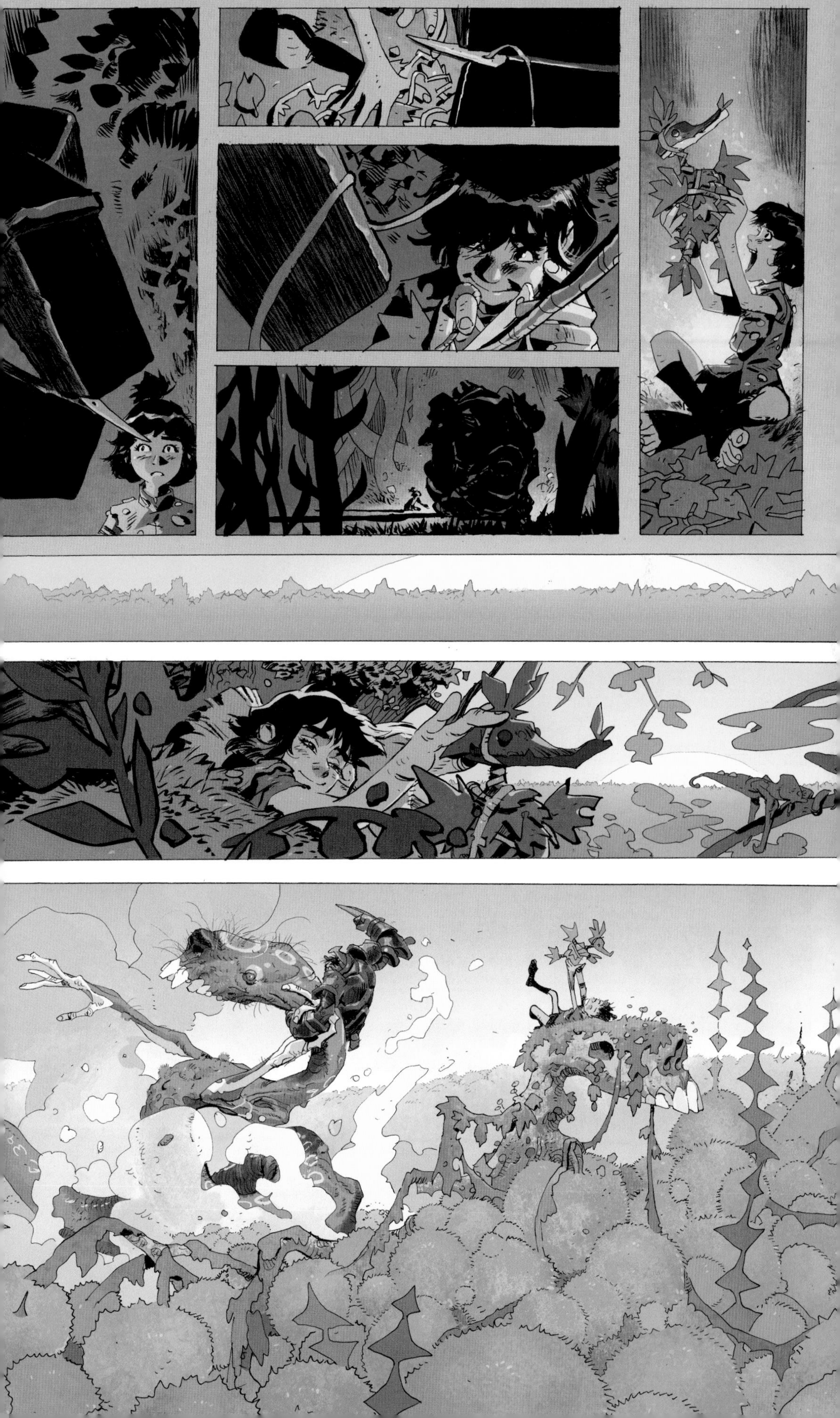

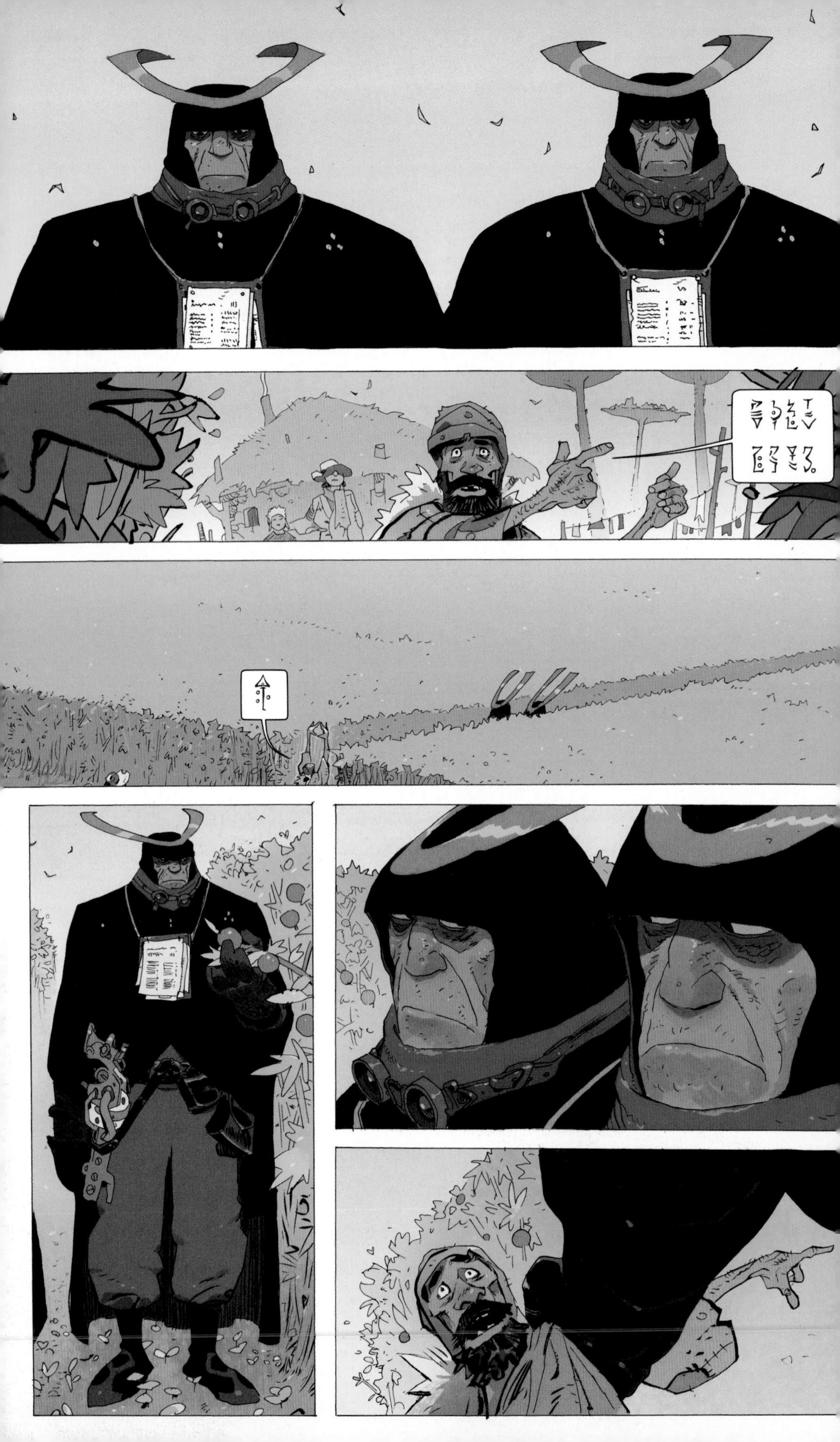

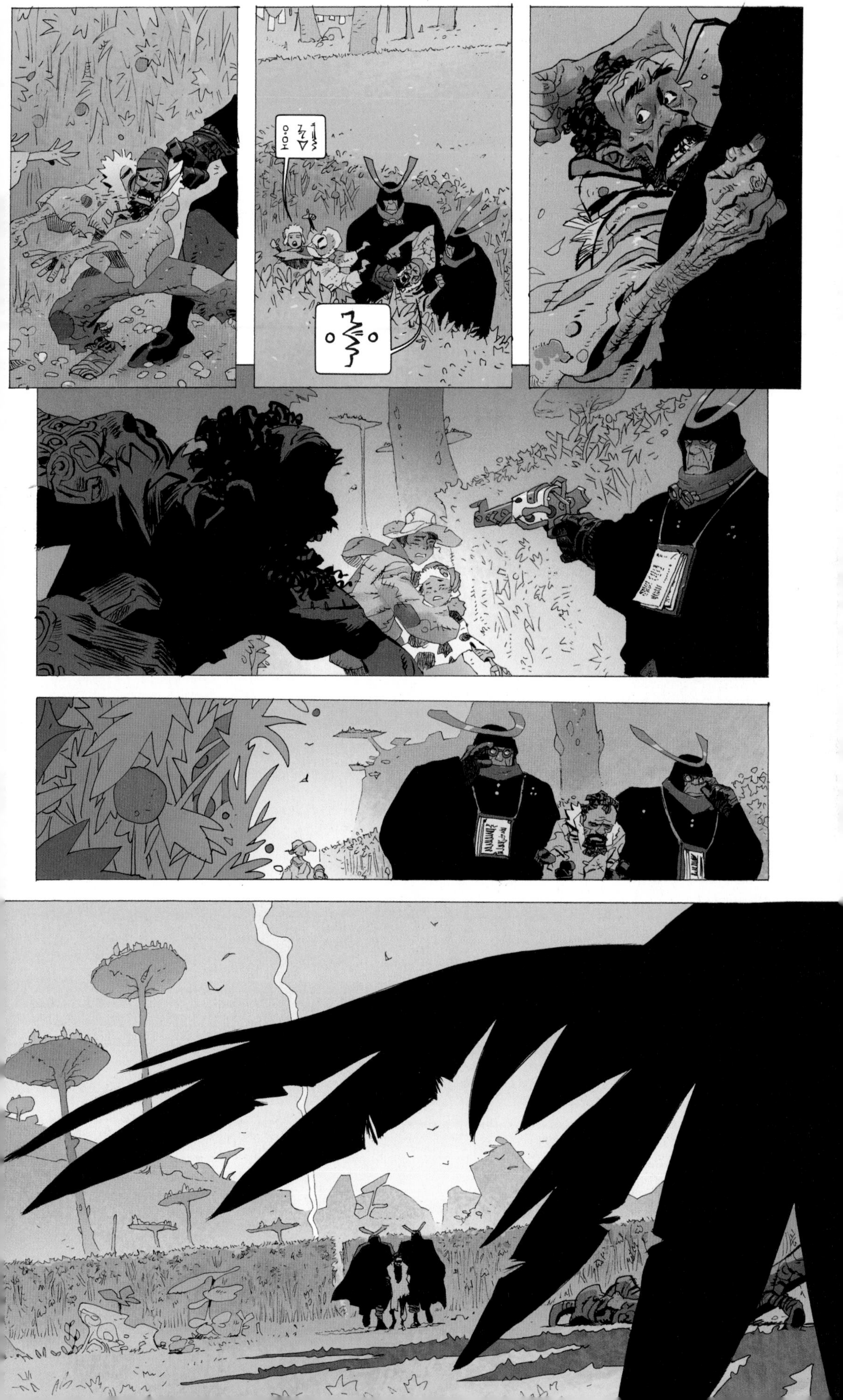

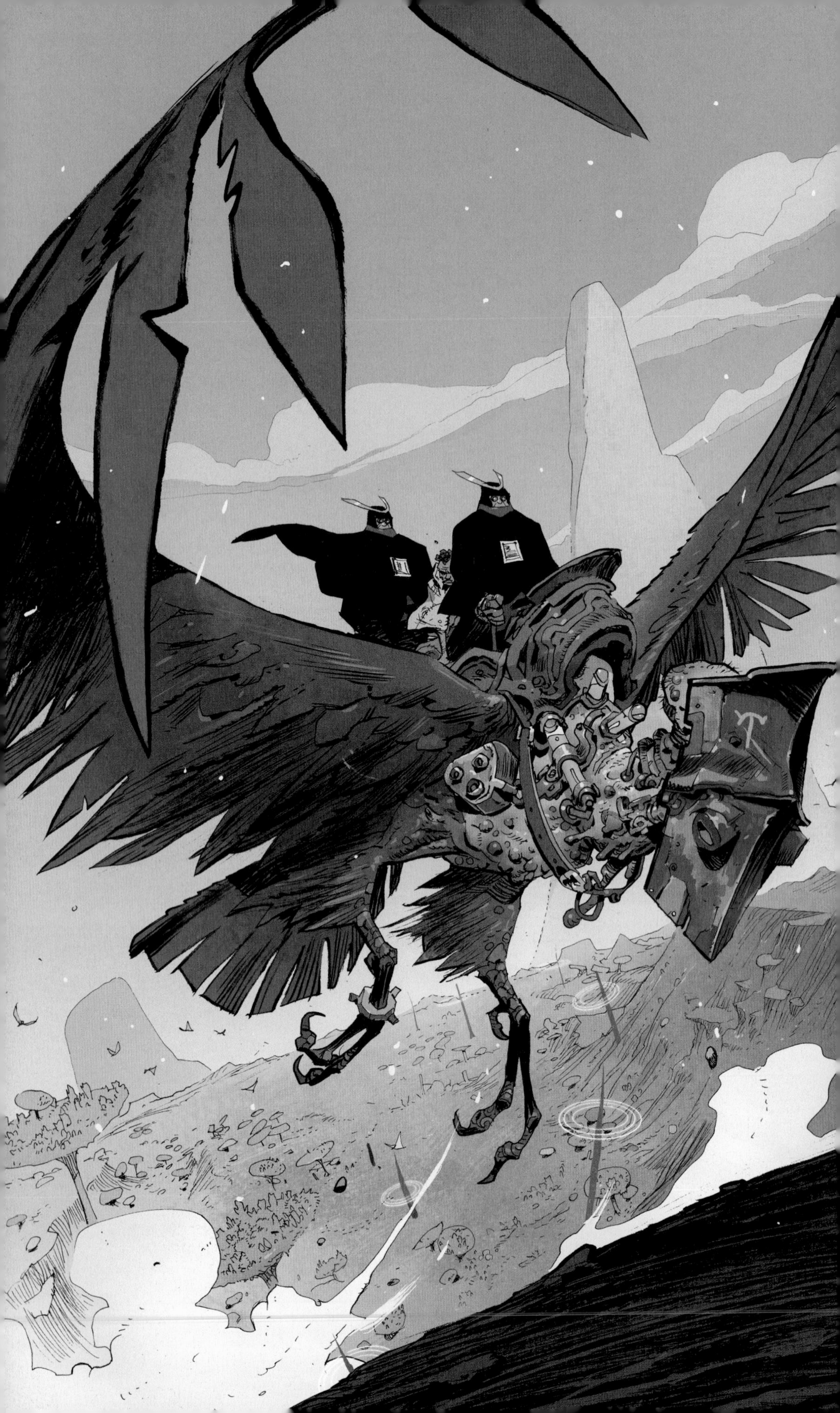

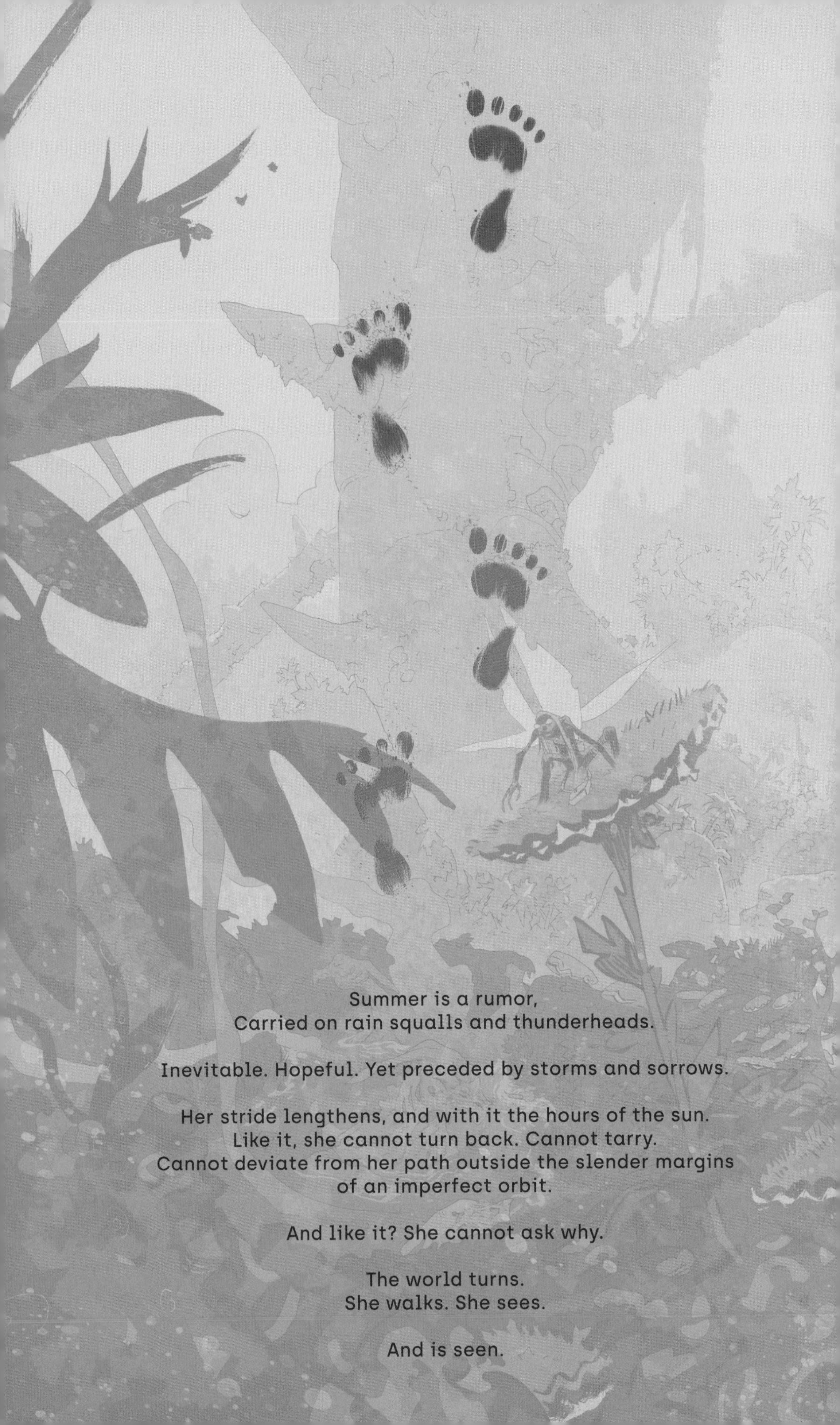

Summer is a rumor,
Carried on rain squalls and thunderheads.

Inevitable. Hopeful. Yet preceded by storms and sorrows.

Her stride lengthens, and with it the hours of the sun.
Like it, she cannot turn back. Cannot tarry.
Cannot deviate from her path outside the slender margins
of an imperfect orbit.

And like it? She cannot ask why.

The world turns.
She walks. She sees.

And is seen.

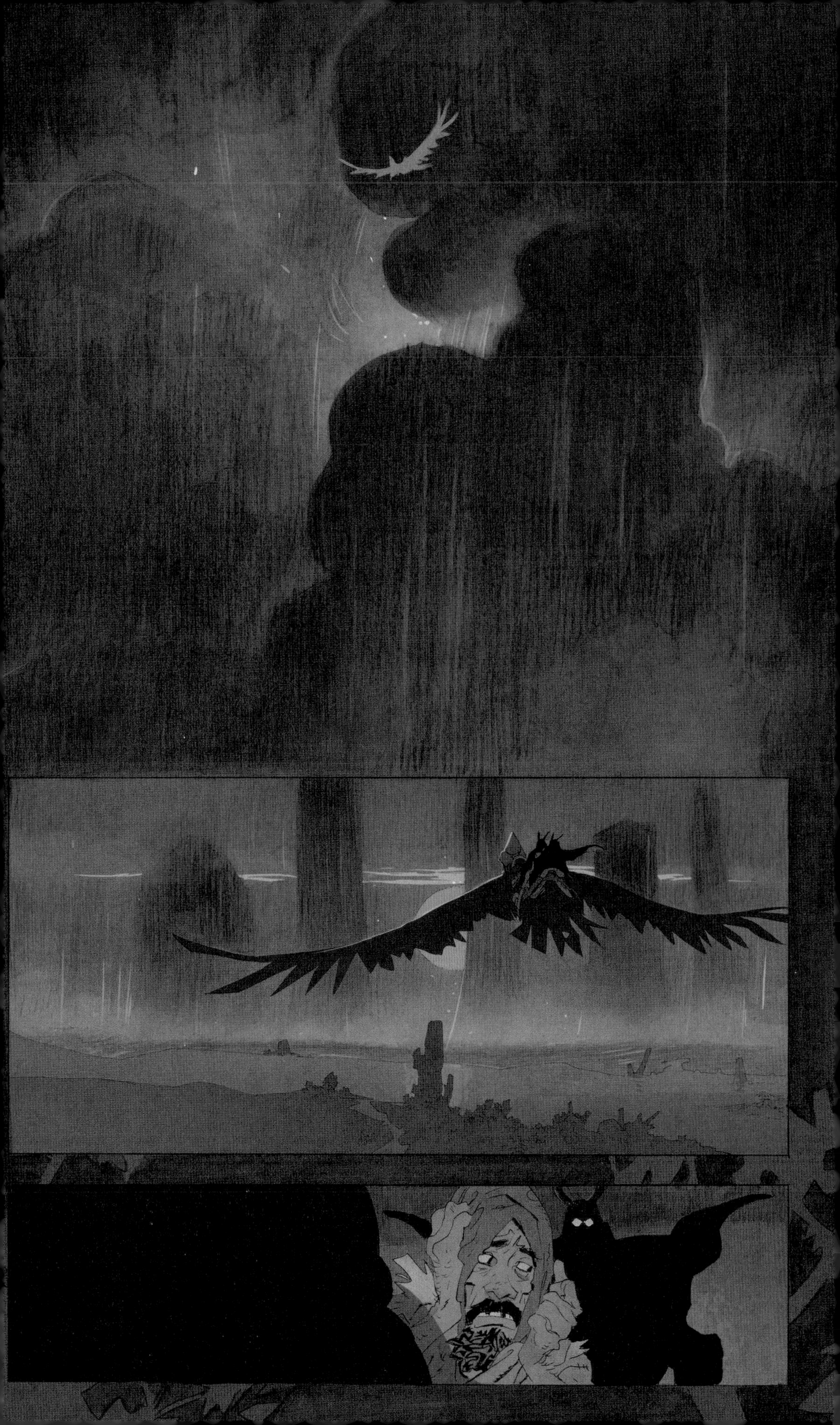

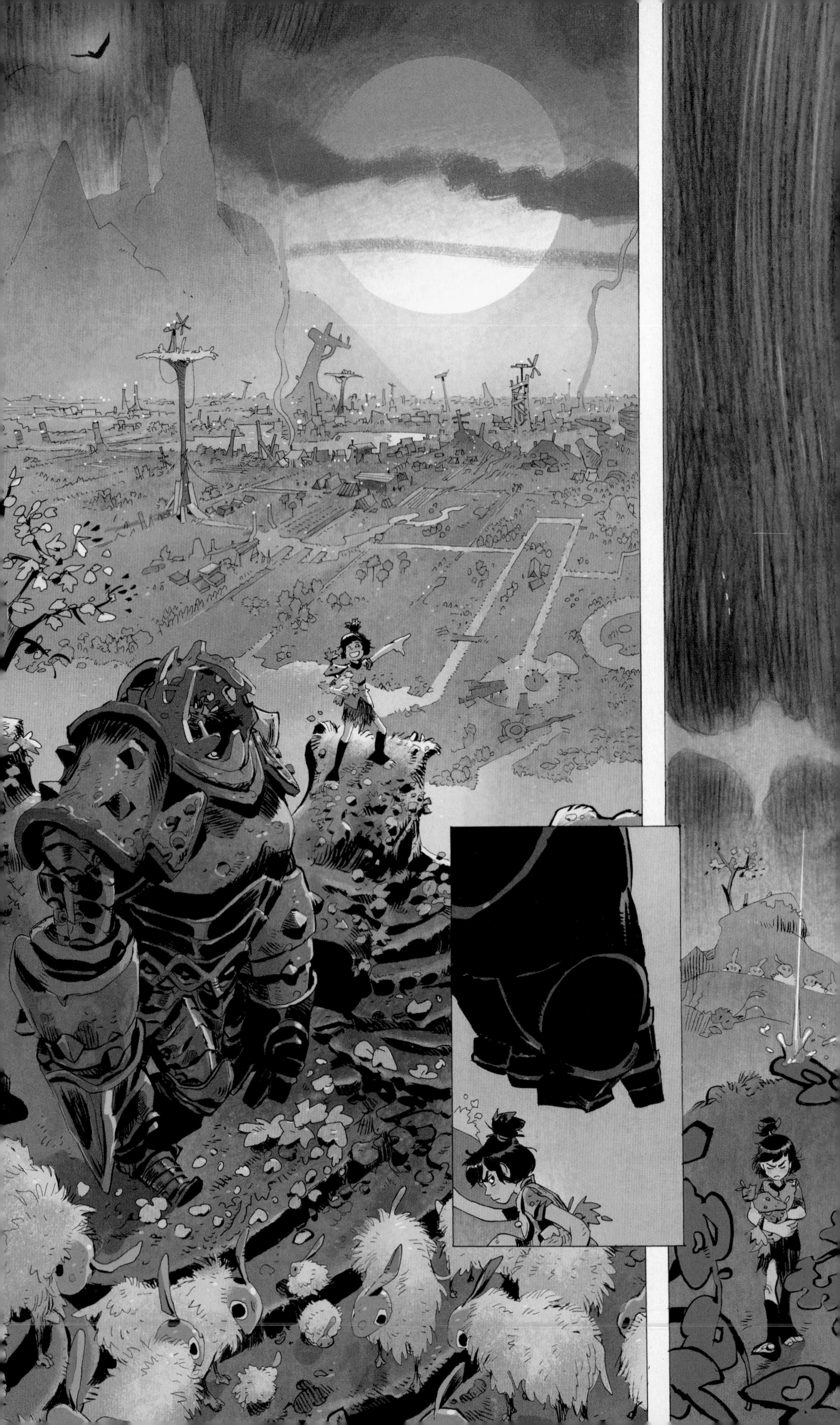

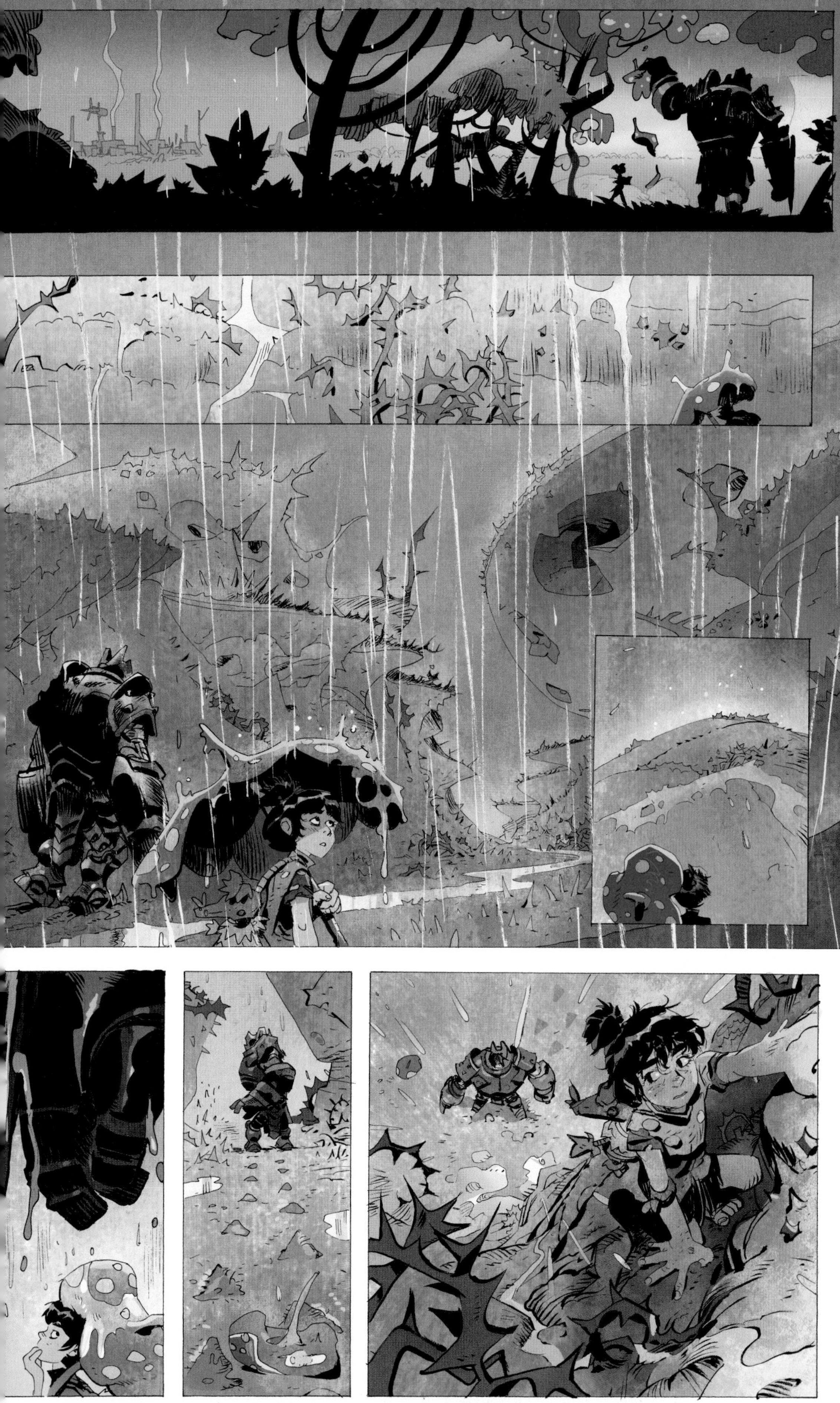

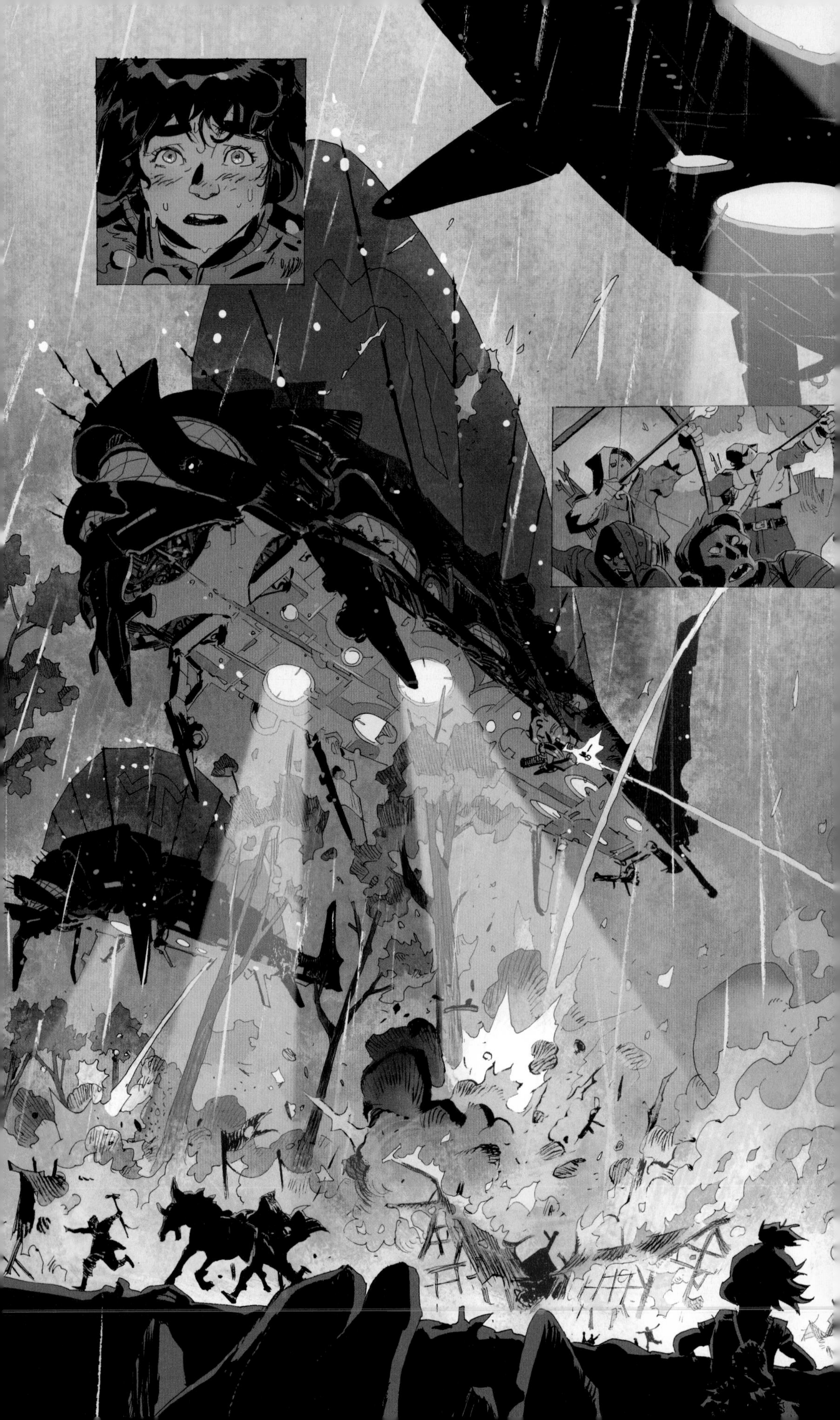

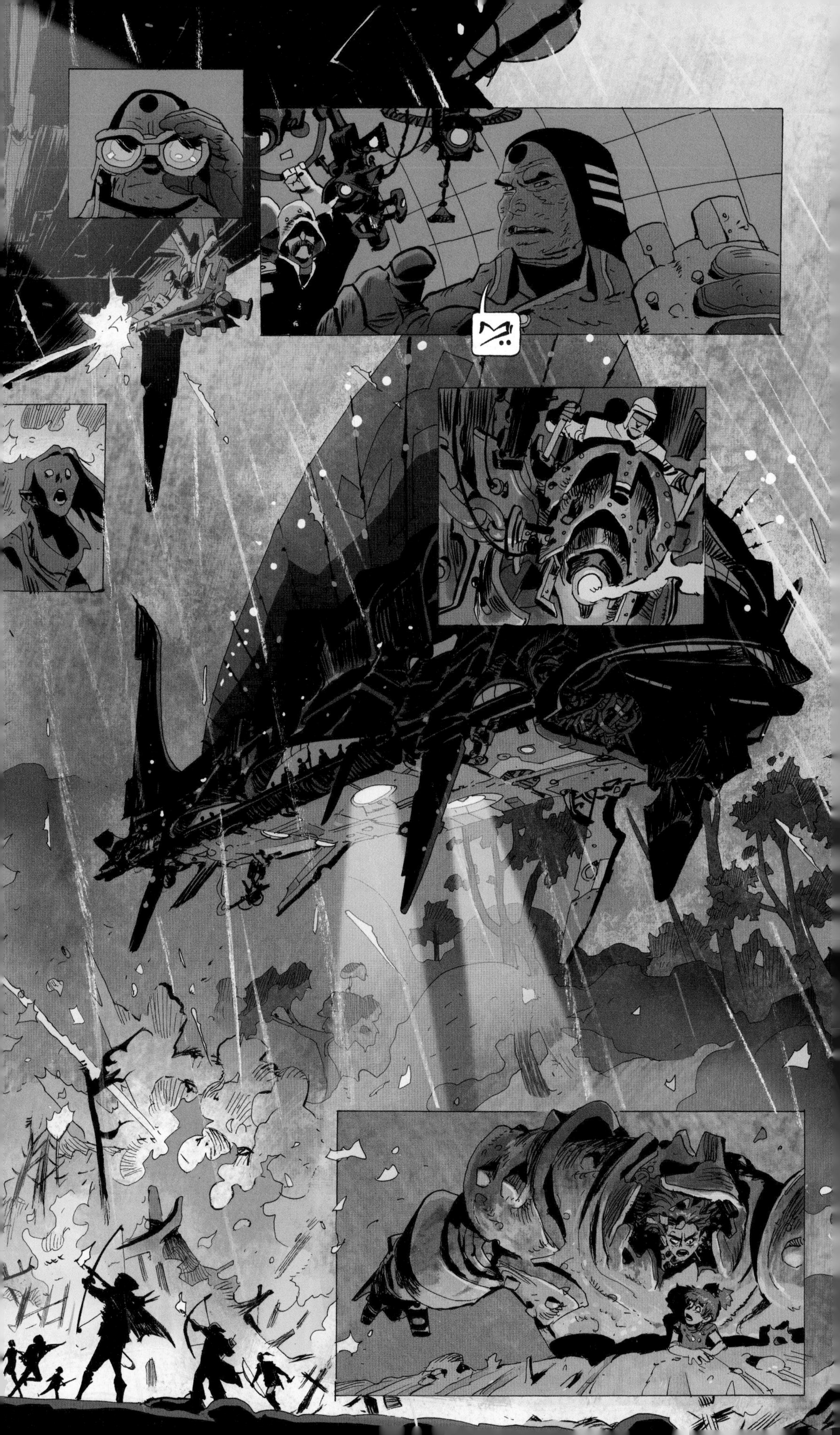

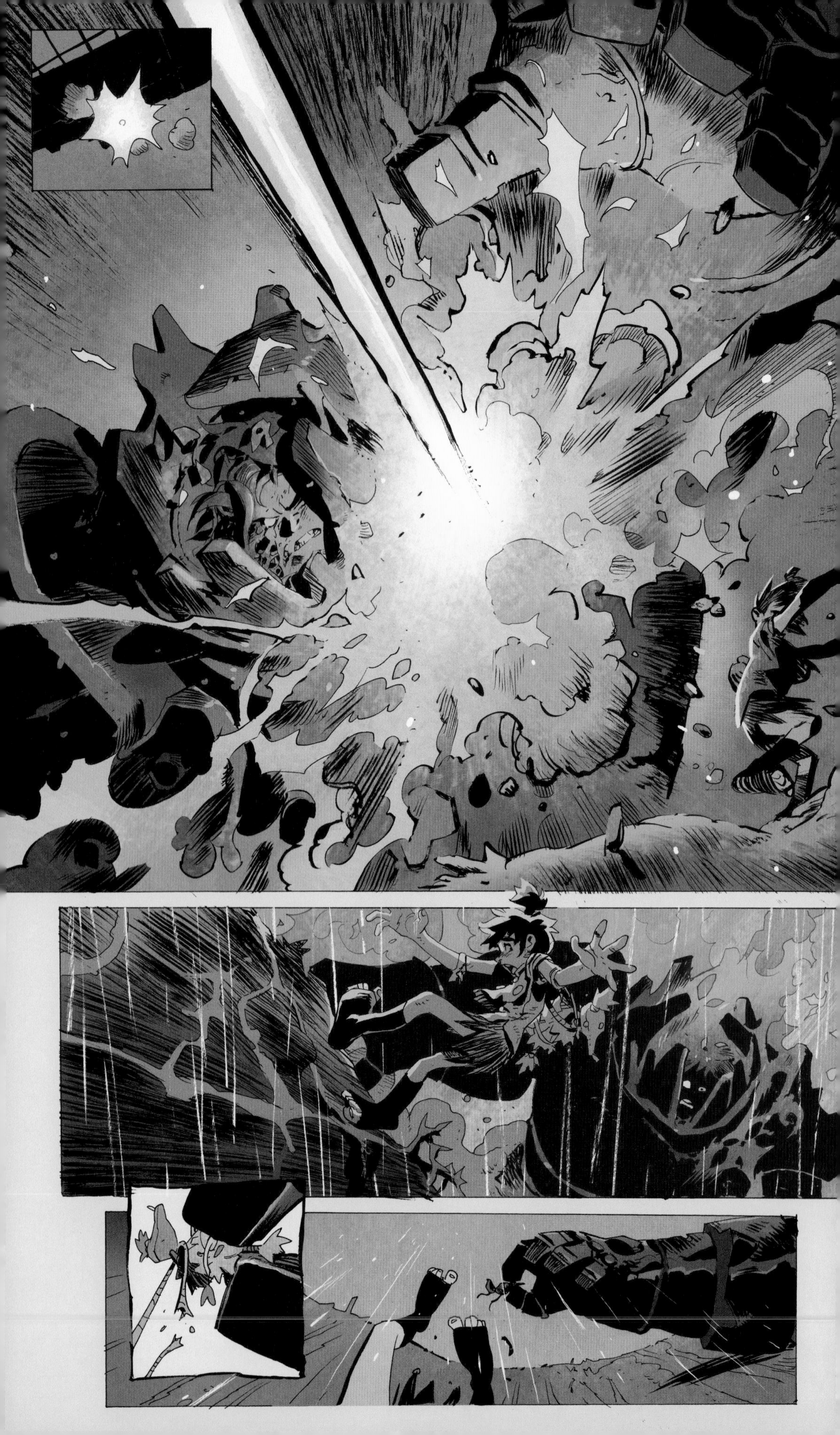

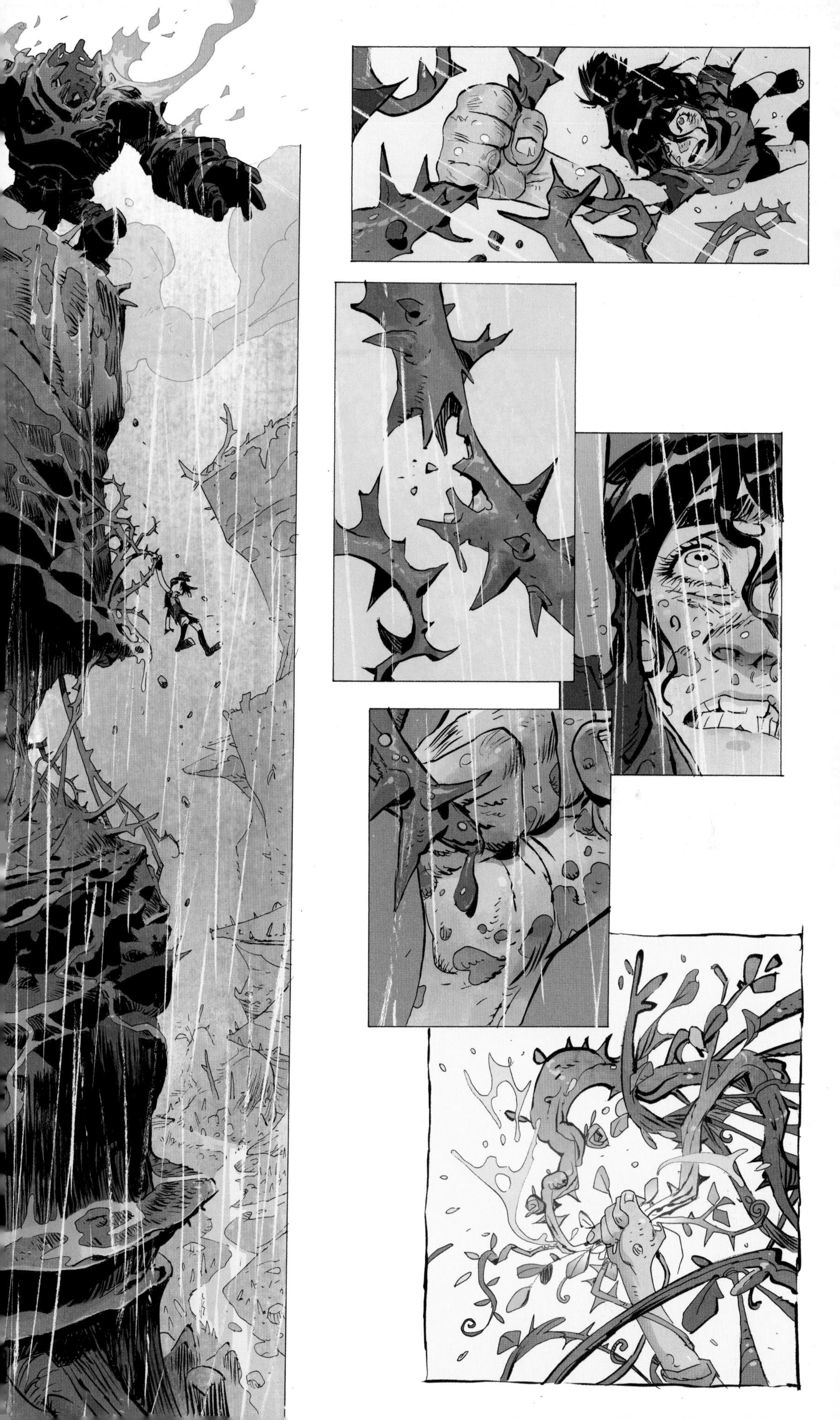

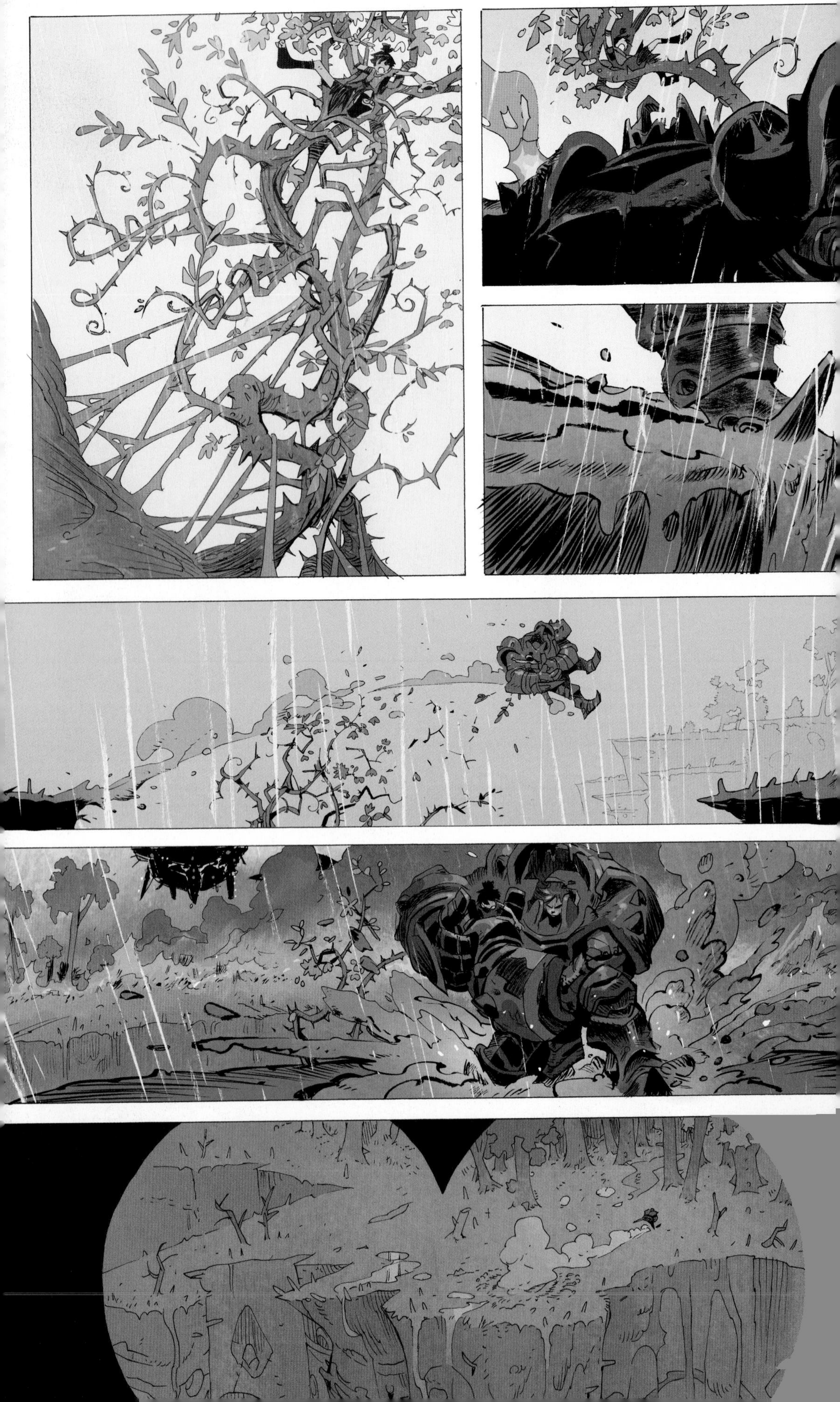

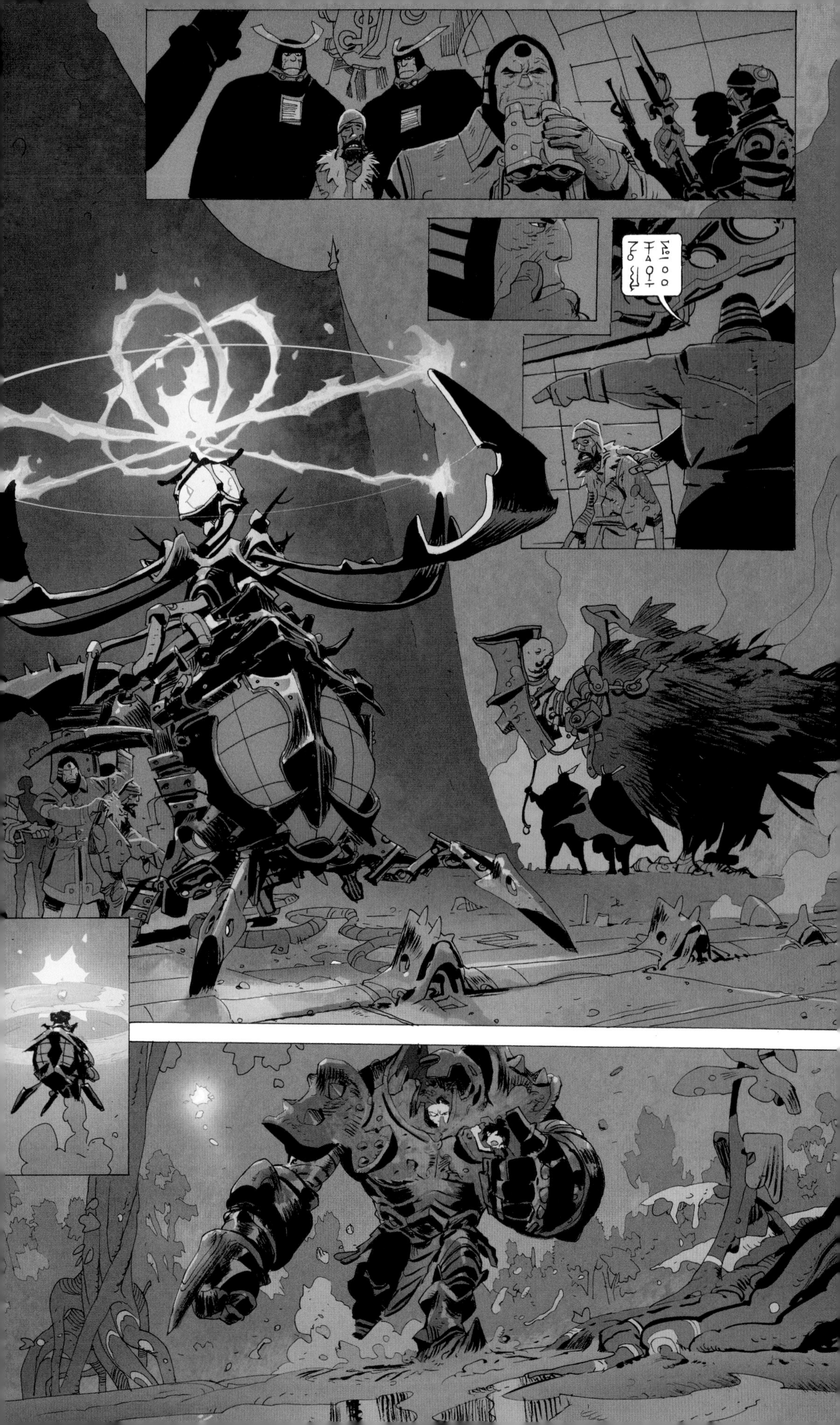

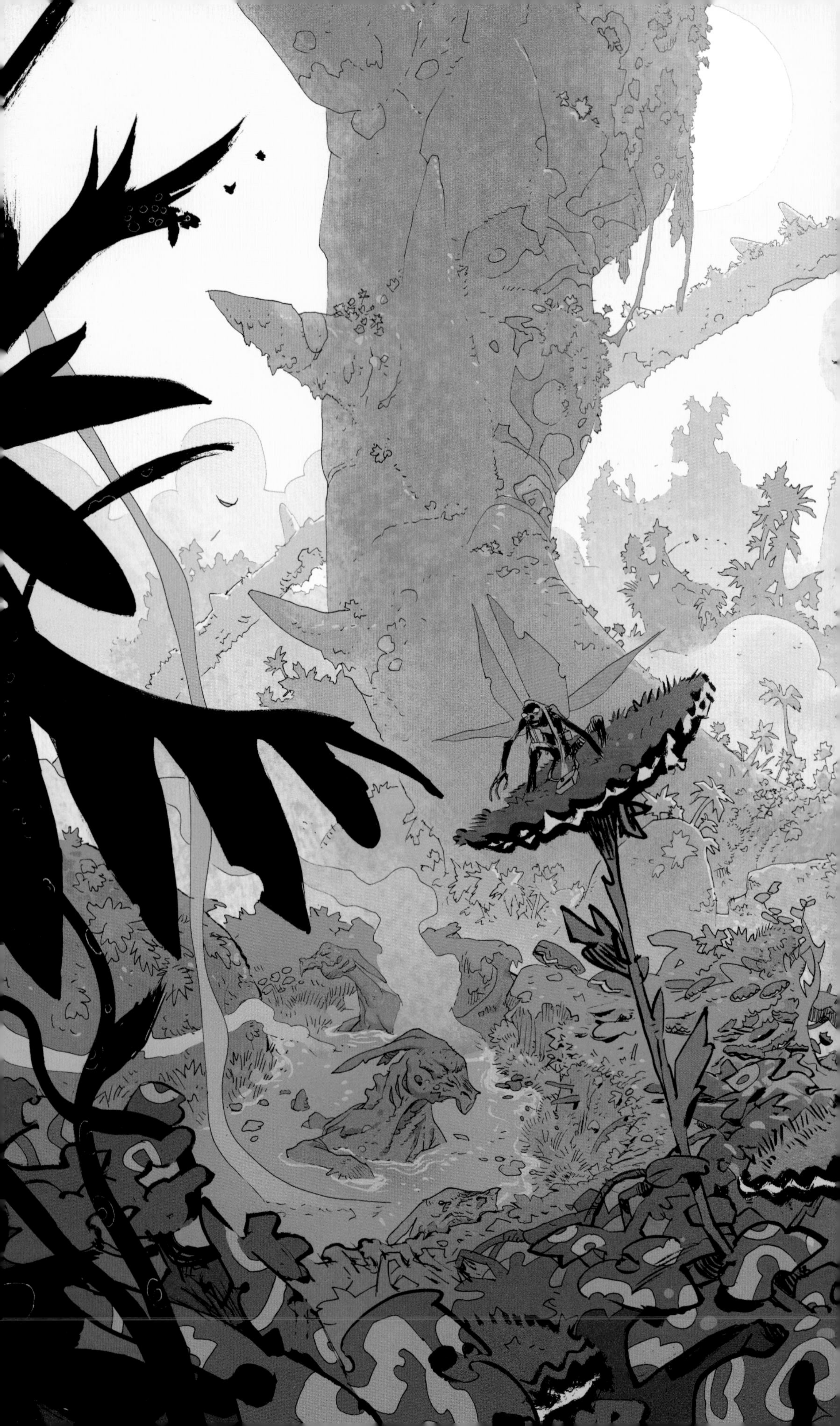

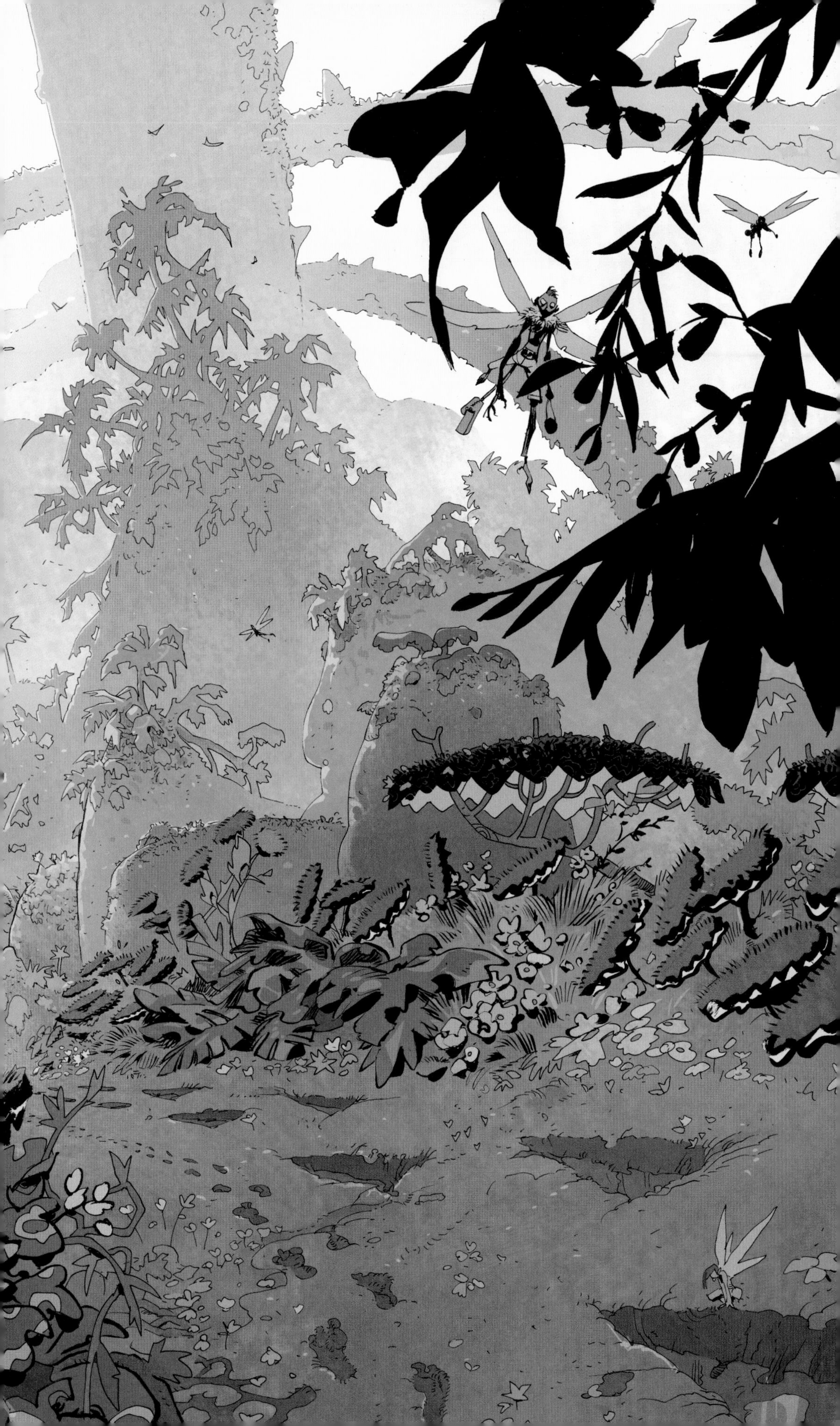

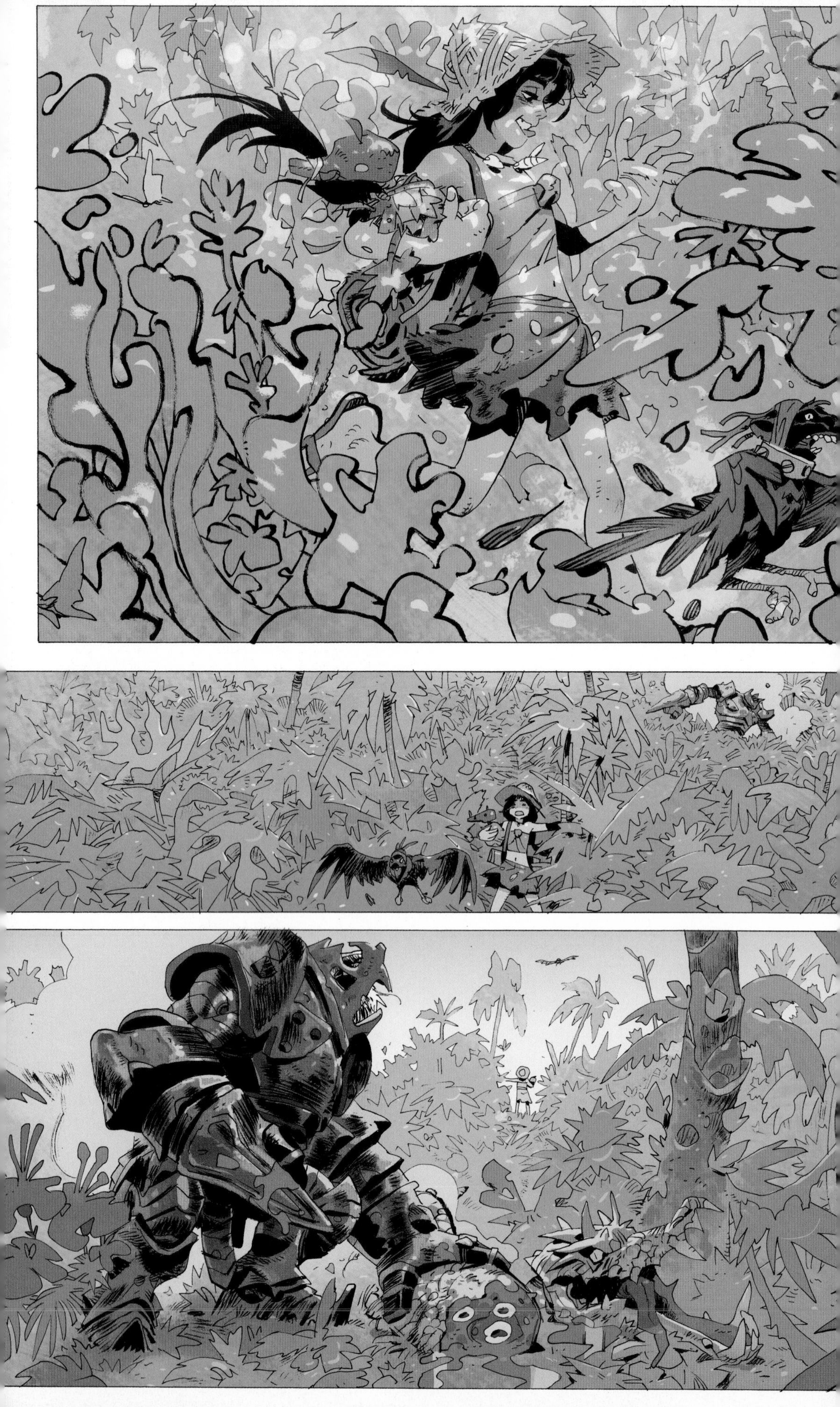

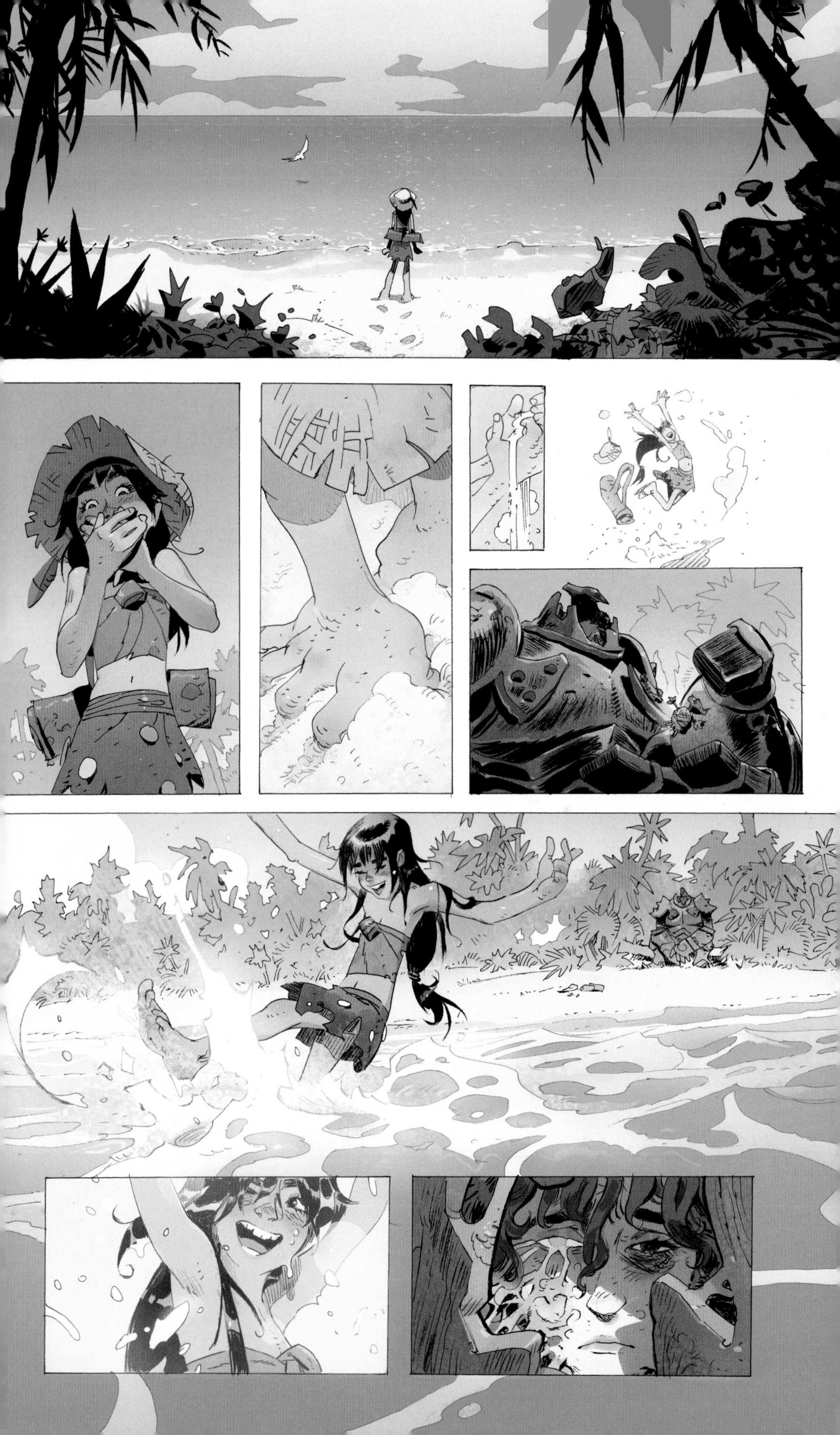

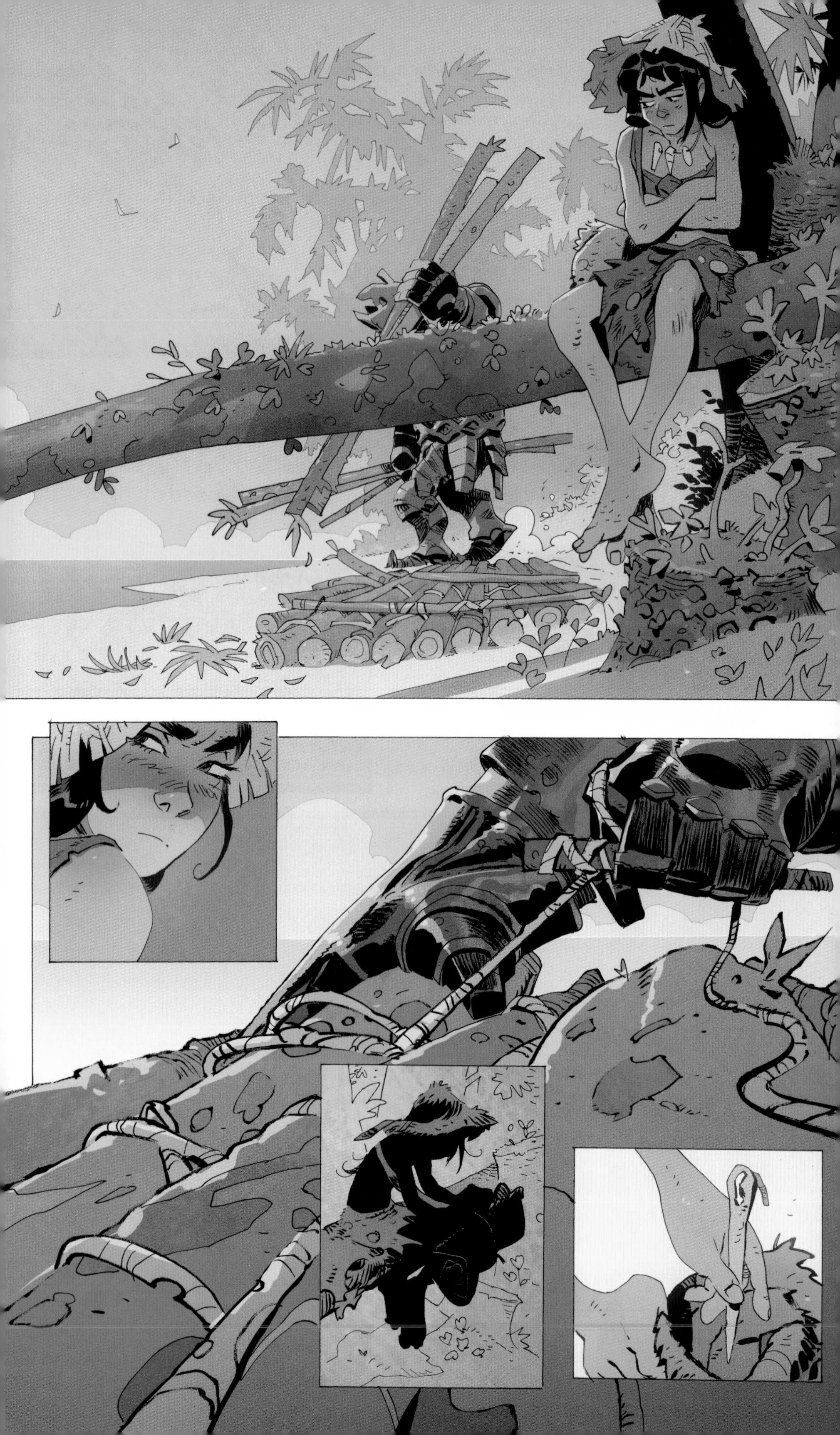

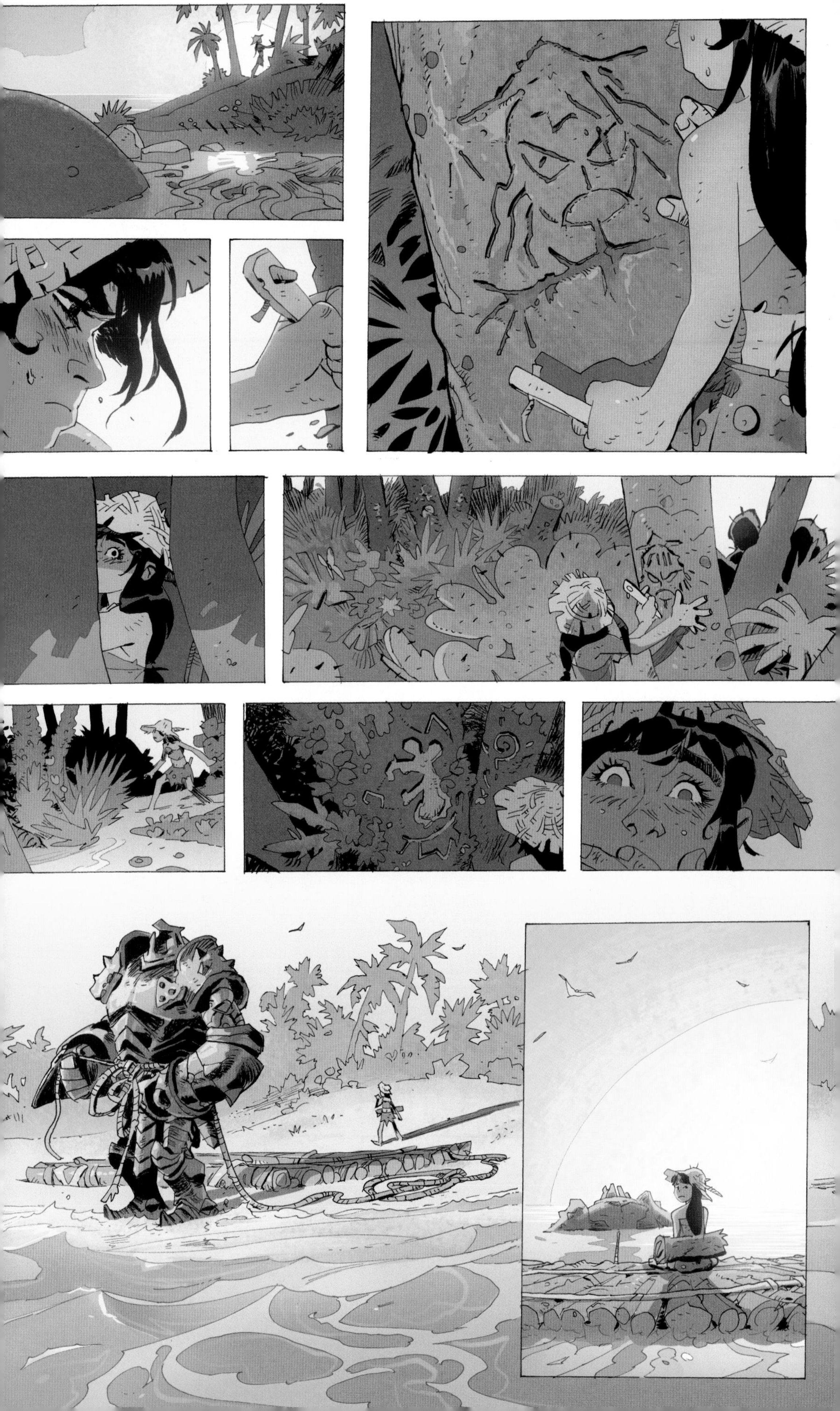

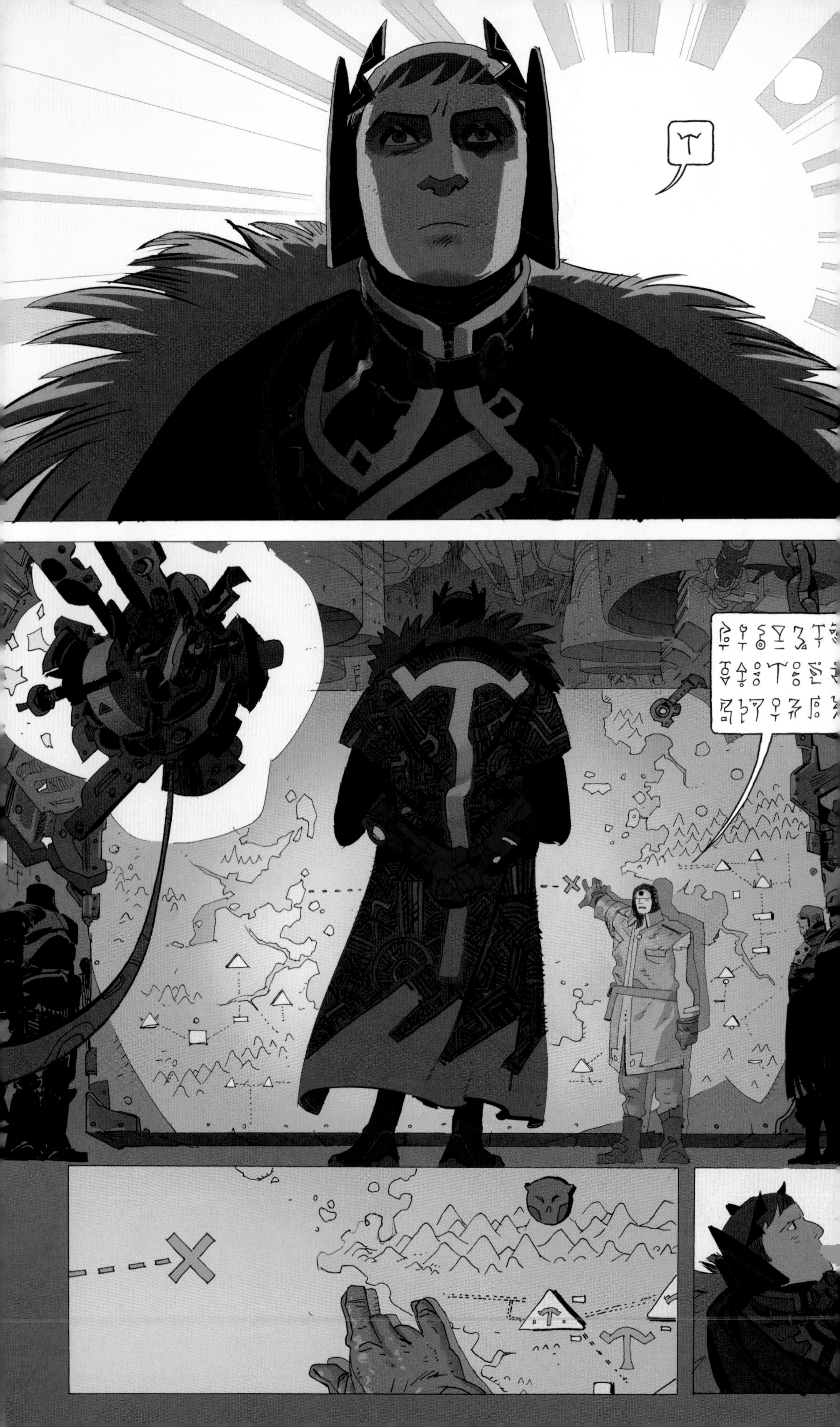

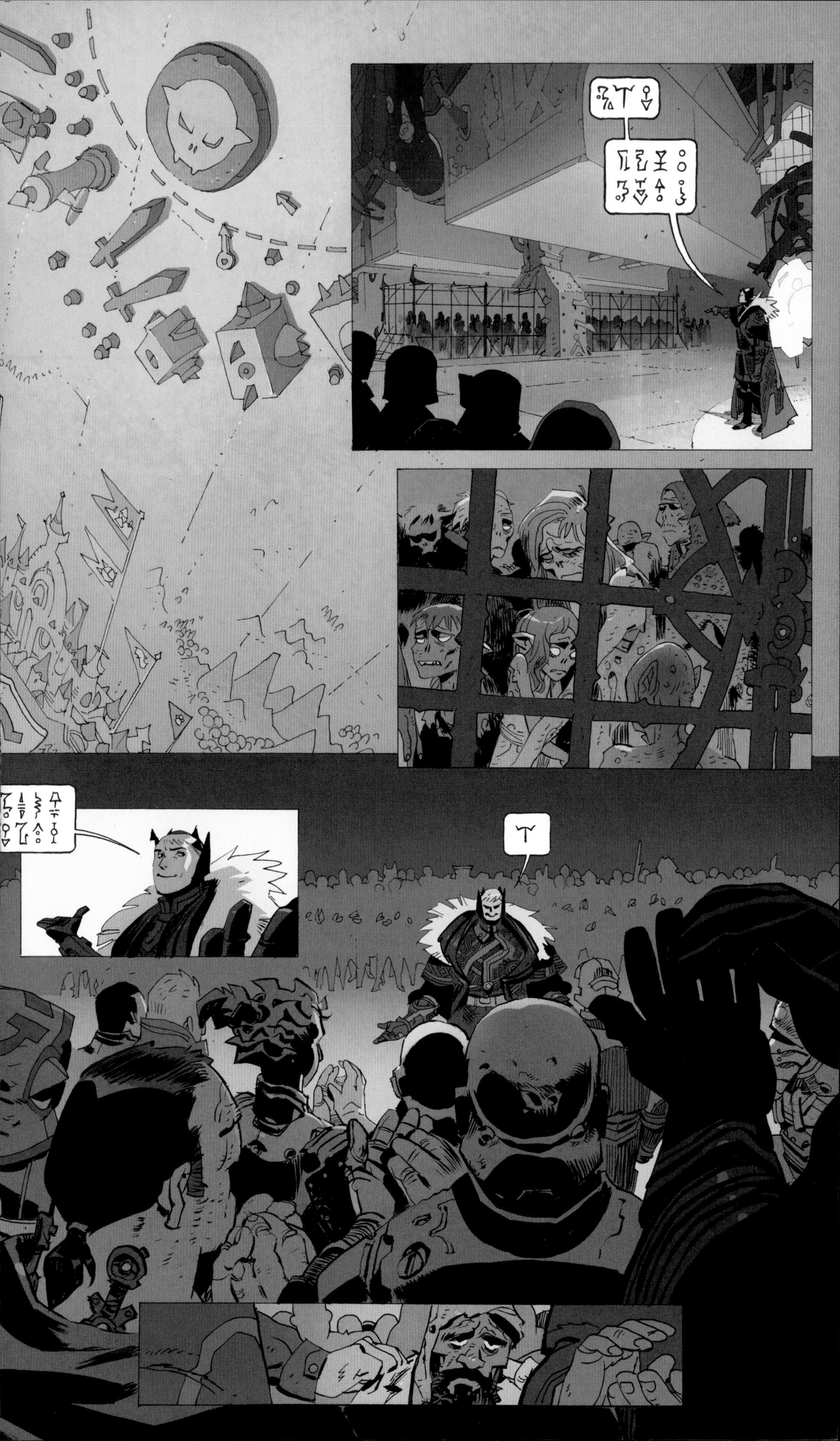

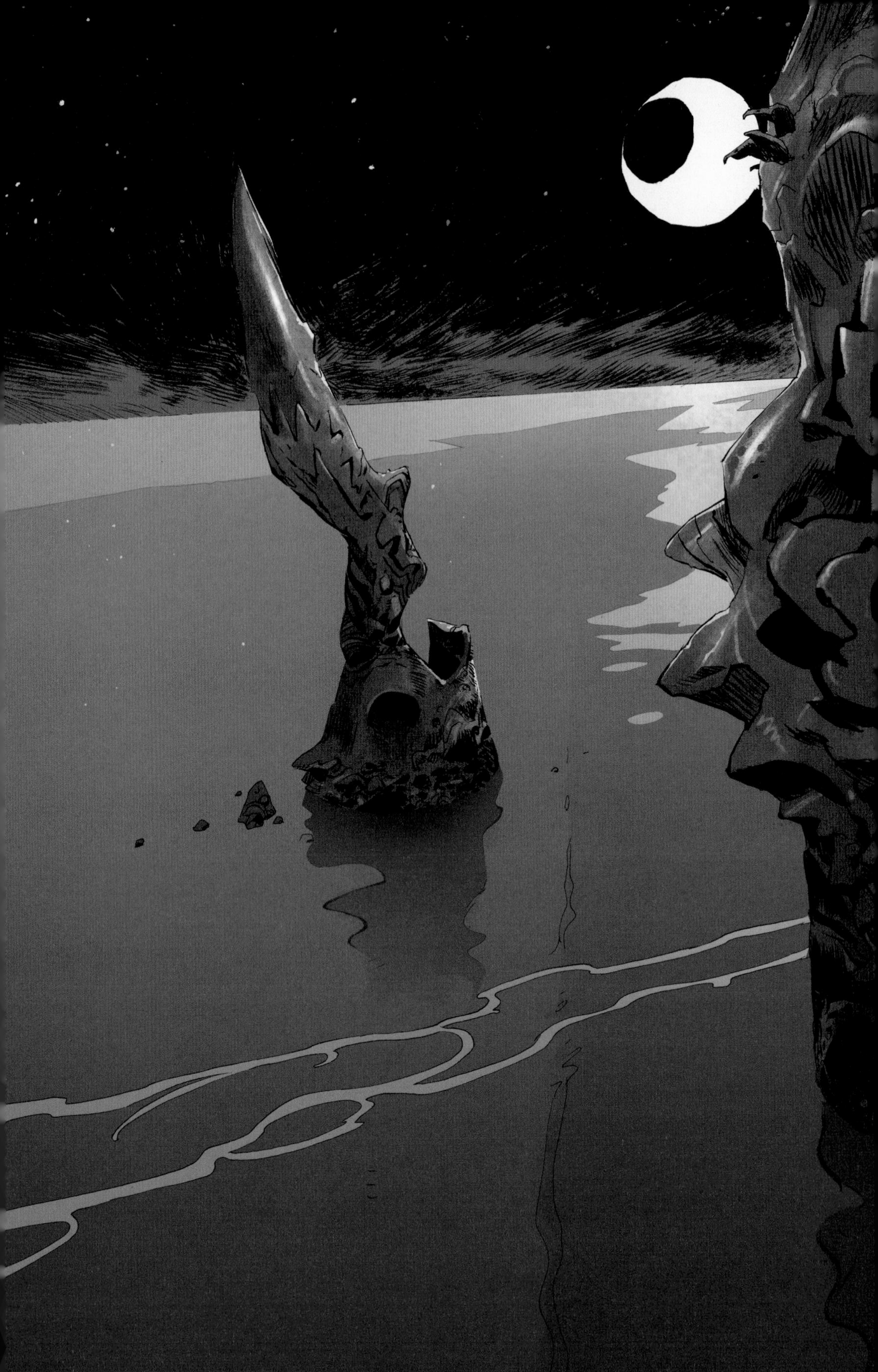

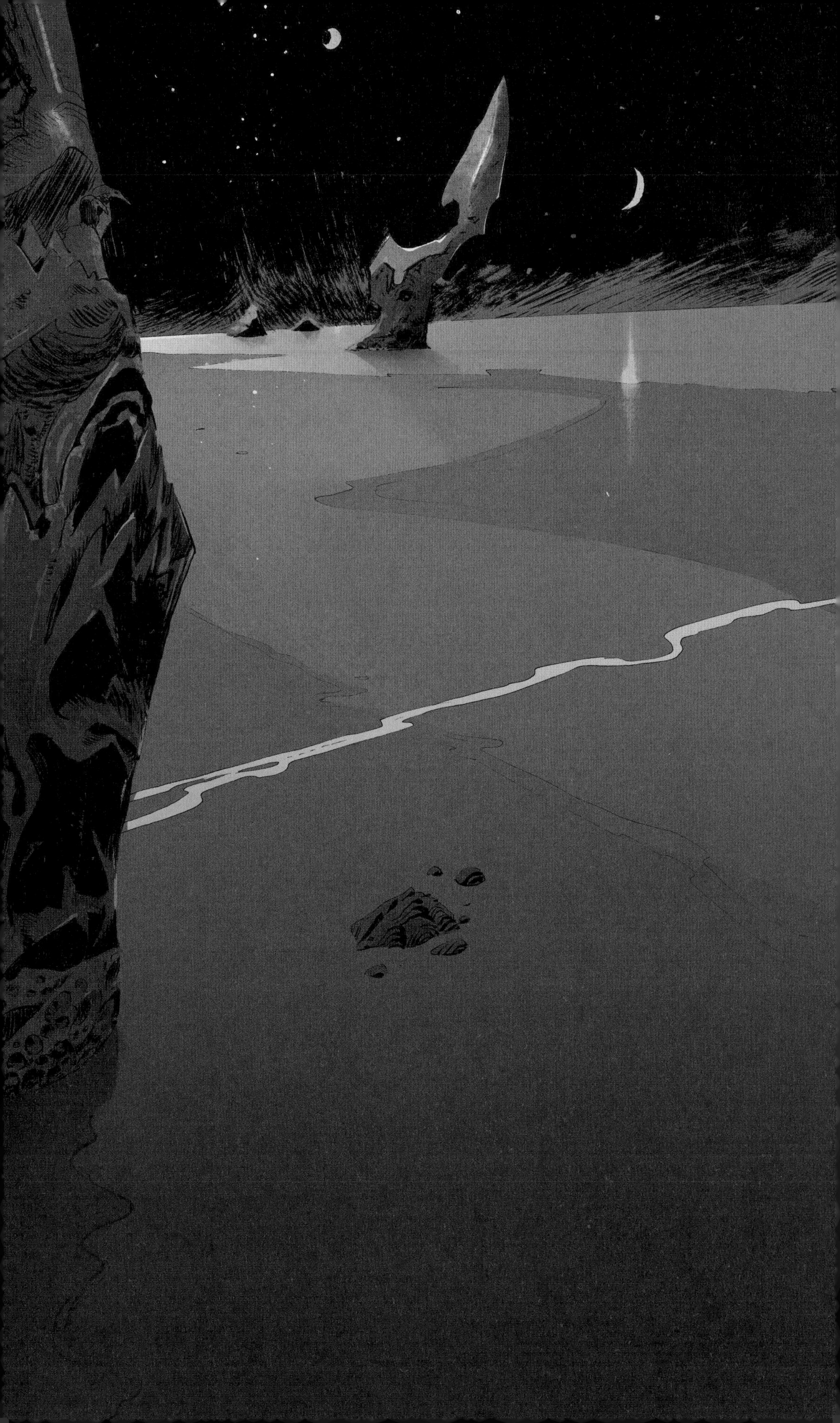

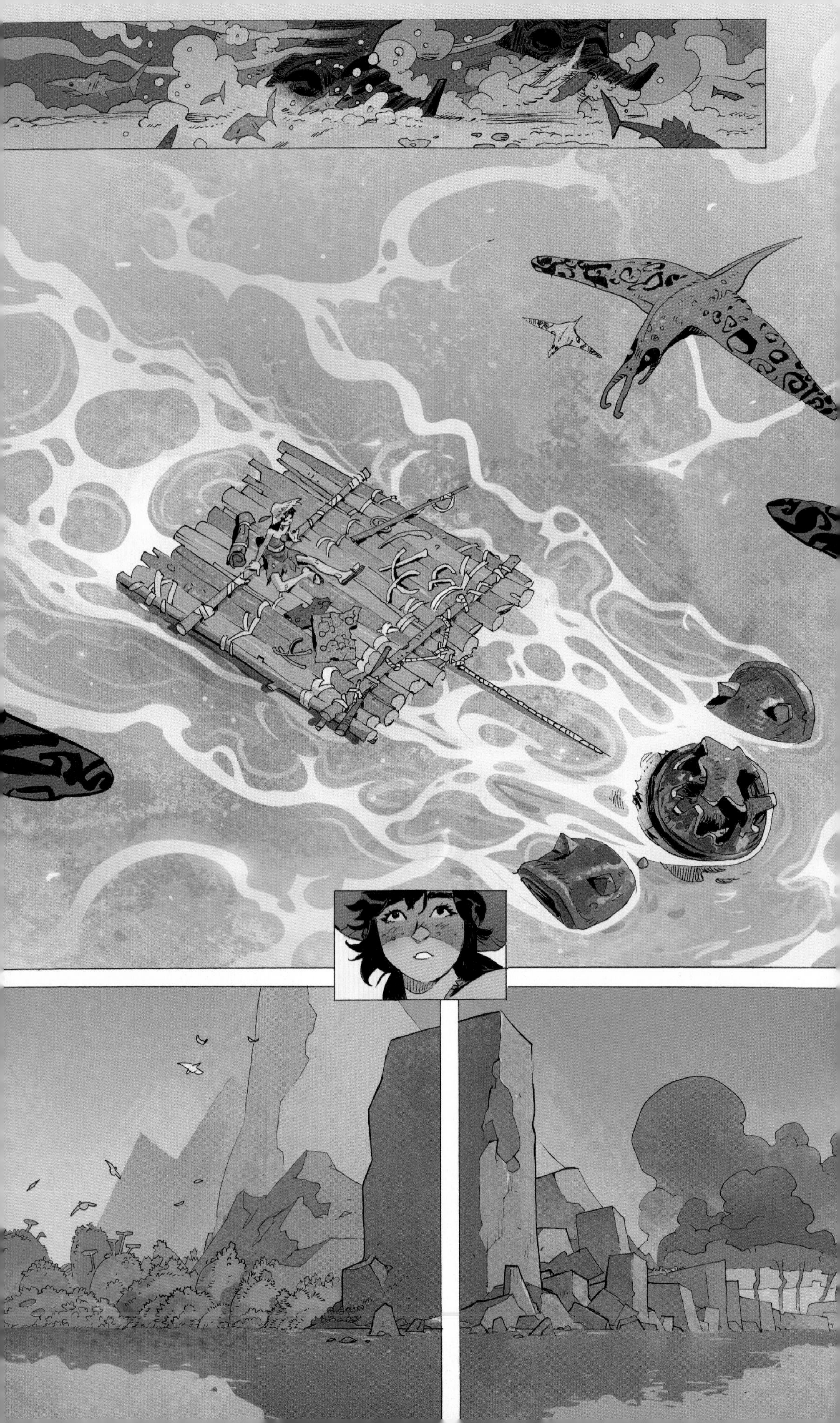

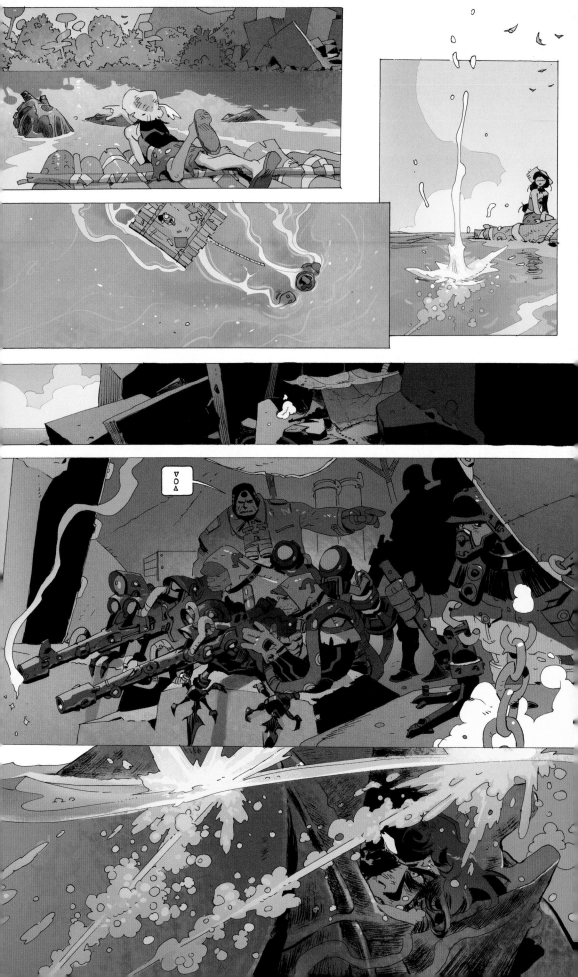

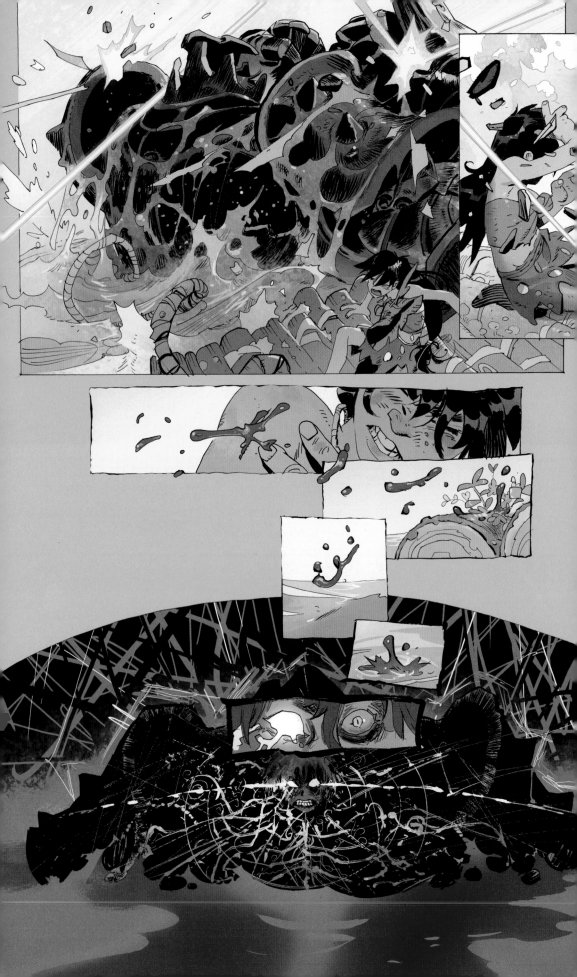

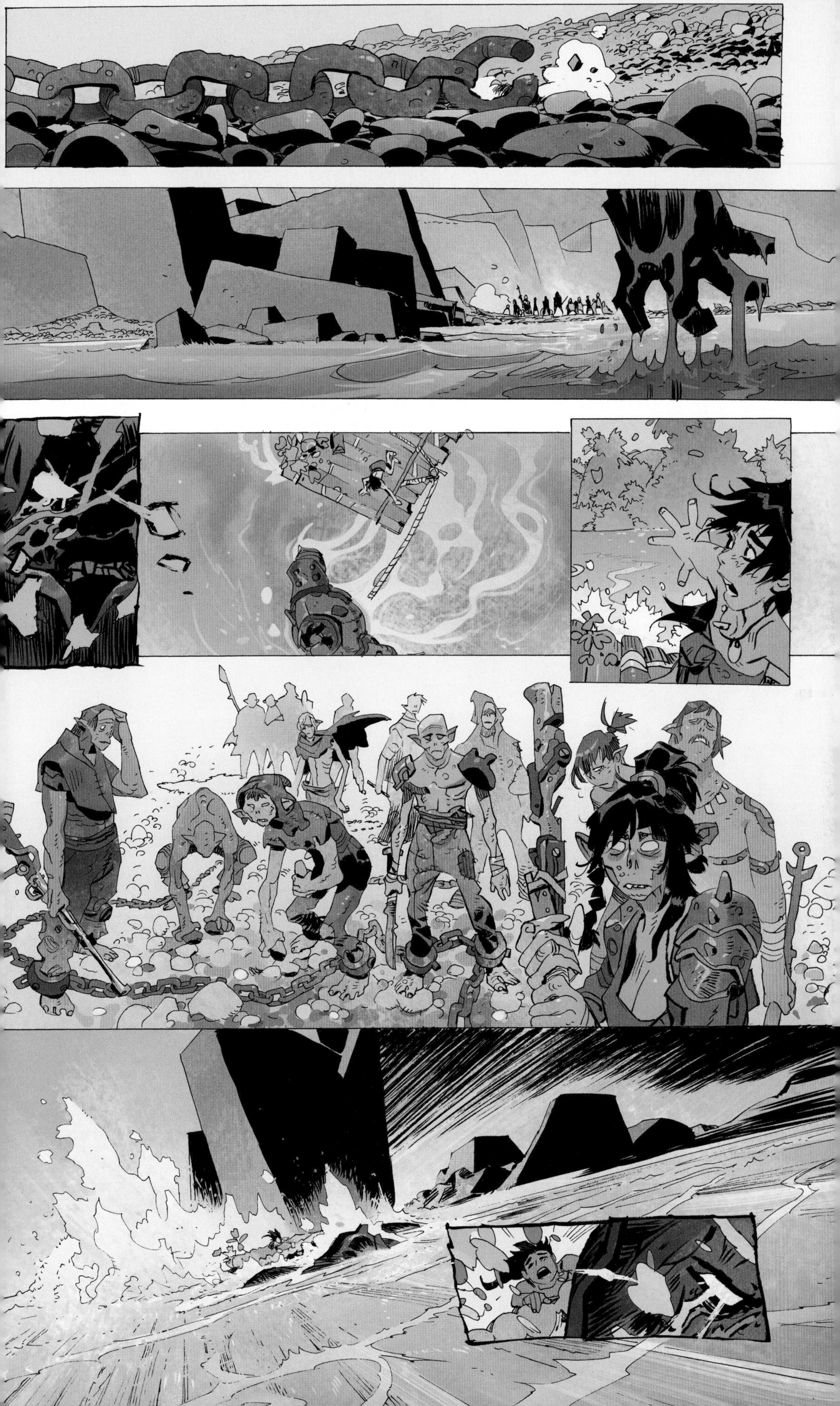

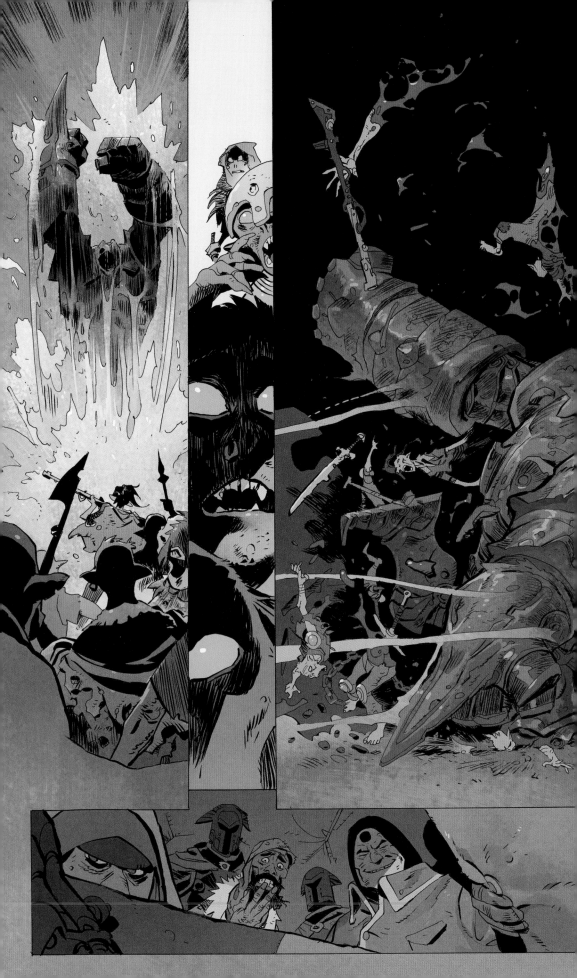

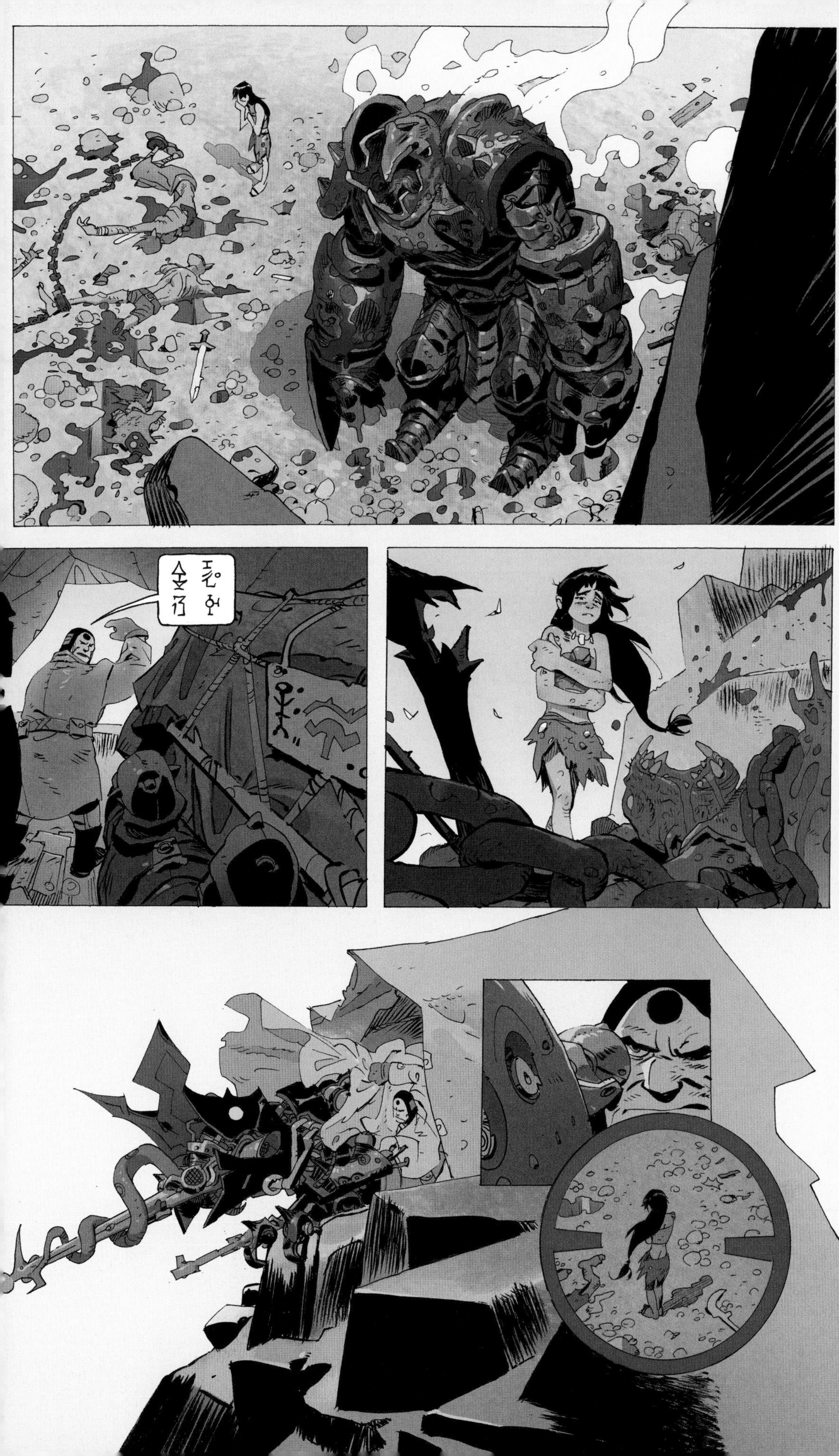

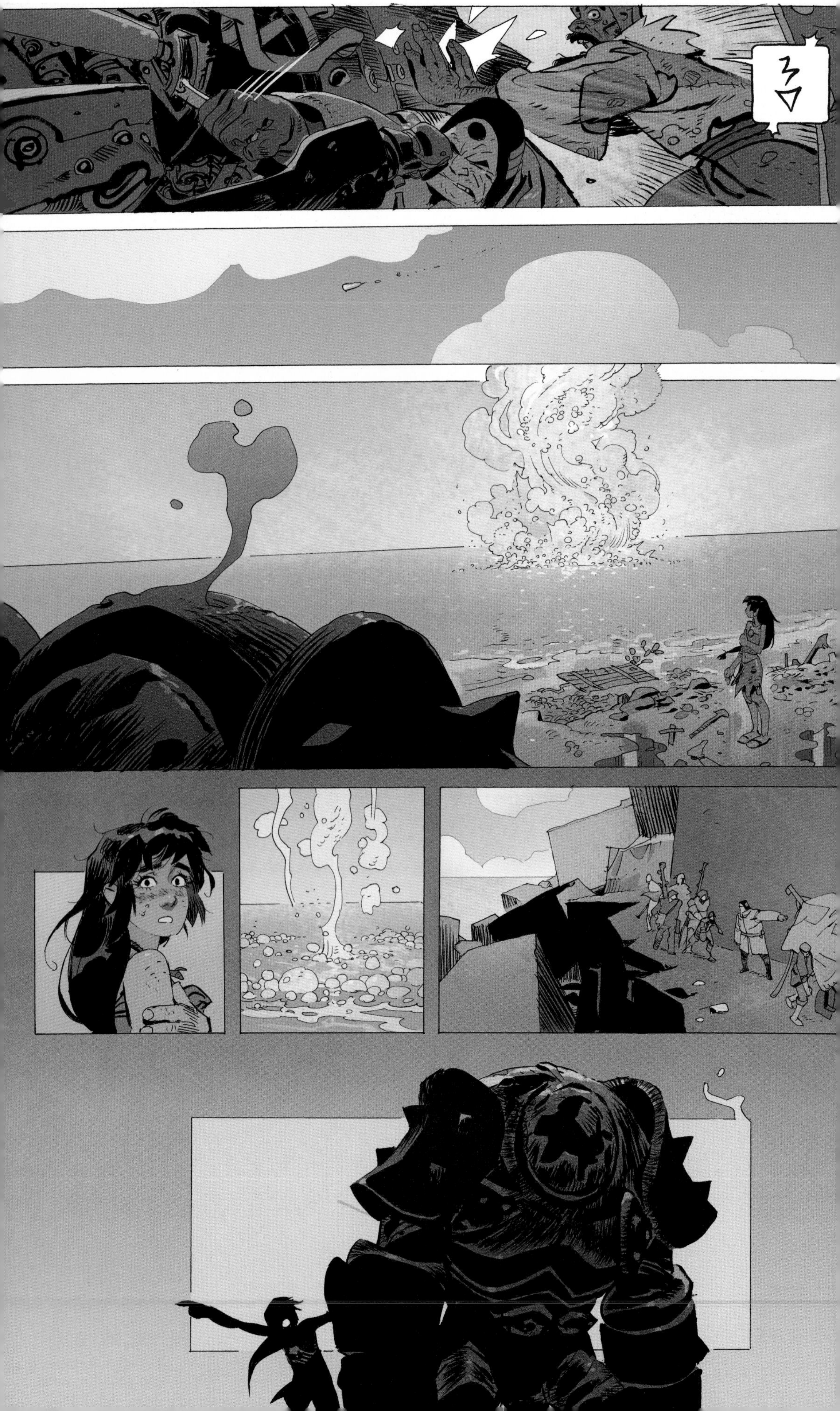

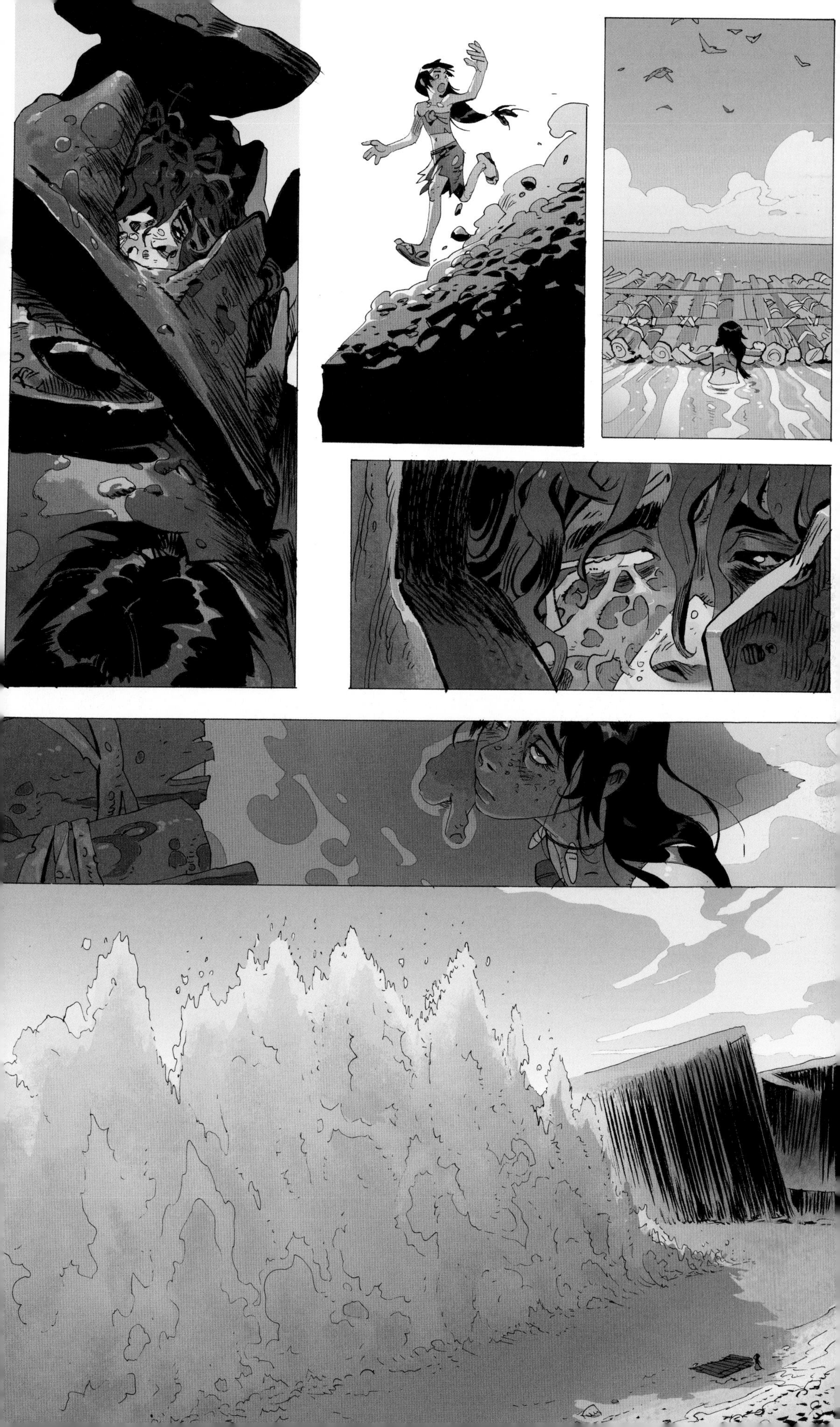

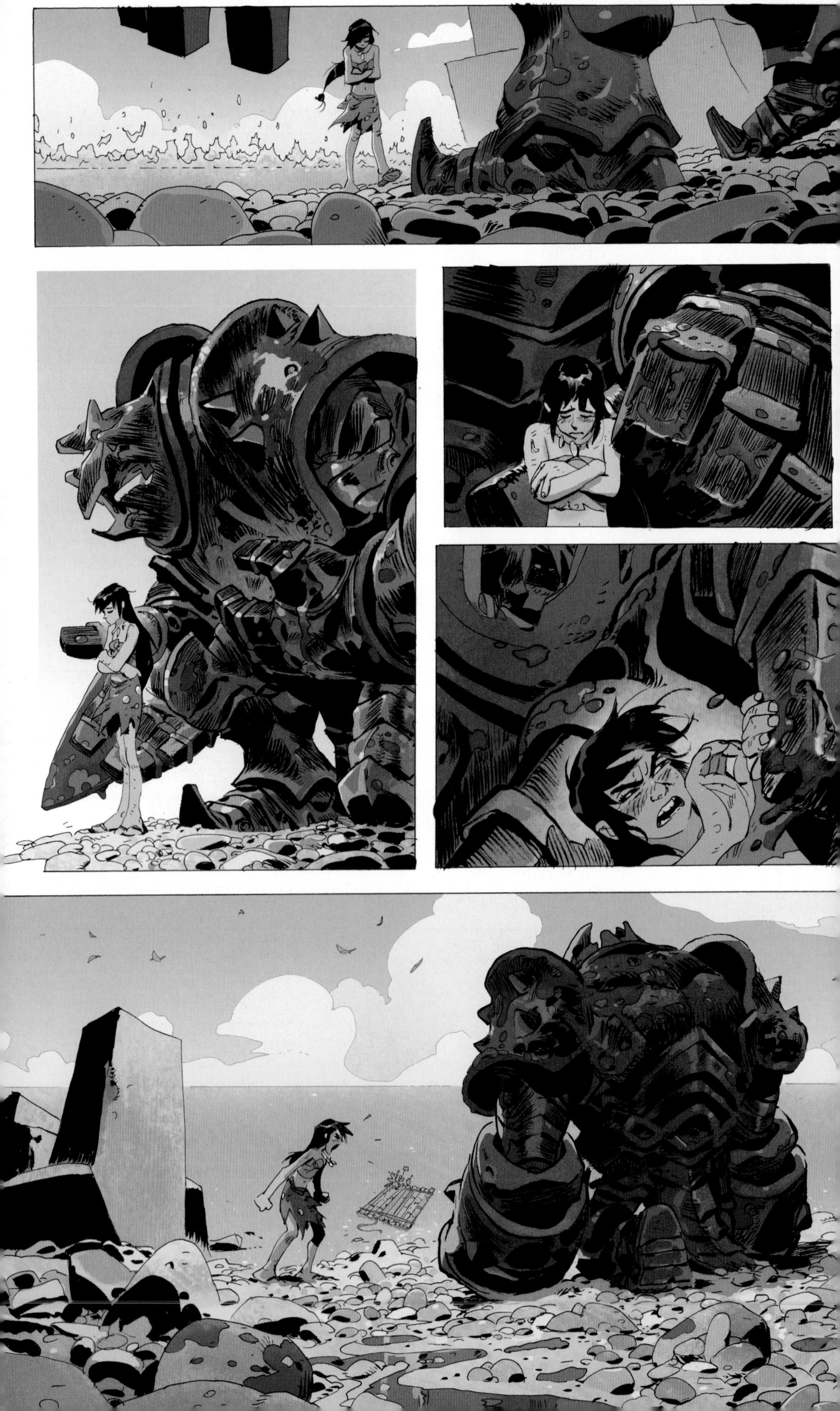

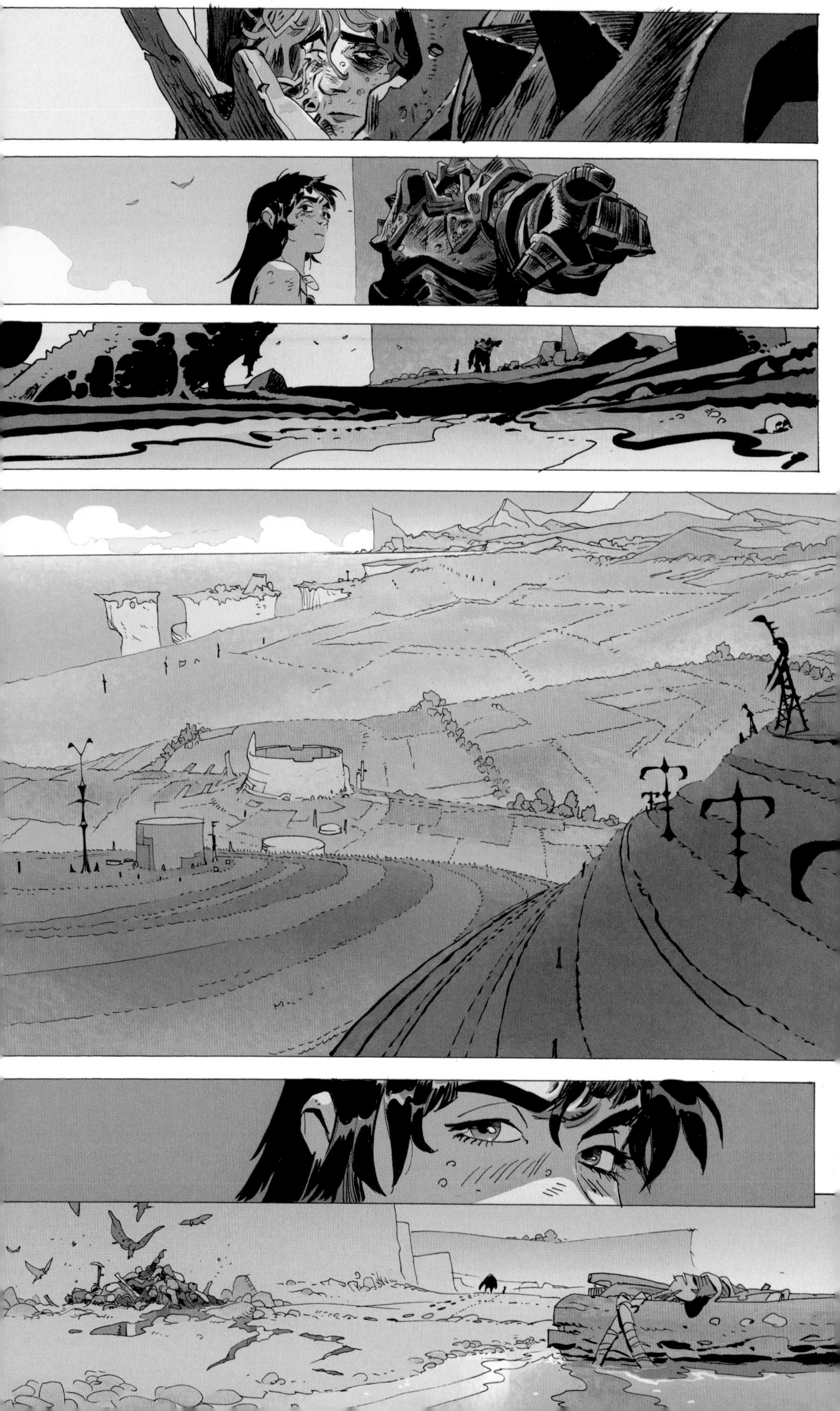

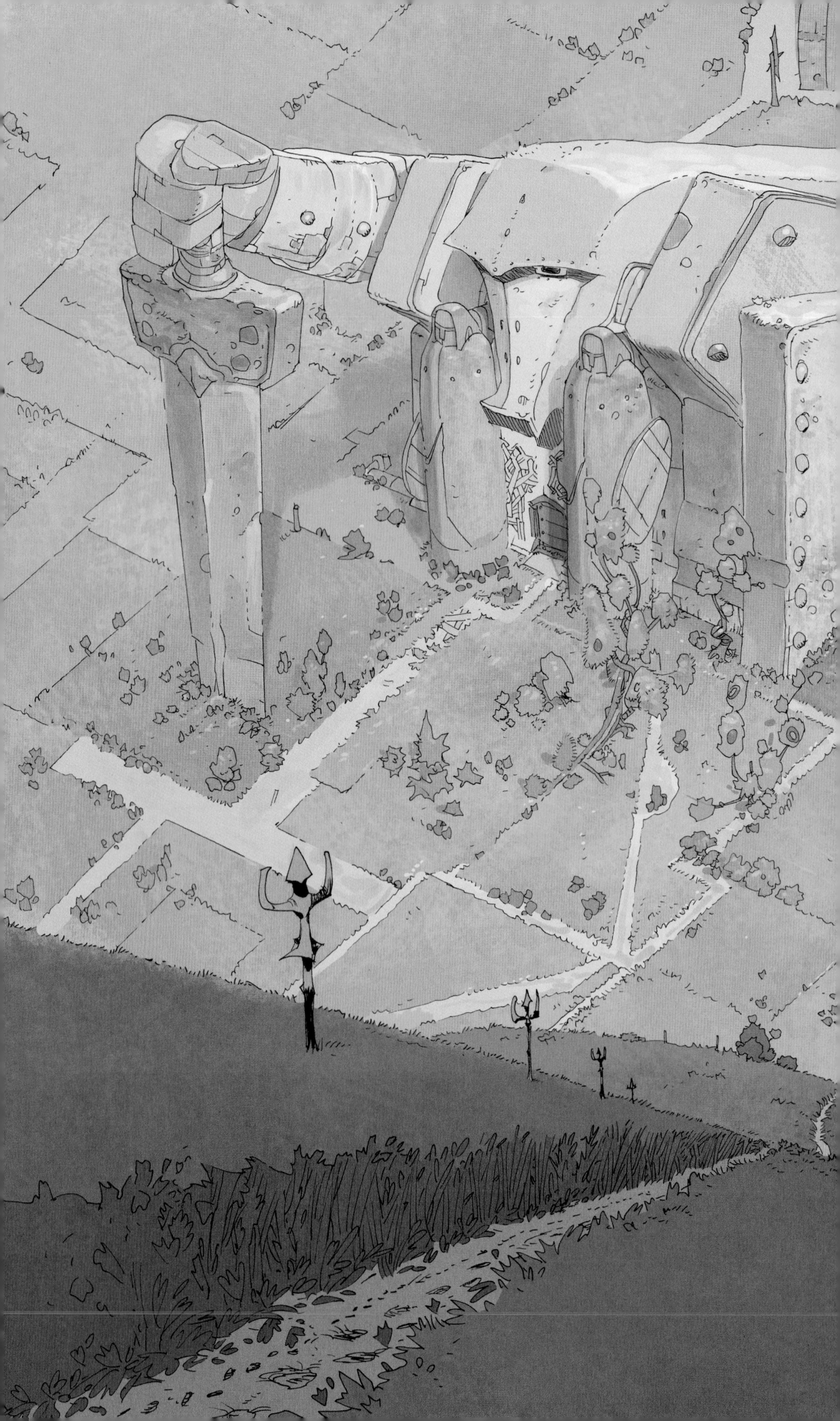

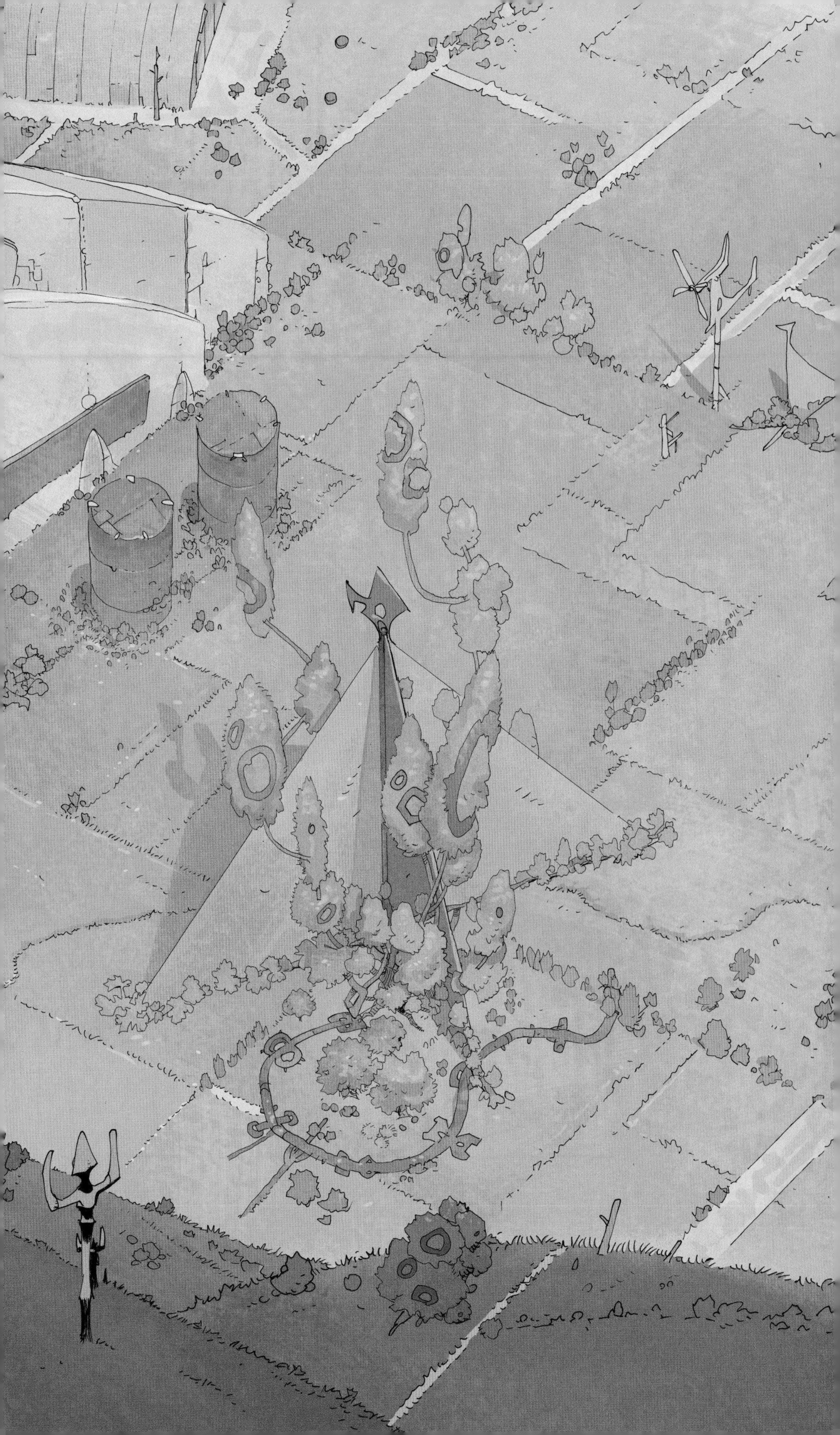

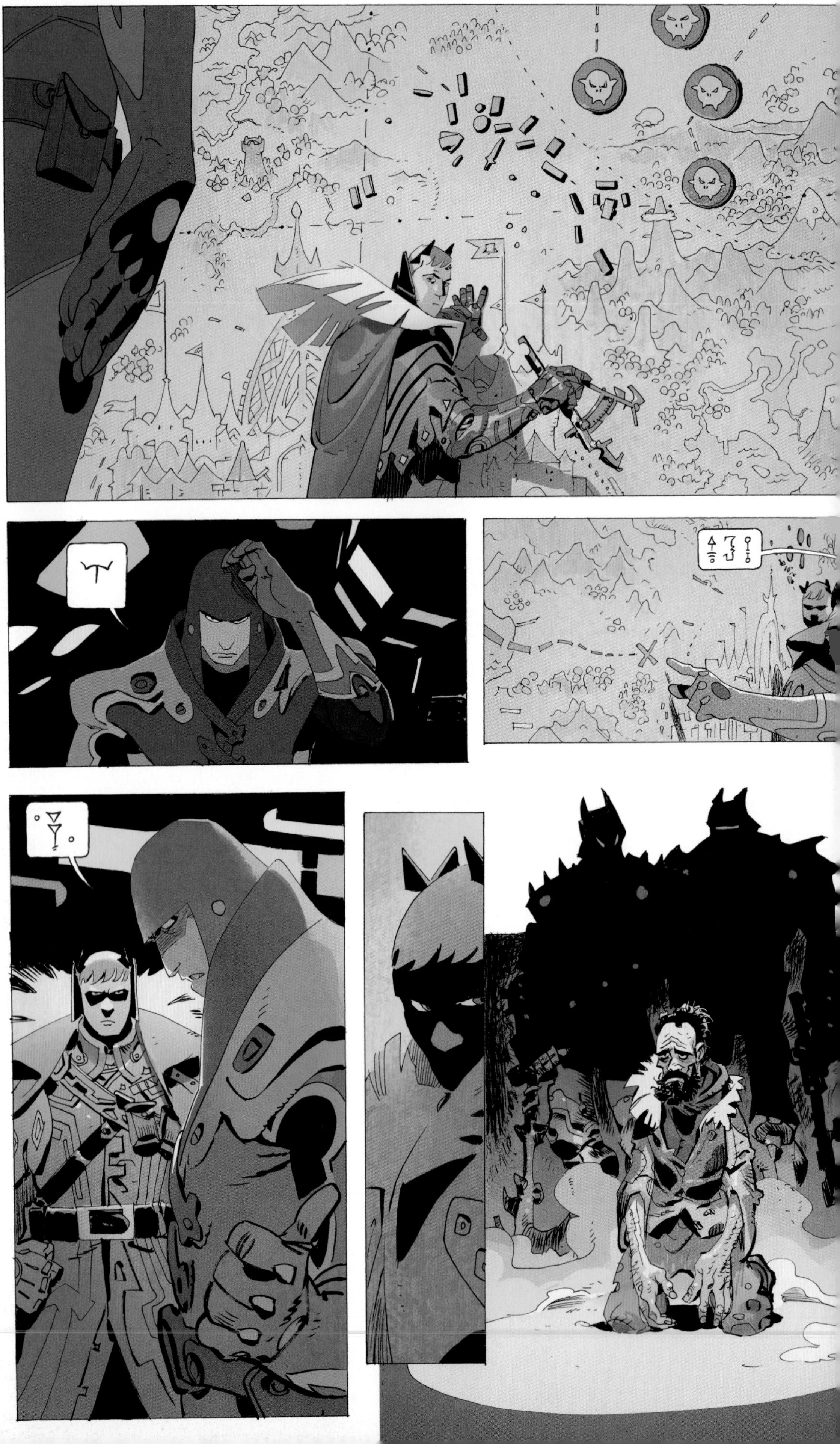

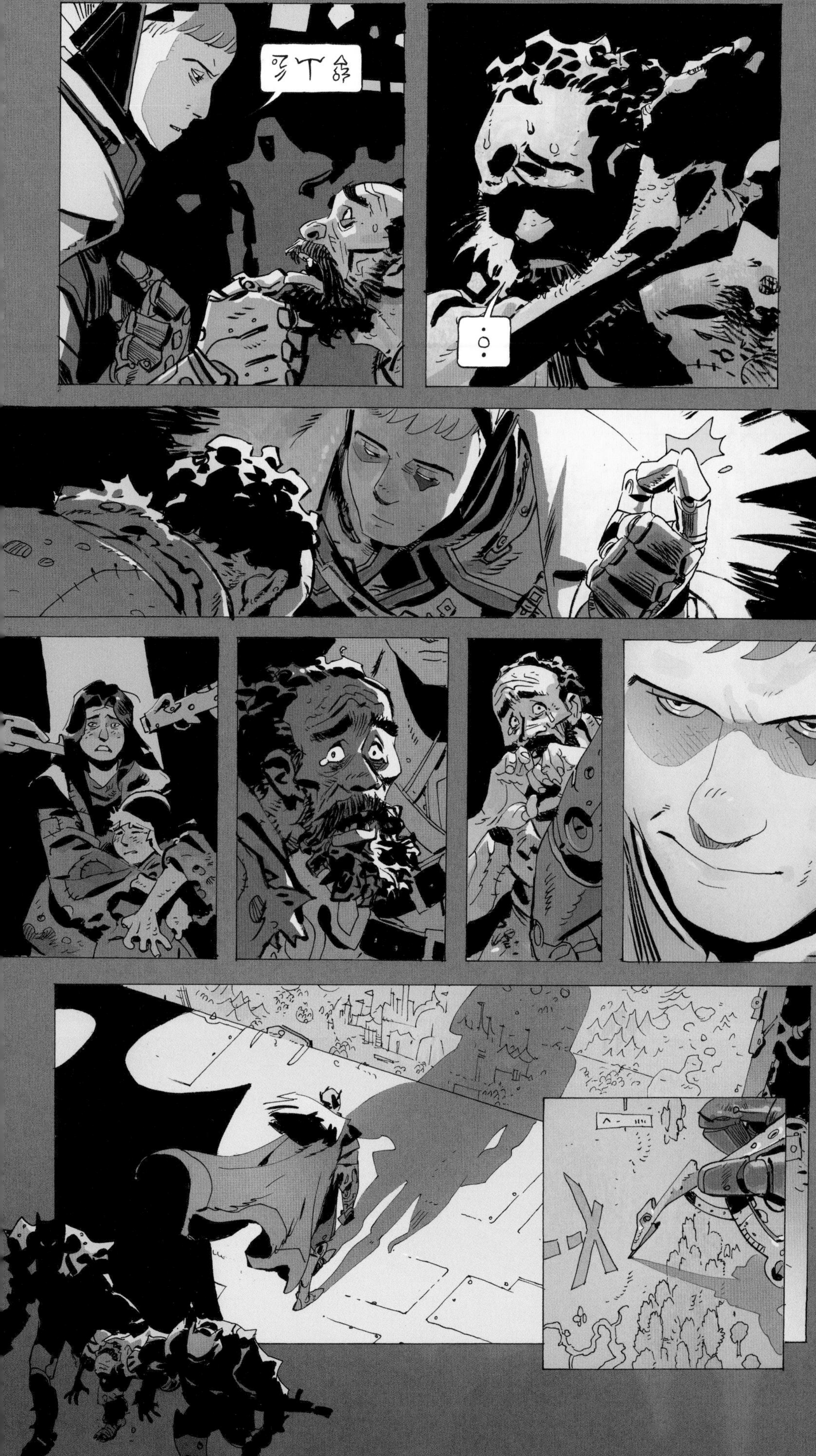

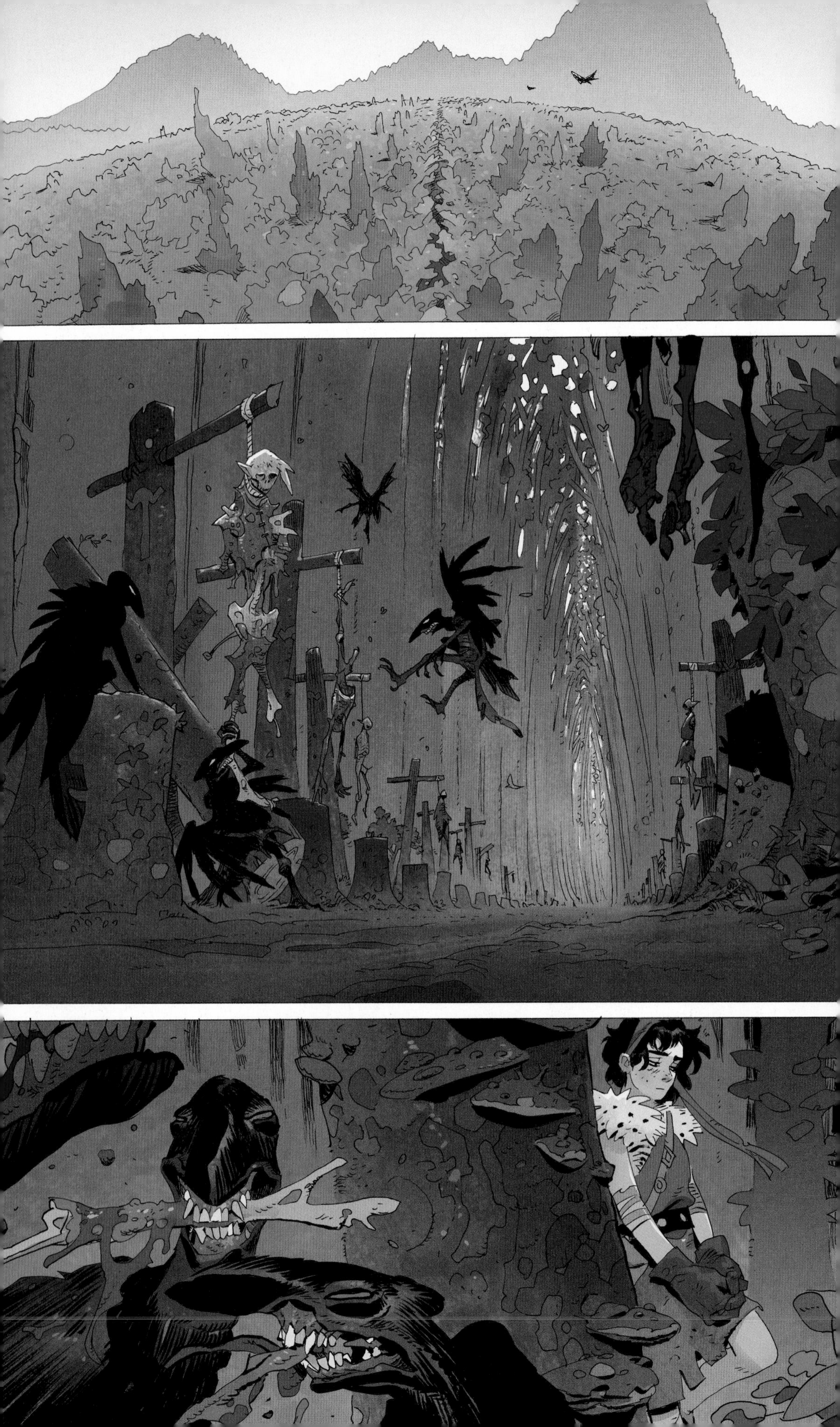

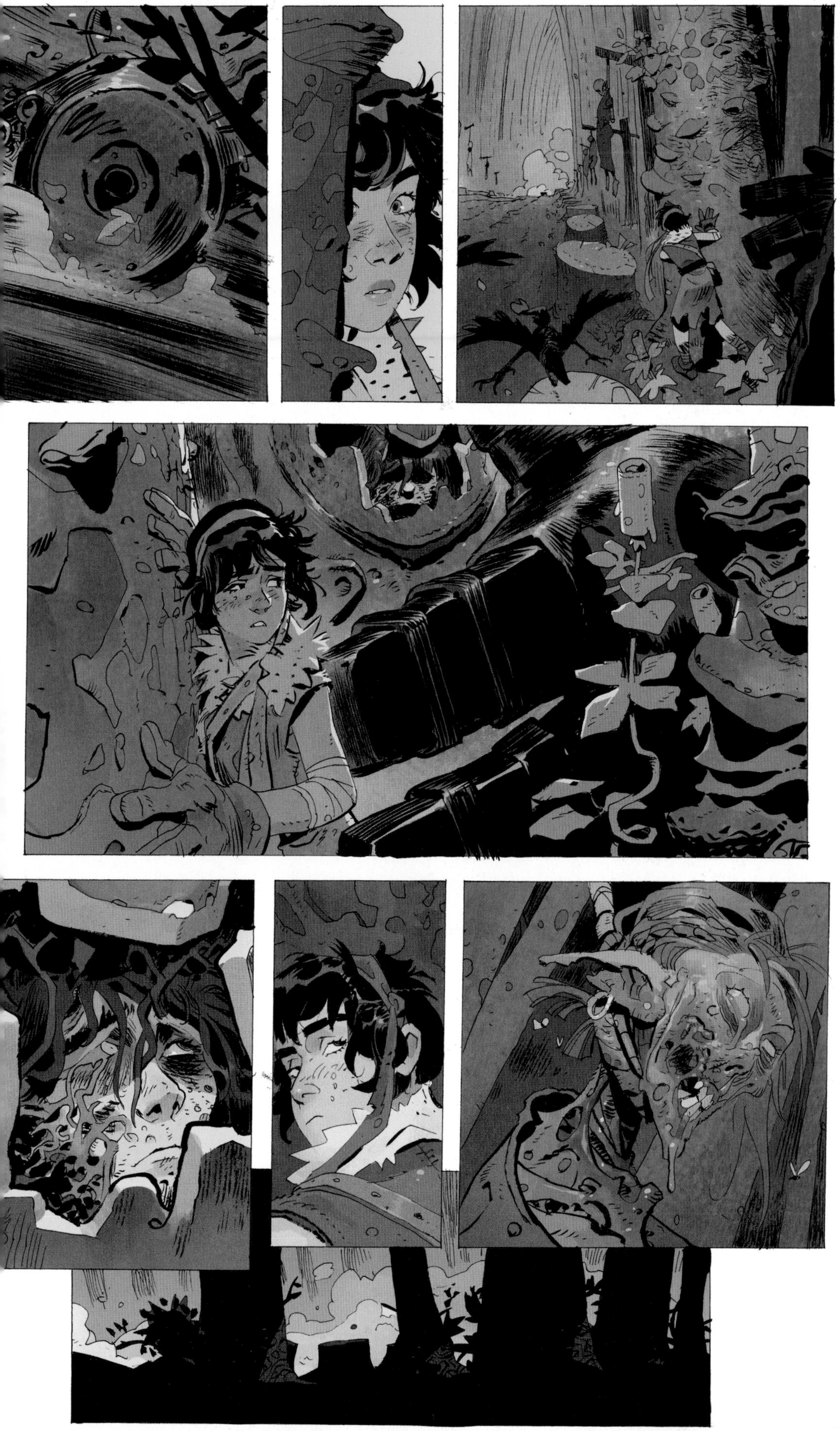

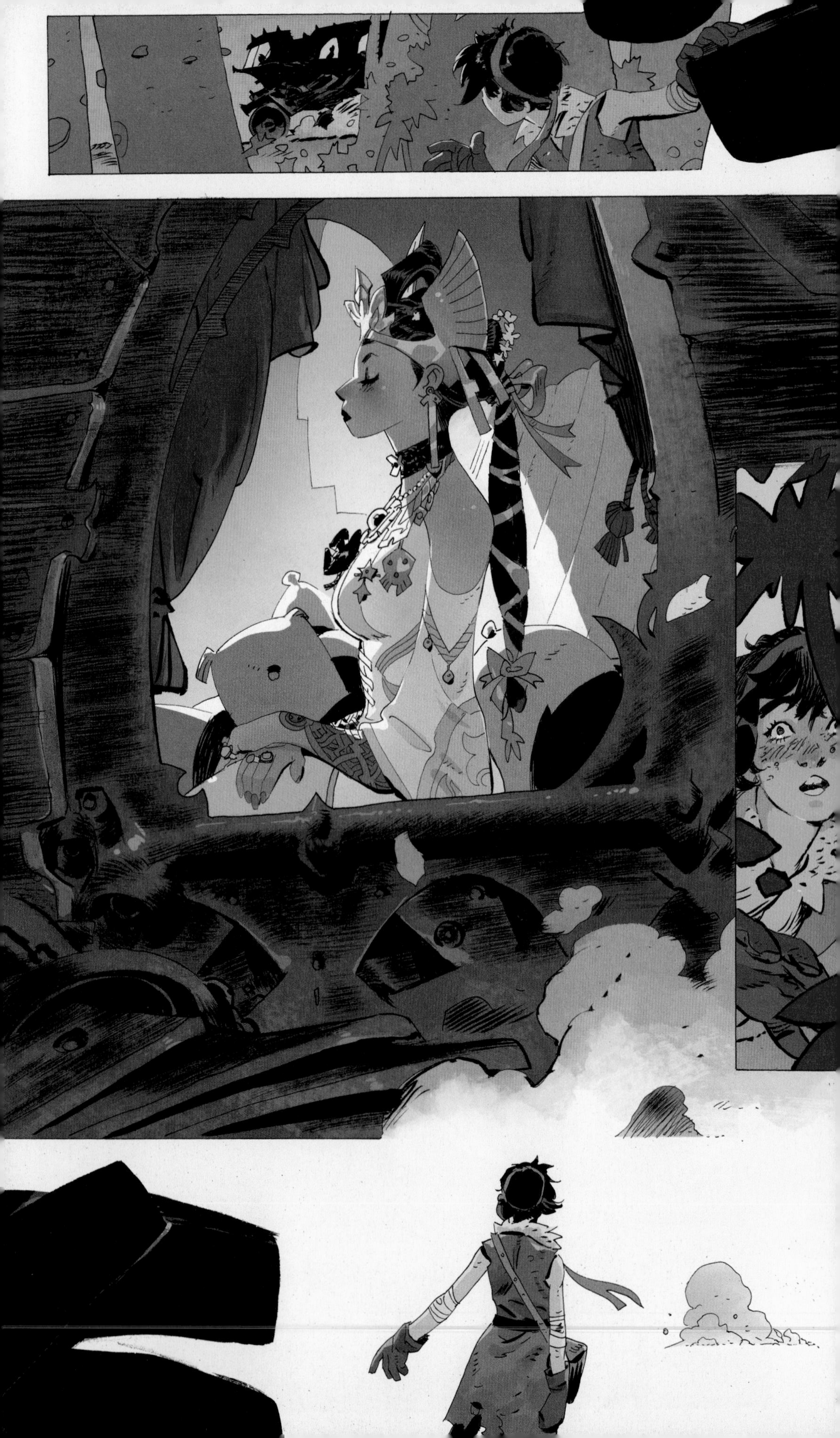

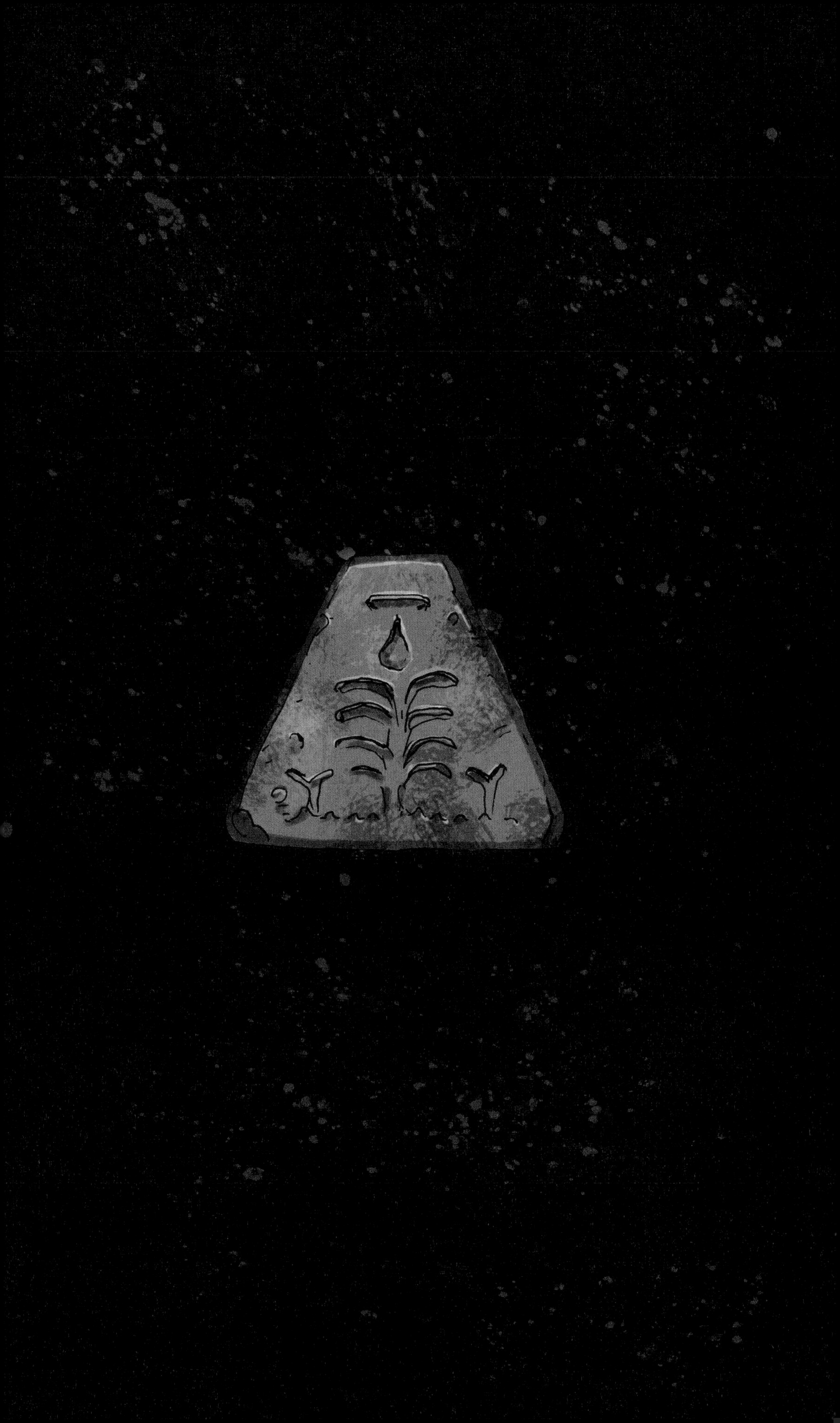

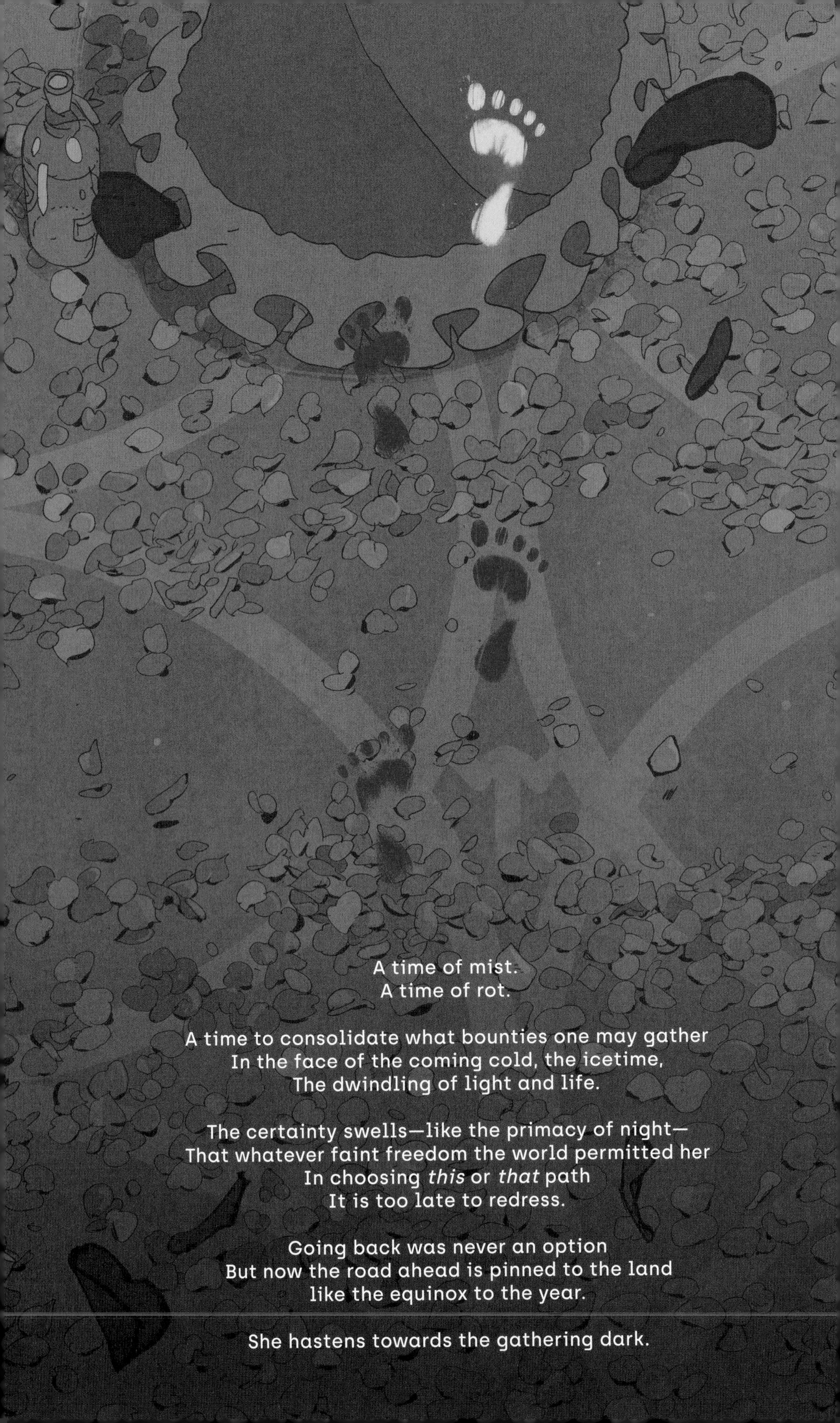

A time of mist.
A time of rot.

A time to consolidate what bounties one may gather
In the face of the coming cold, the icetime,
The dwindling of light and life.

The certainty swells—like the primacy of night—
That whatever faint freedom the world permitted her
In choosing *this* or *that* path
It is too late to redress.

Going back was never an option
But now the road ahead is pinned to the land
like the equinox to the year.

She hastens towards the gathering dark.

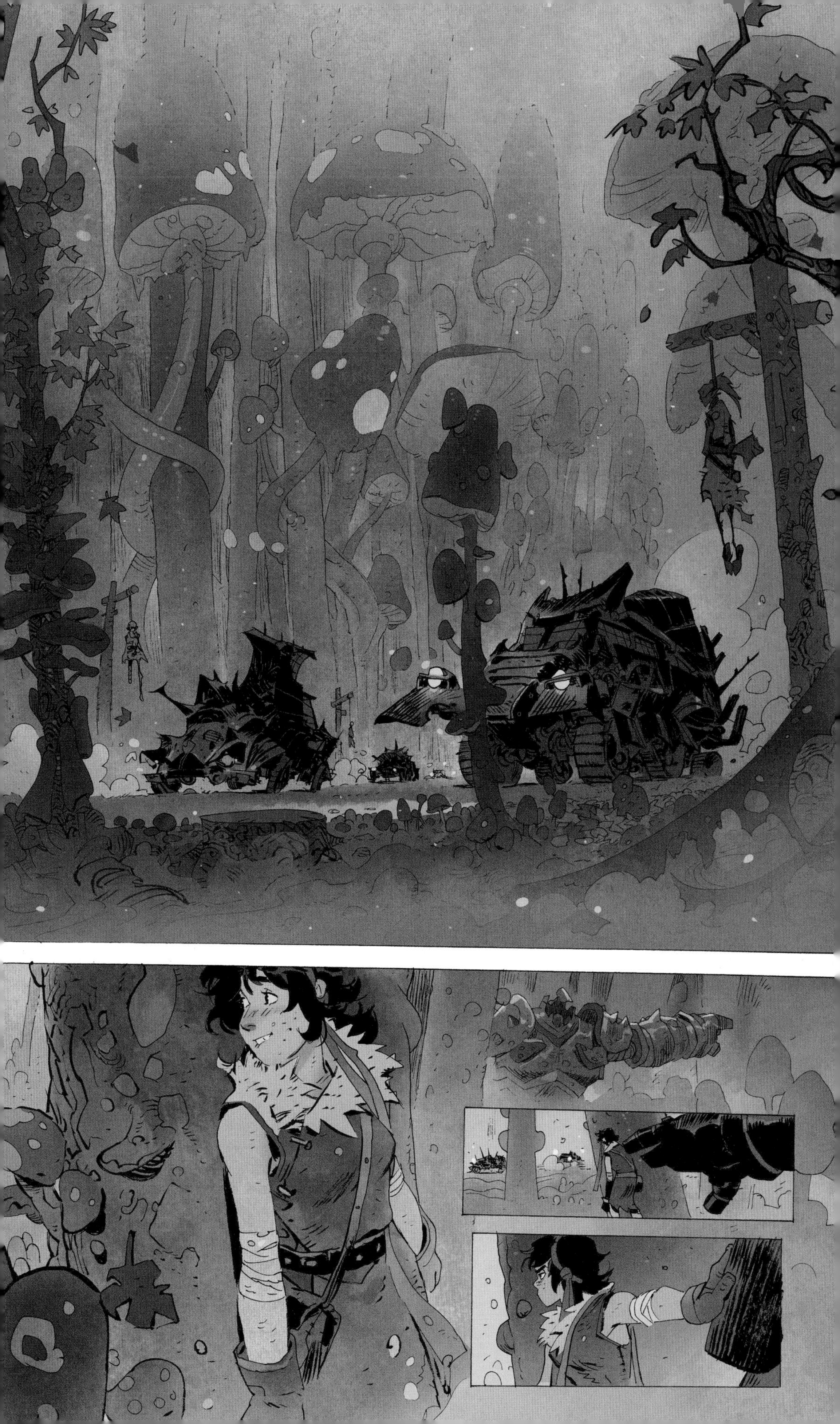

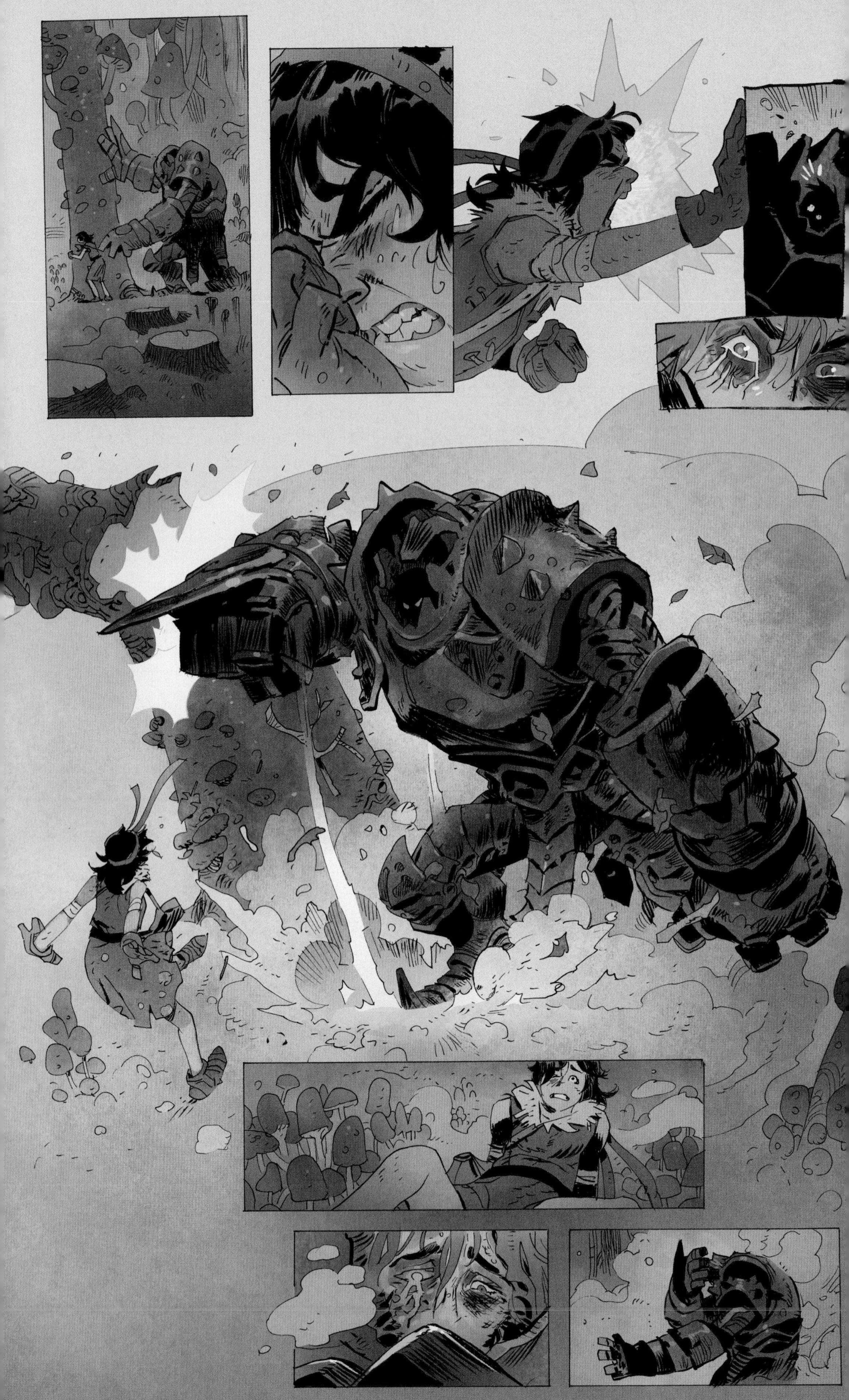

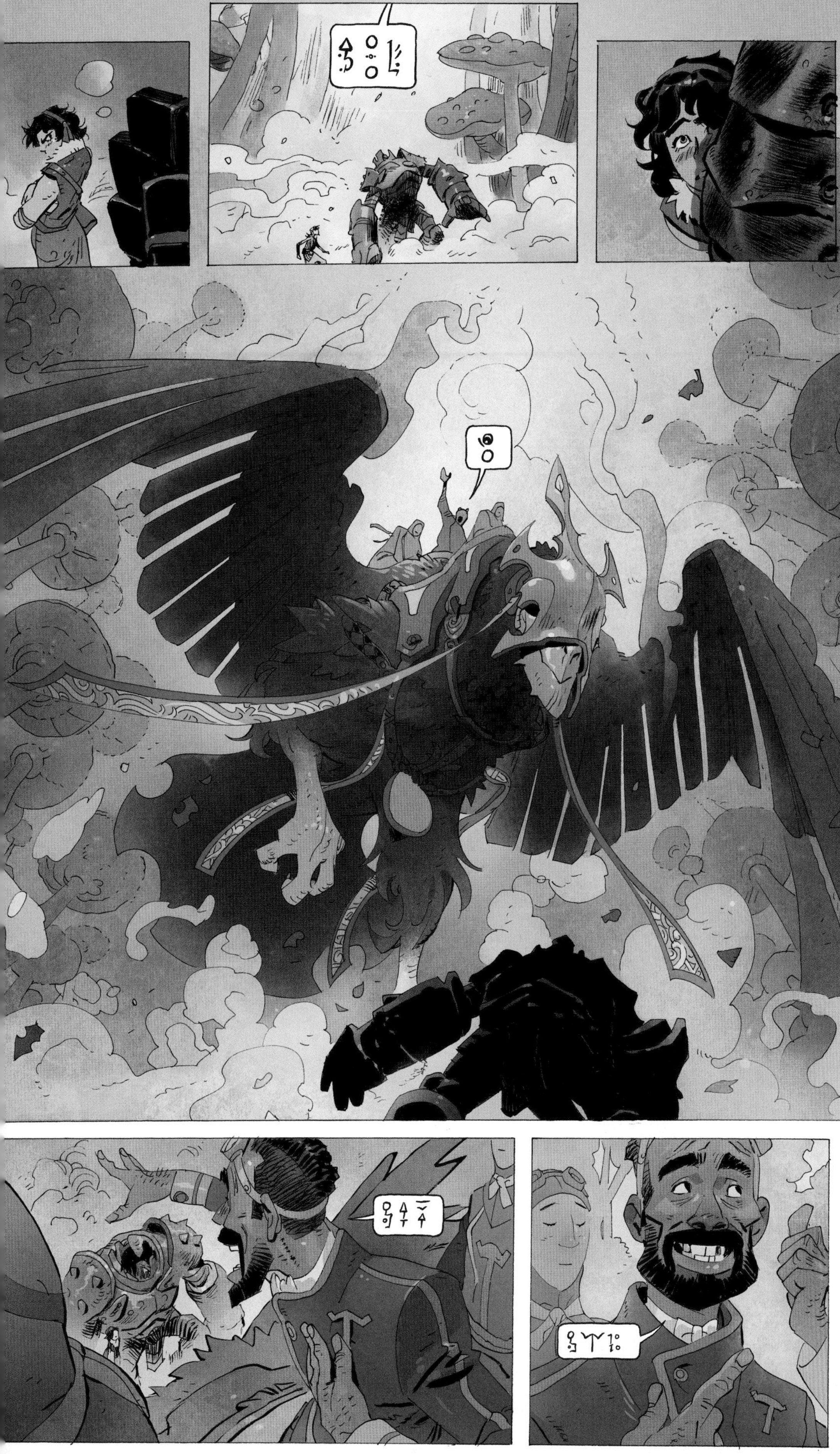

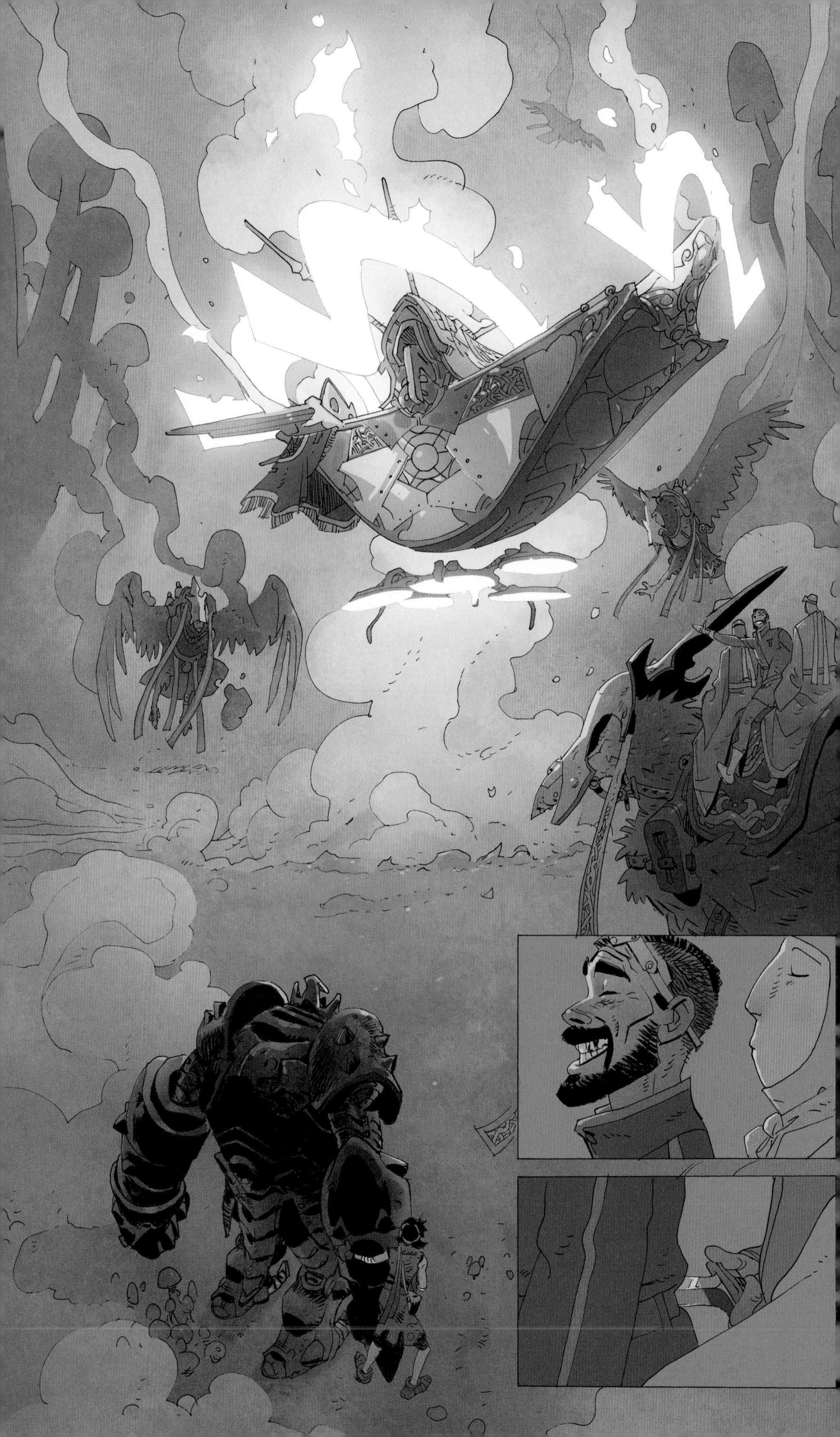

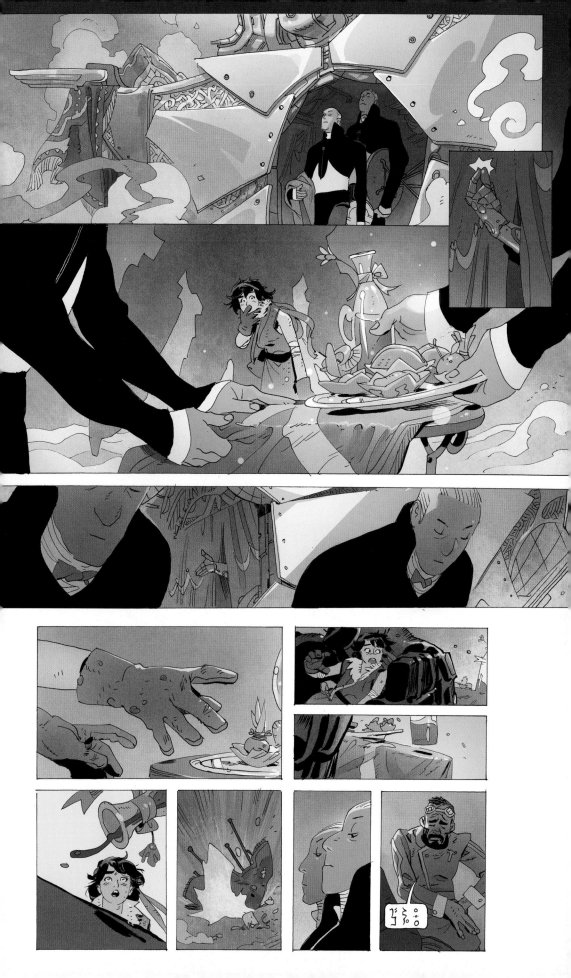

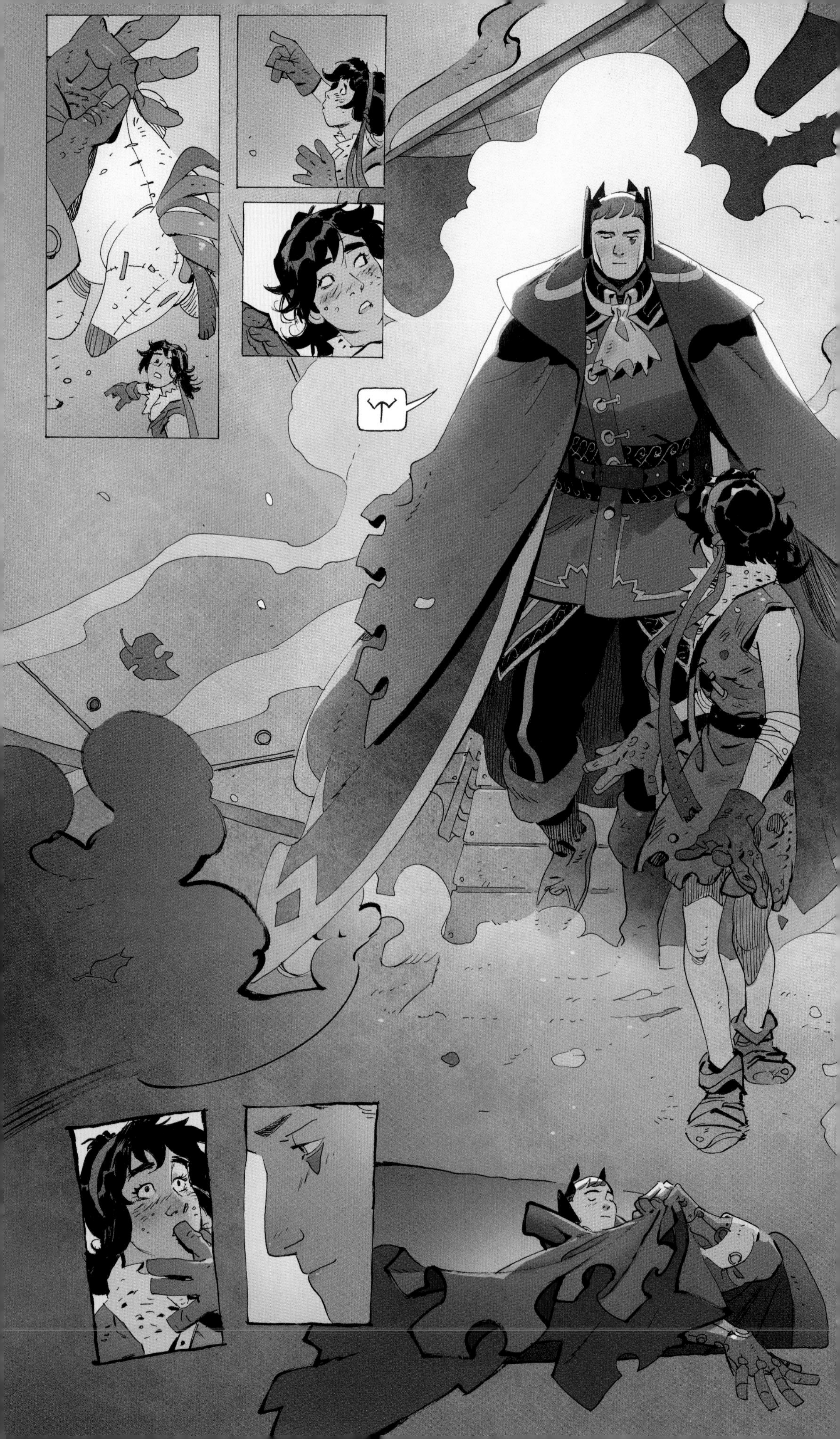

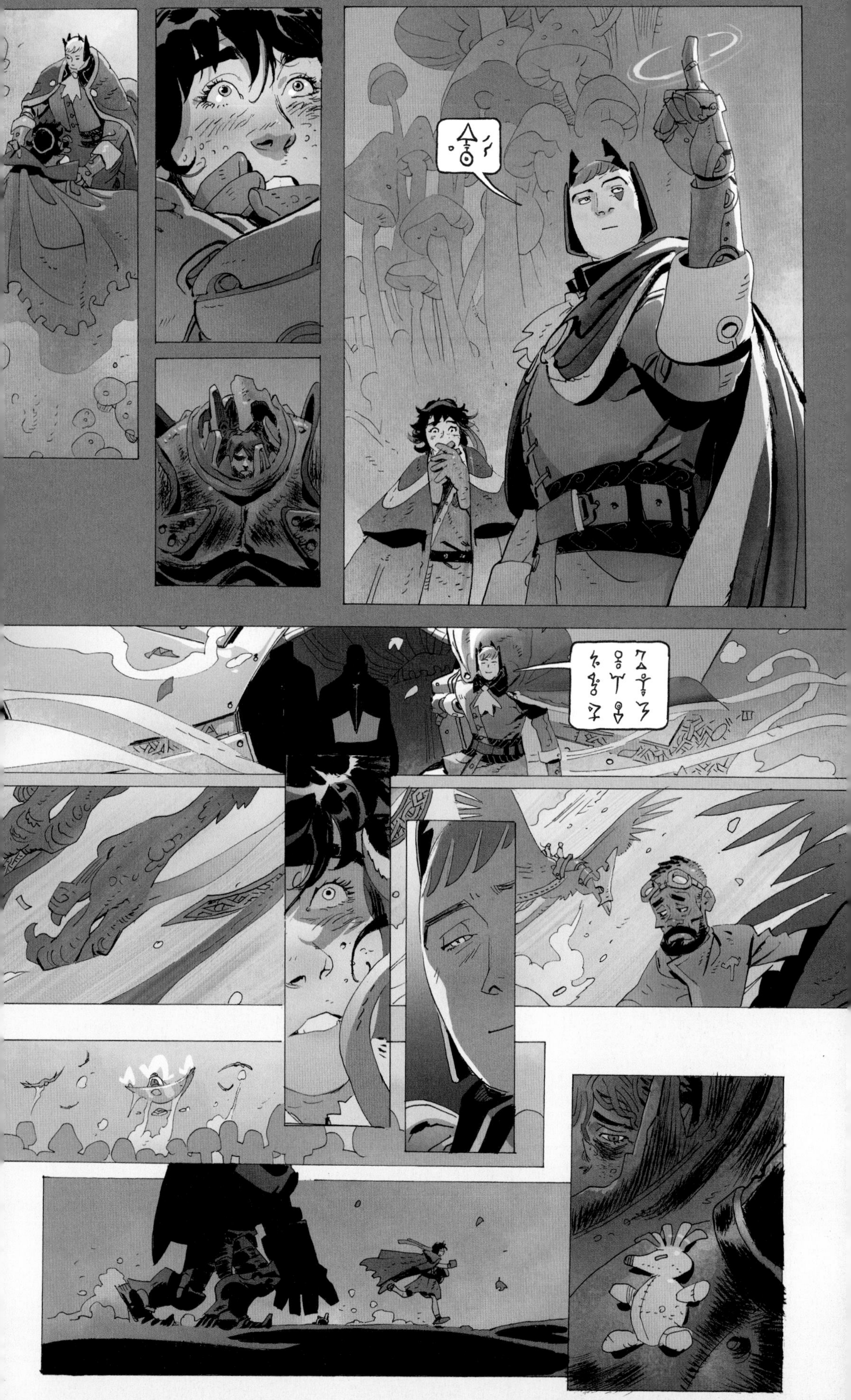

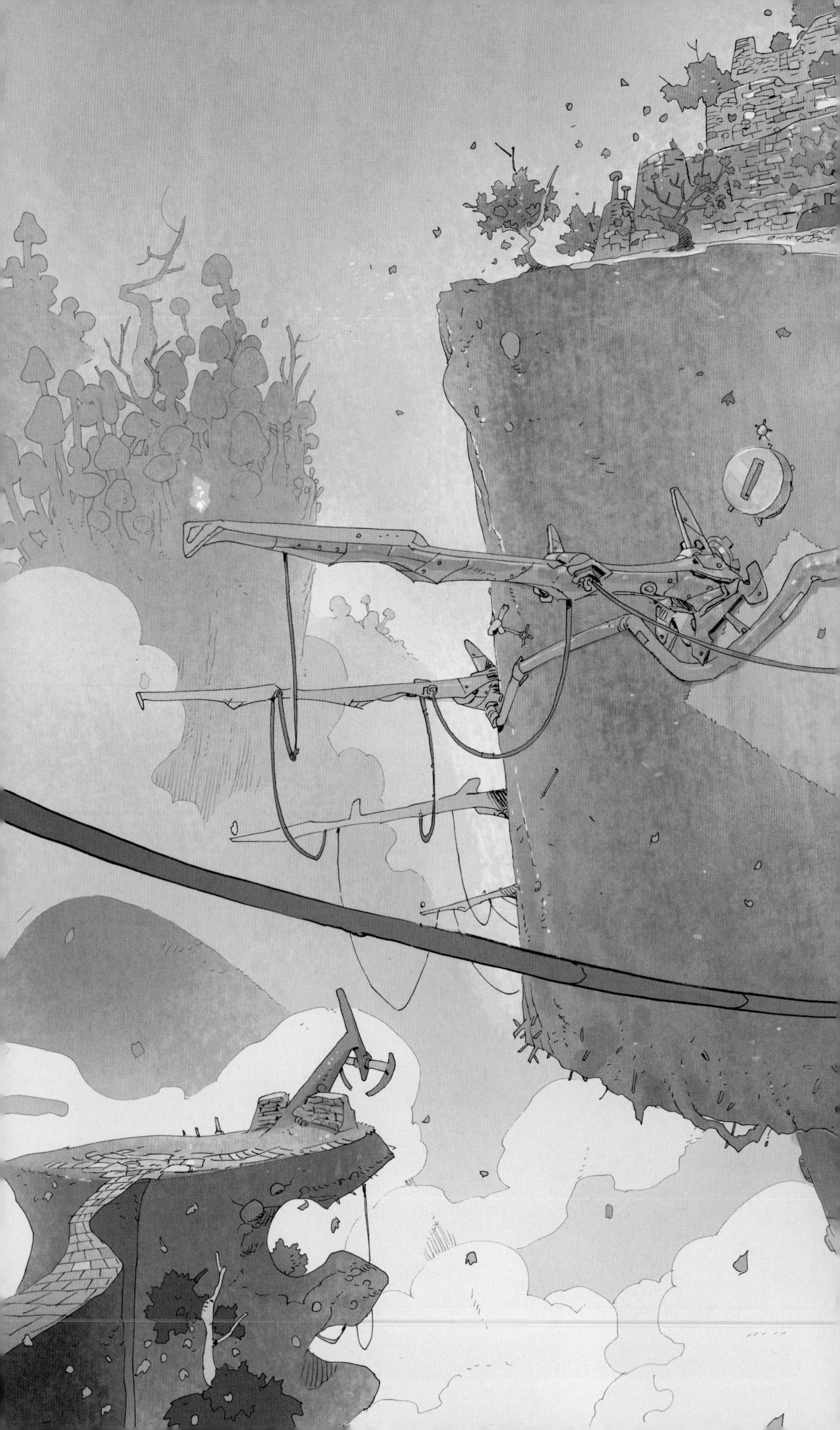

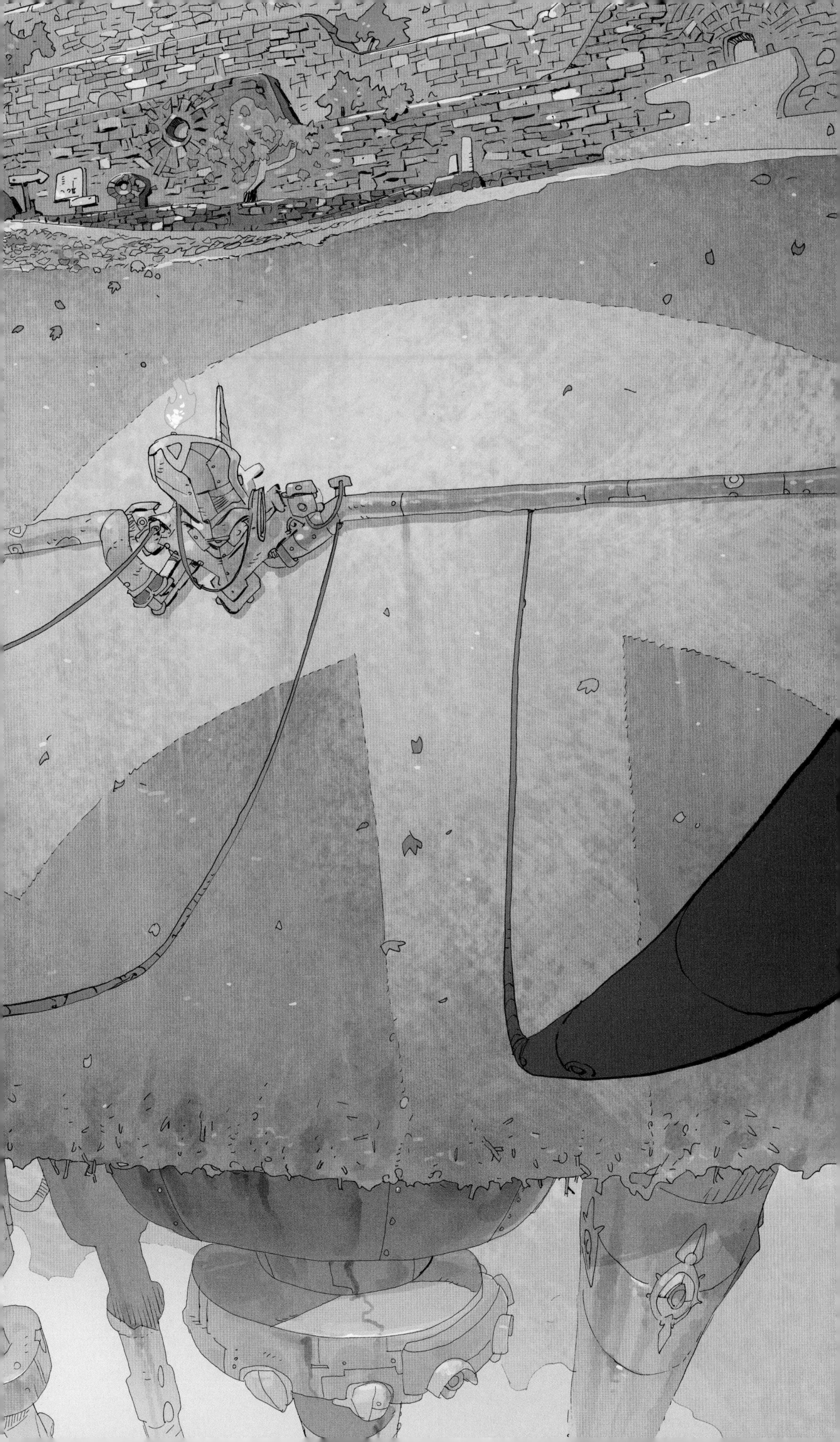

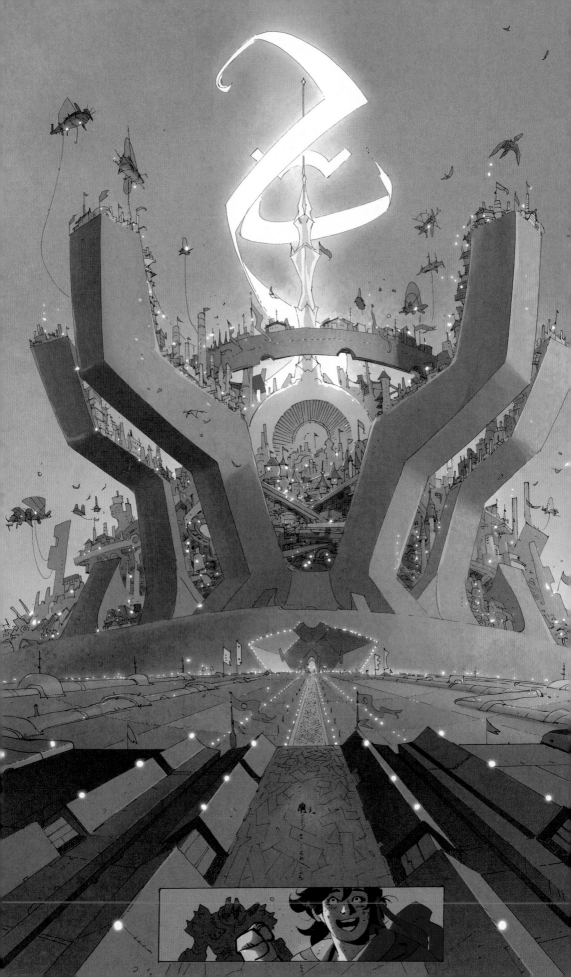

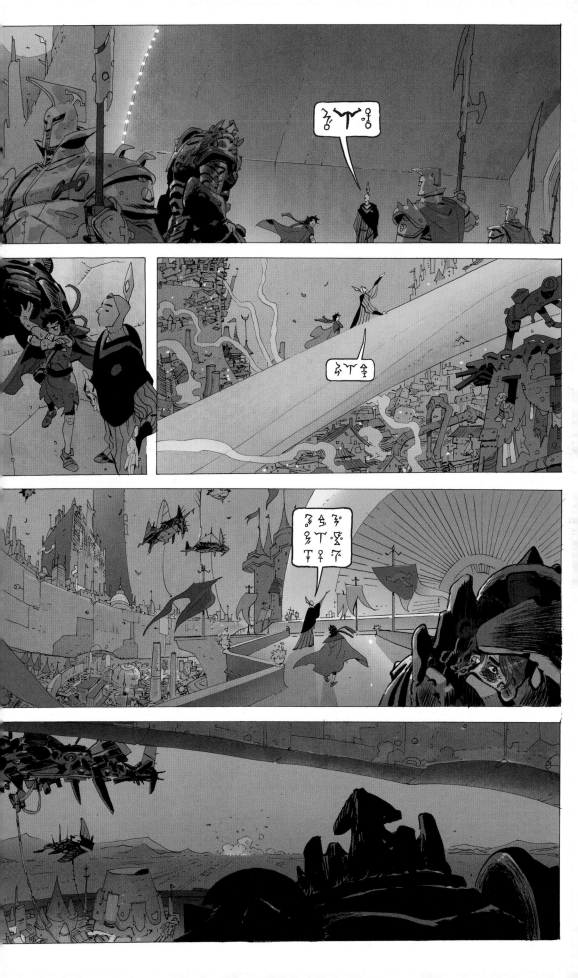

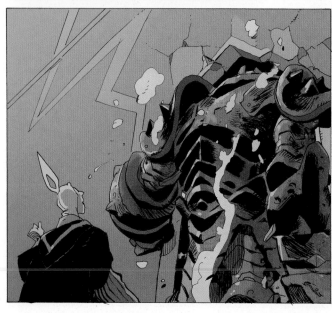

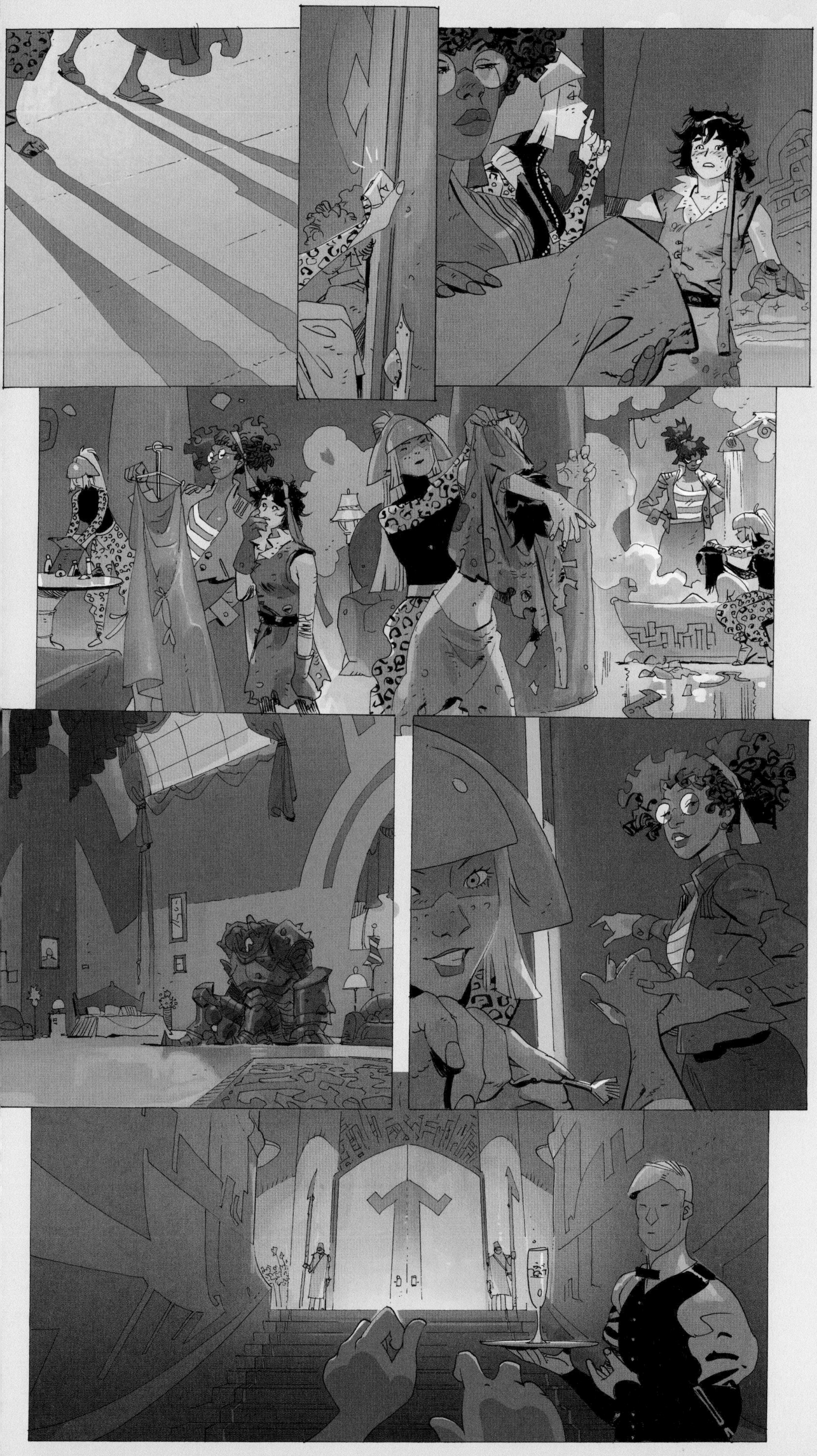

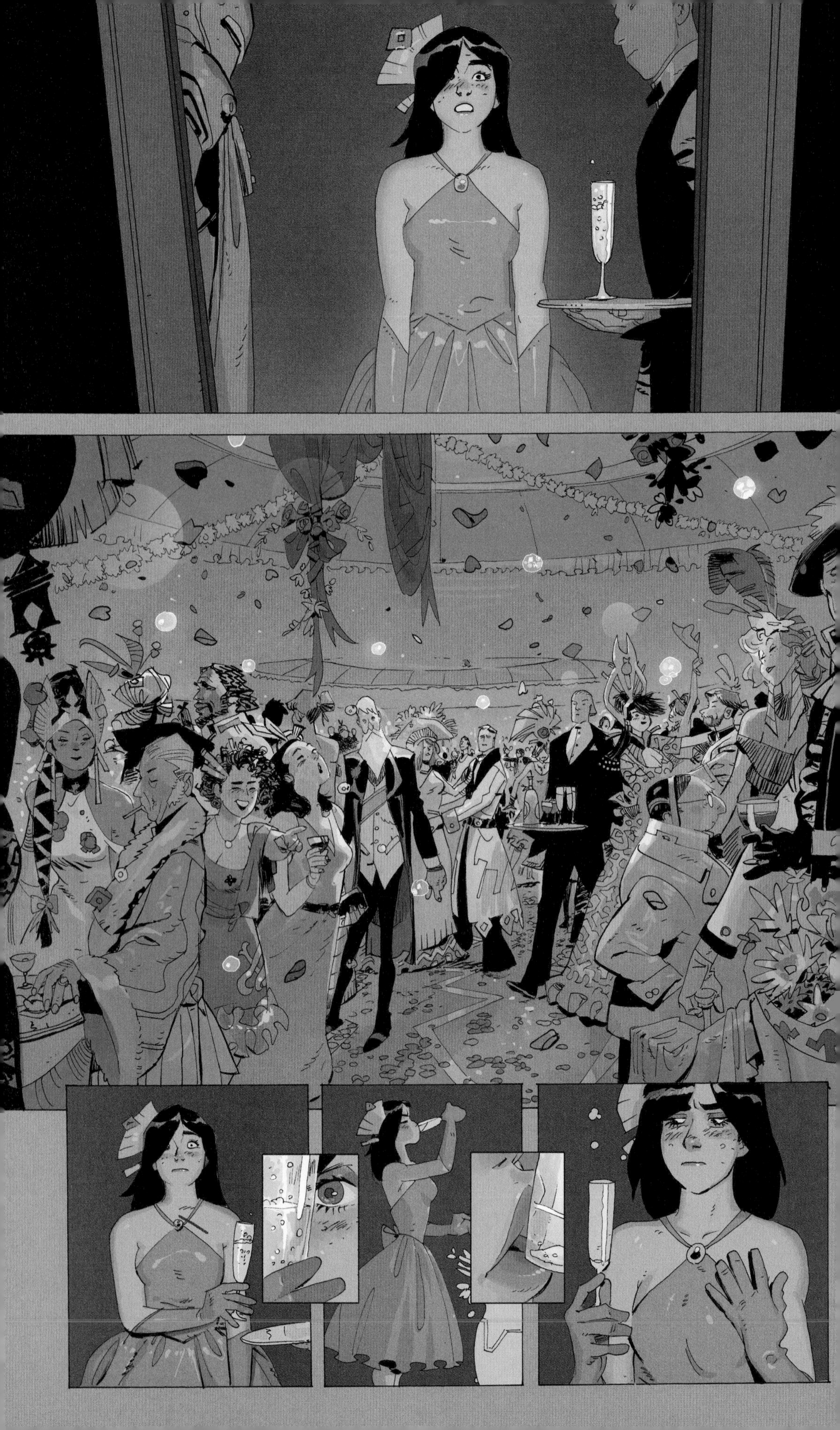

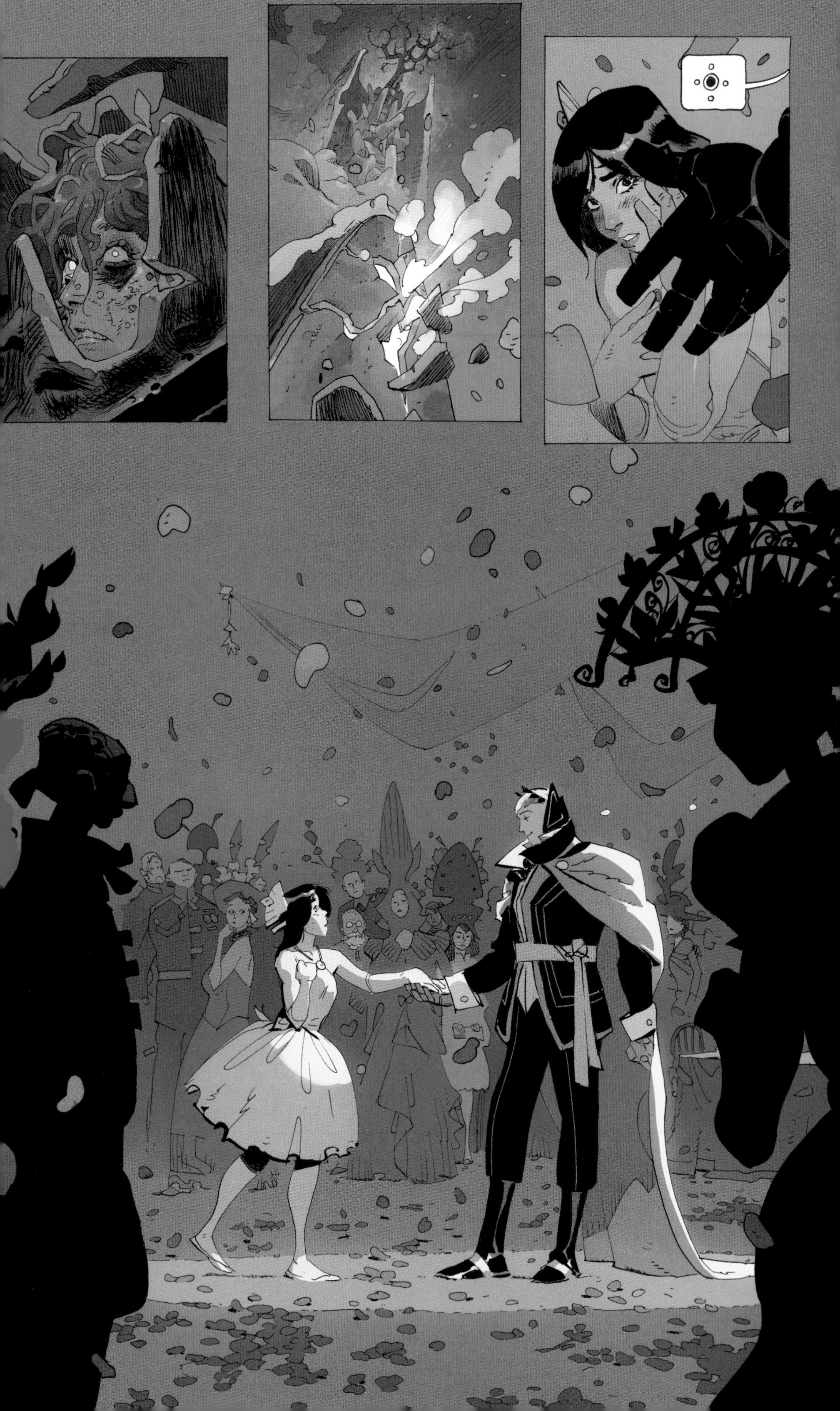

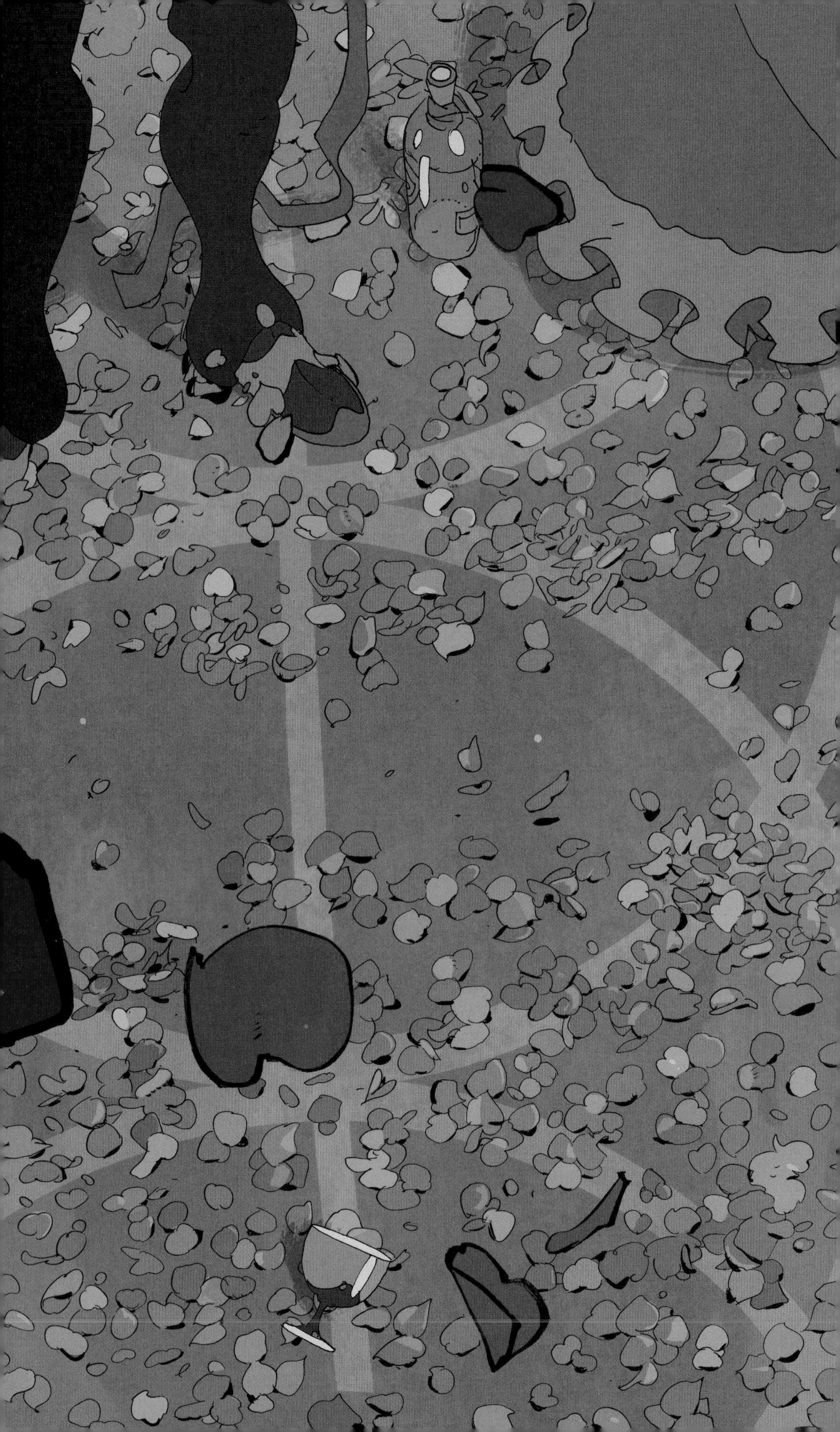

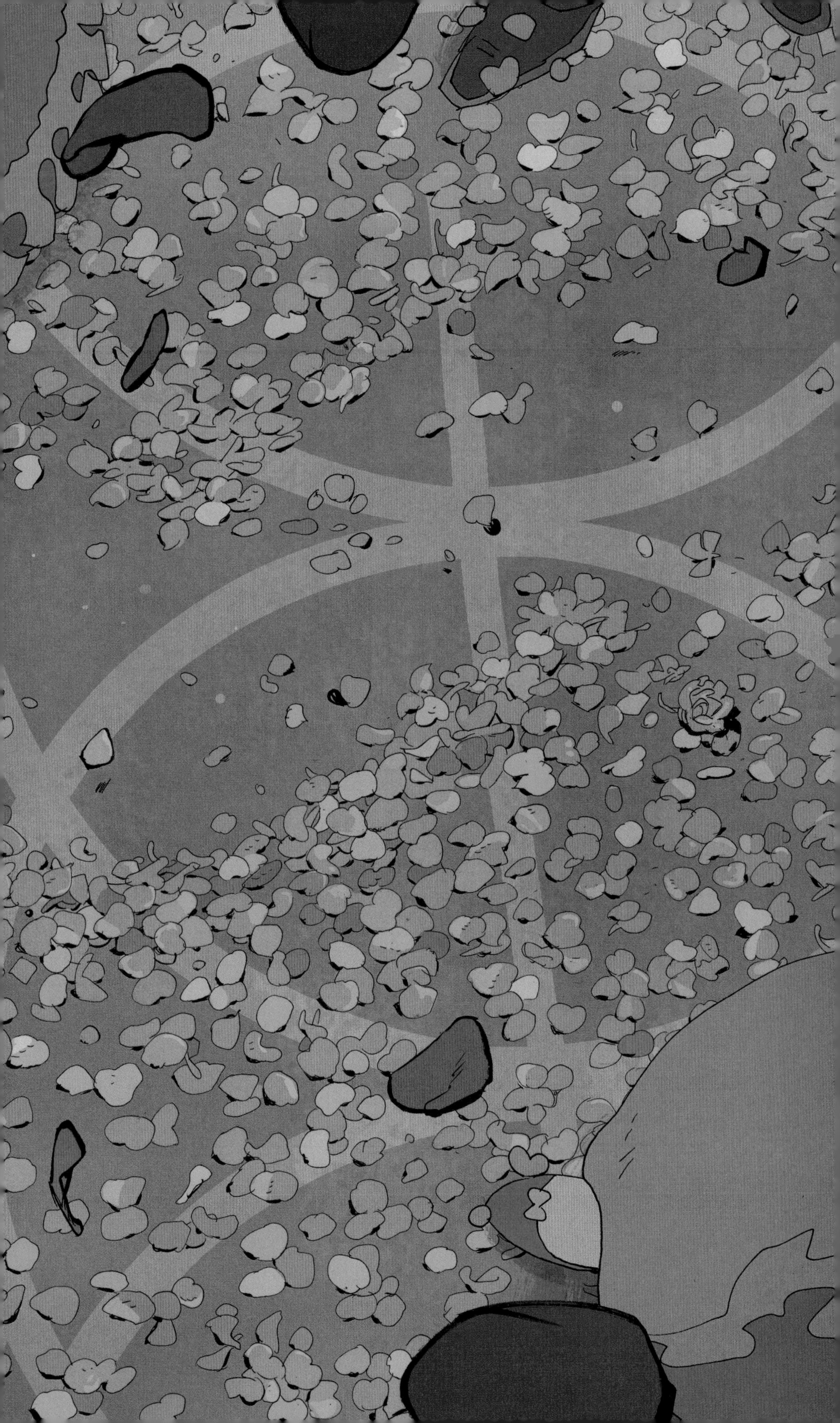

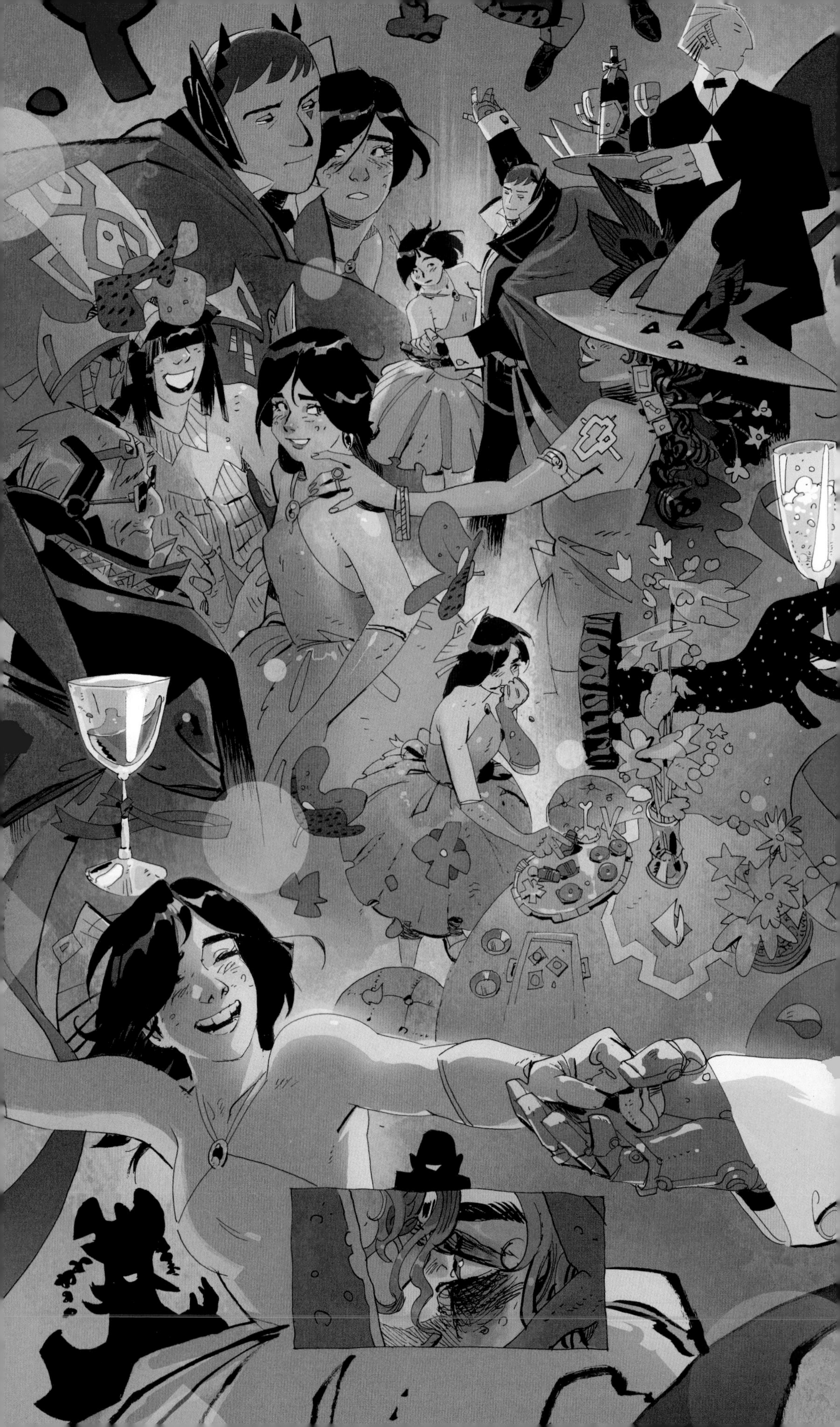

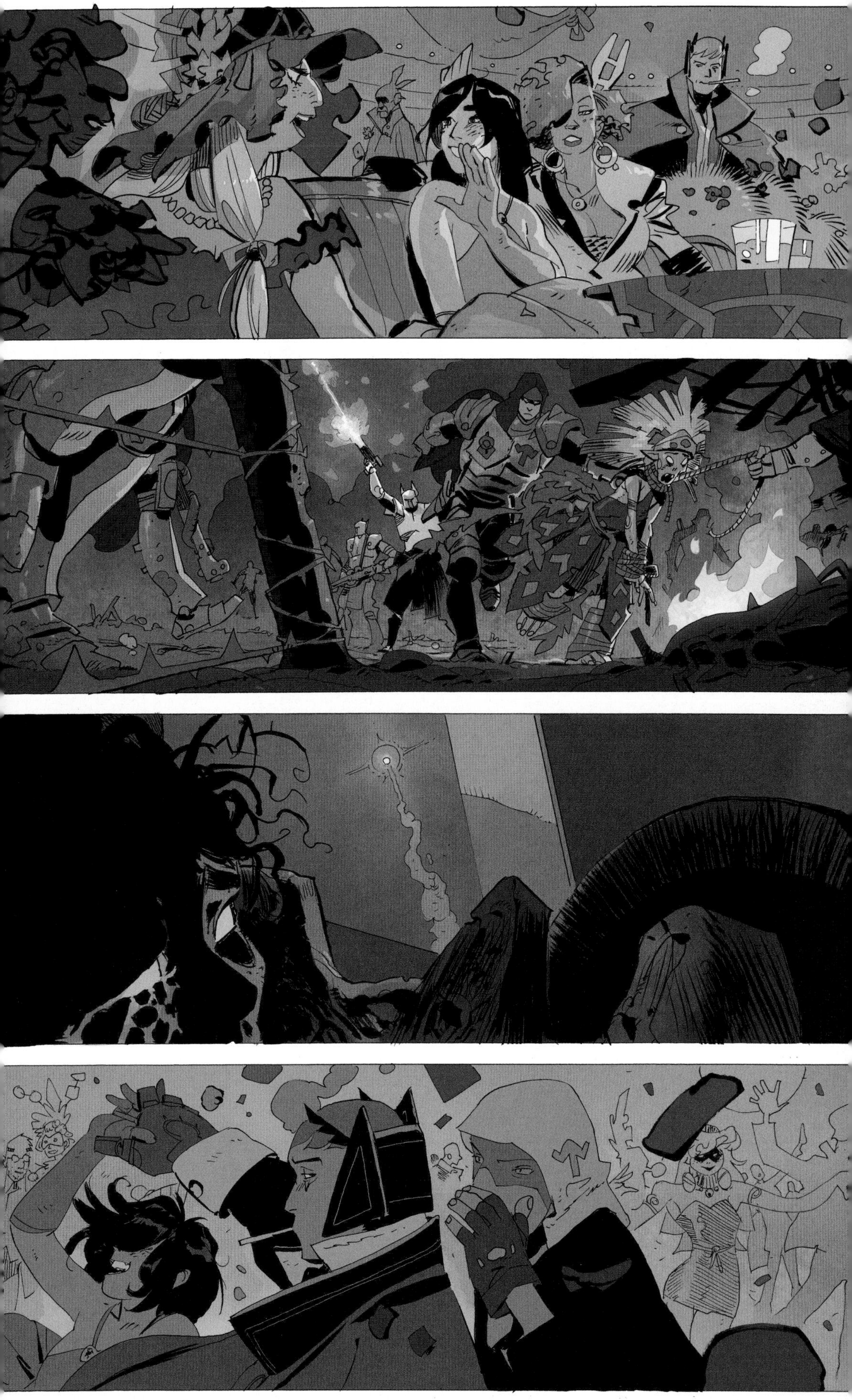

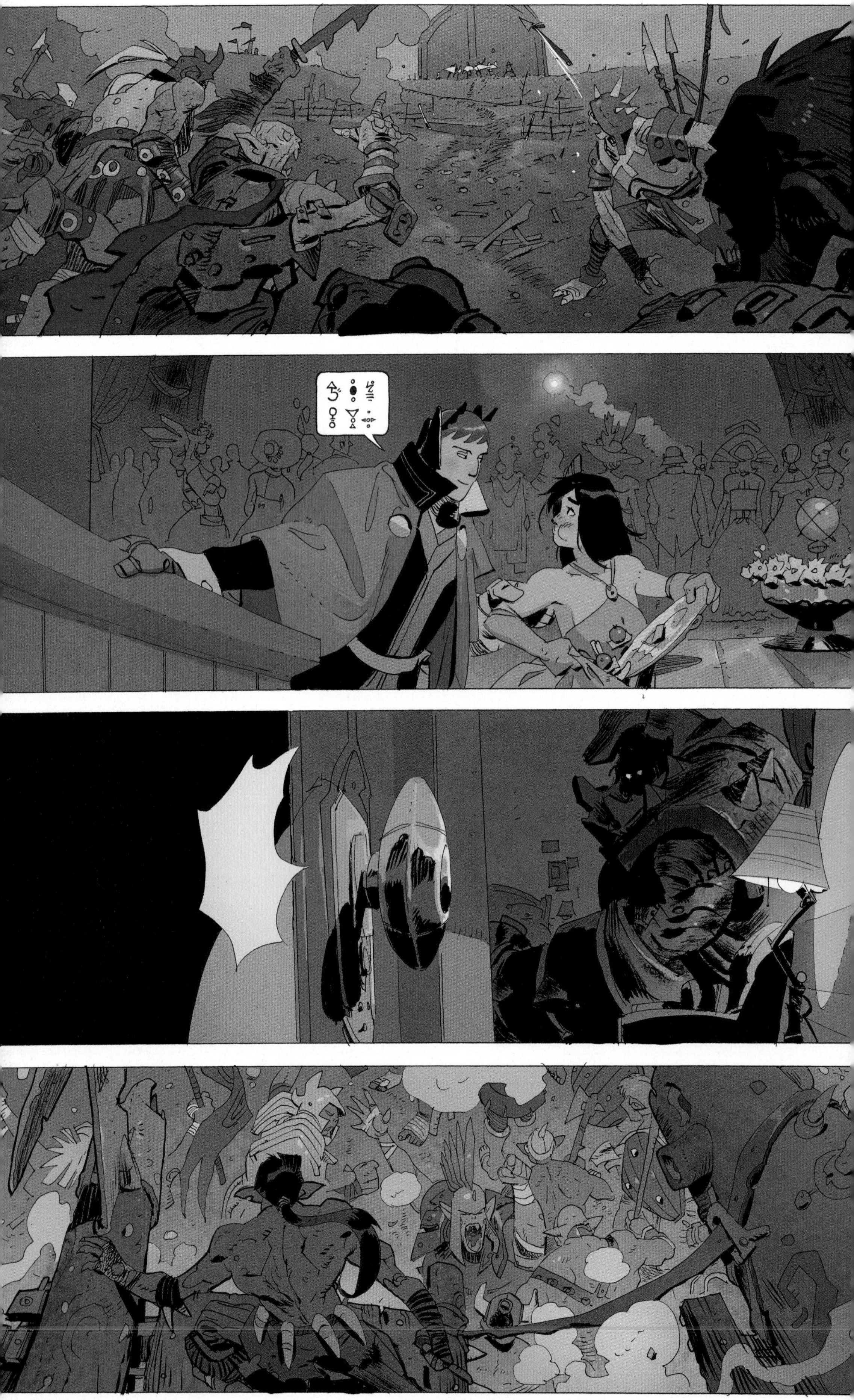

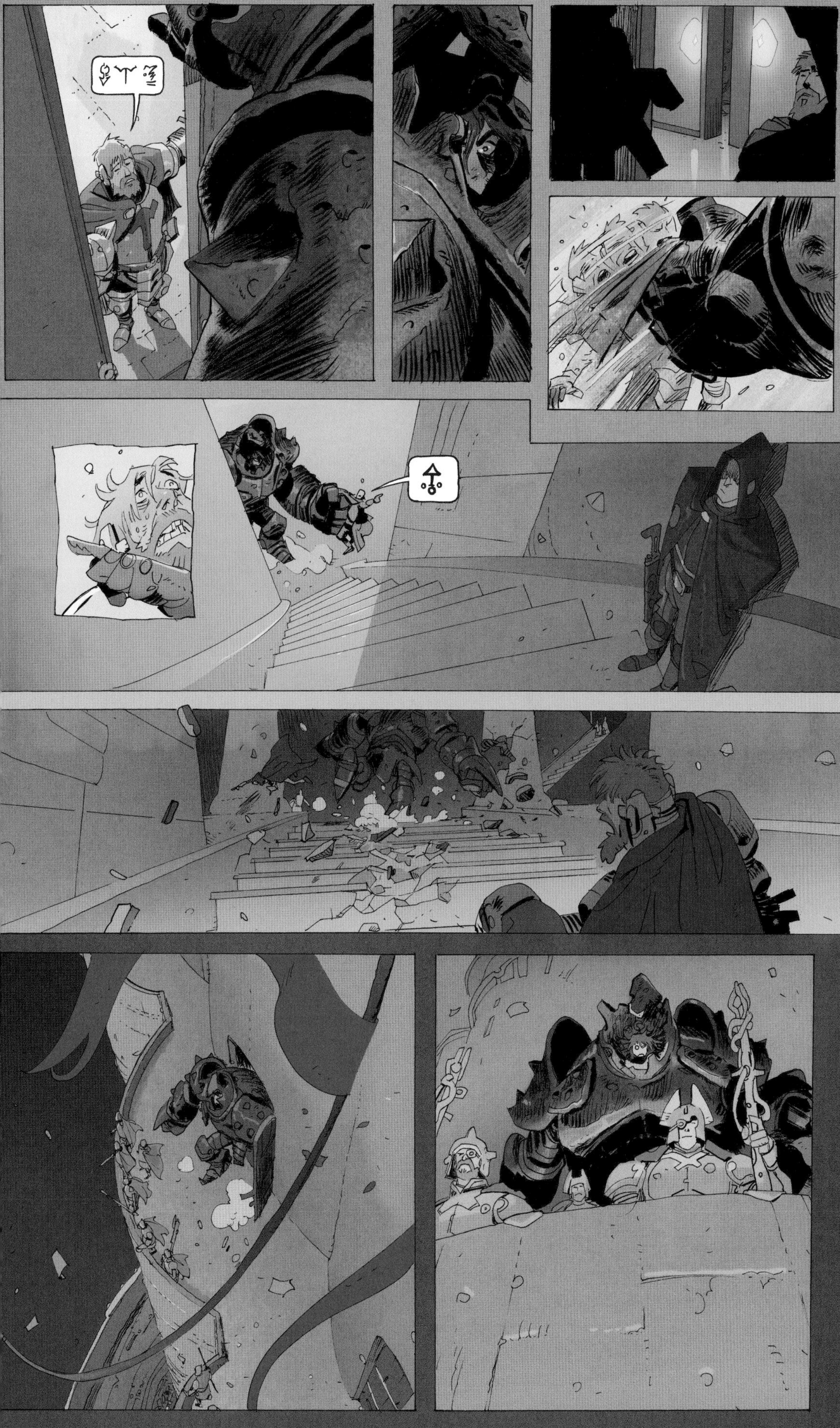

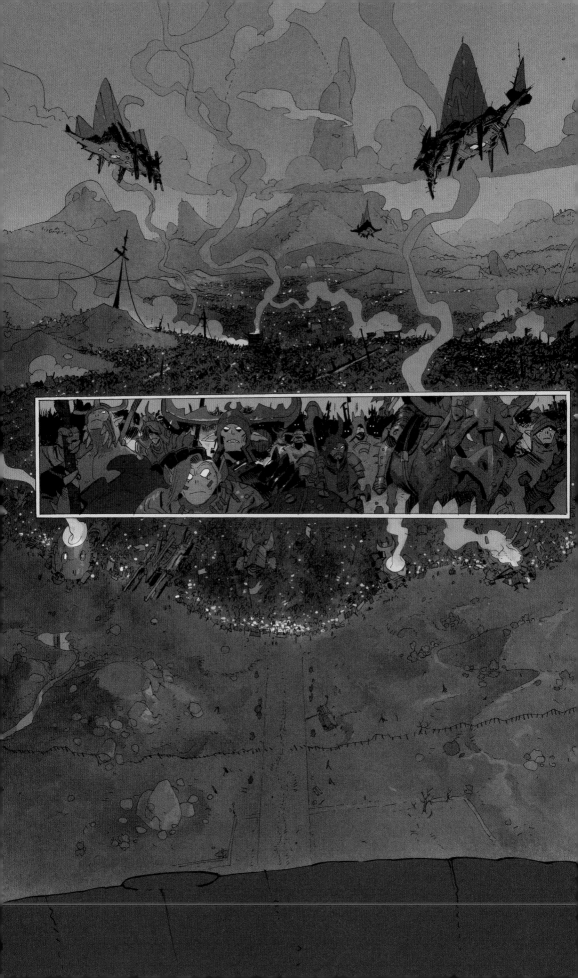

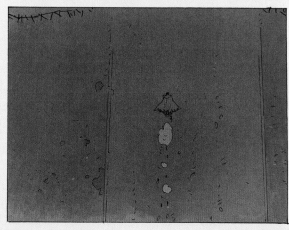

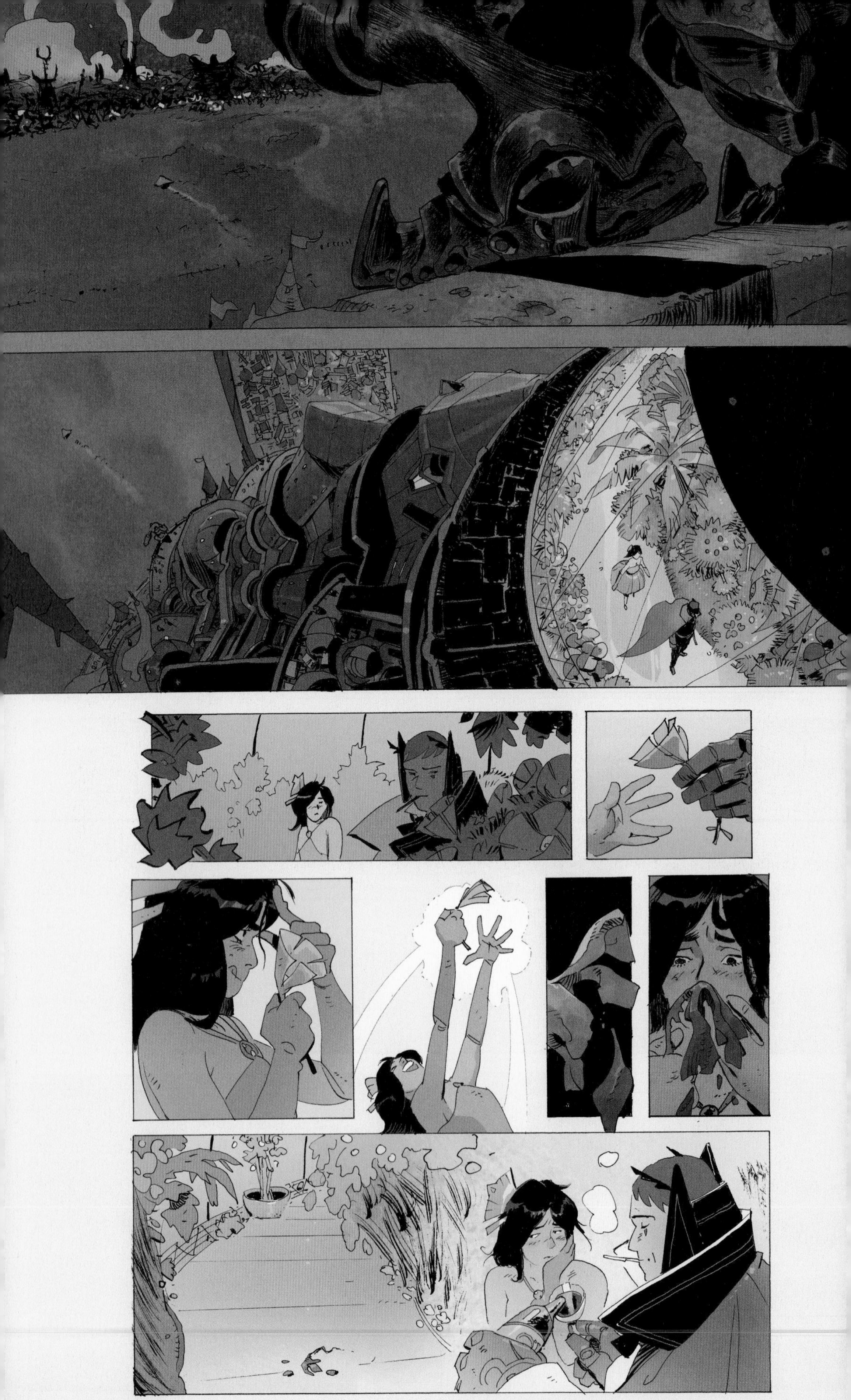

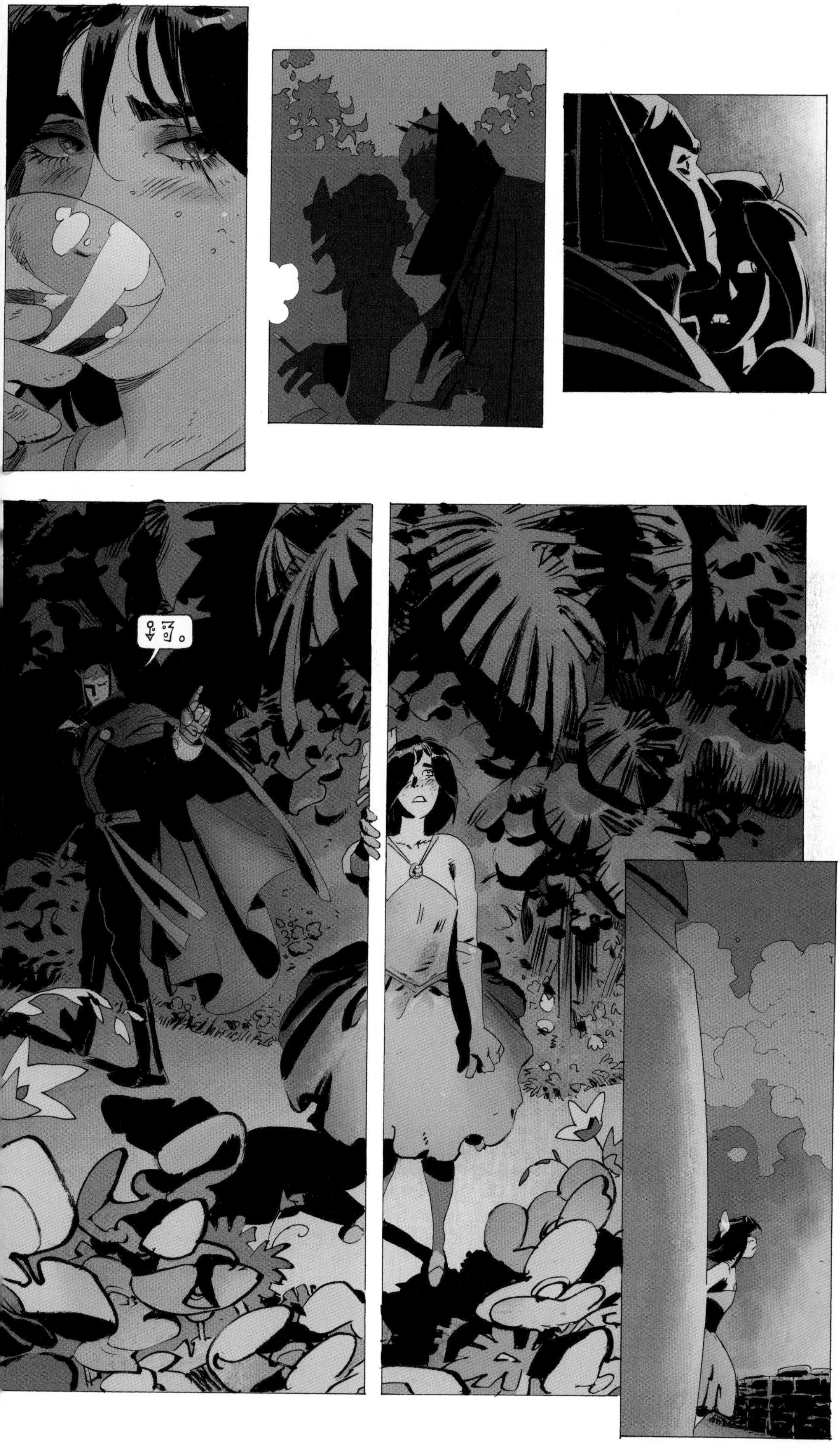

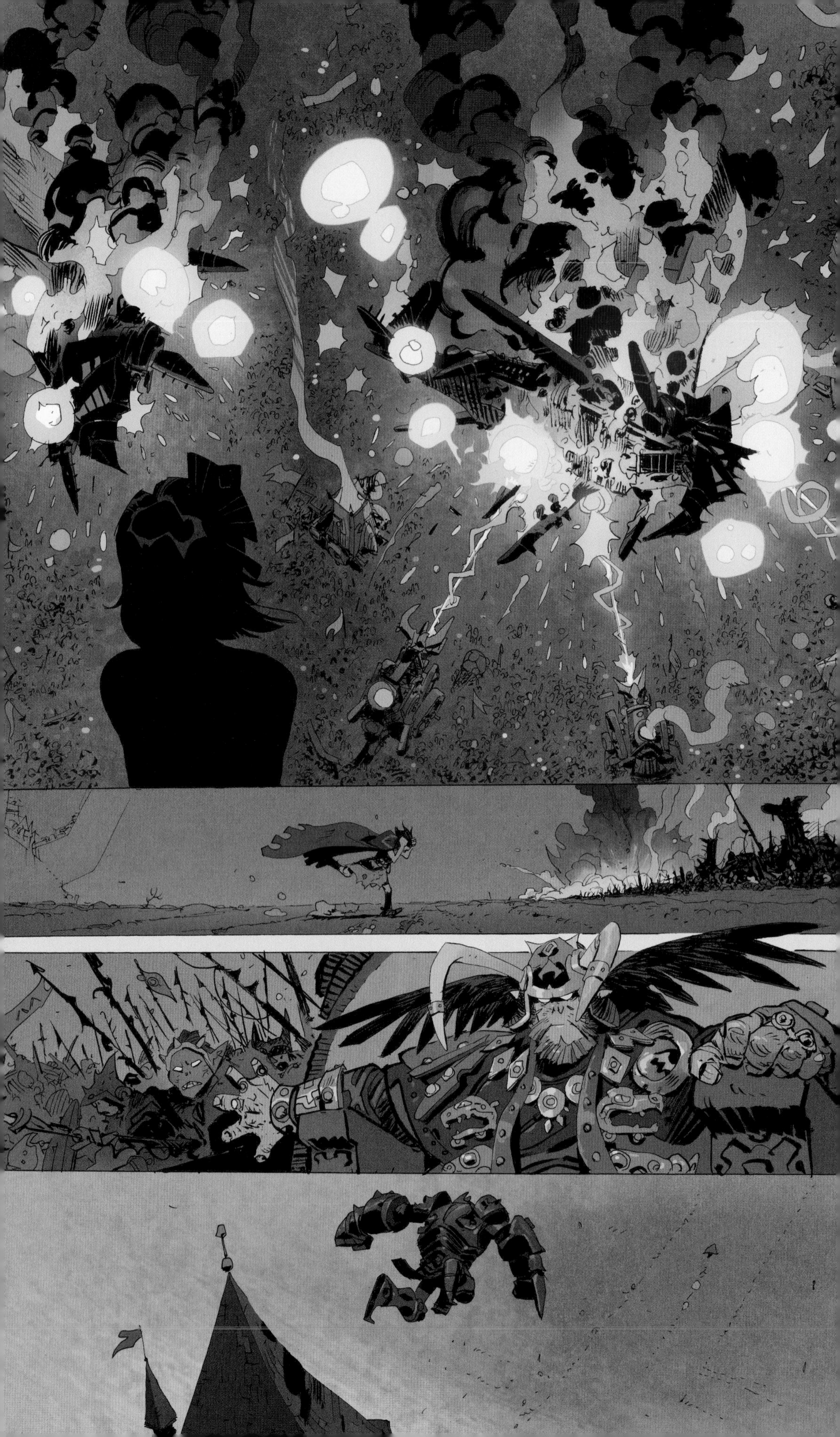

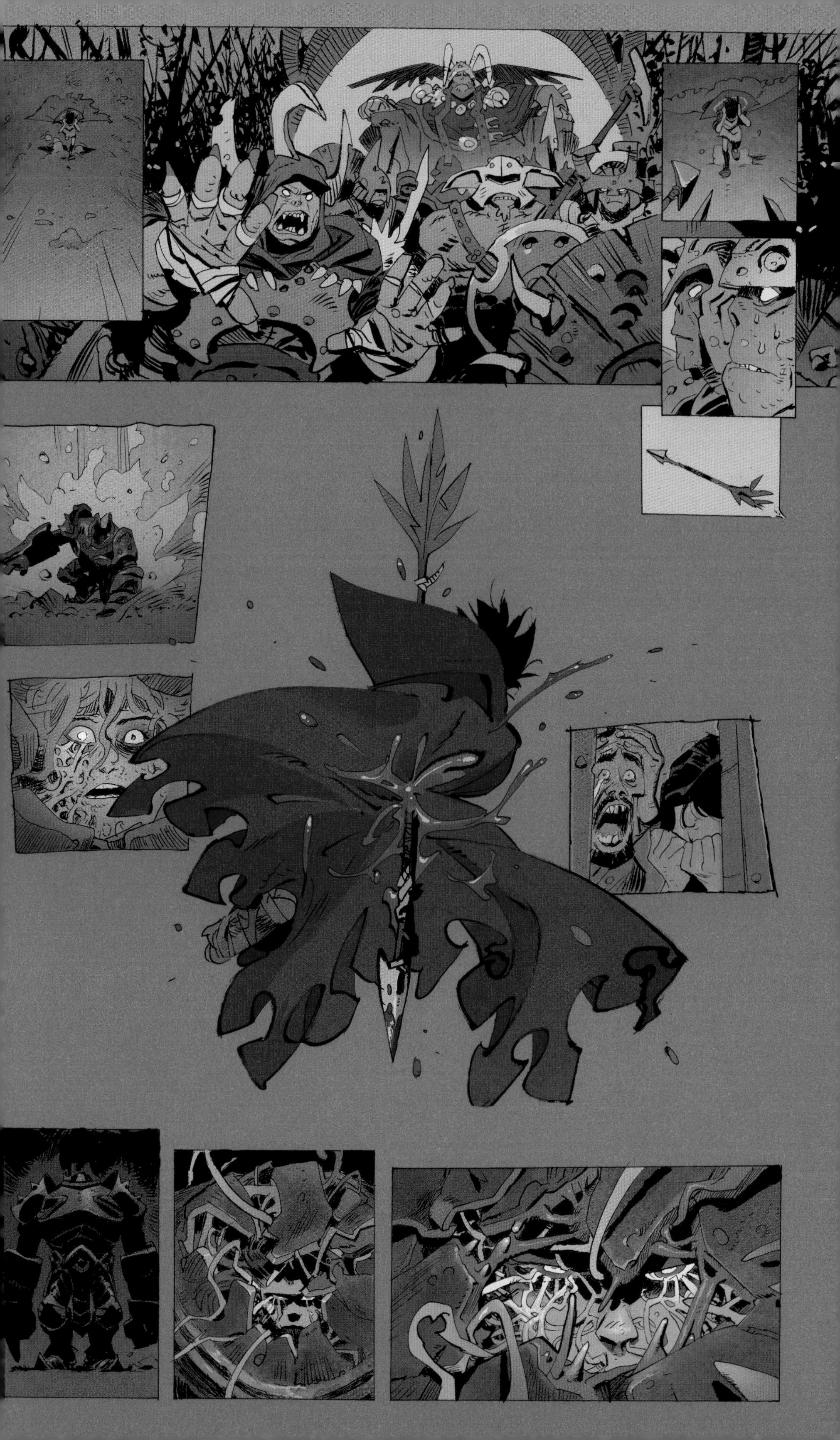

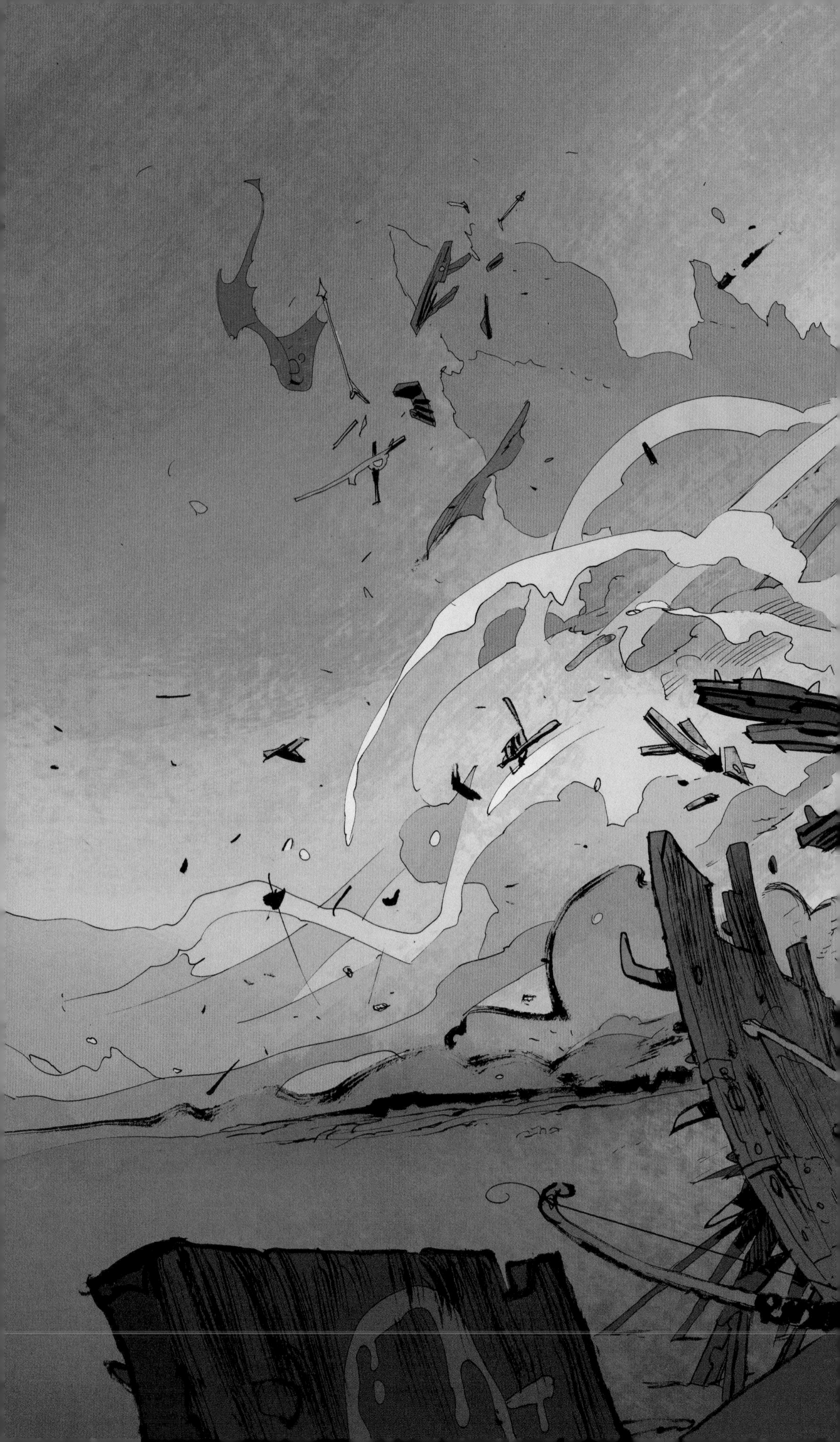

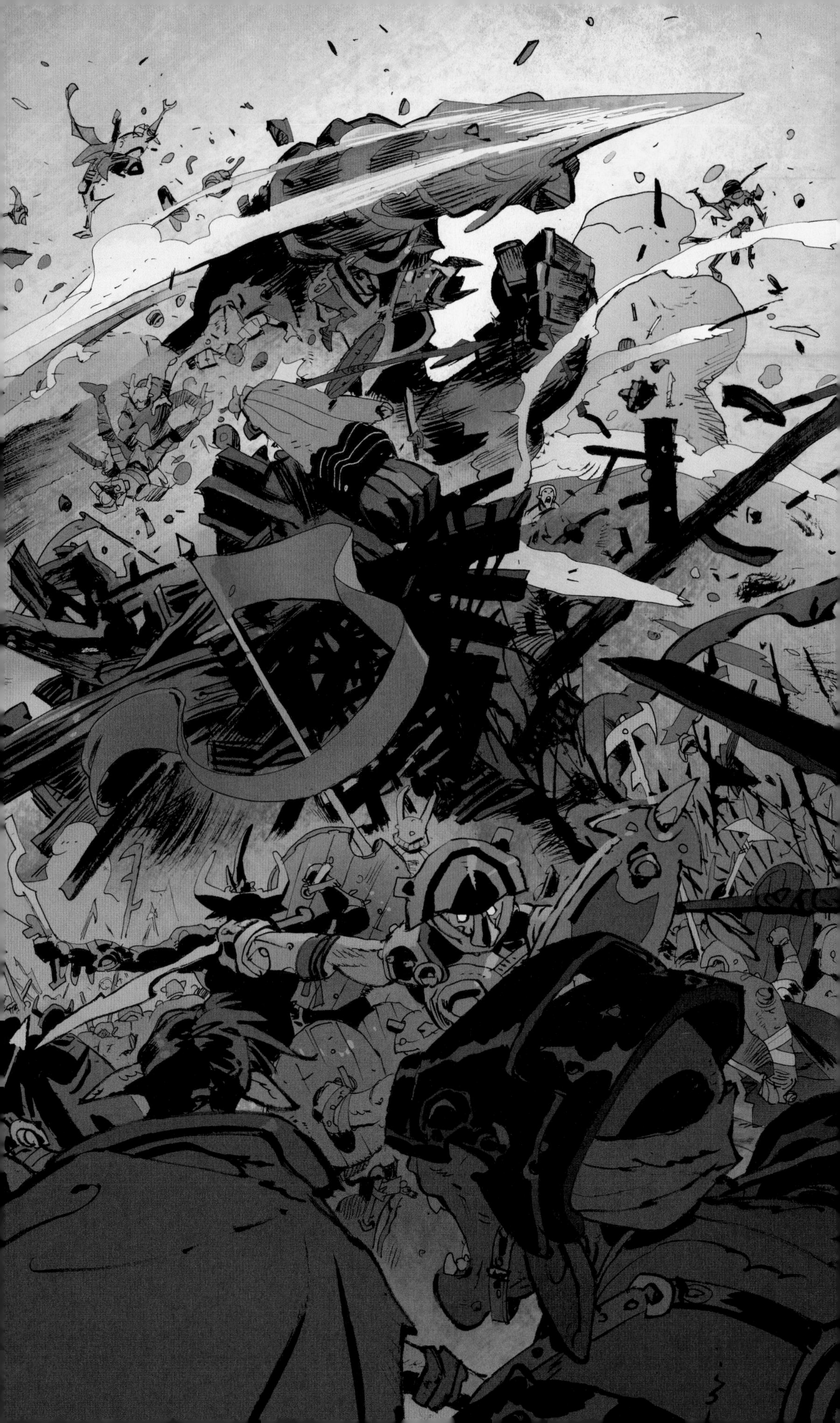

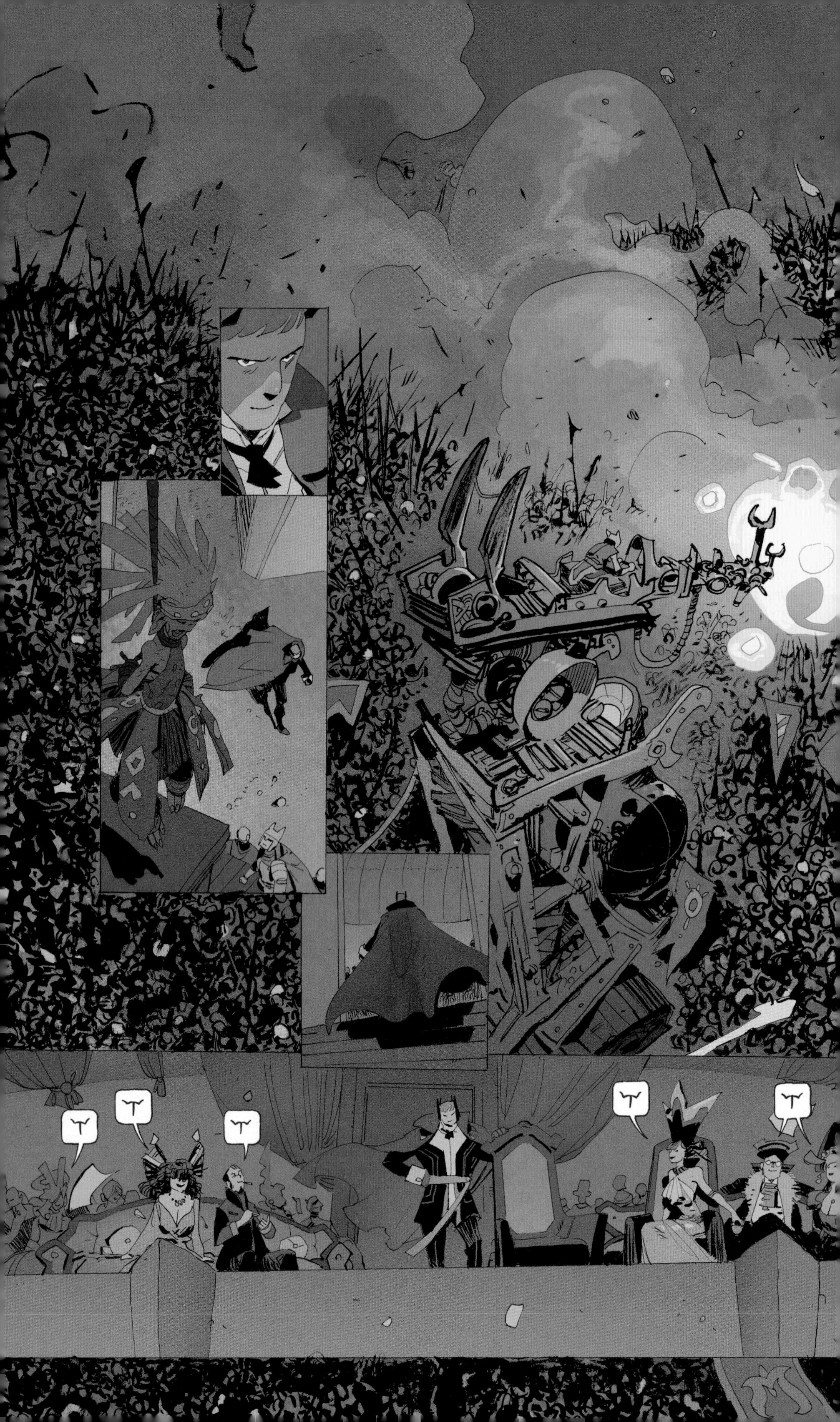

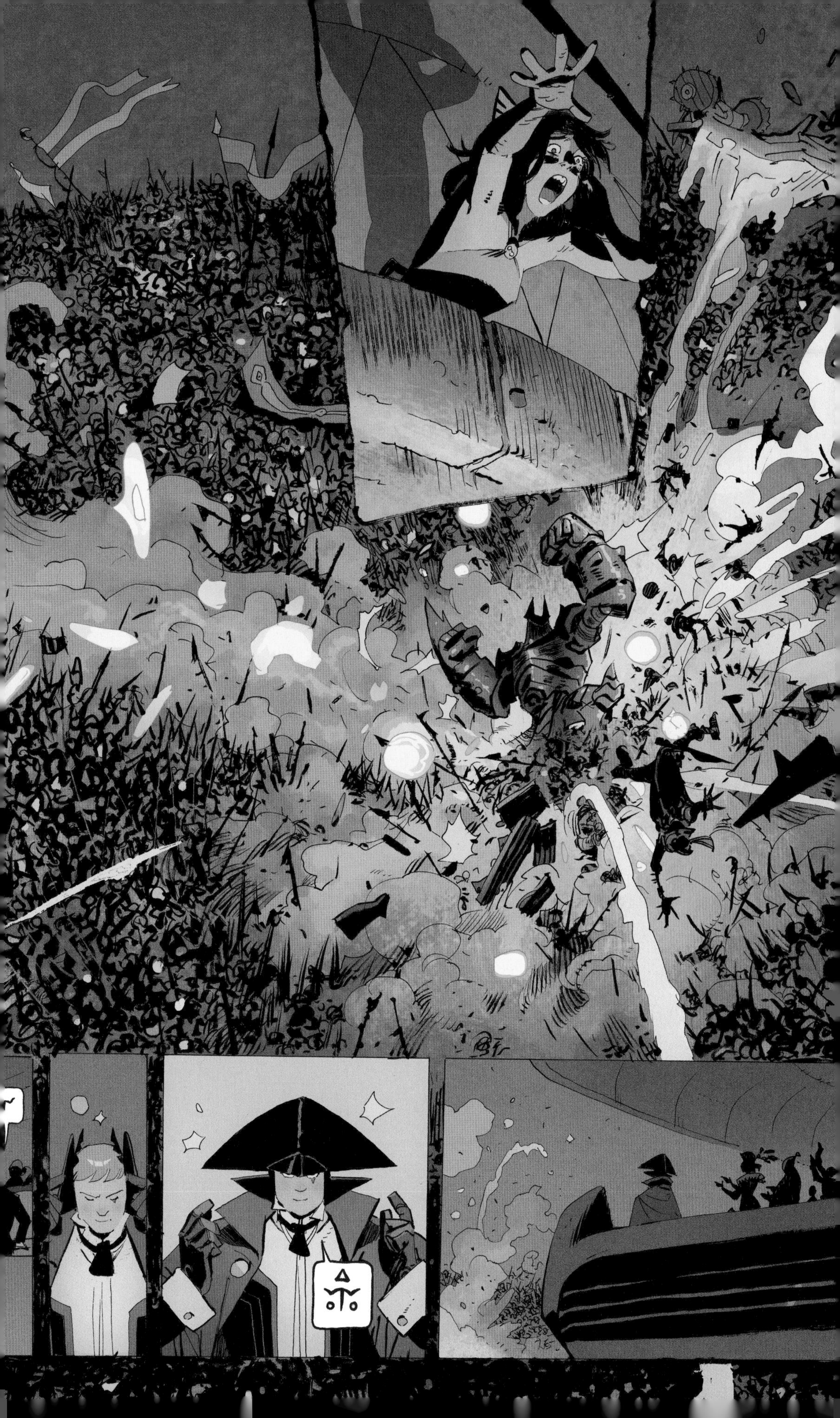

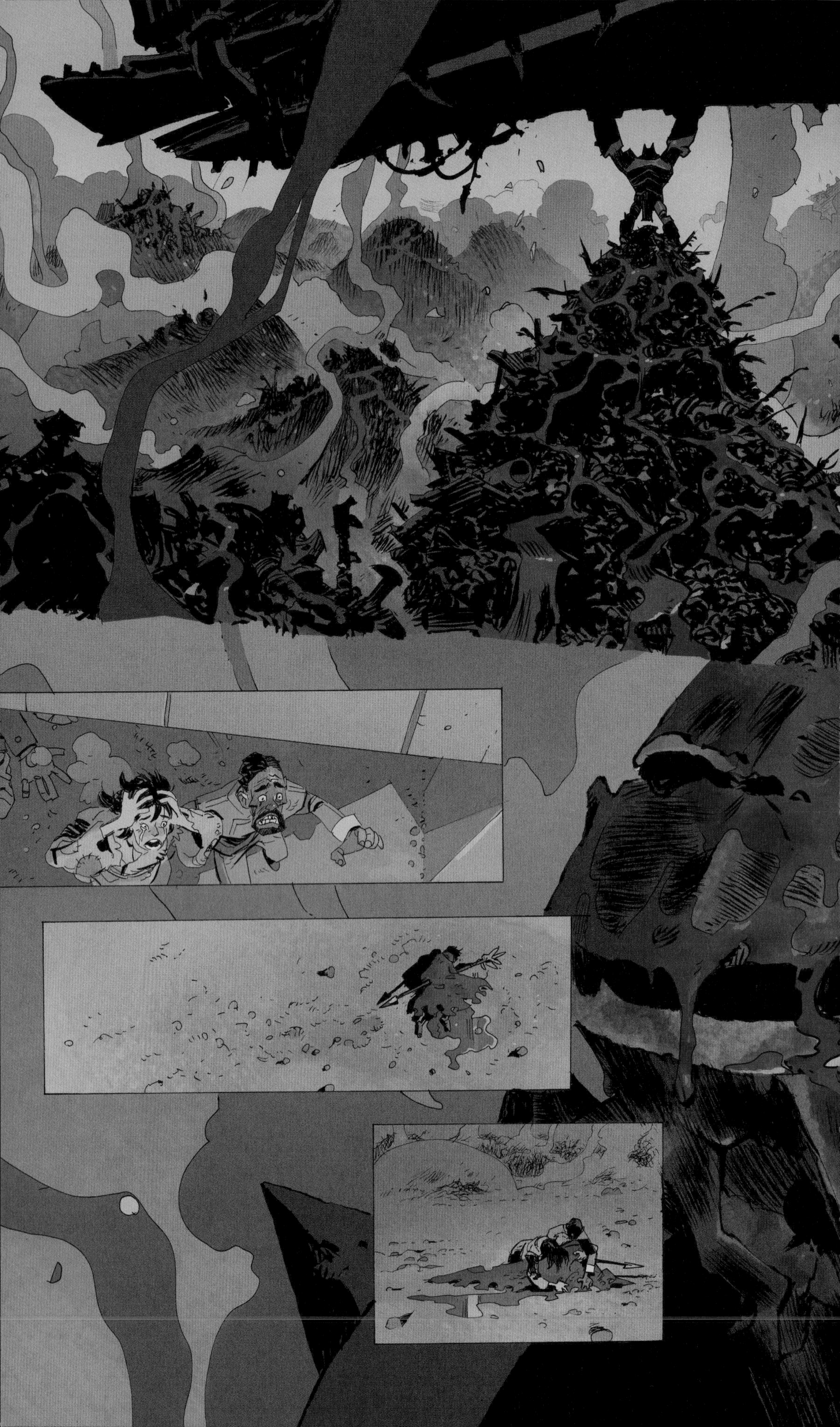

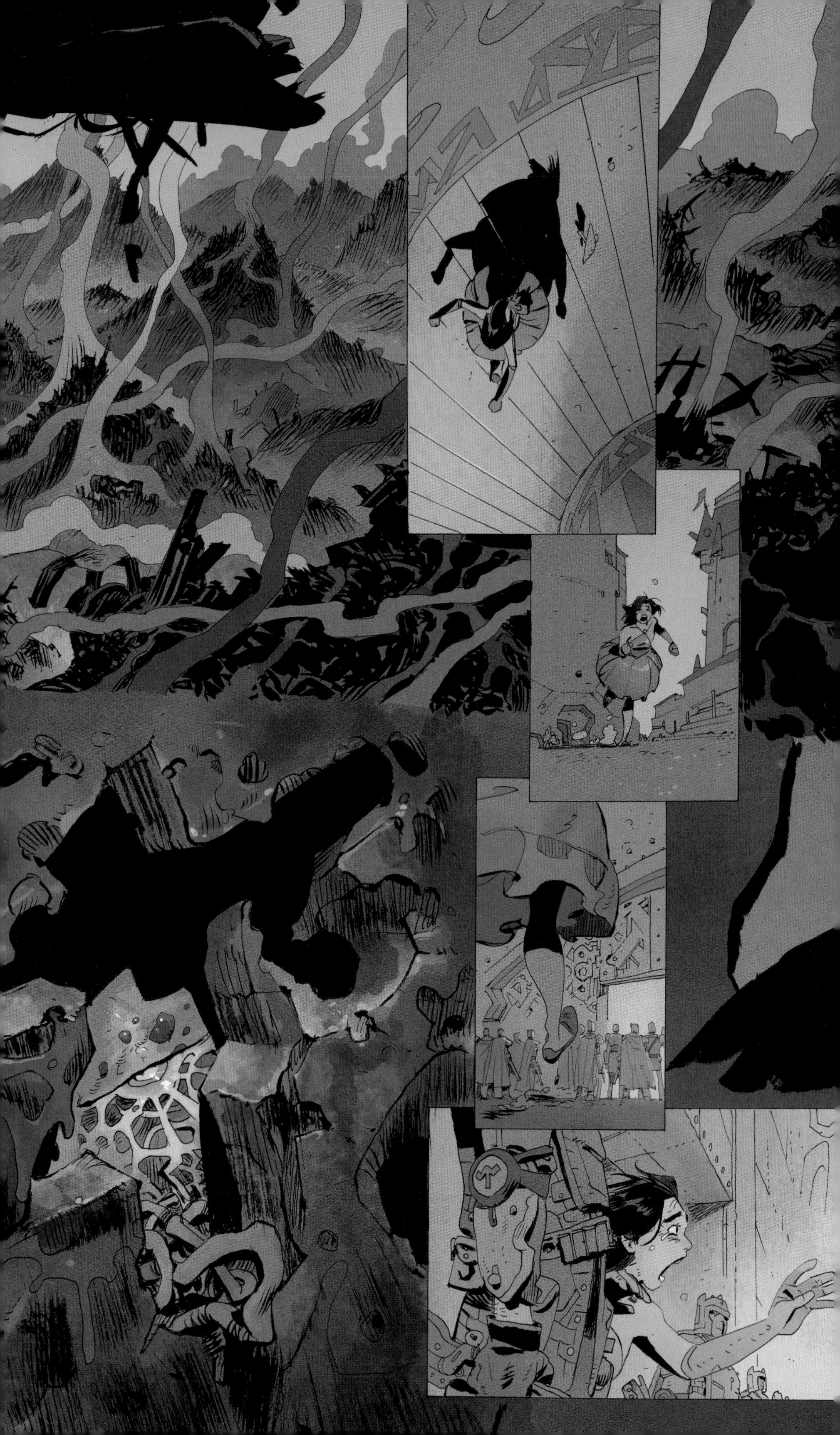

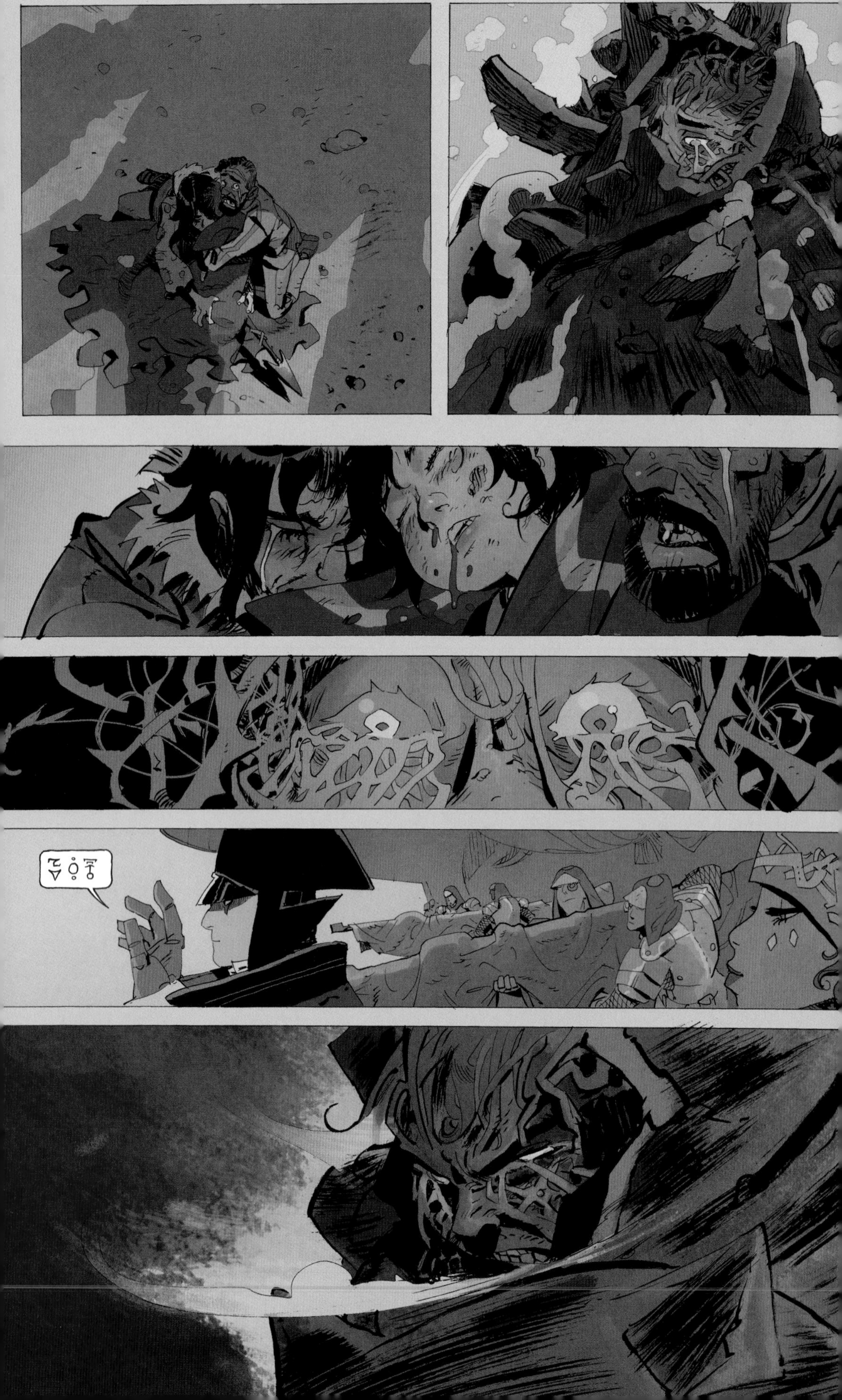

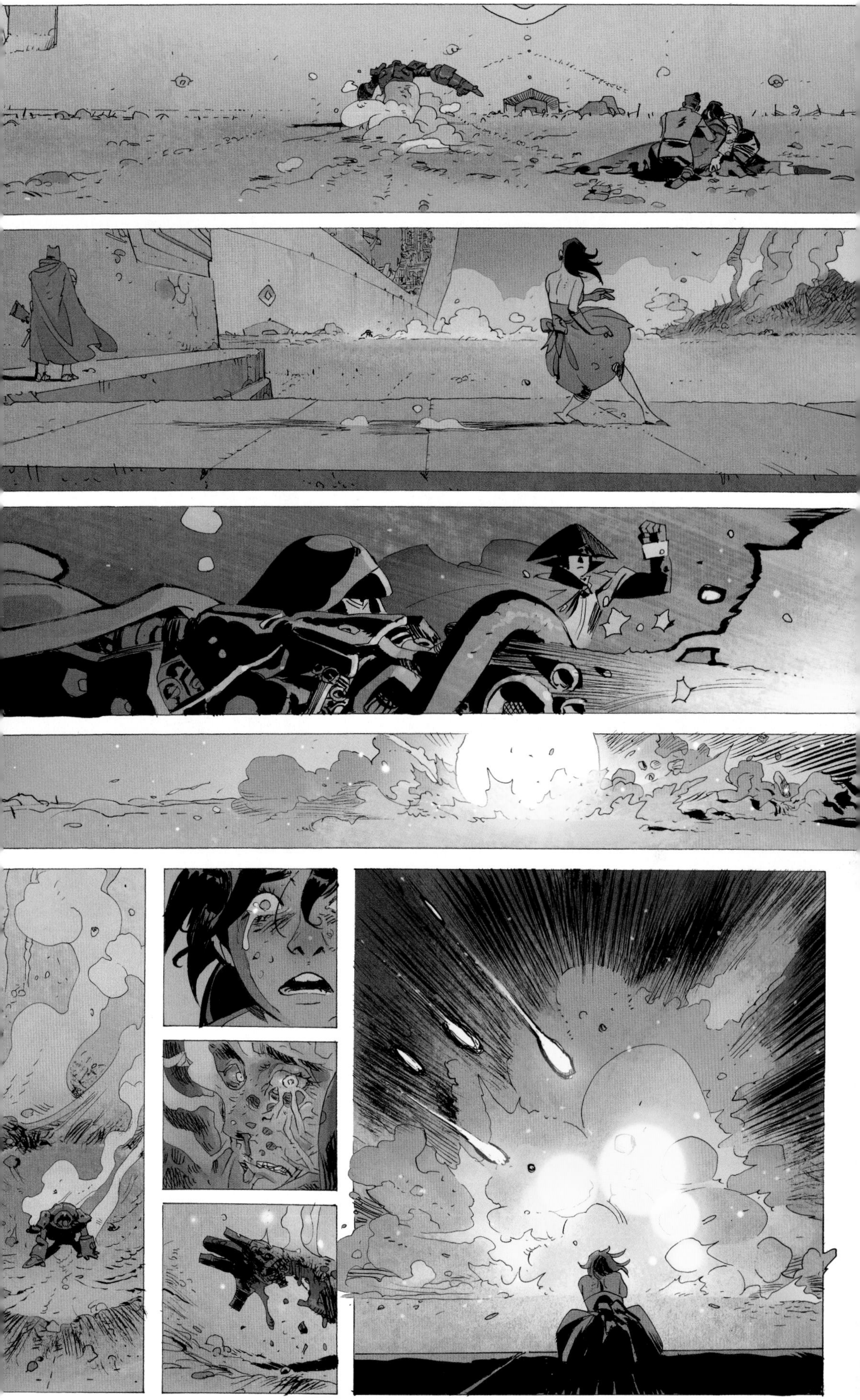

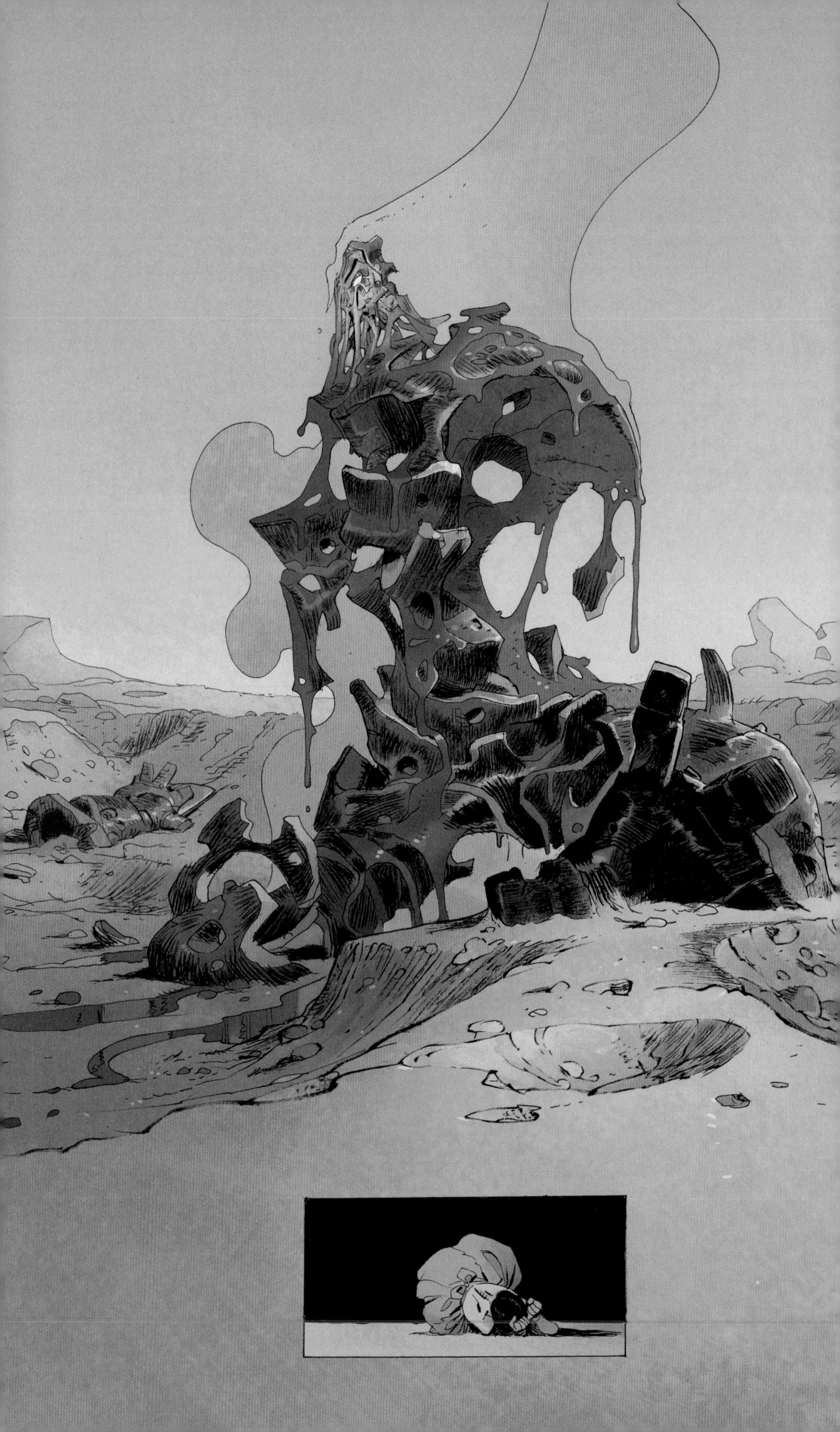

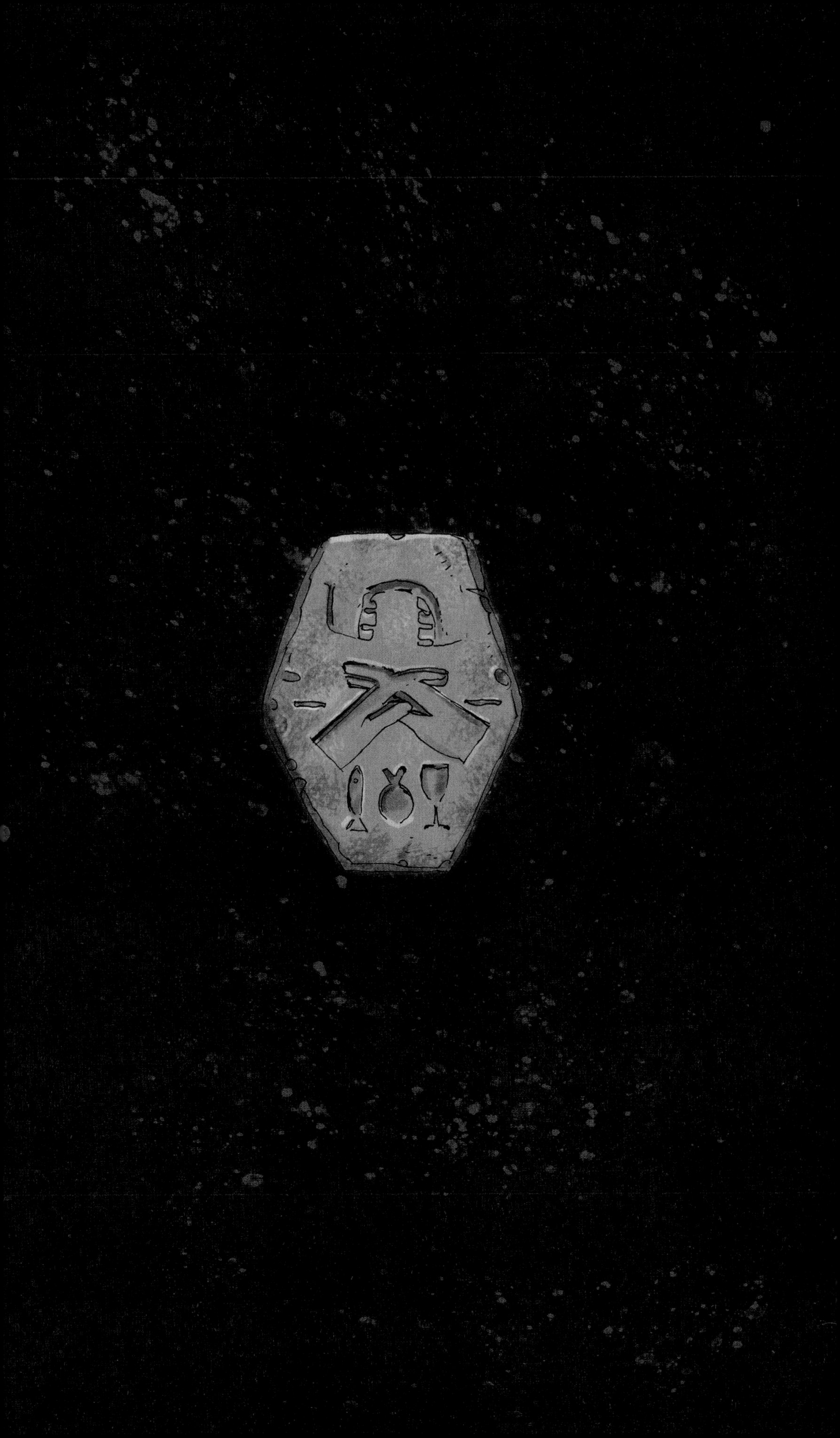

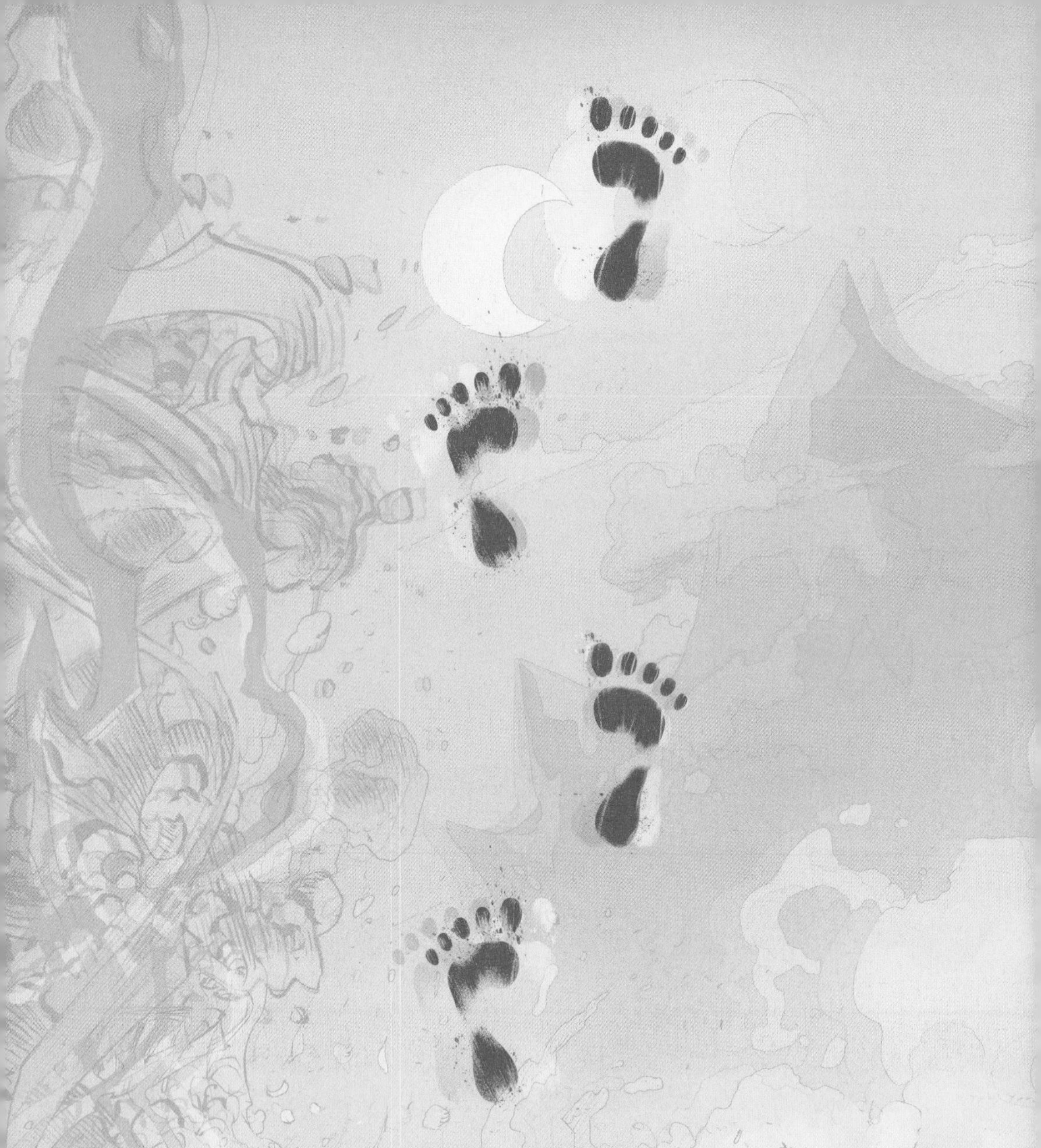

She sees at last that she has not been walking.
She has been falling.

Falling towards Winter.

But the world is rolling askew,
There is no sun waiting to dawn behind the ice,
Spring will not come.

Nobody will help her.
Nobody could.

Time turns for nobody's sake but its own.
But what—*who*—is time?

She was never meant to fall alone.

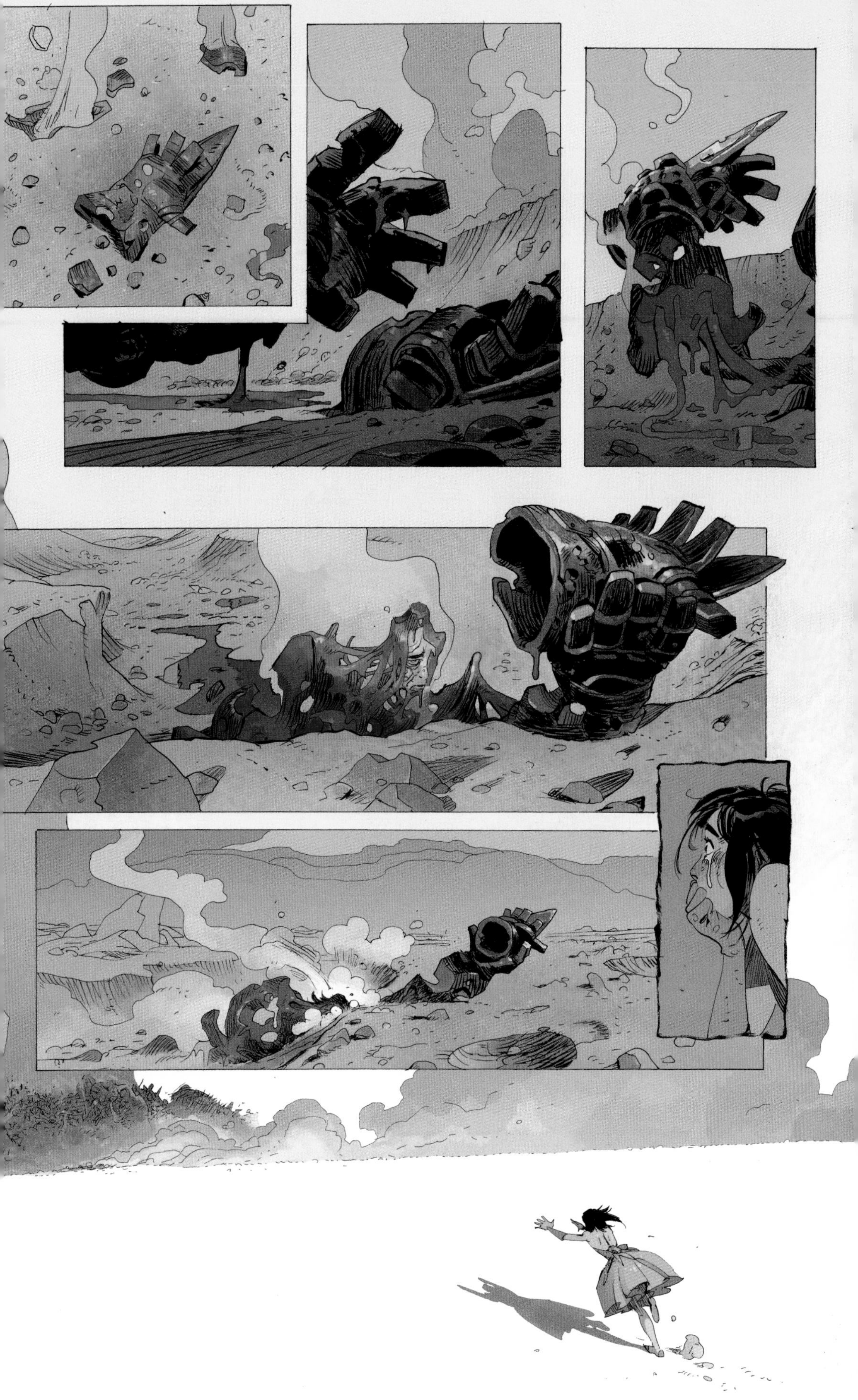

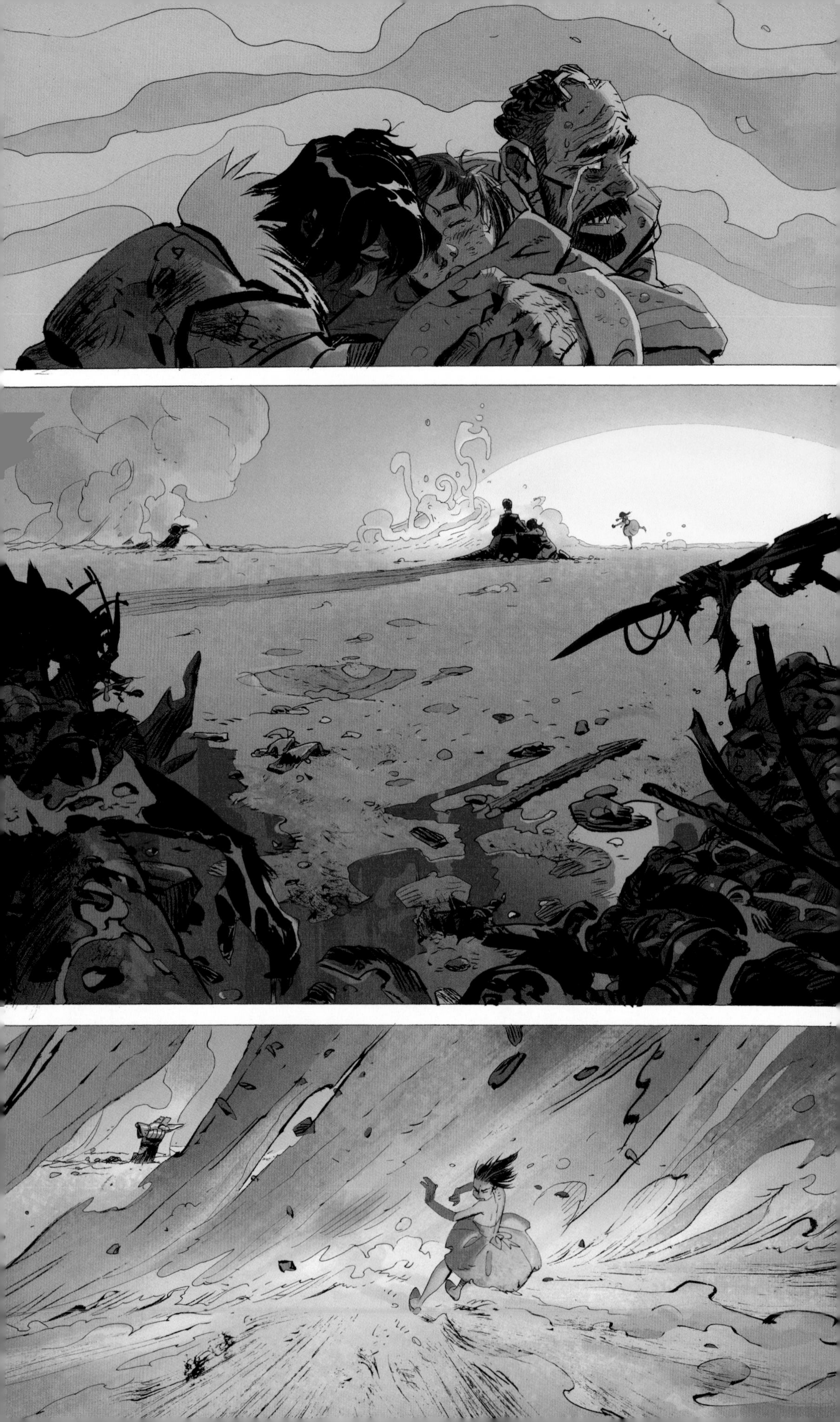

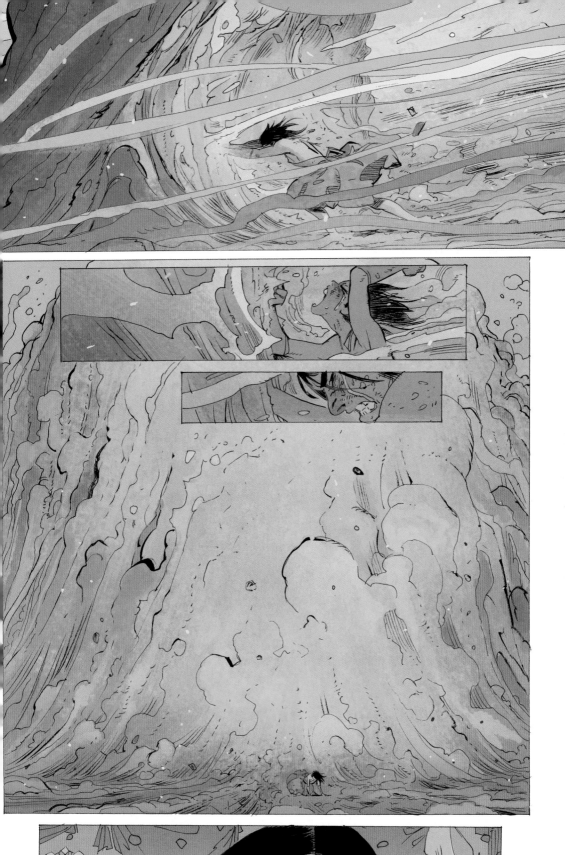

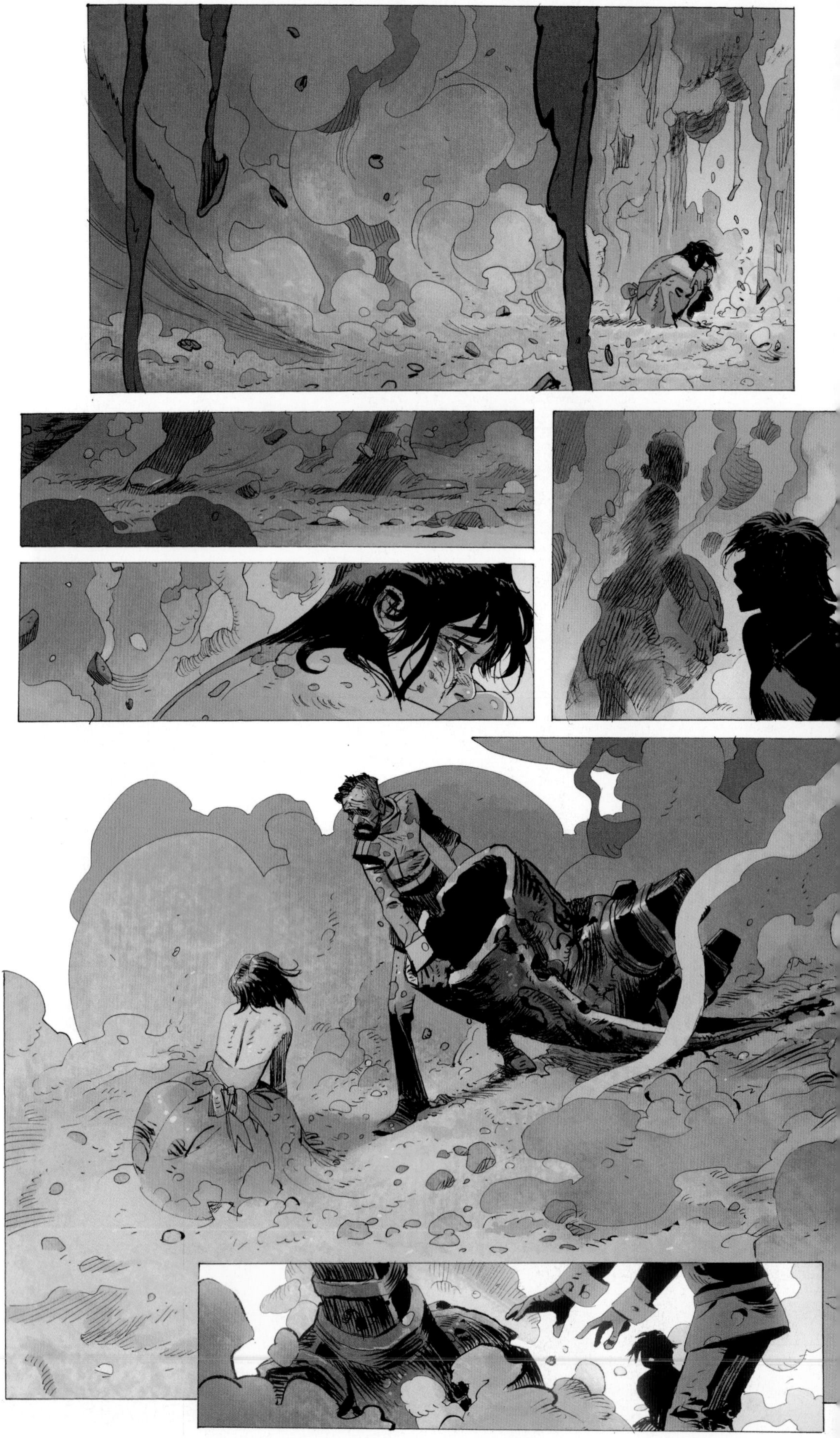

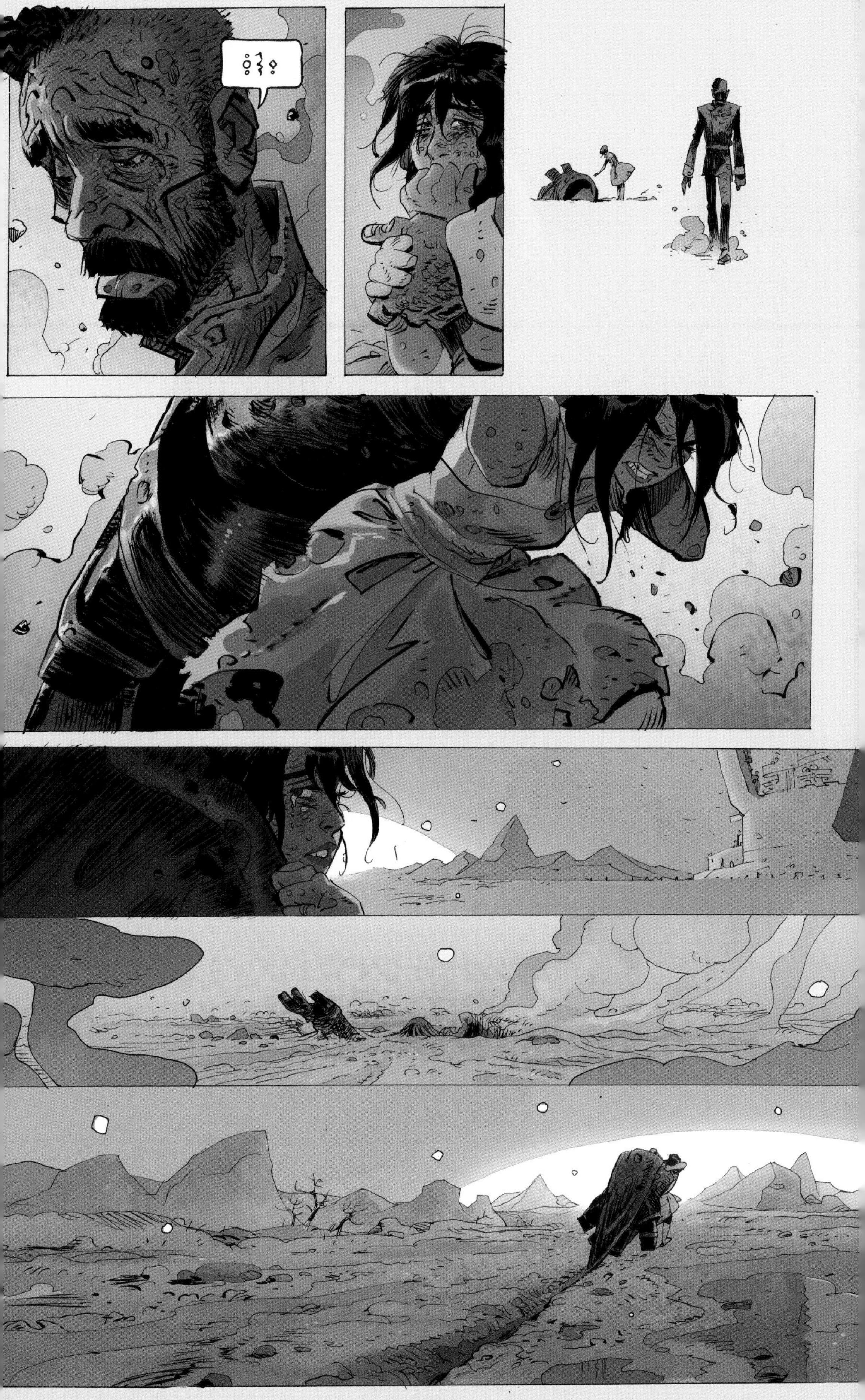

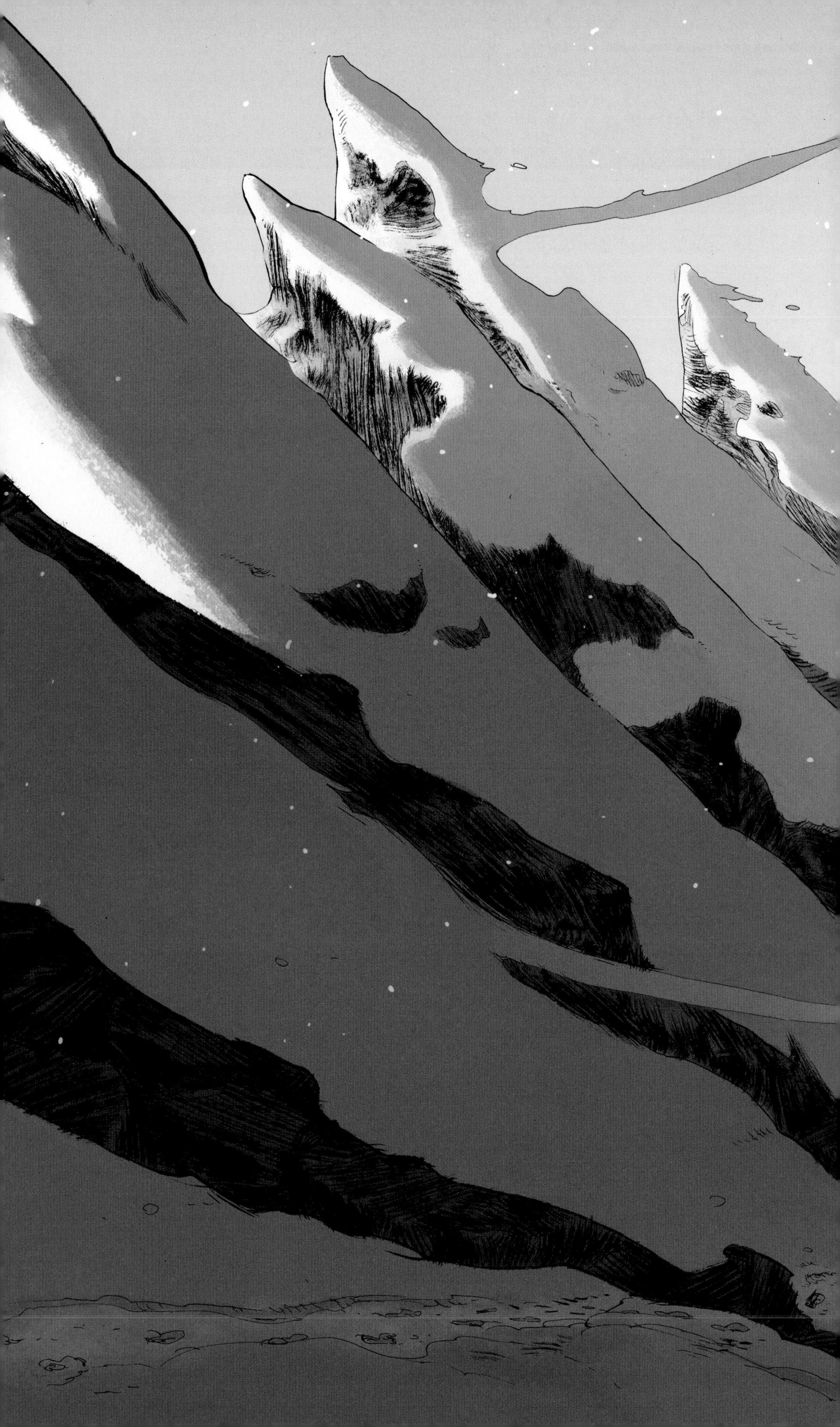

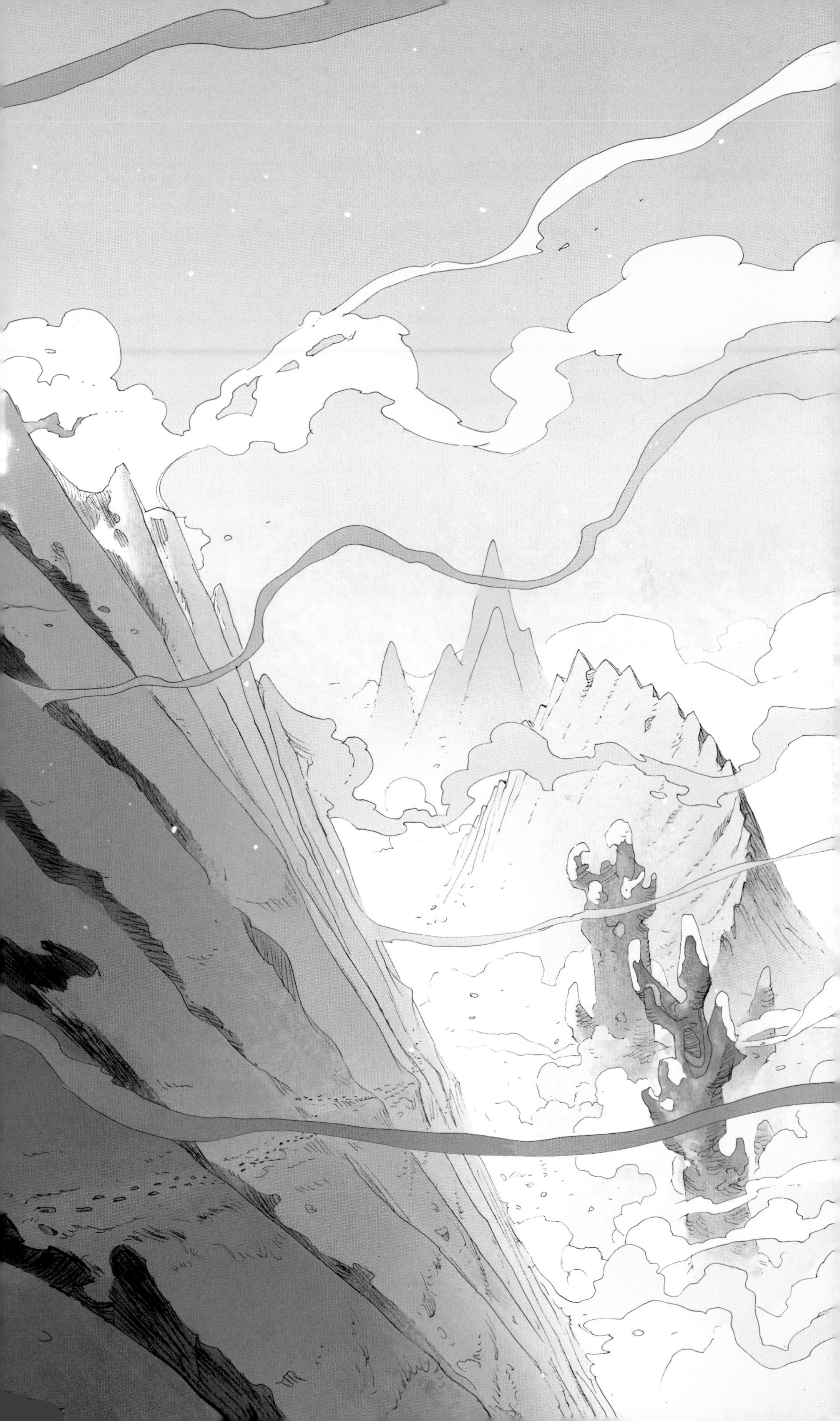

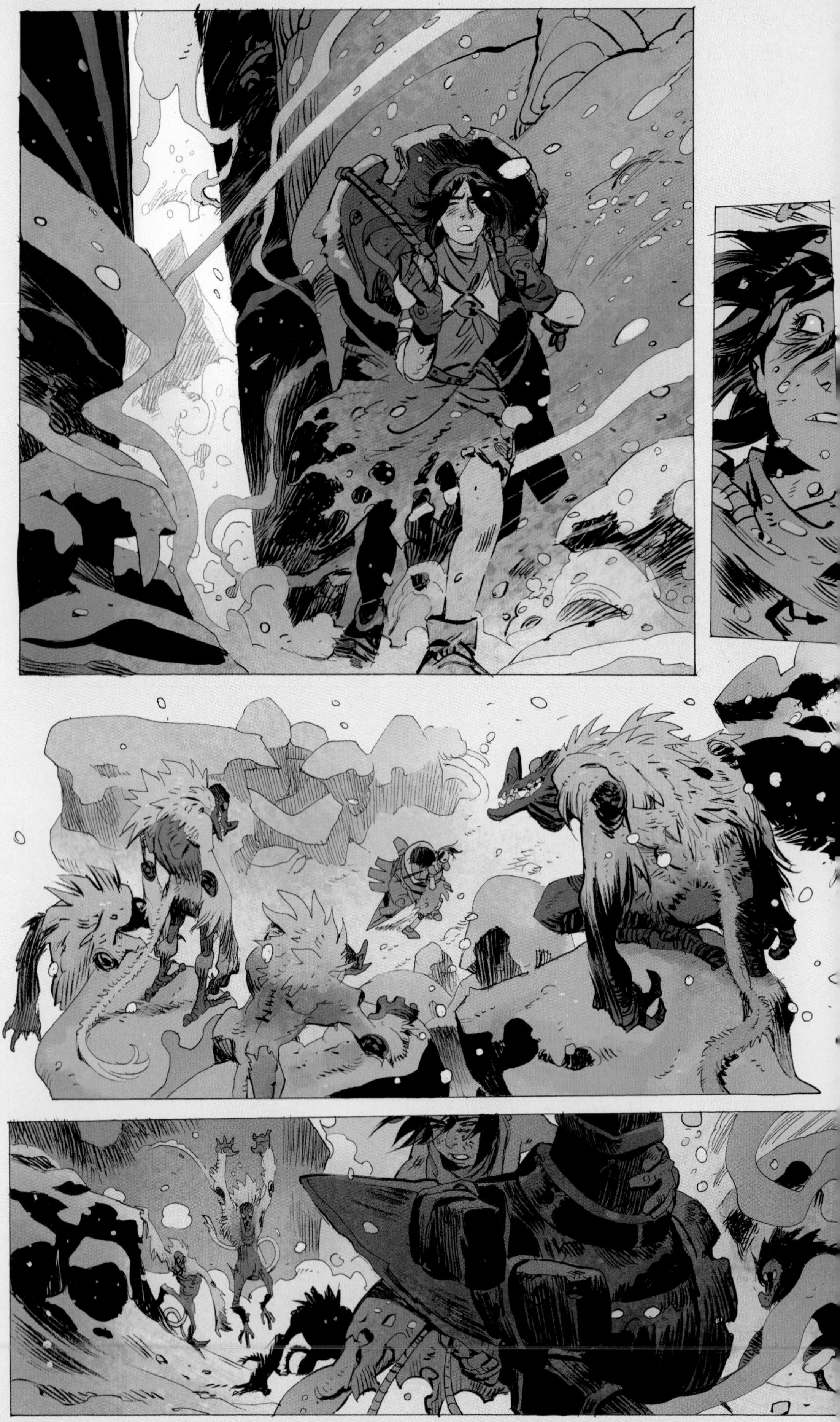

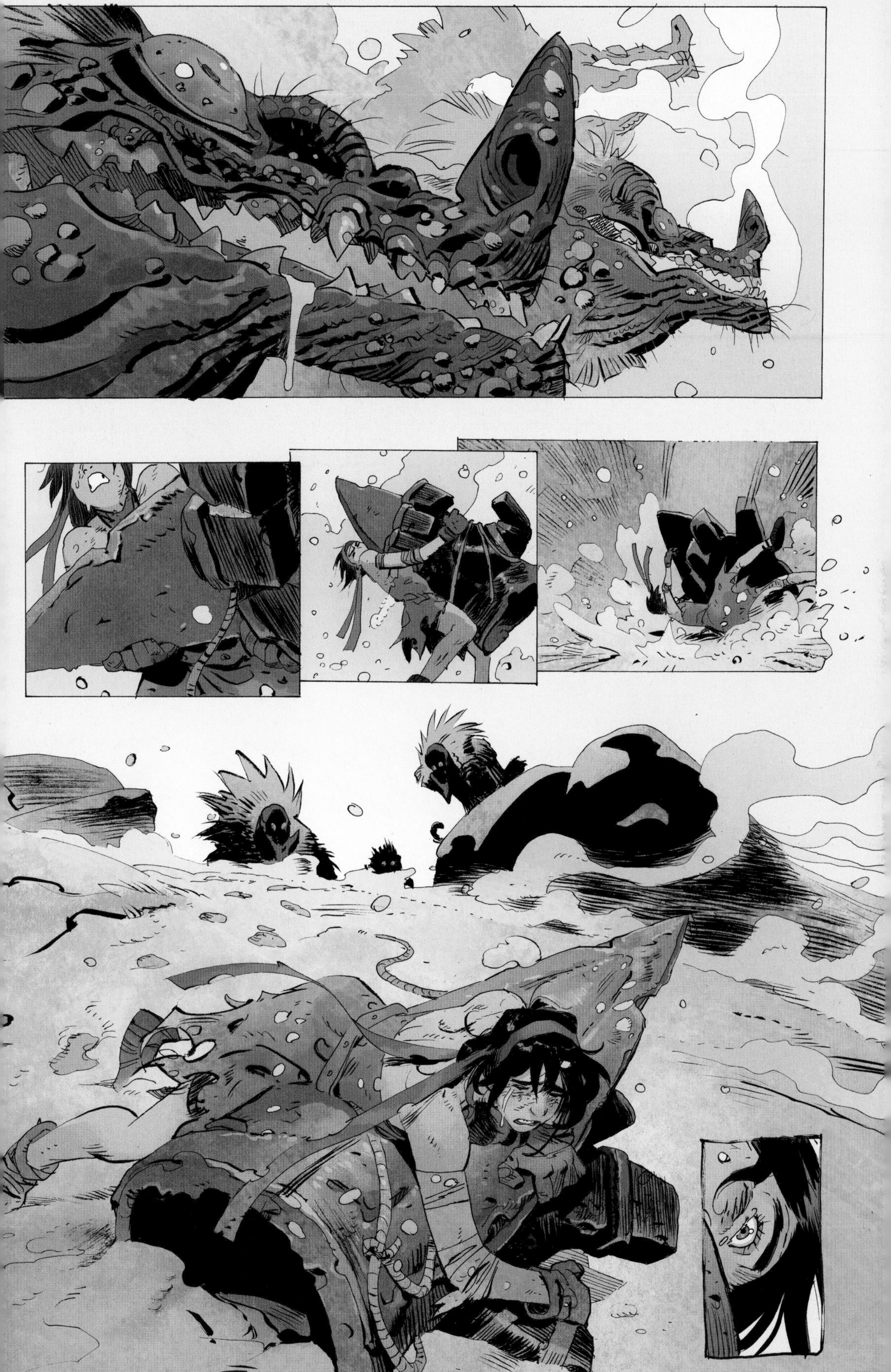

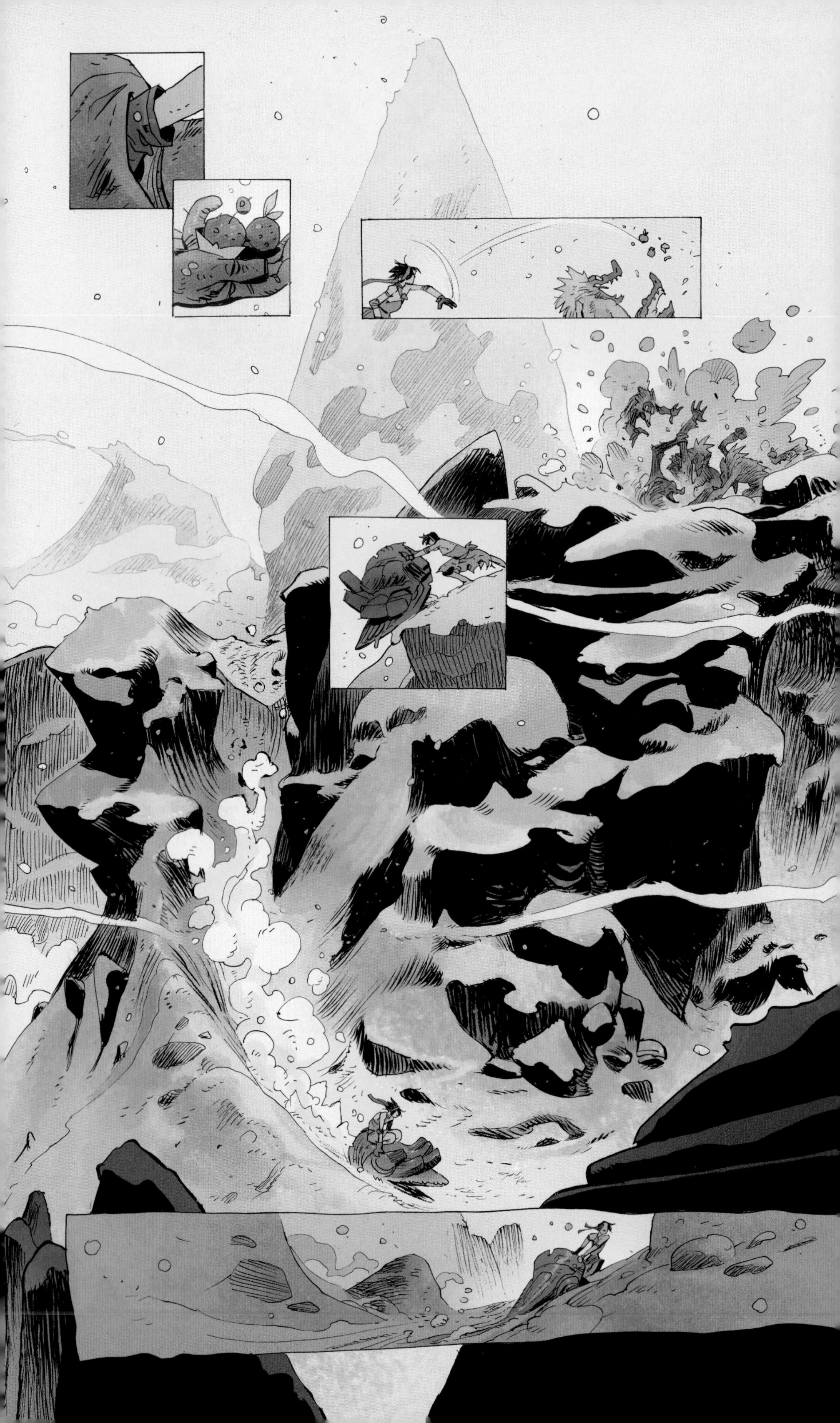

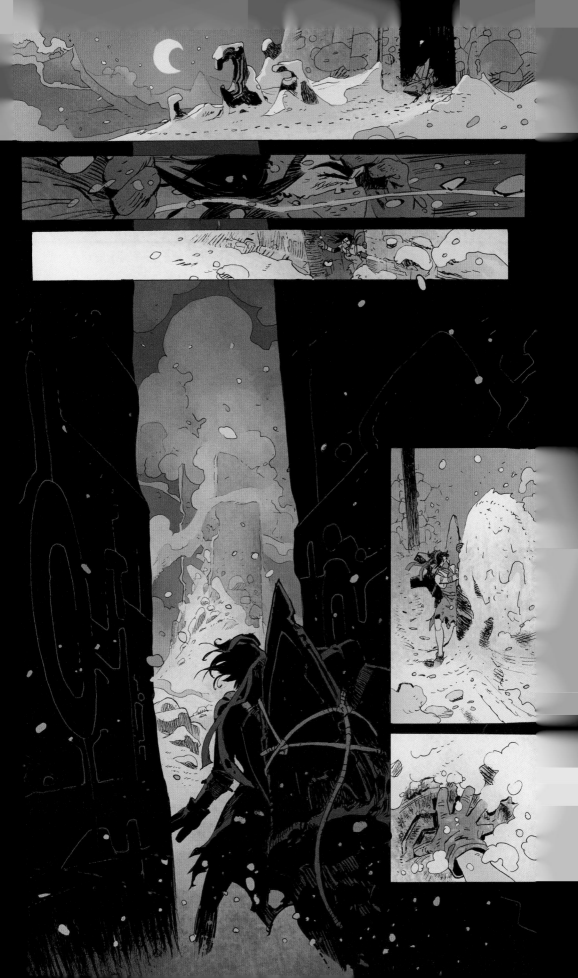

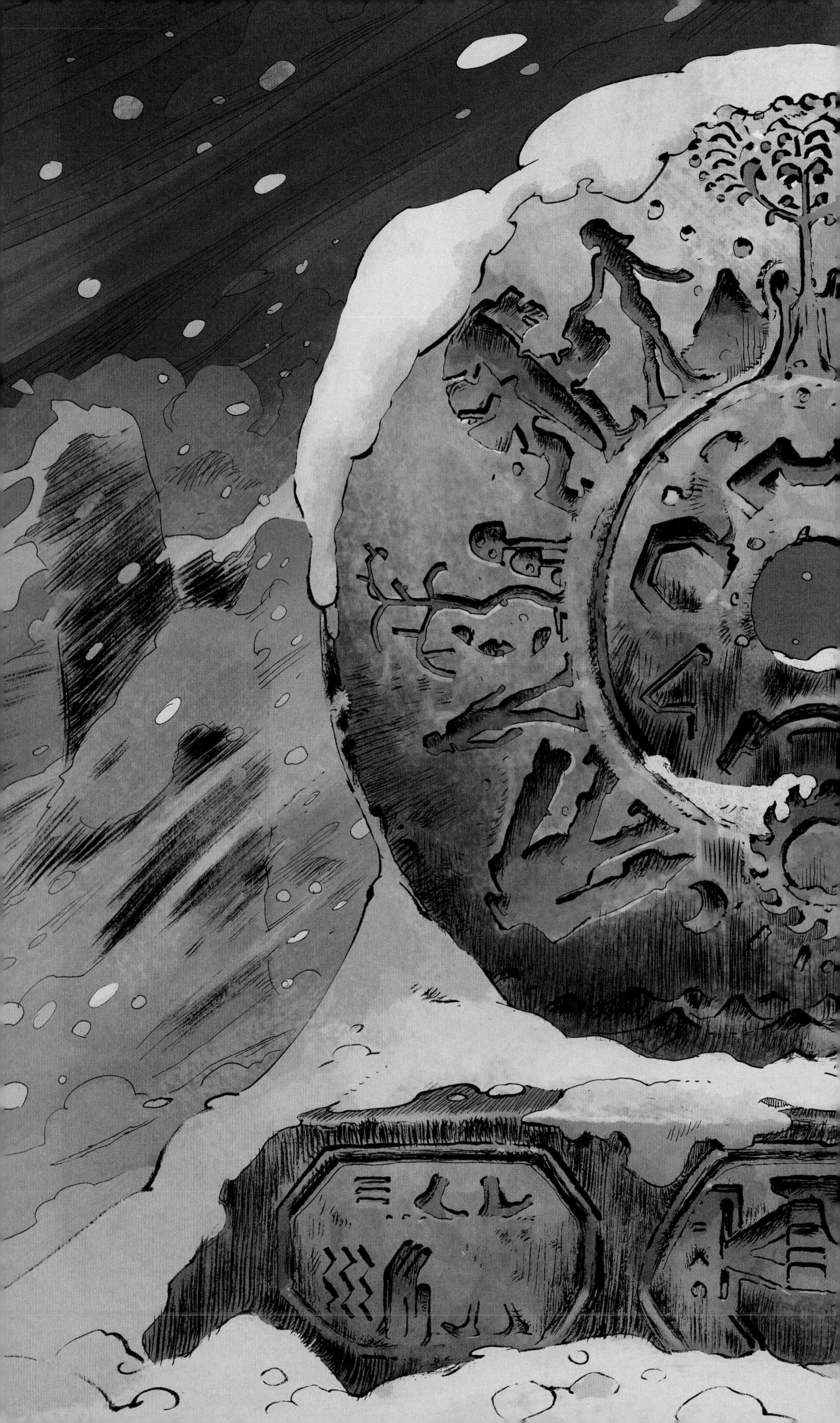

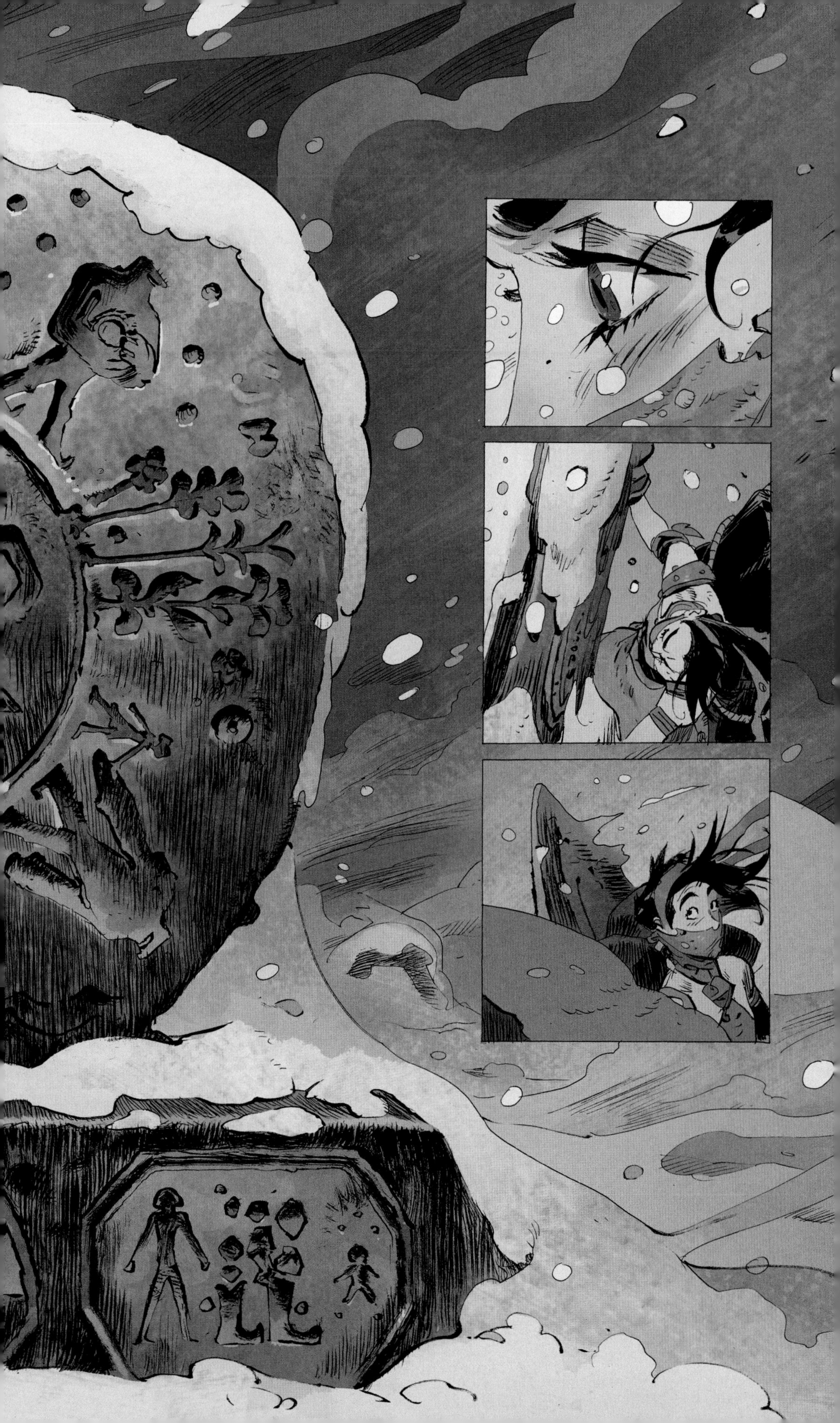

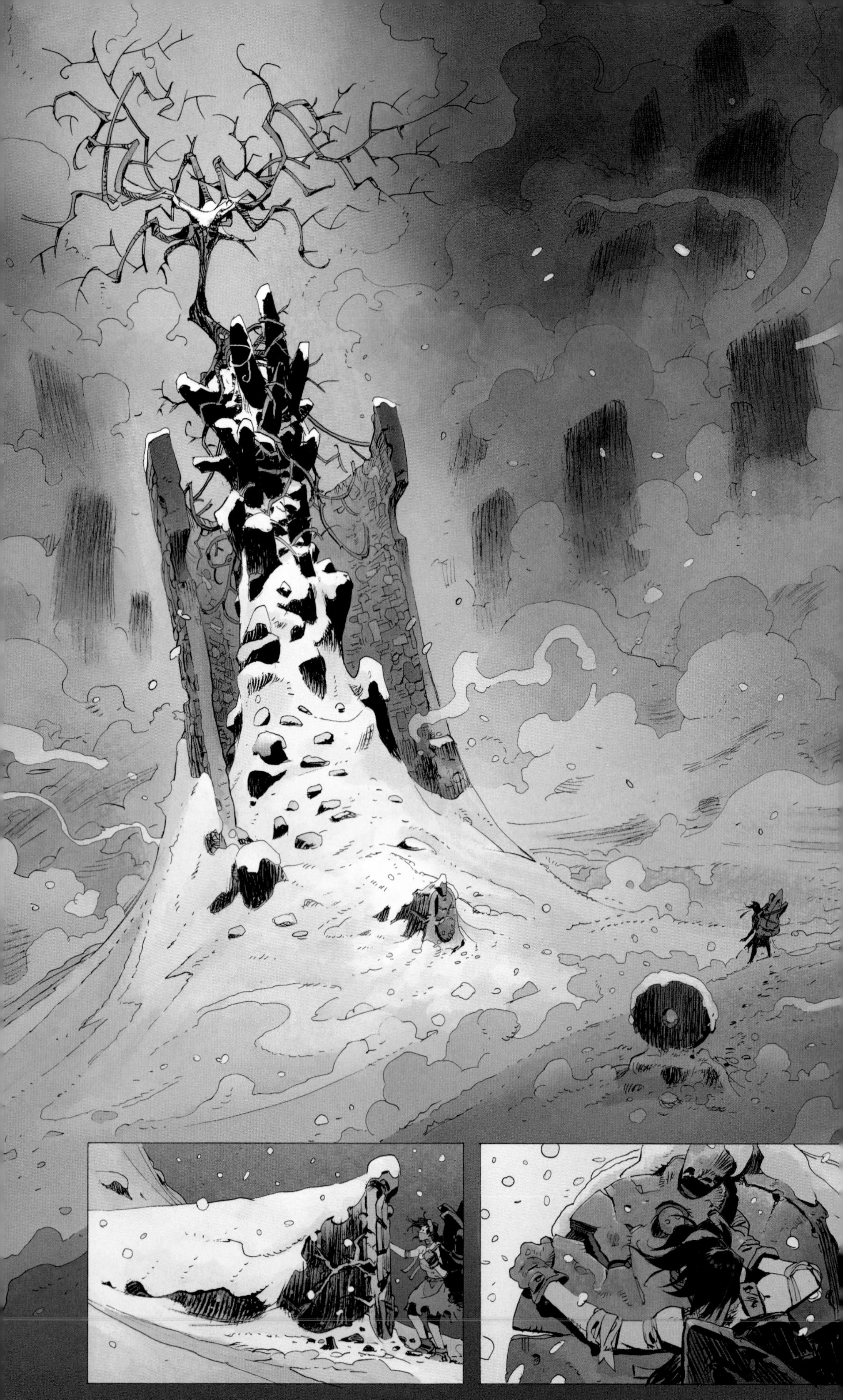

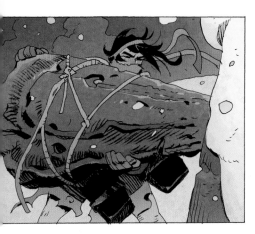

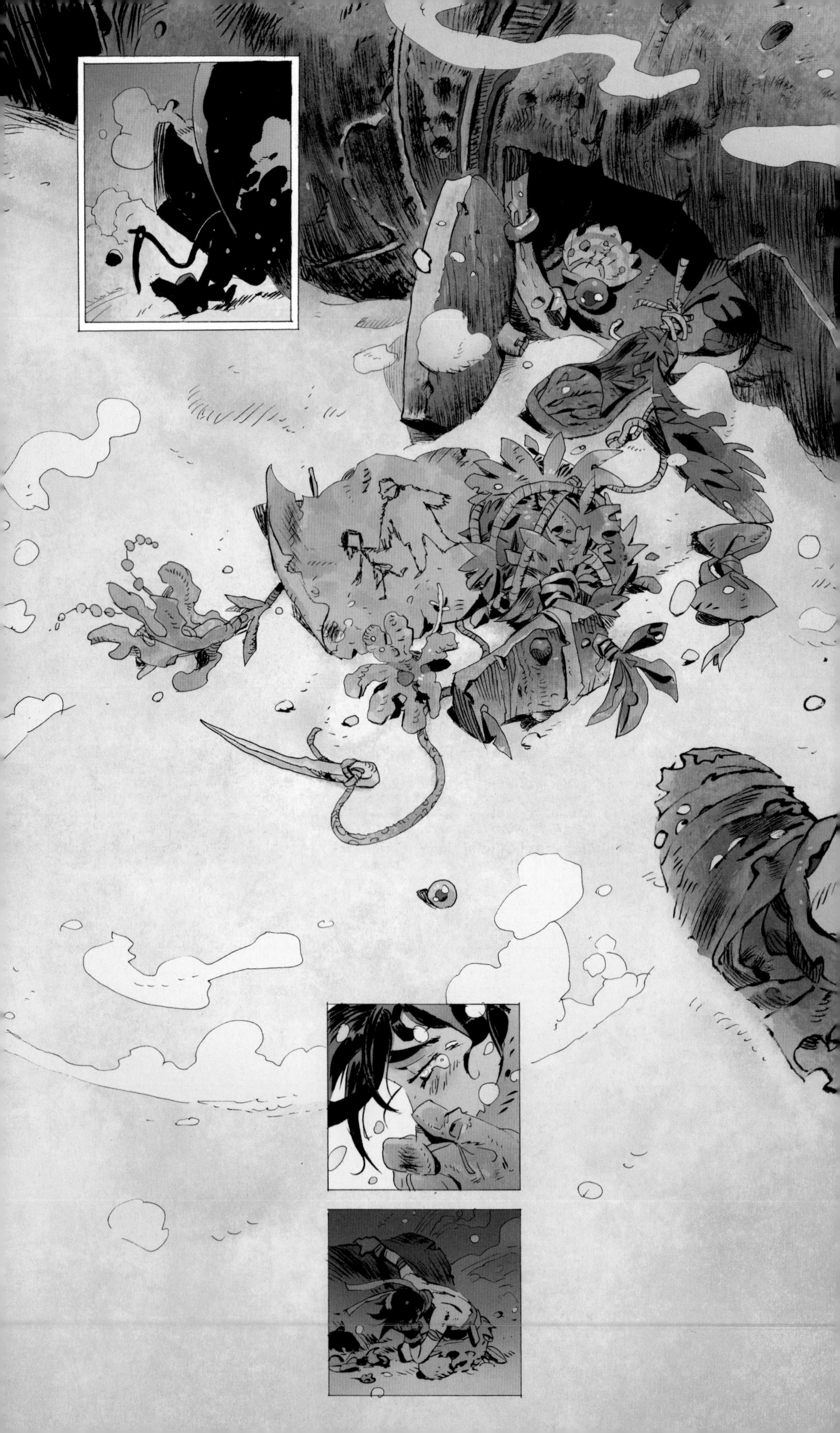

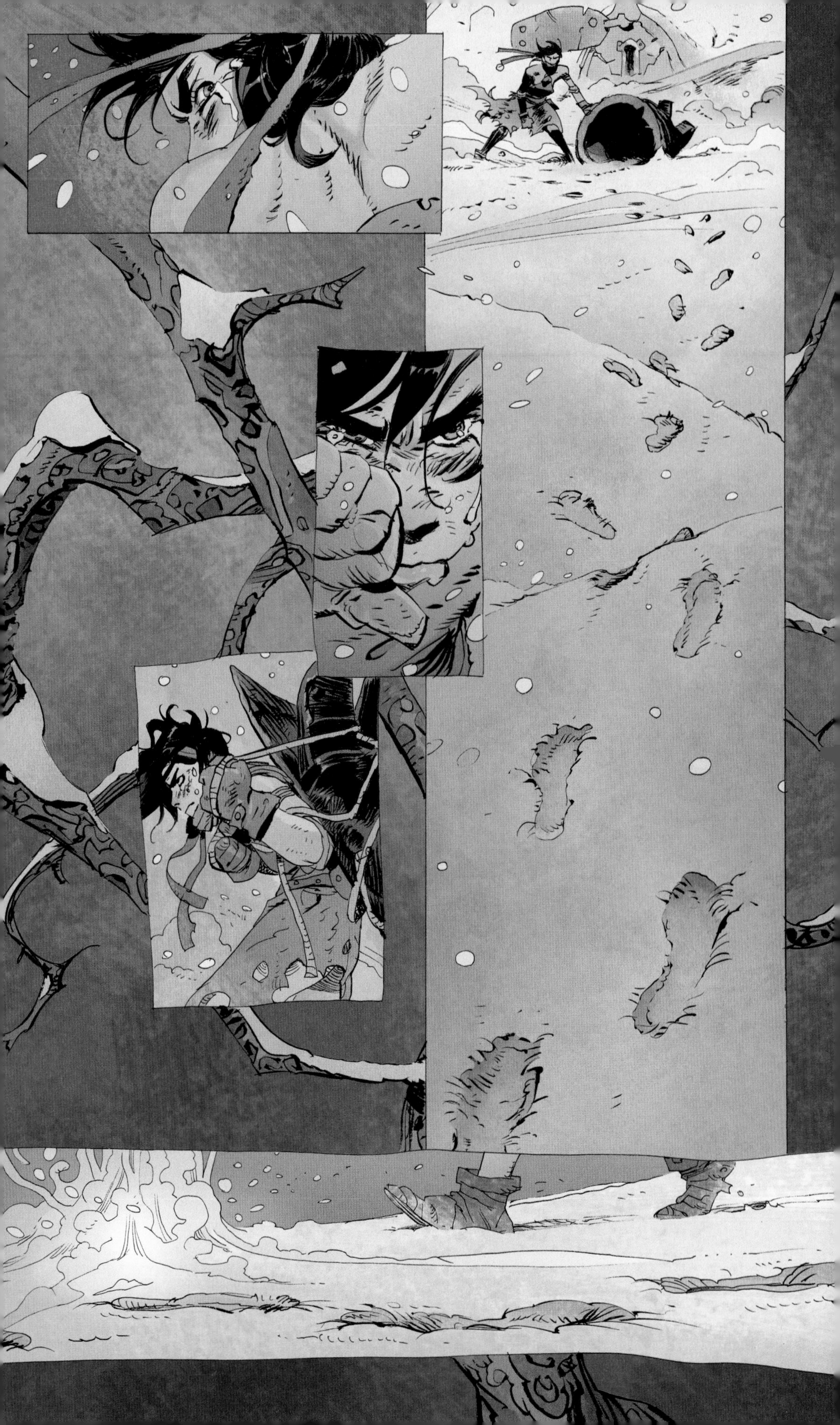

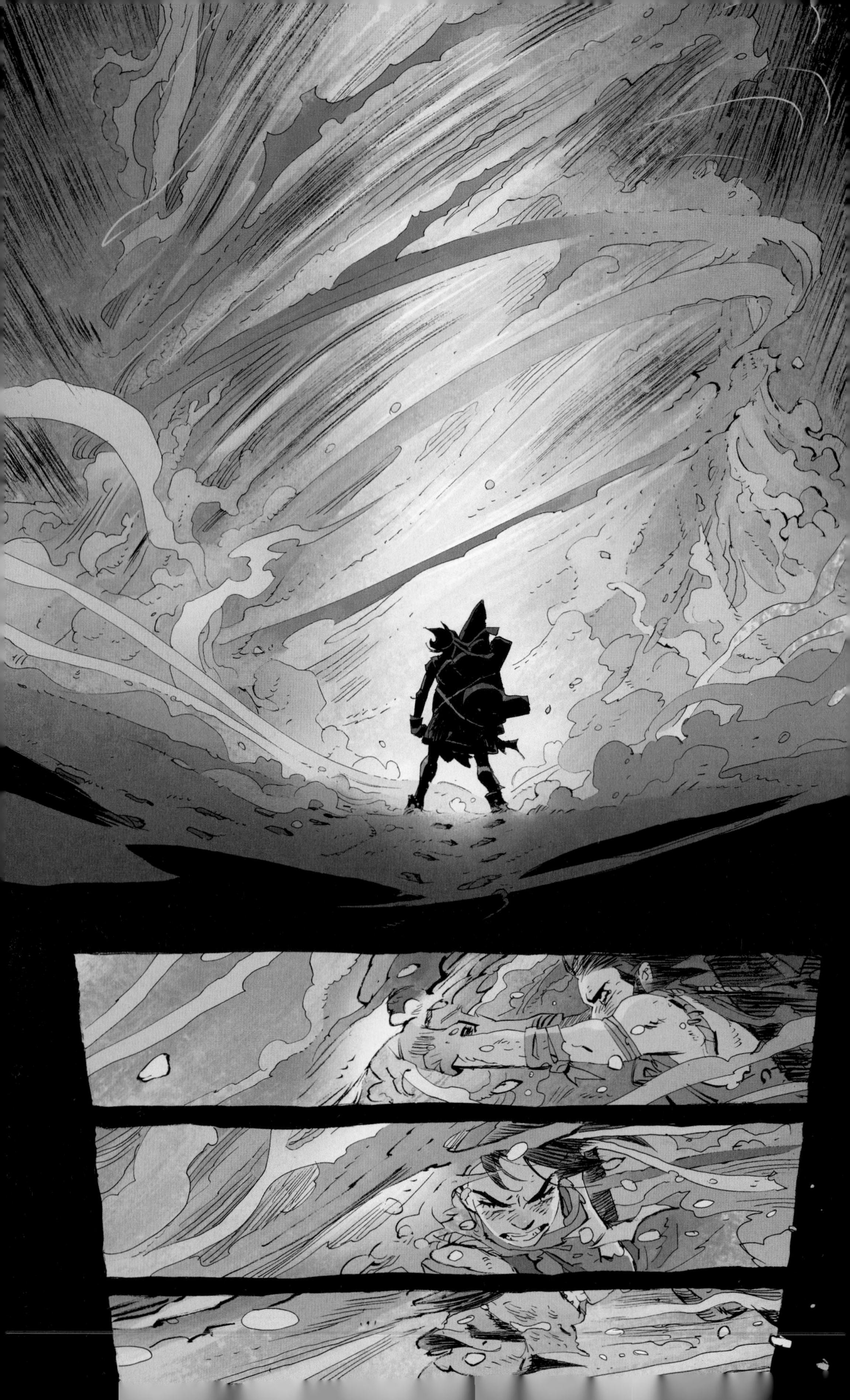

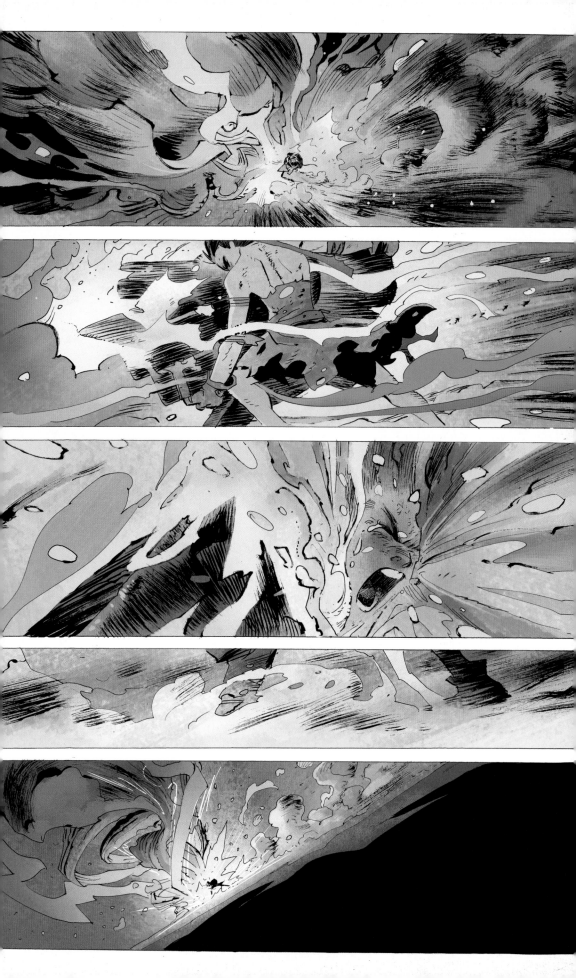

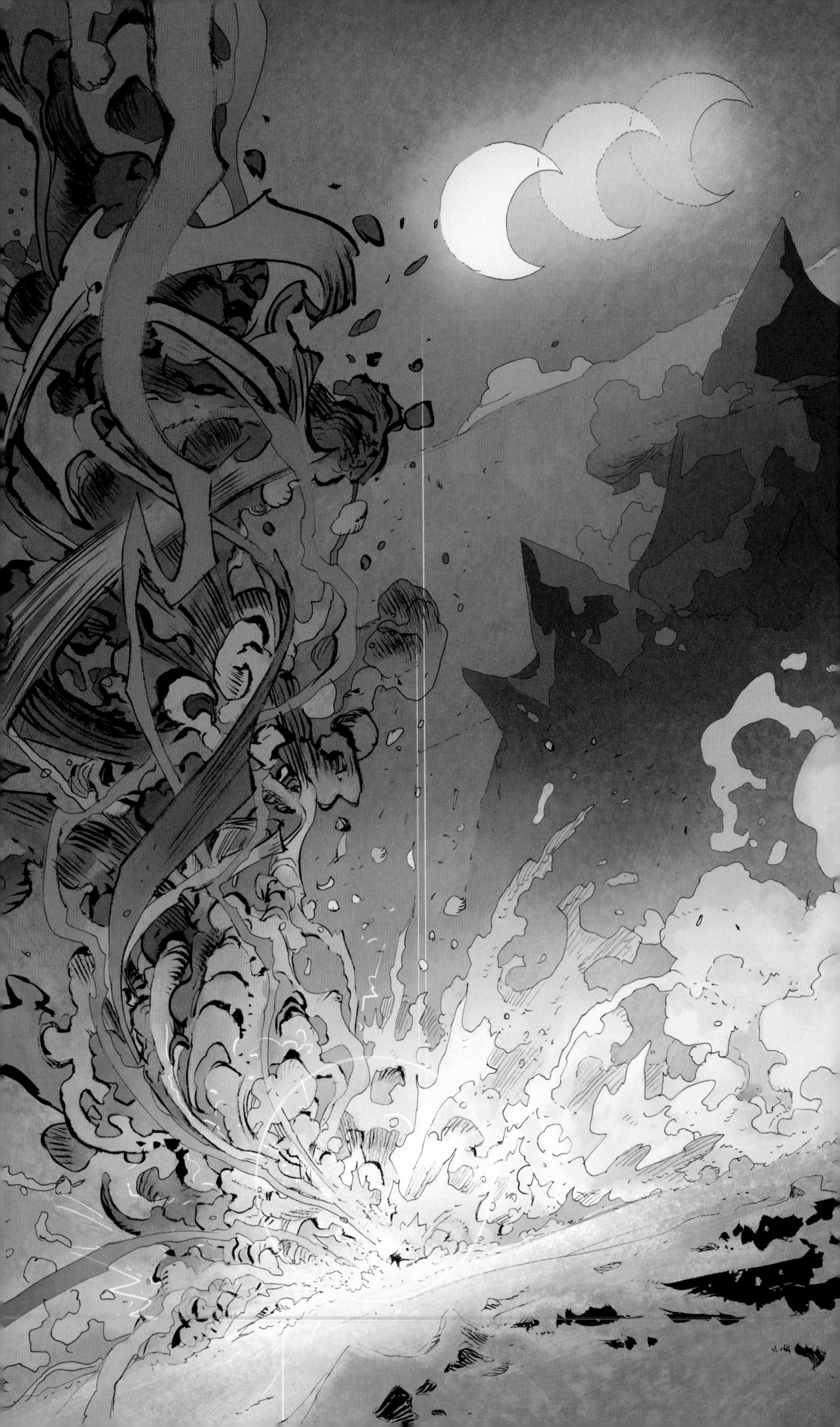

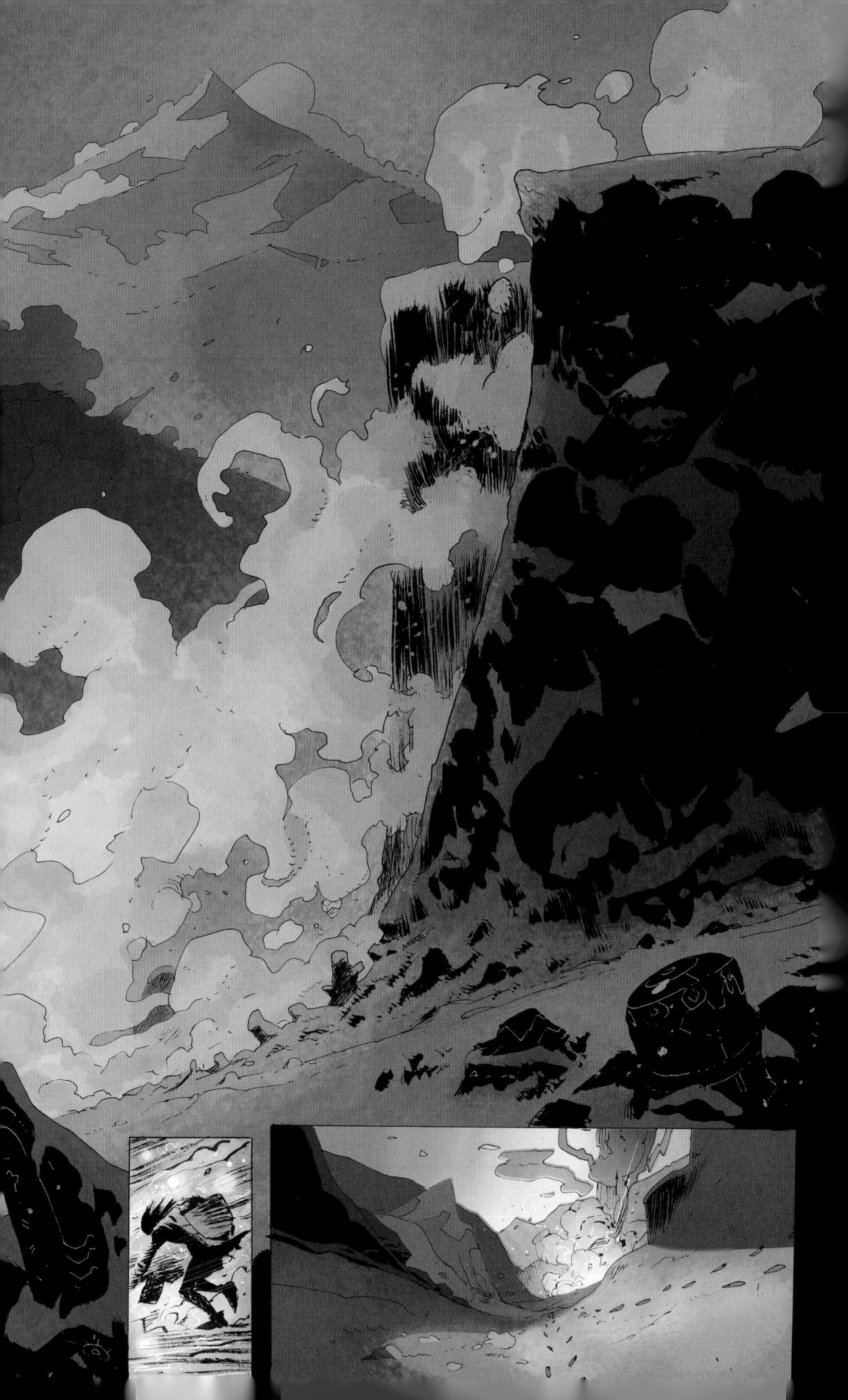

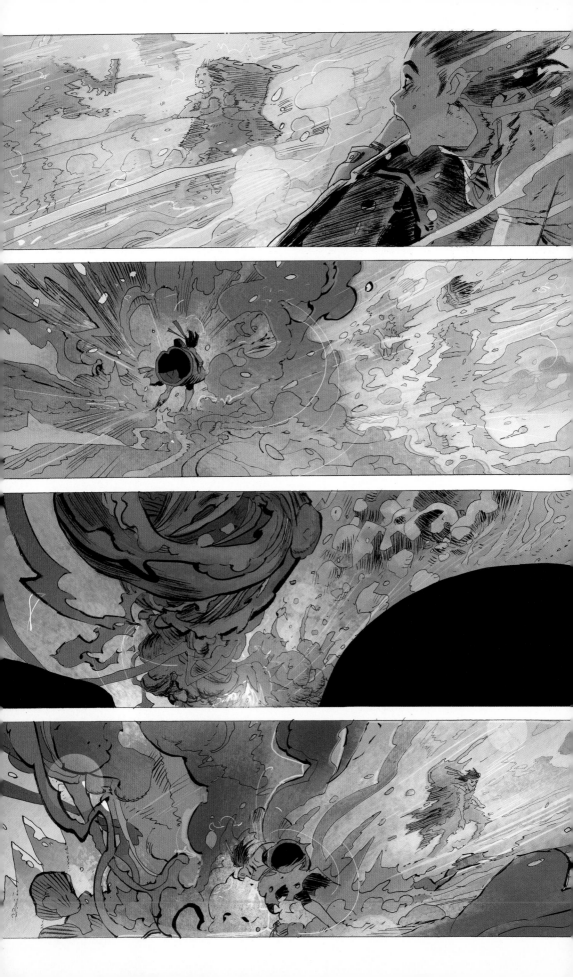

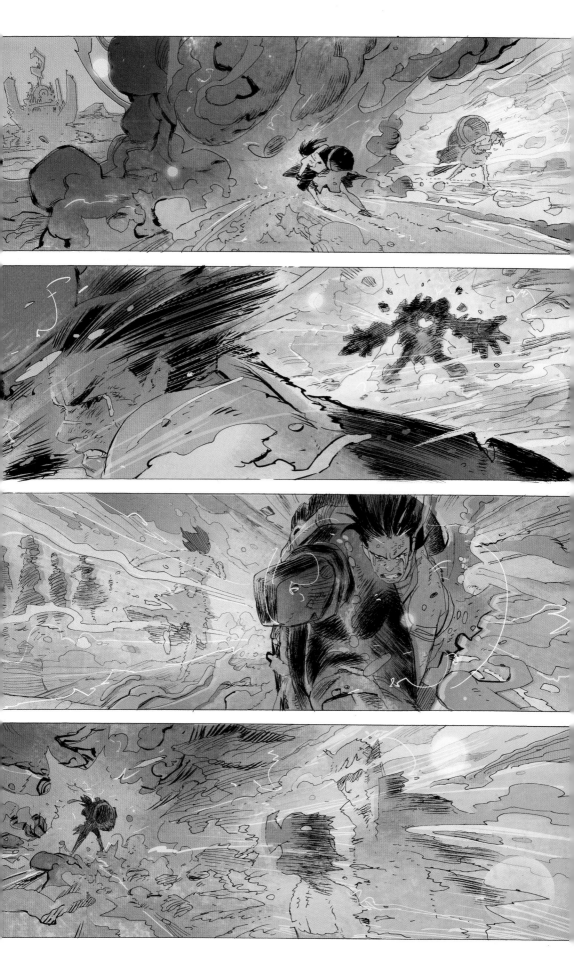

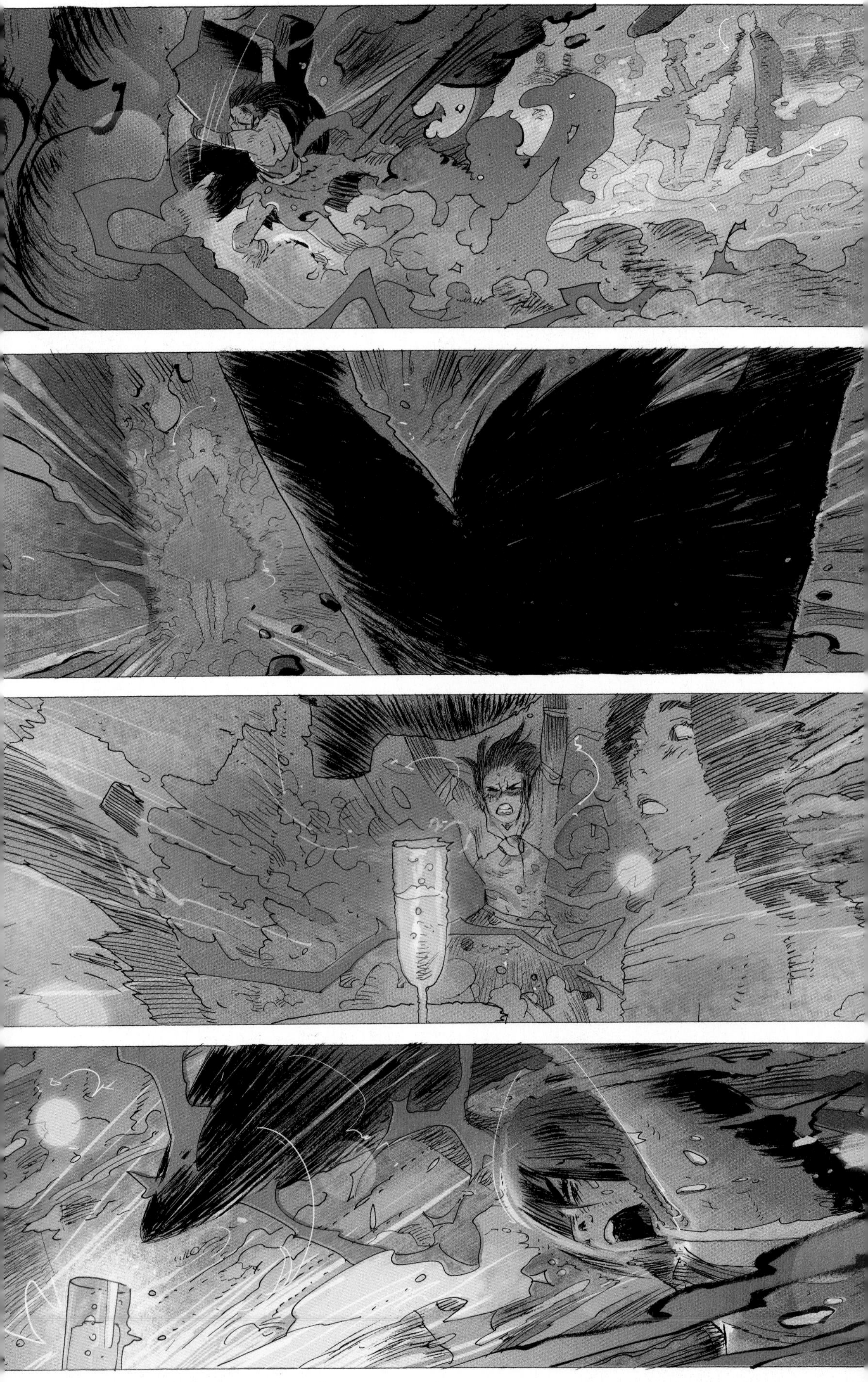

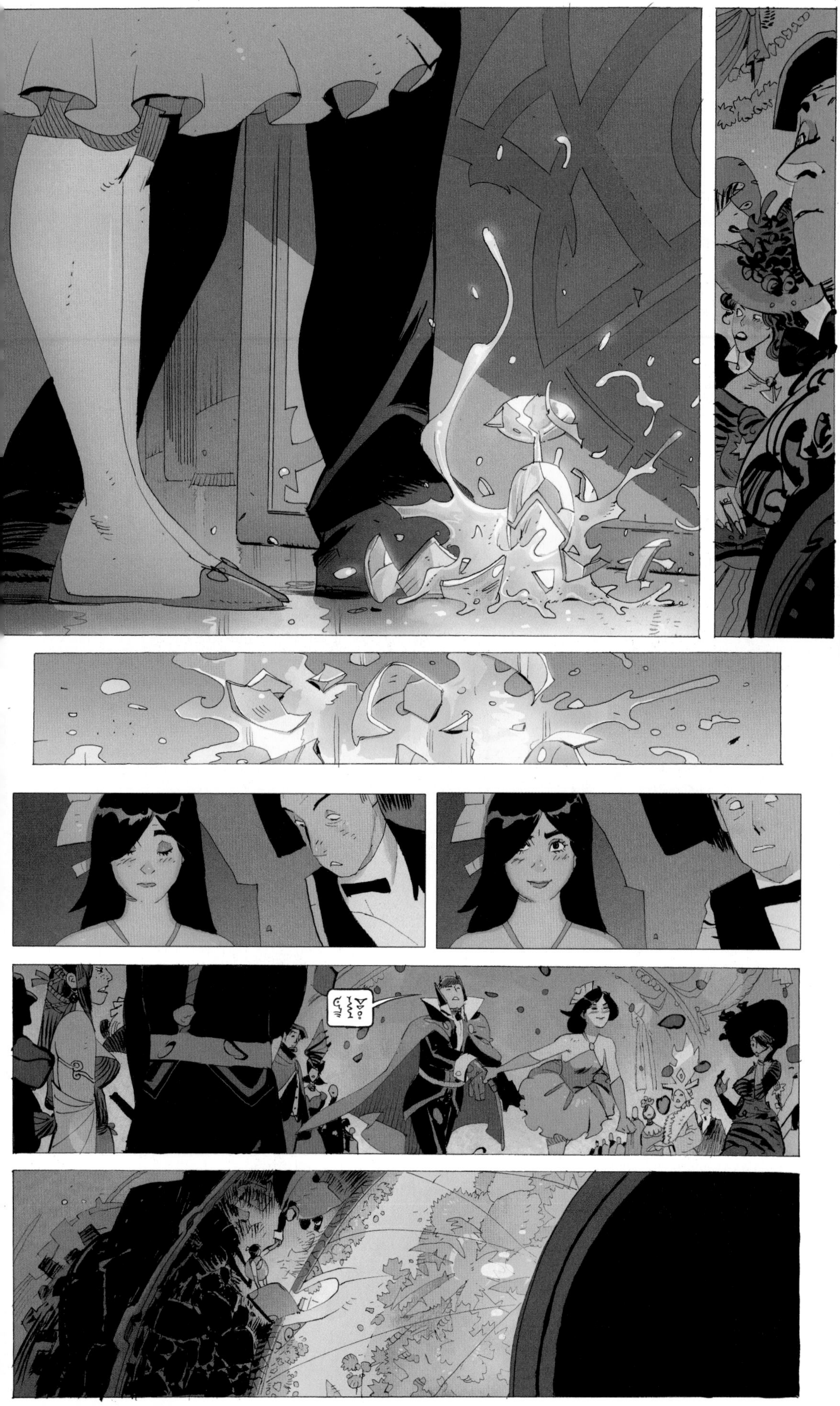

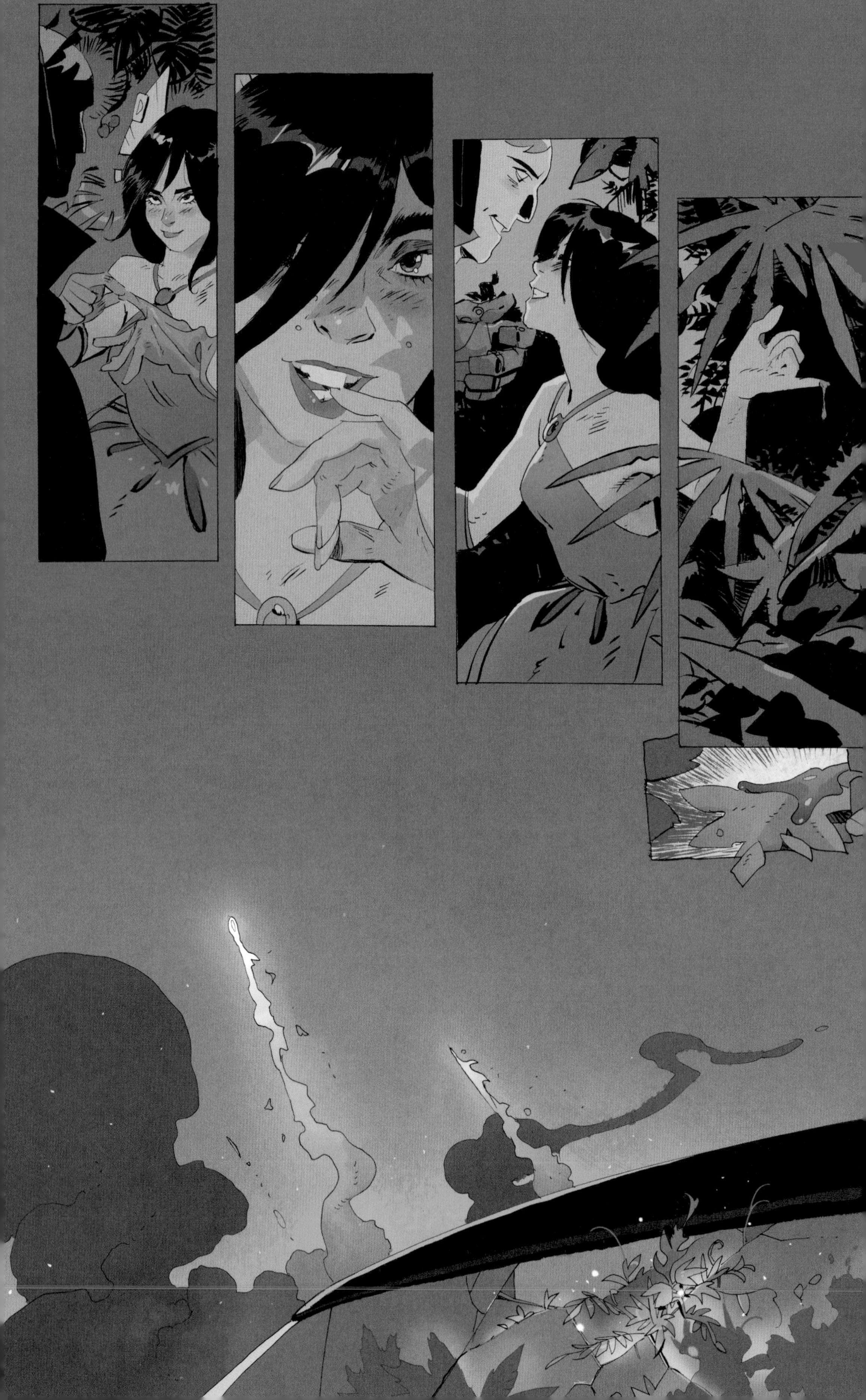

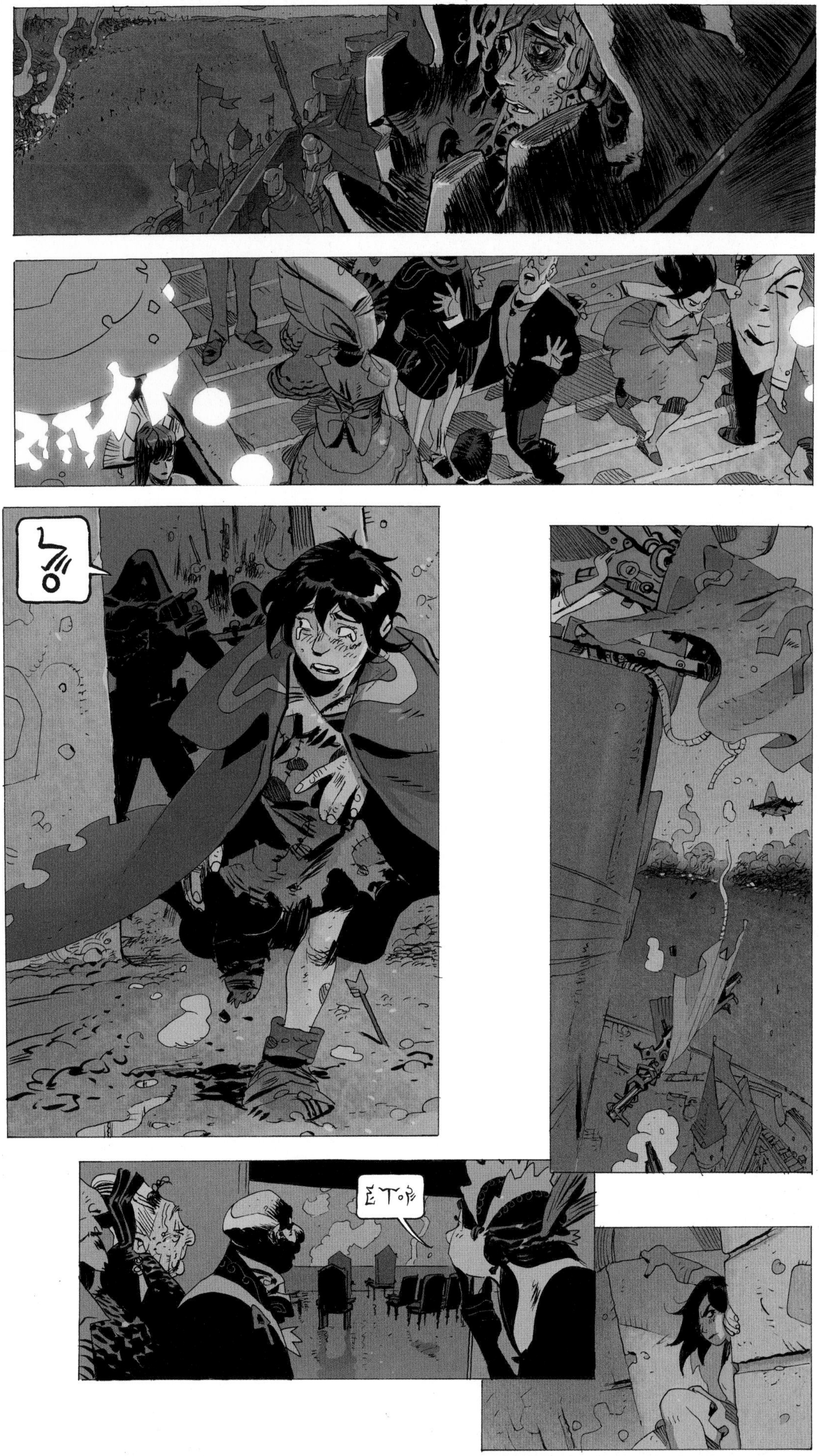

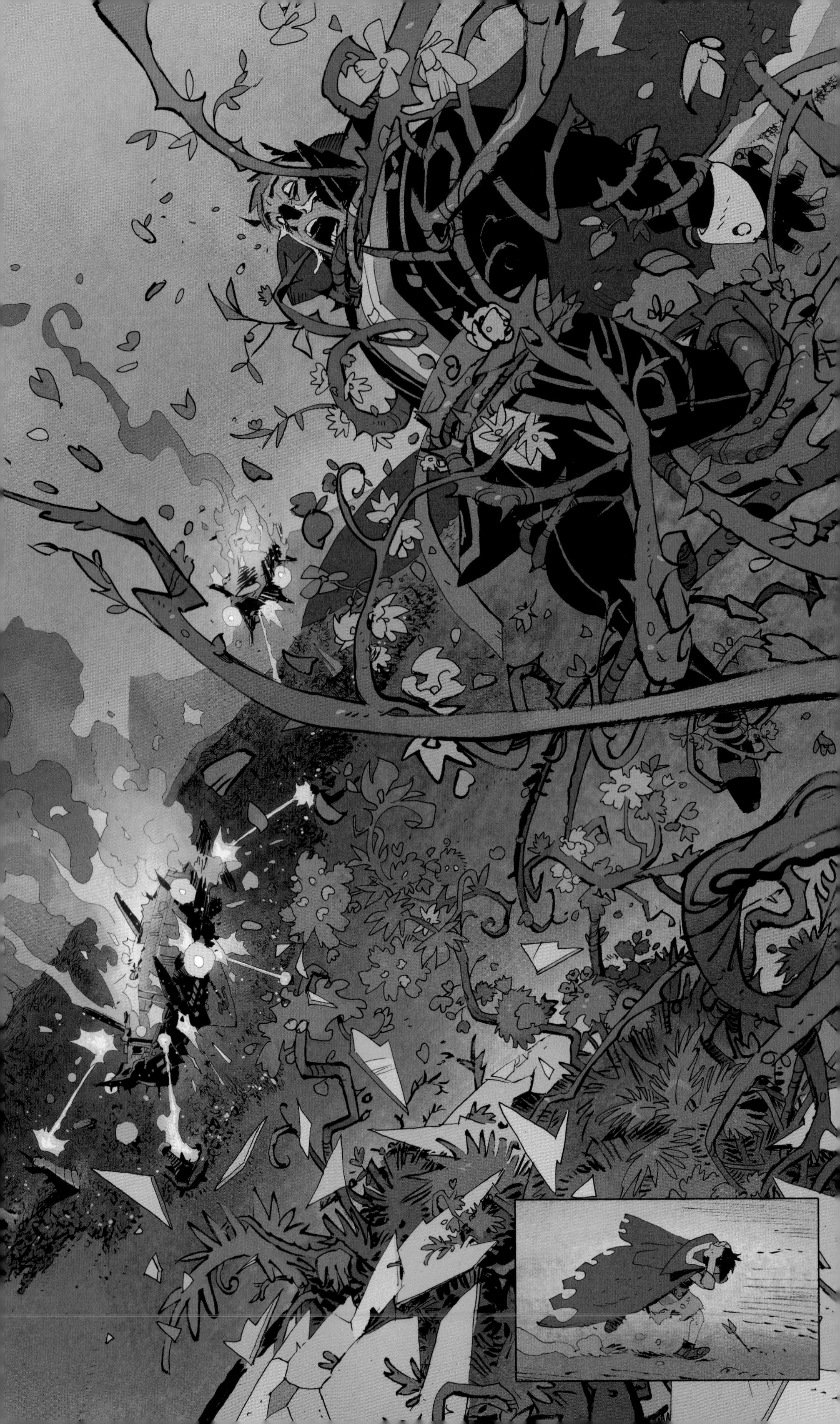

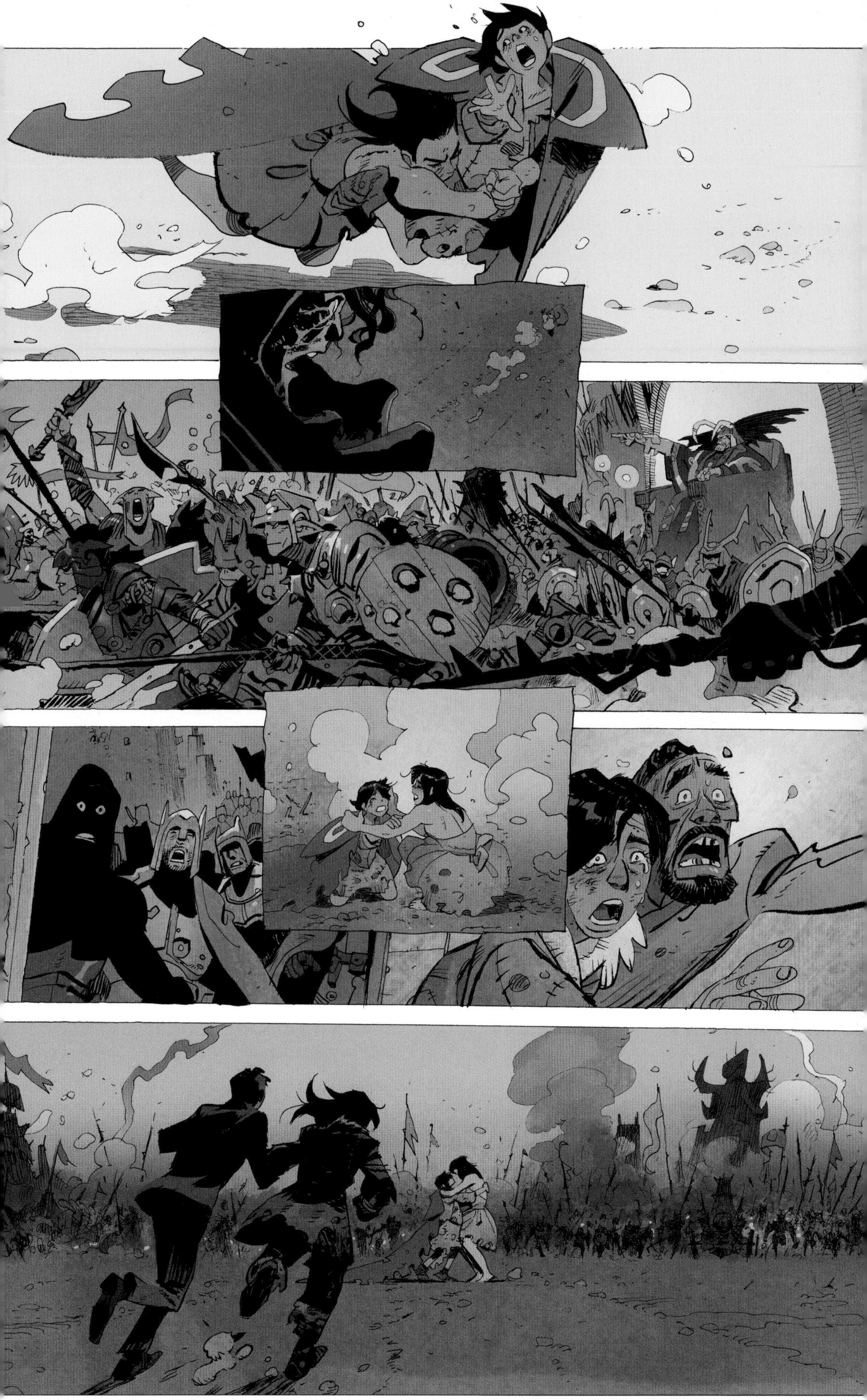

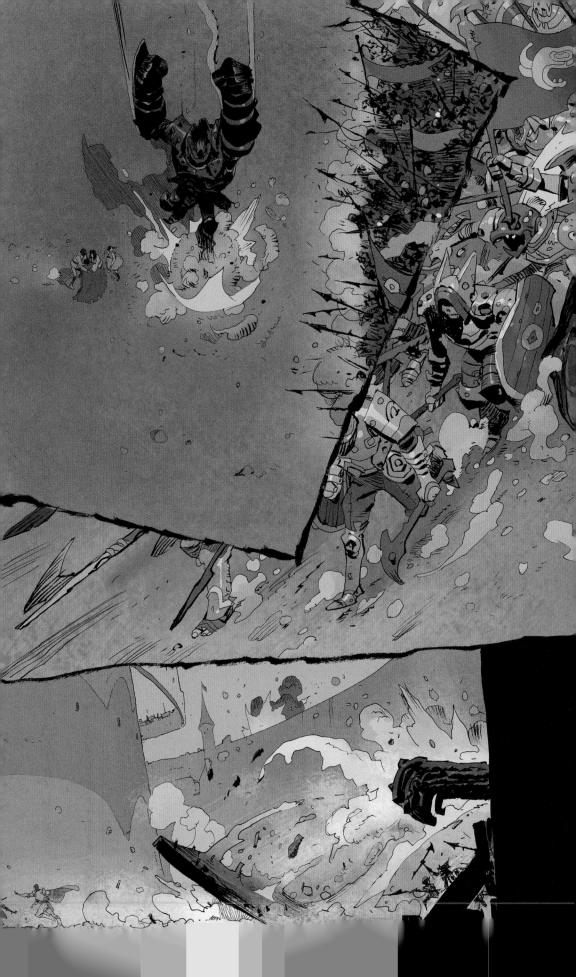

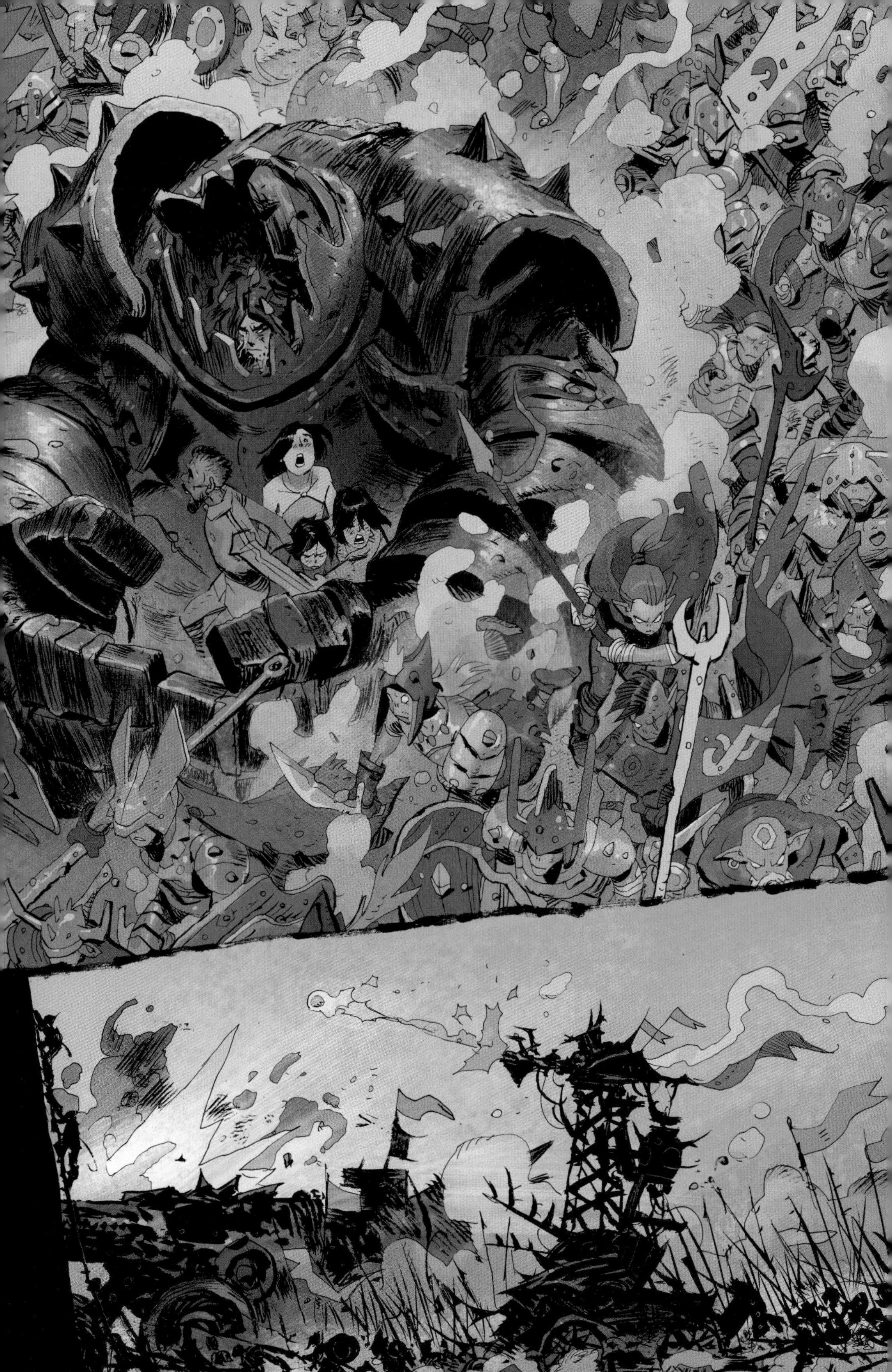

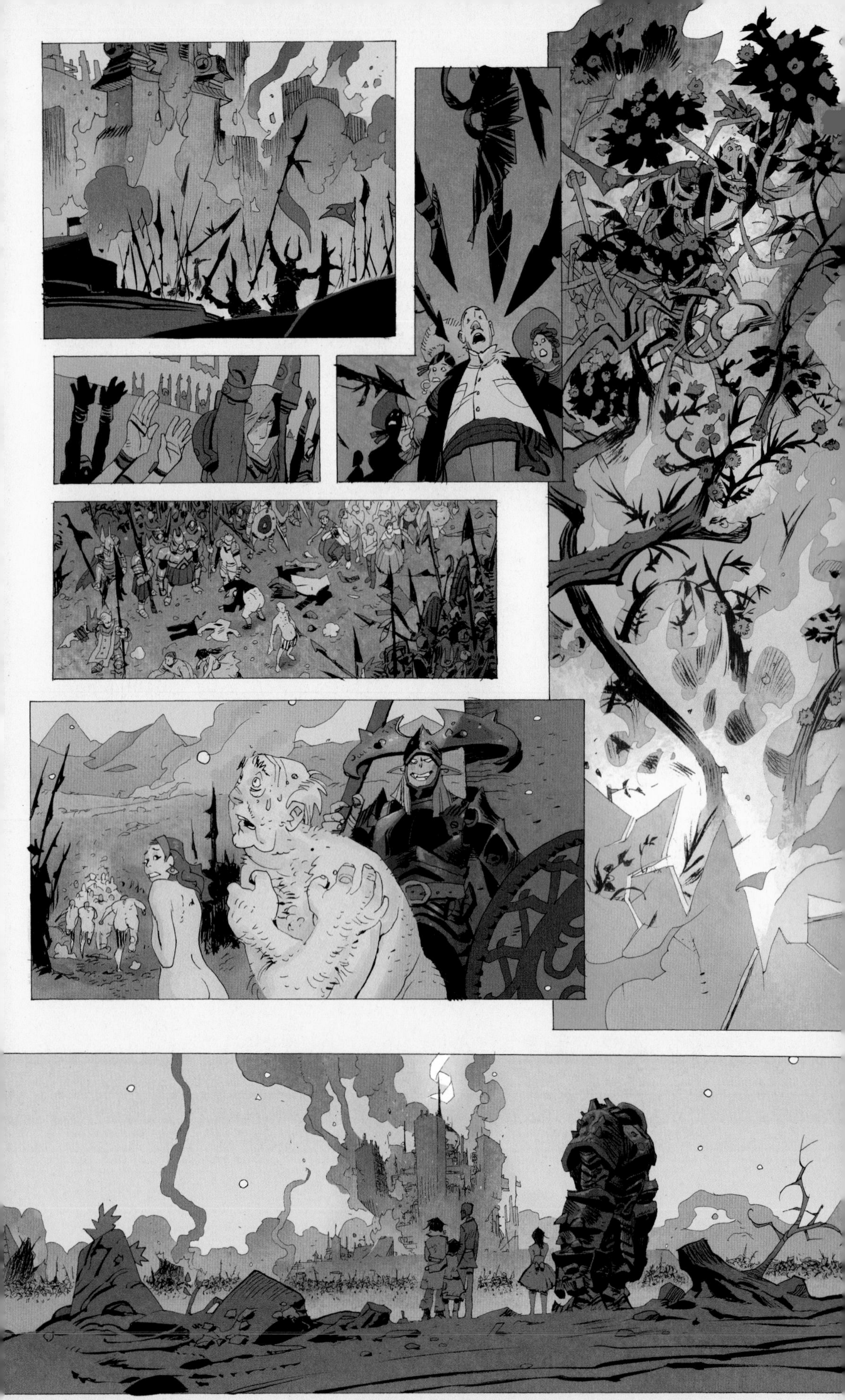

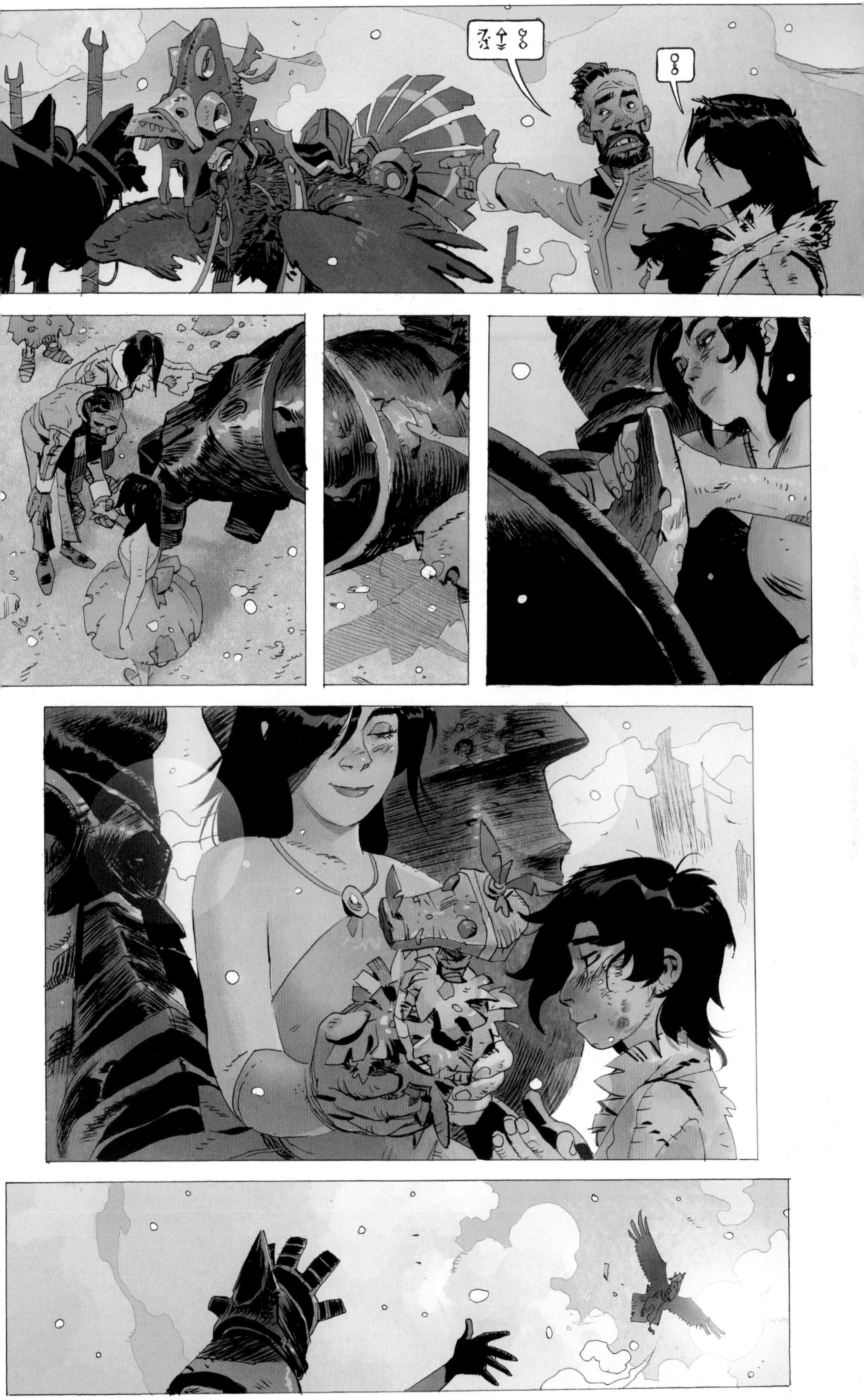

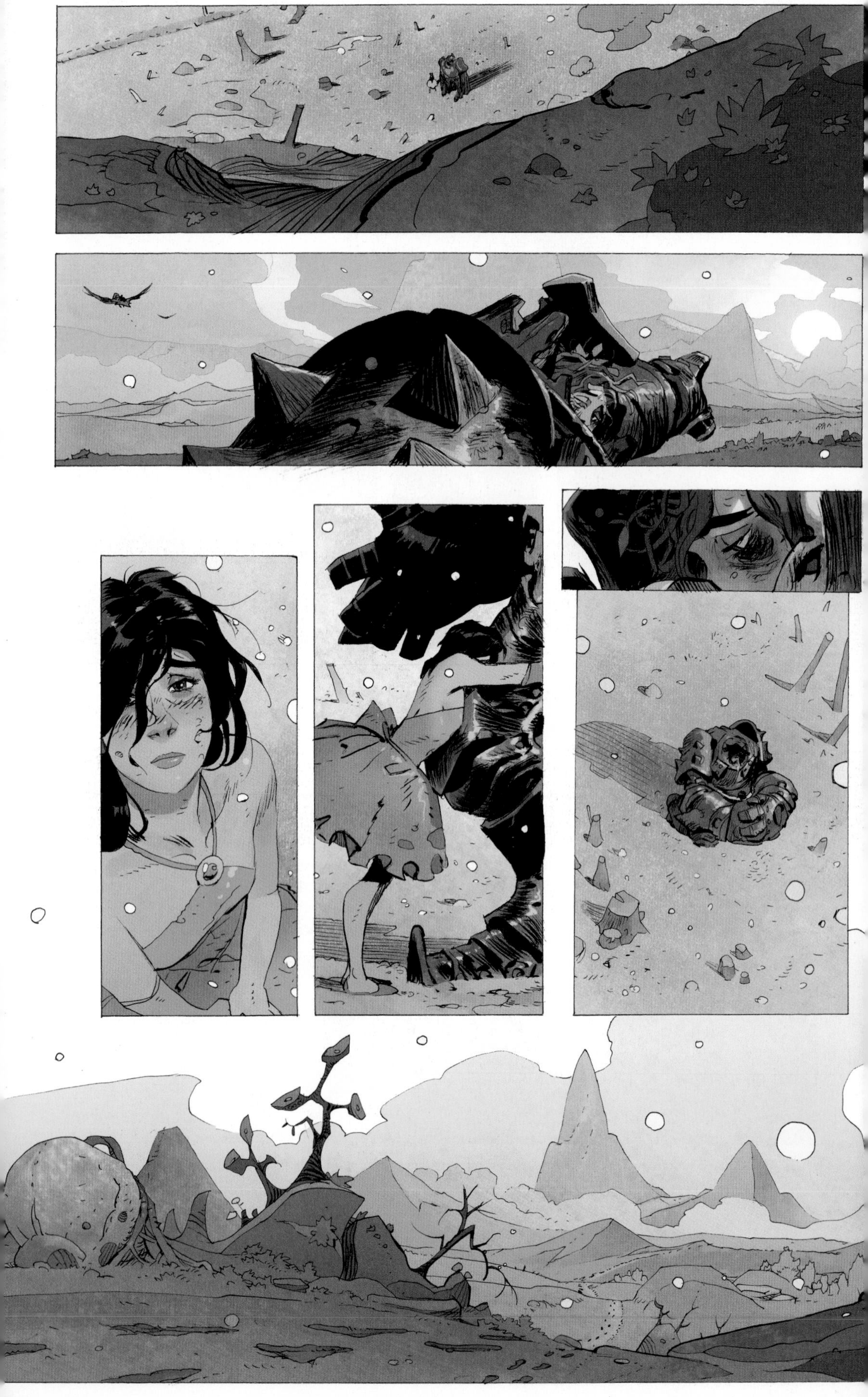

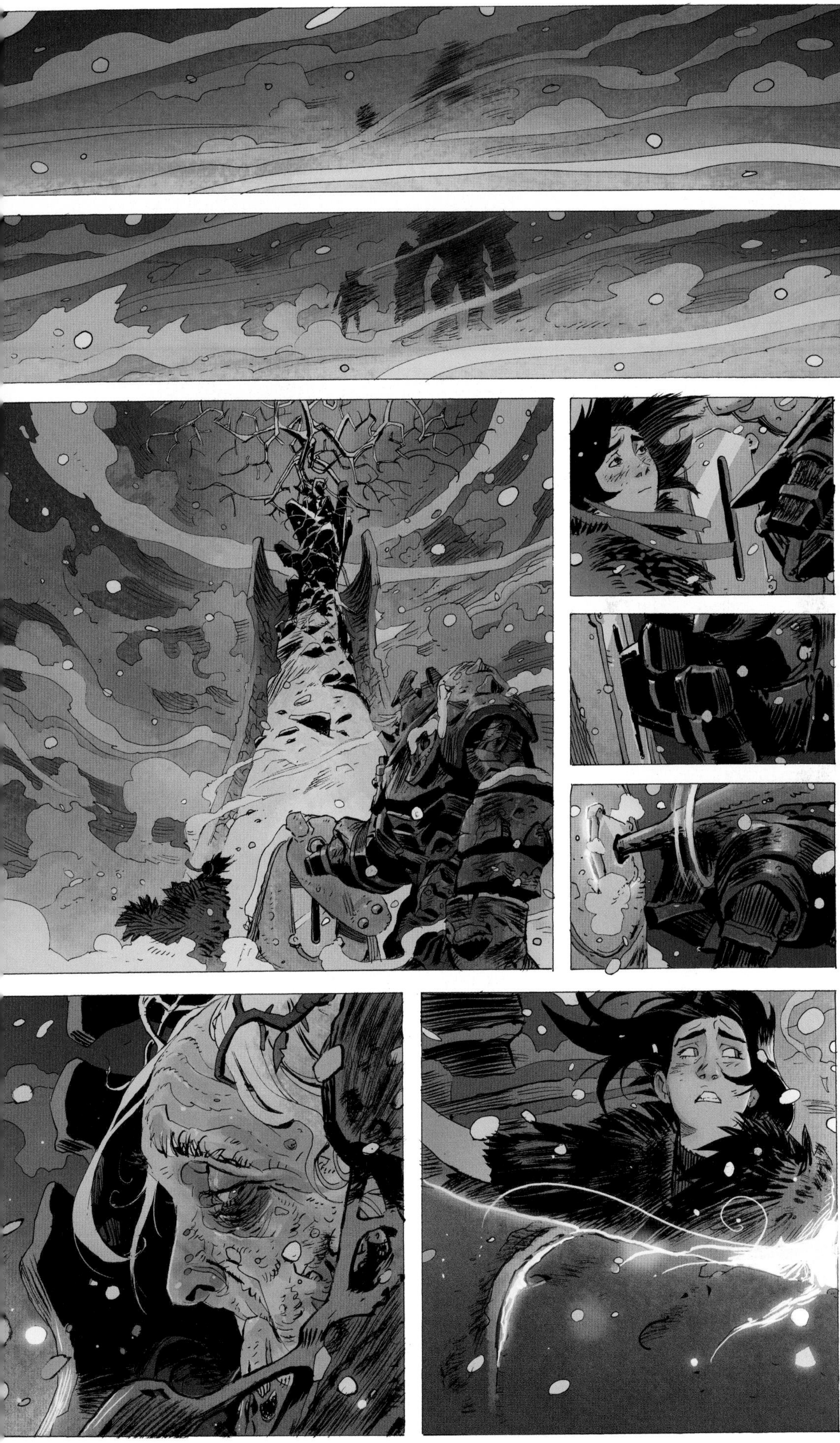

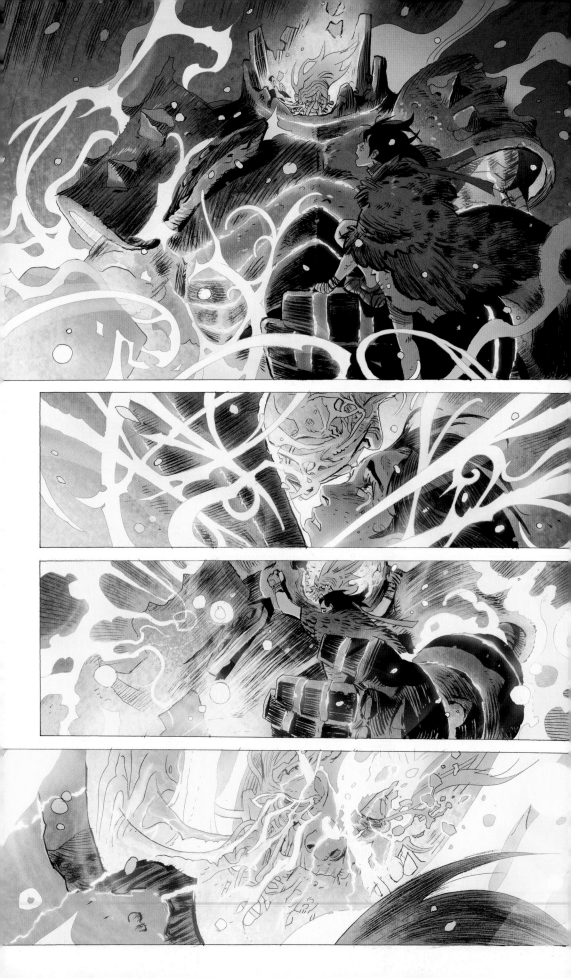

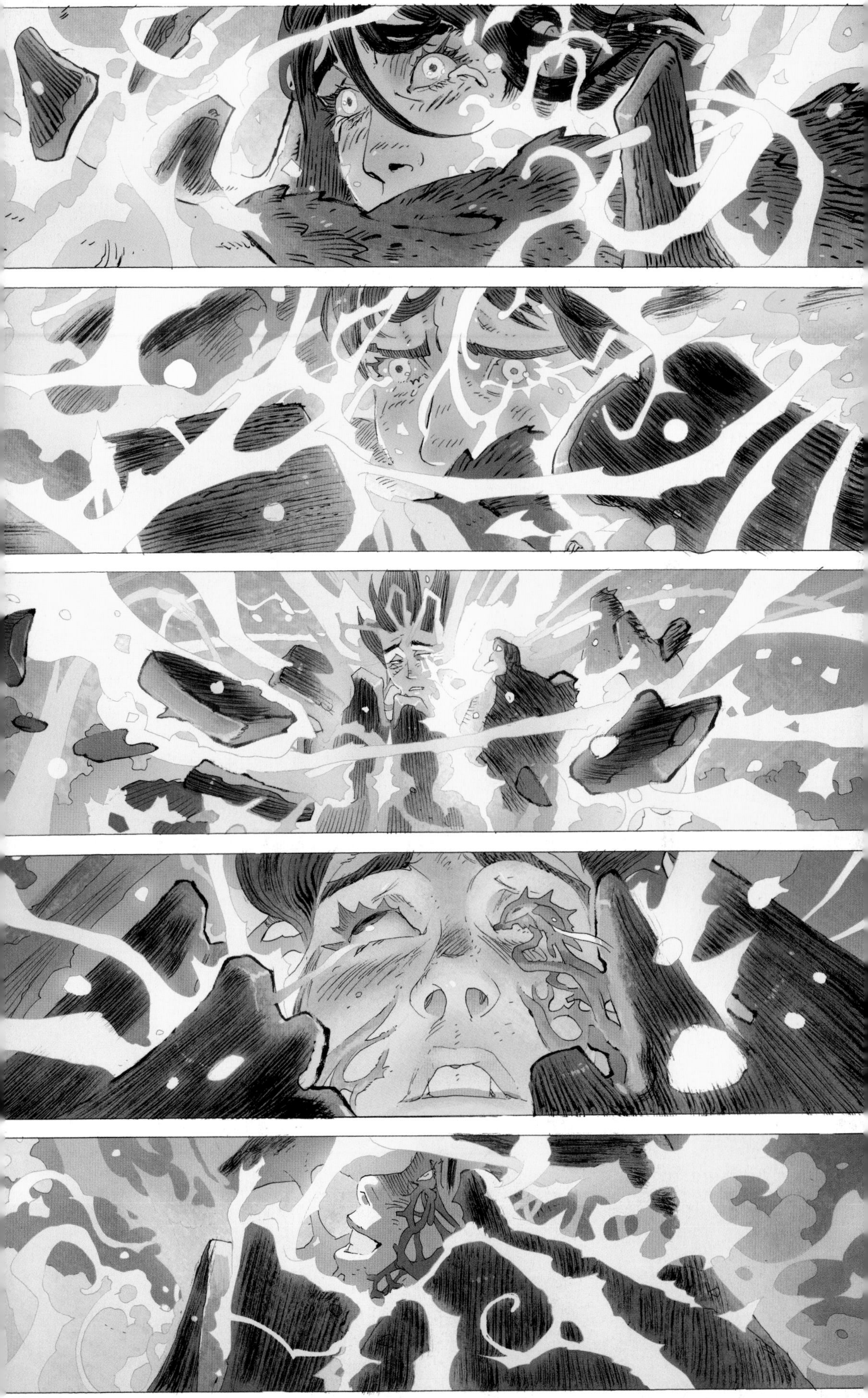

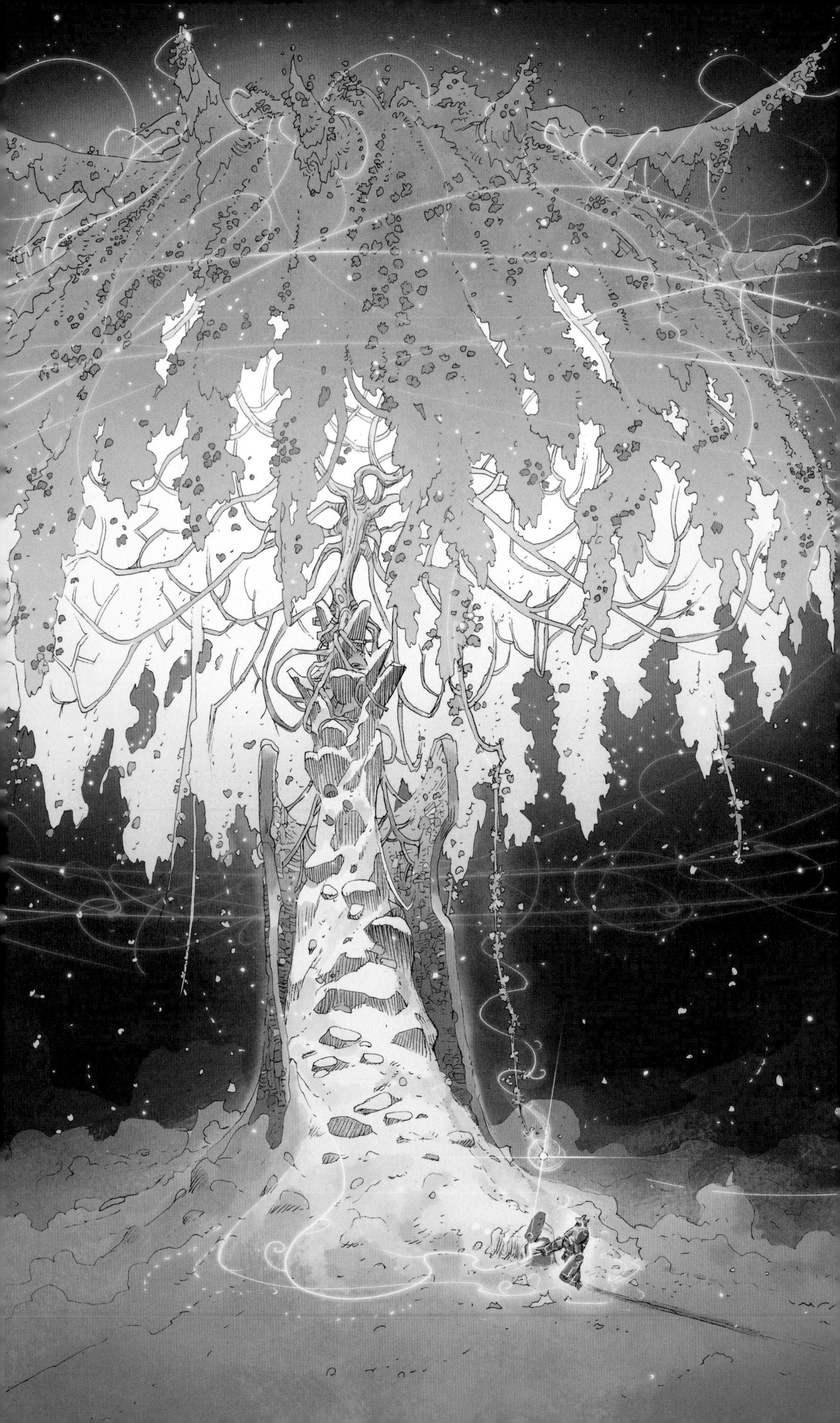

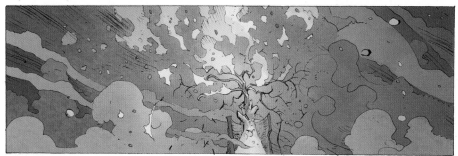

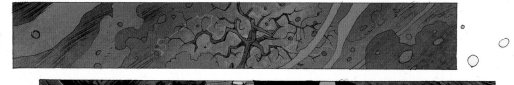

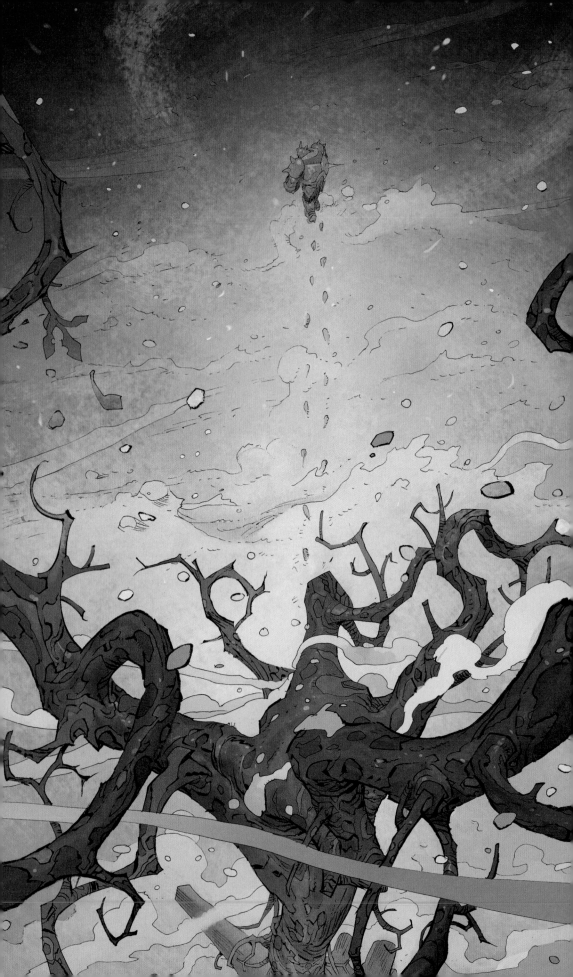

Faint.
Faint promises of Spring.
But promises still.

A girl wakes.

# Cover Gallery

## FEATURING

## Matías Bergara

### AND SPECIAL GUEST ARTISTS

**#1**
Ian Bertram
James Harren
Jock

**#2**
Peach Momoko

**#3**
Jamie McKelvie

**#4**
Tula Lotay

**ISSUE 1, COVER A**
Matías Bergara

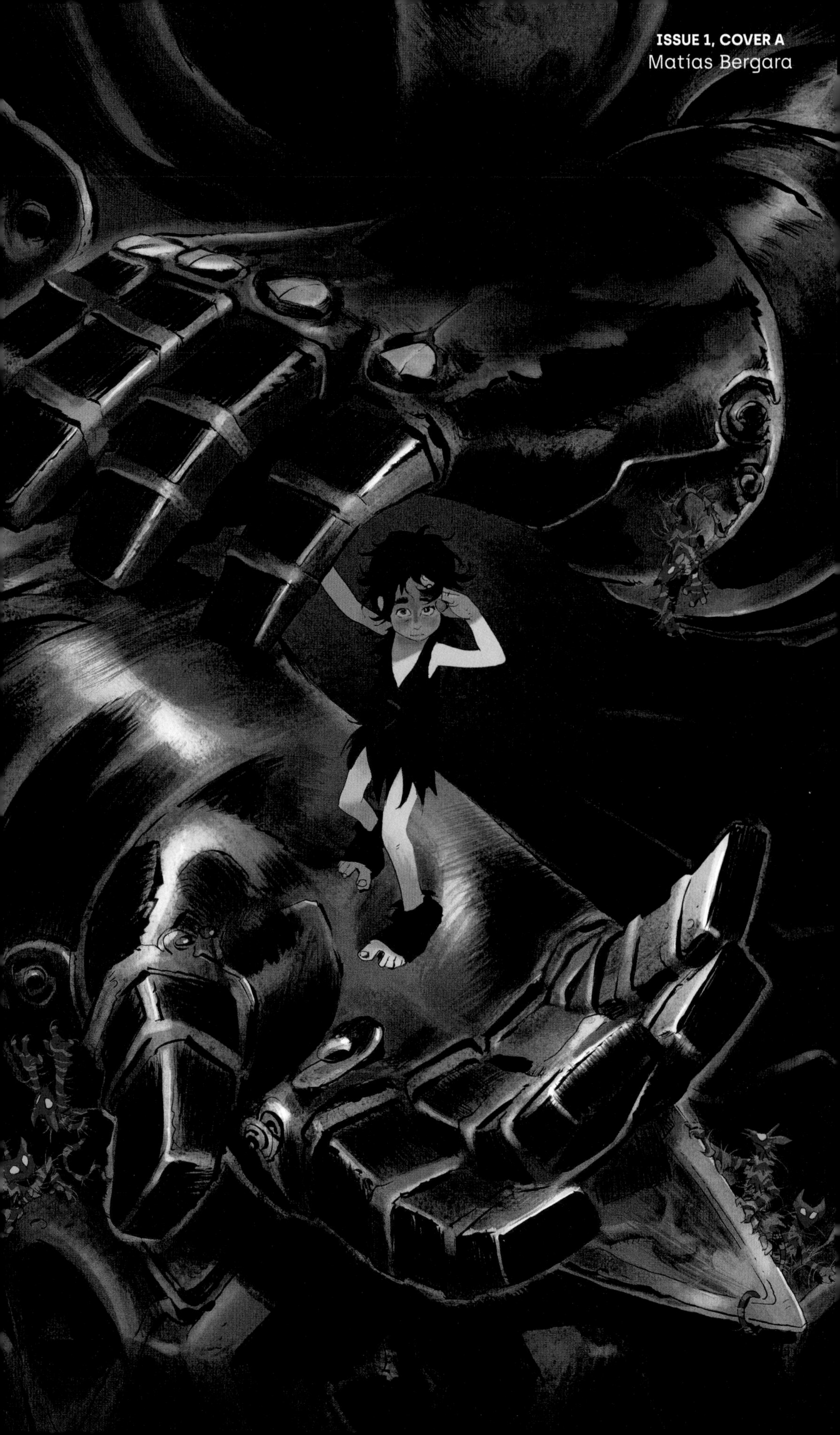

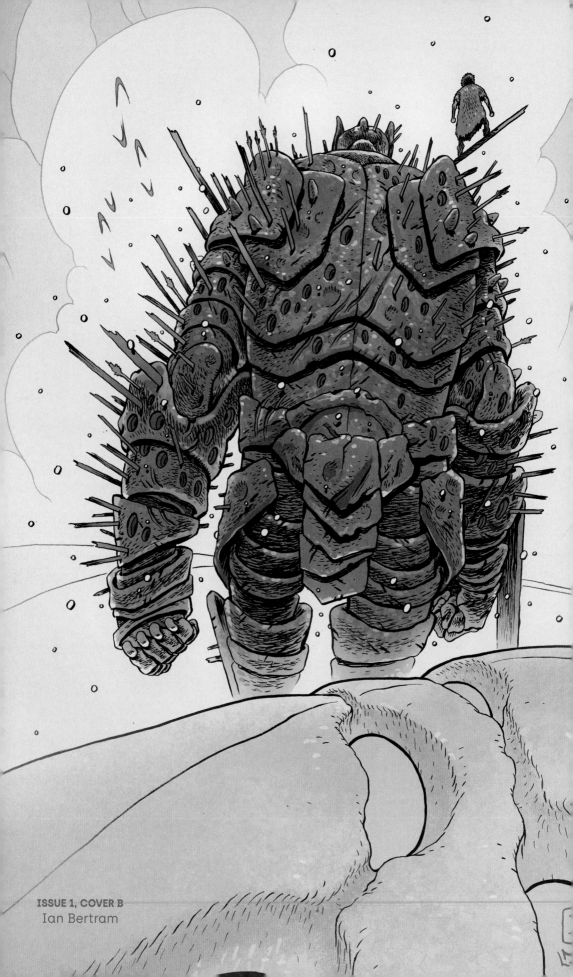

ISSUE 1, COVER B
Ian Bertram

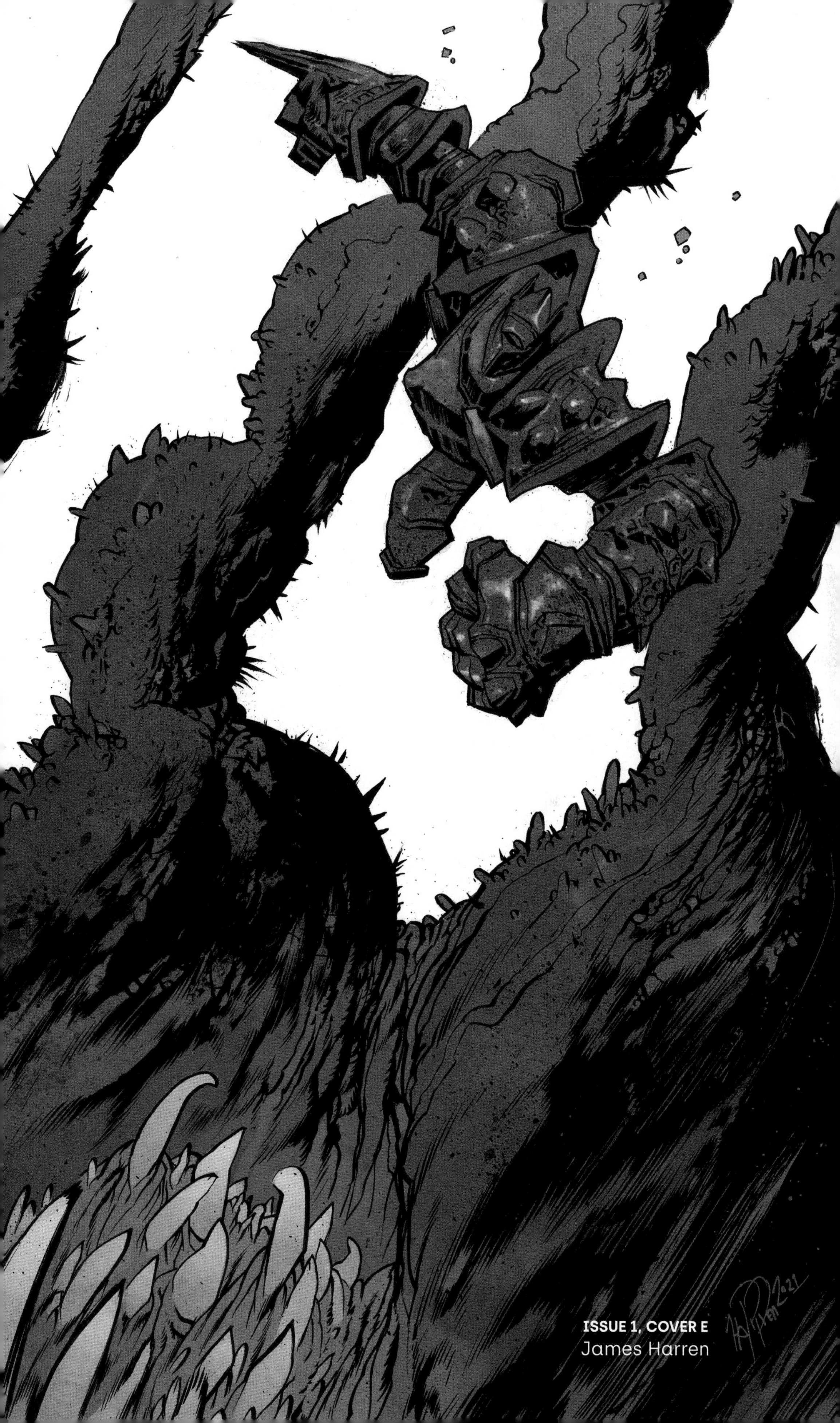

**ISSUE 1, COVER E**
James Harren

**ISSUE 1, COVER D**
Matías Bergara

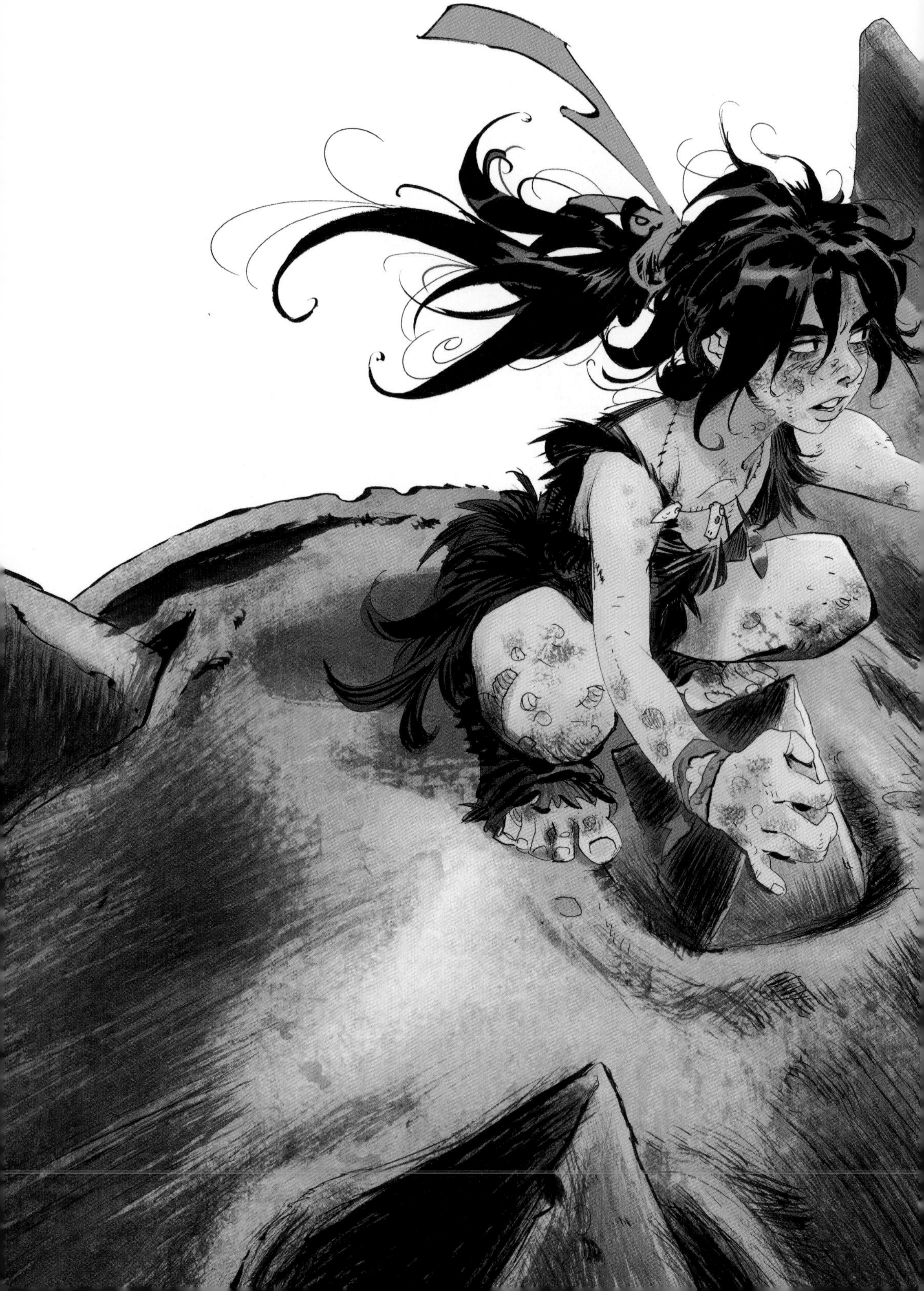

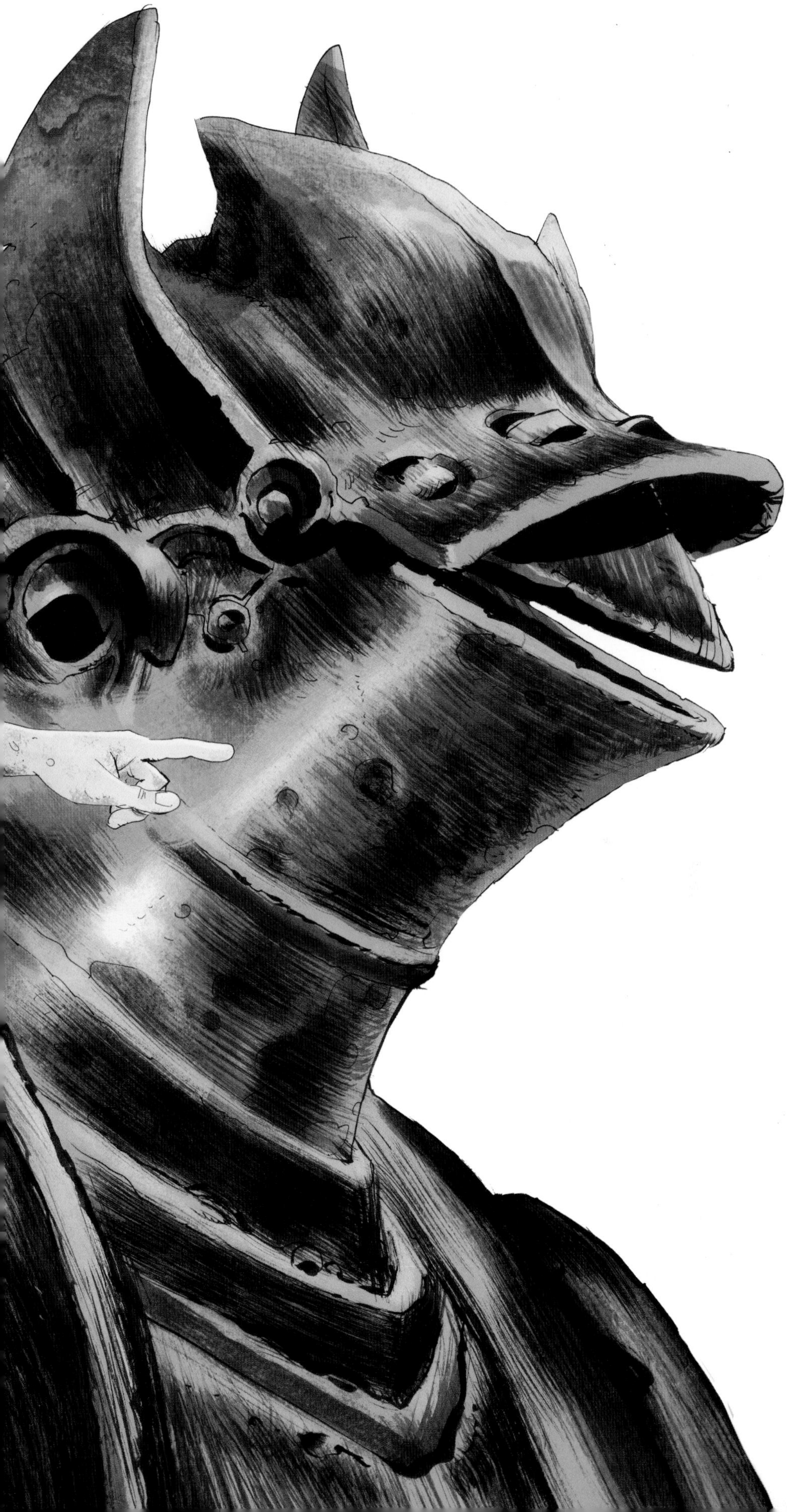

**ISSUE 1, COVER F**
Jock

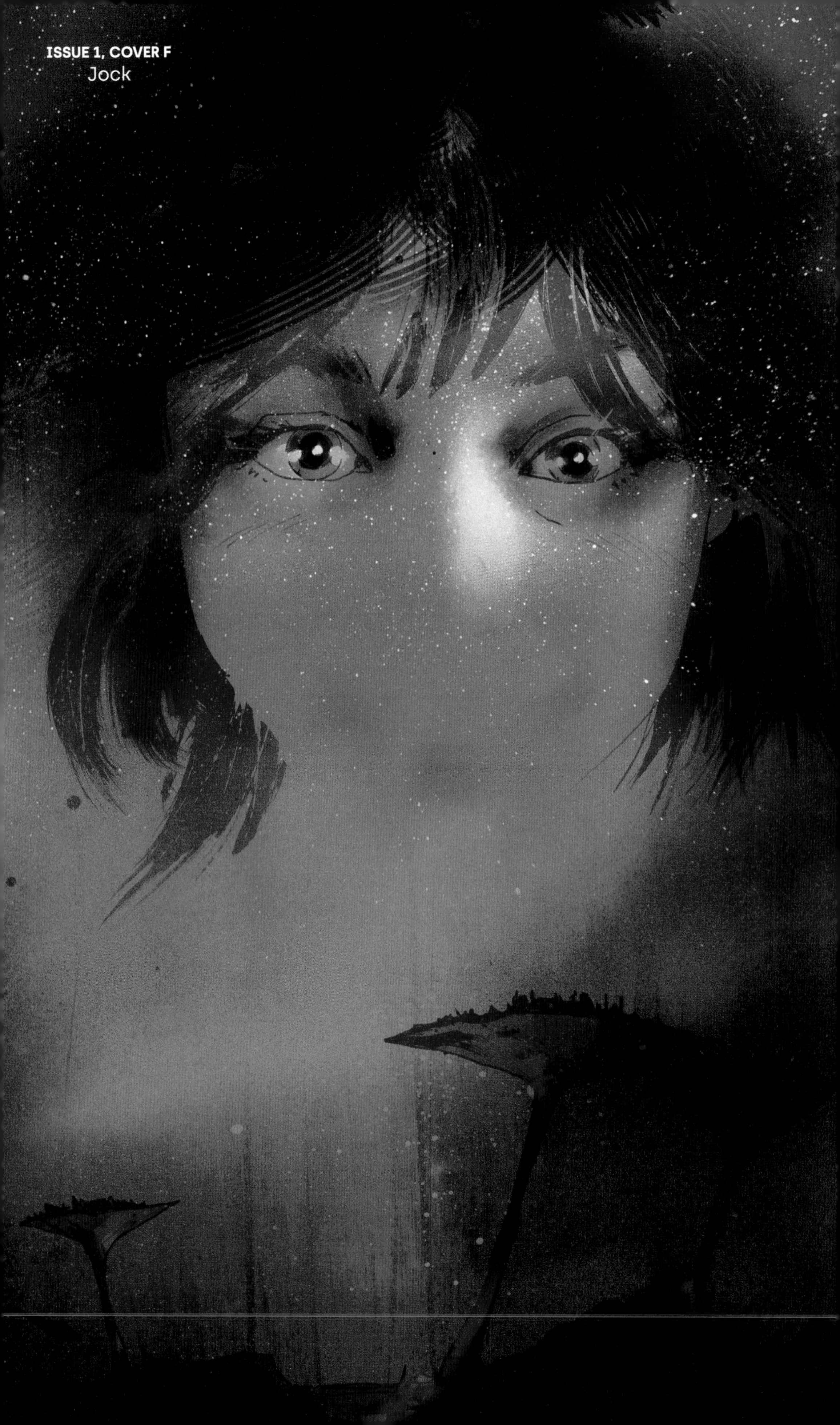

**ISSUE 2, COVER A**
Matías Bergara

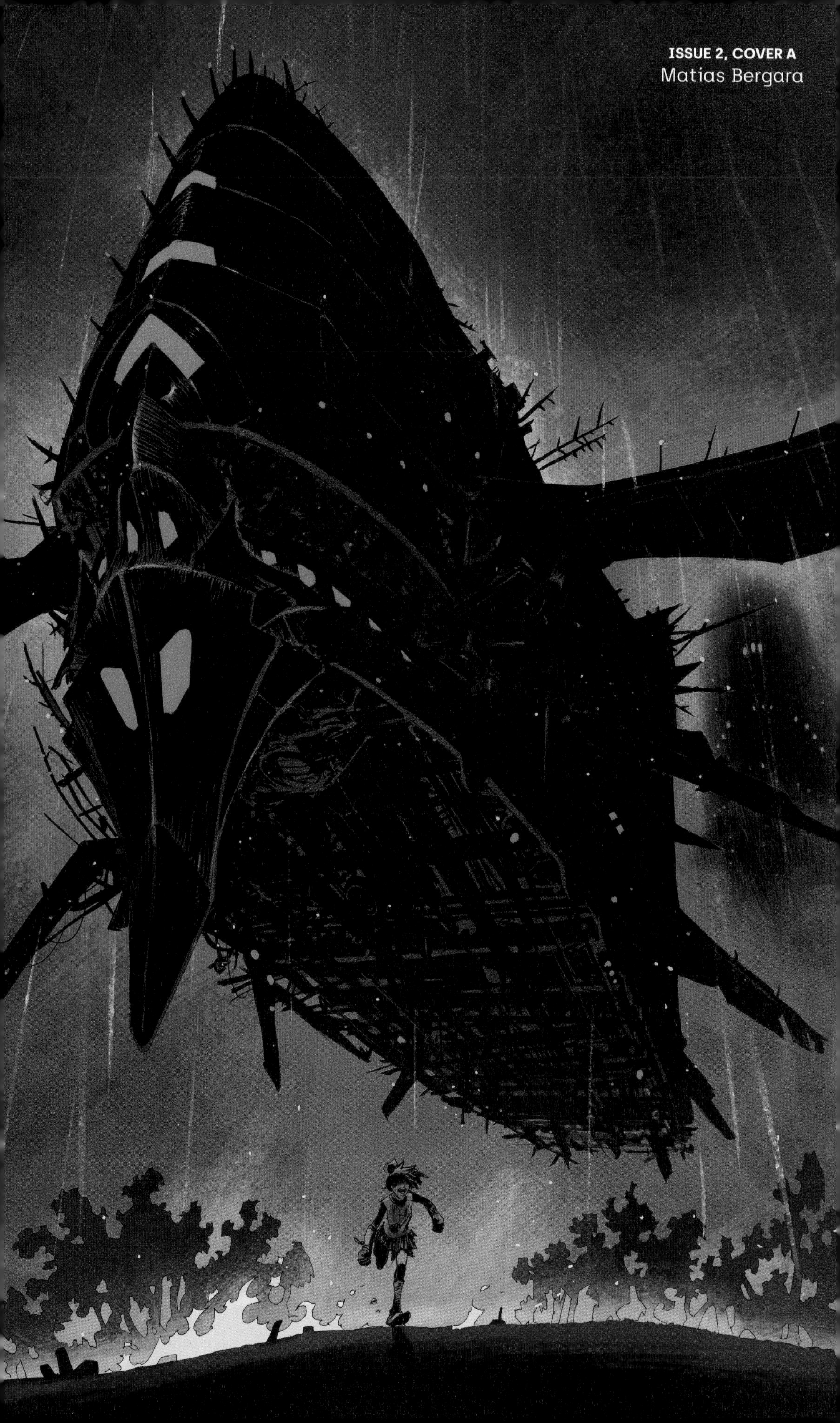

**ISSUE 2, COVER B**
Peach Momoko

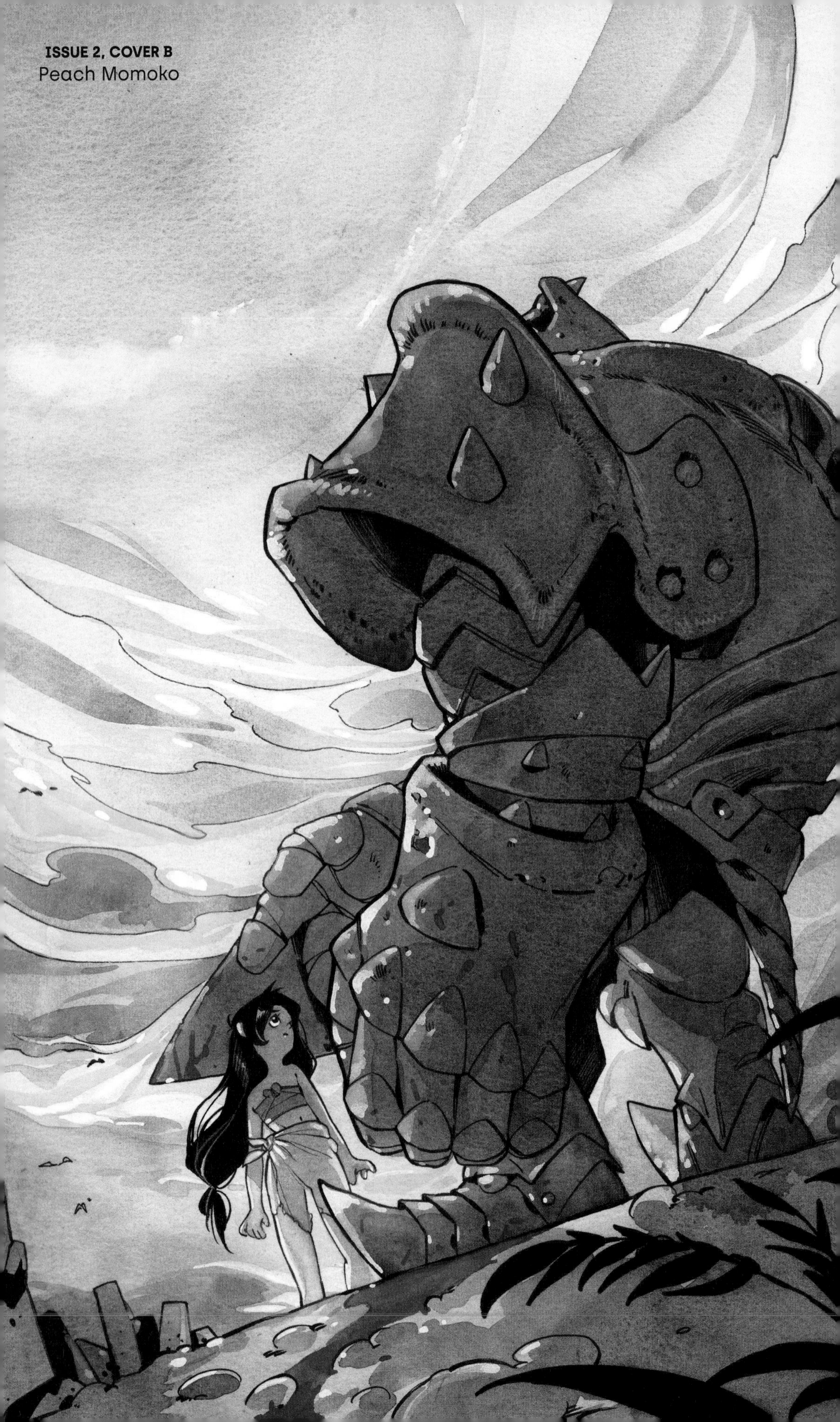

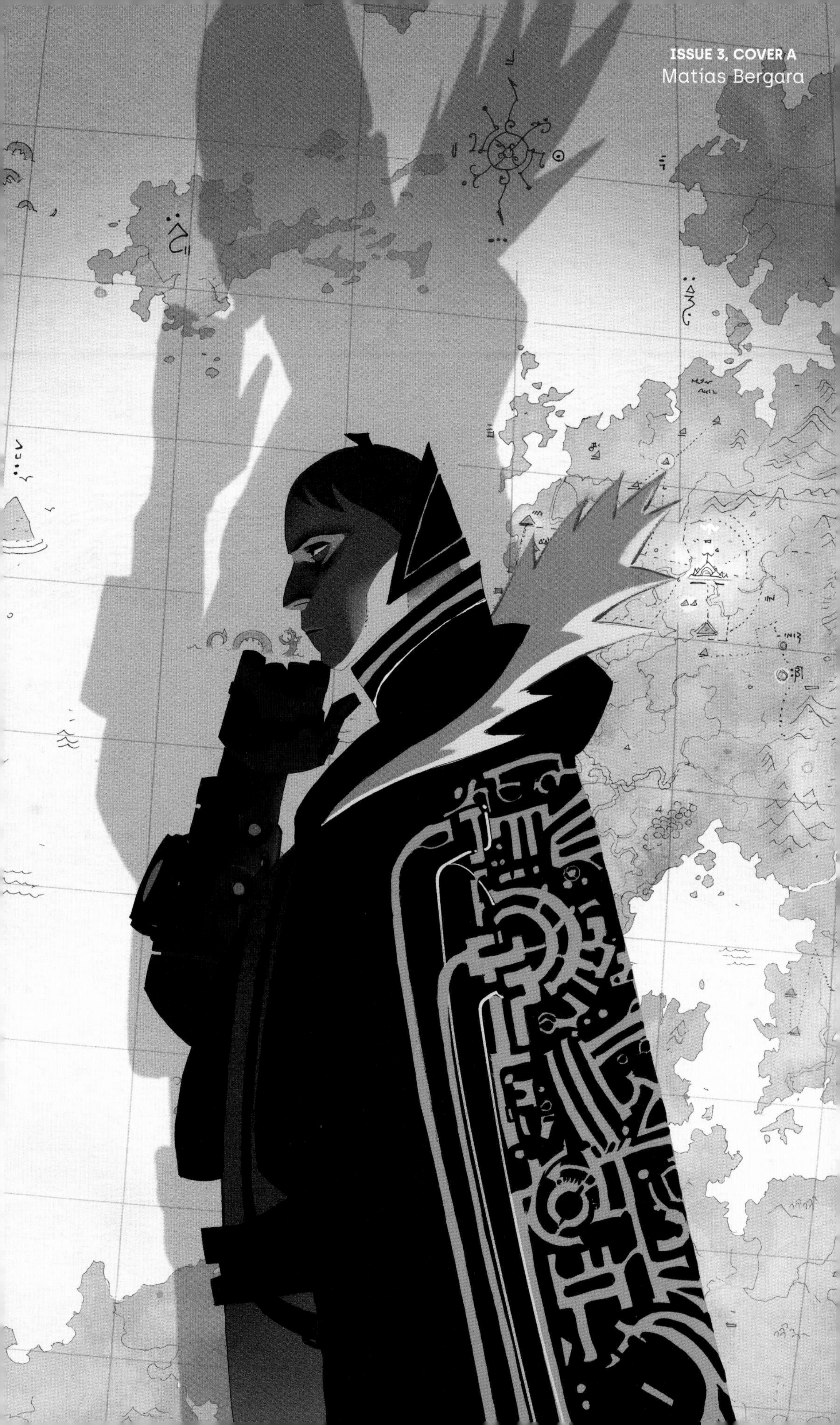

**ISSUE 3, COVER A**
Matías Bergara

**ISSUE 3, COVER B**
Jamie McKelvie

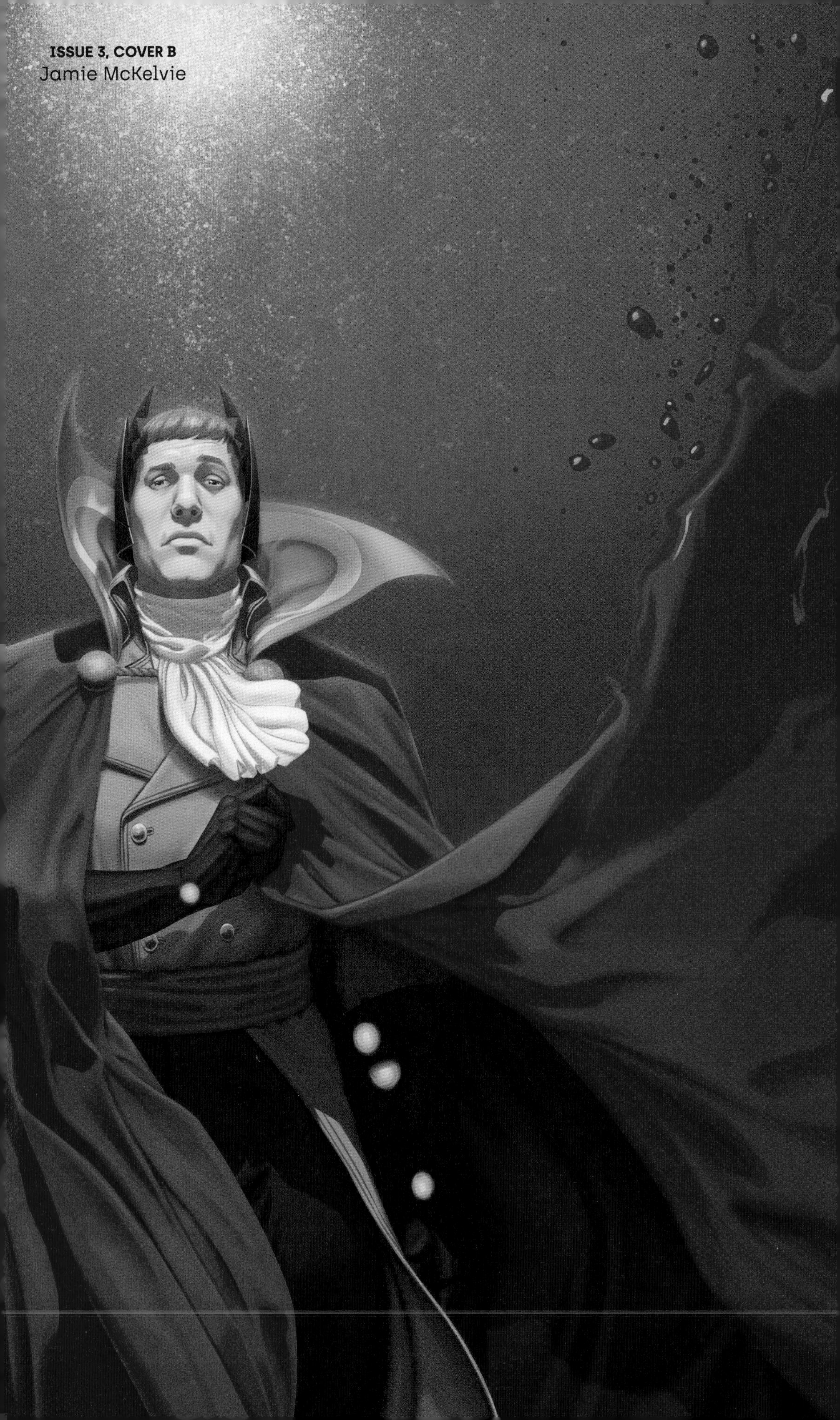

**ISSUE 4, COVER A**
Matías Bergara

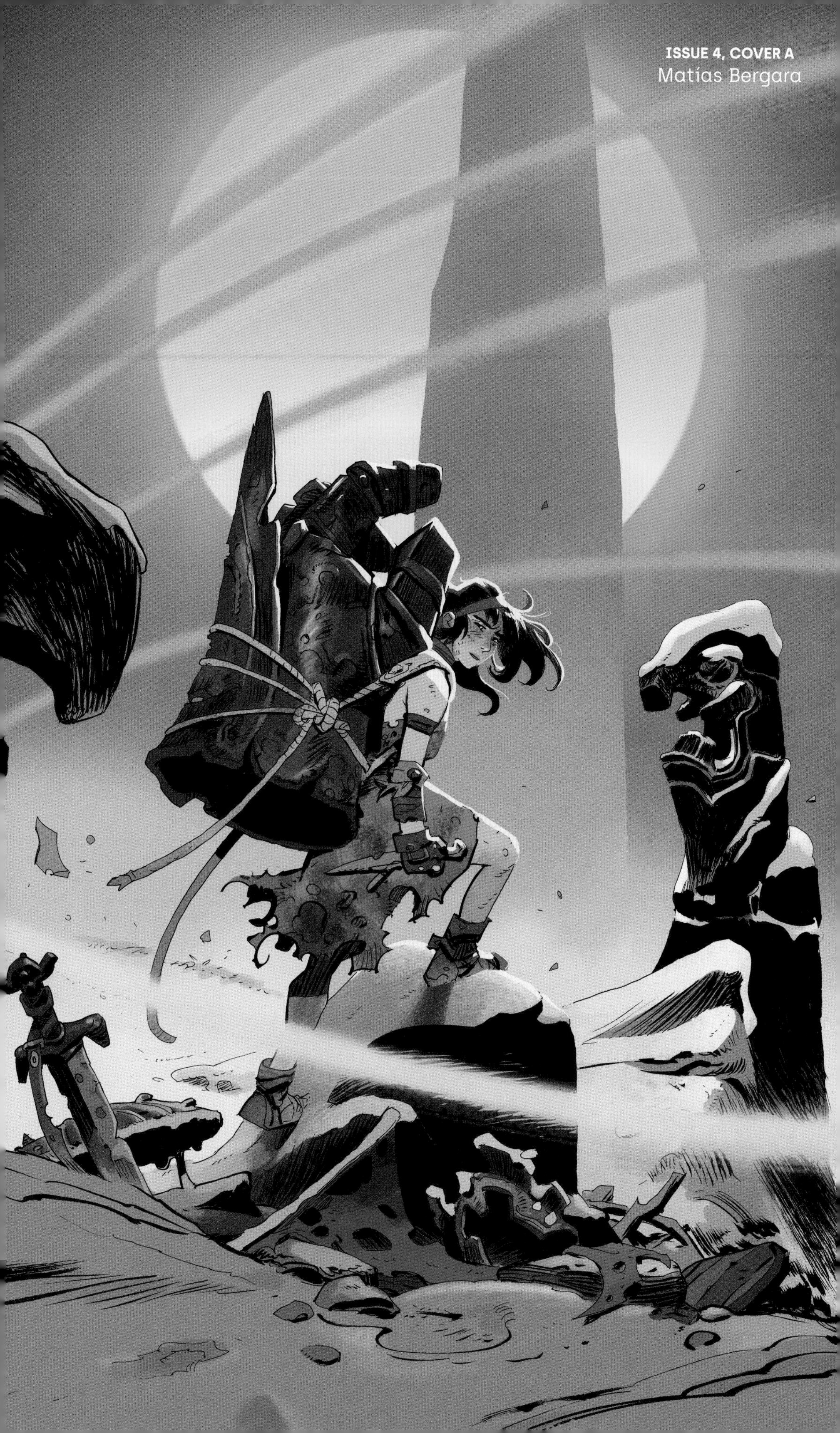

**ISSUE 4, COVER B**
Tula Lotay

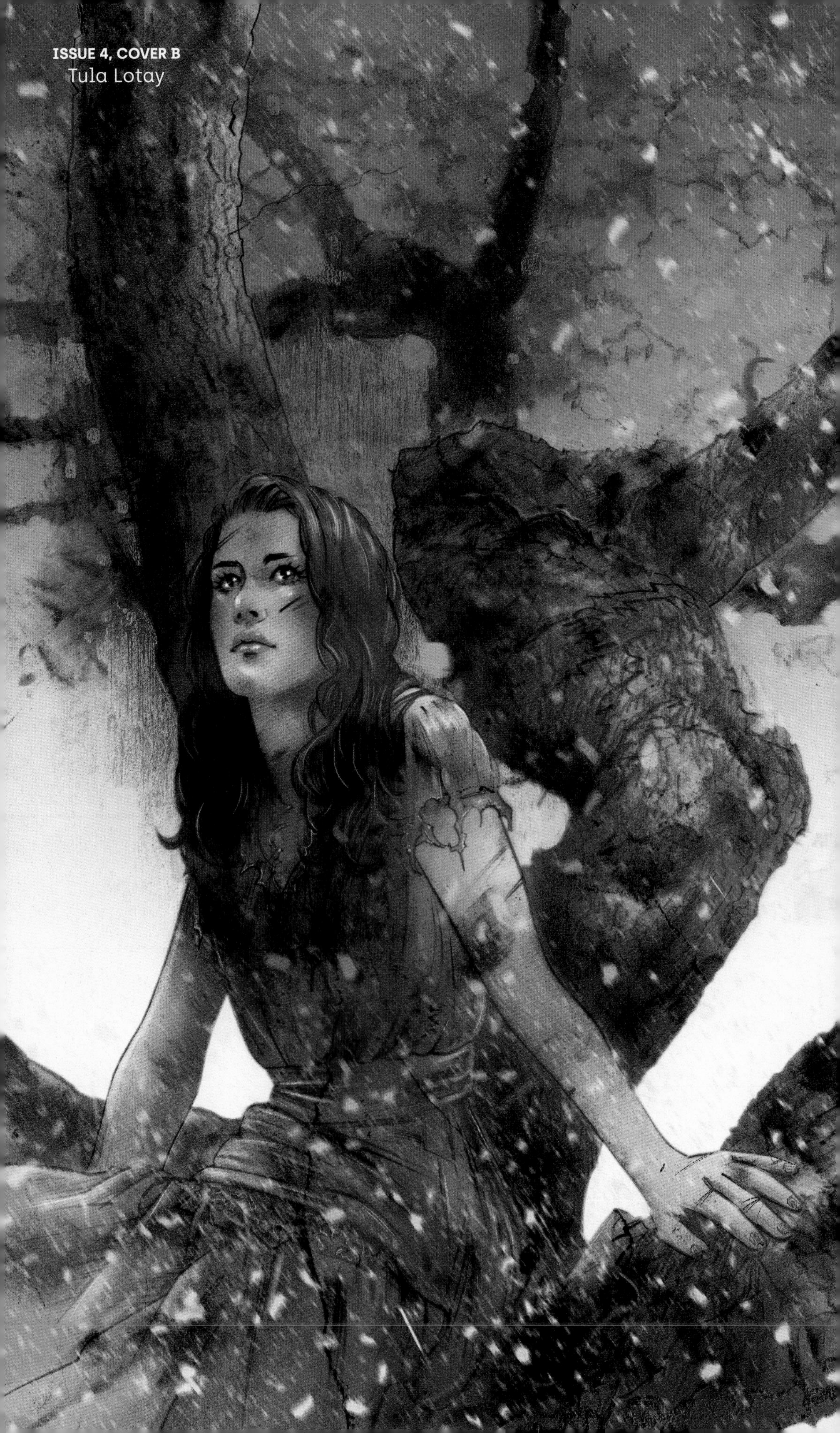

# Script To Art

**FEATURING**

Si Spurrier & Matías Bergara

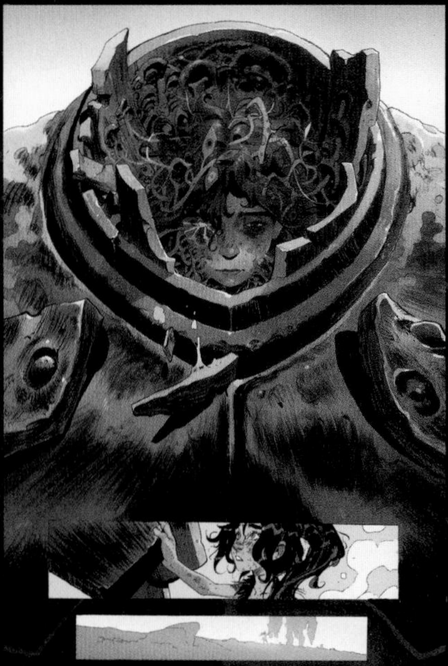

## ISSUE 1, PAGE 28

**28.1:** Large - most of the page. 2/3rds at least. Beauty shot of the WARRIOR, still looking towards us and the GIRL -- but now with no helmet. There's a HUMAN HEAD underneath it. A woman. She looks remarkably similar to the GIRL – albeit in her mid-to-late twenties. We should be immediately thinking: IS THIS HER MOM? AN OLDER SISTER? WHO *IS* SHE...? The family resemblance is clear.

She has tears on her cheeks too -- sharing the girl's sadness. And yet, also: resolve. She's accepted her fate and won't rage against it. She's pointing ahead. *We have to keep going.*

**28.2:** Small. On the girl's face. Amazed, moved, confused, about what she's seeing. She had no idea there was a person under there, let alone one who looked like her.

**28.3:** Wide. The farmer's family watches as the girl sprints off in the warrior's wake. The warrior already marching onwards through the melting snow. Towards warmer lands.

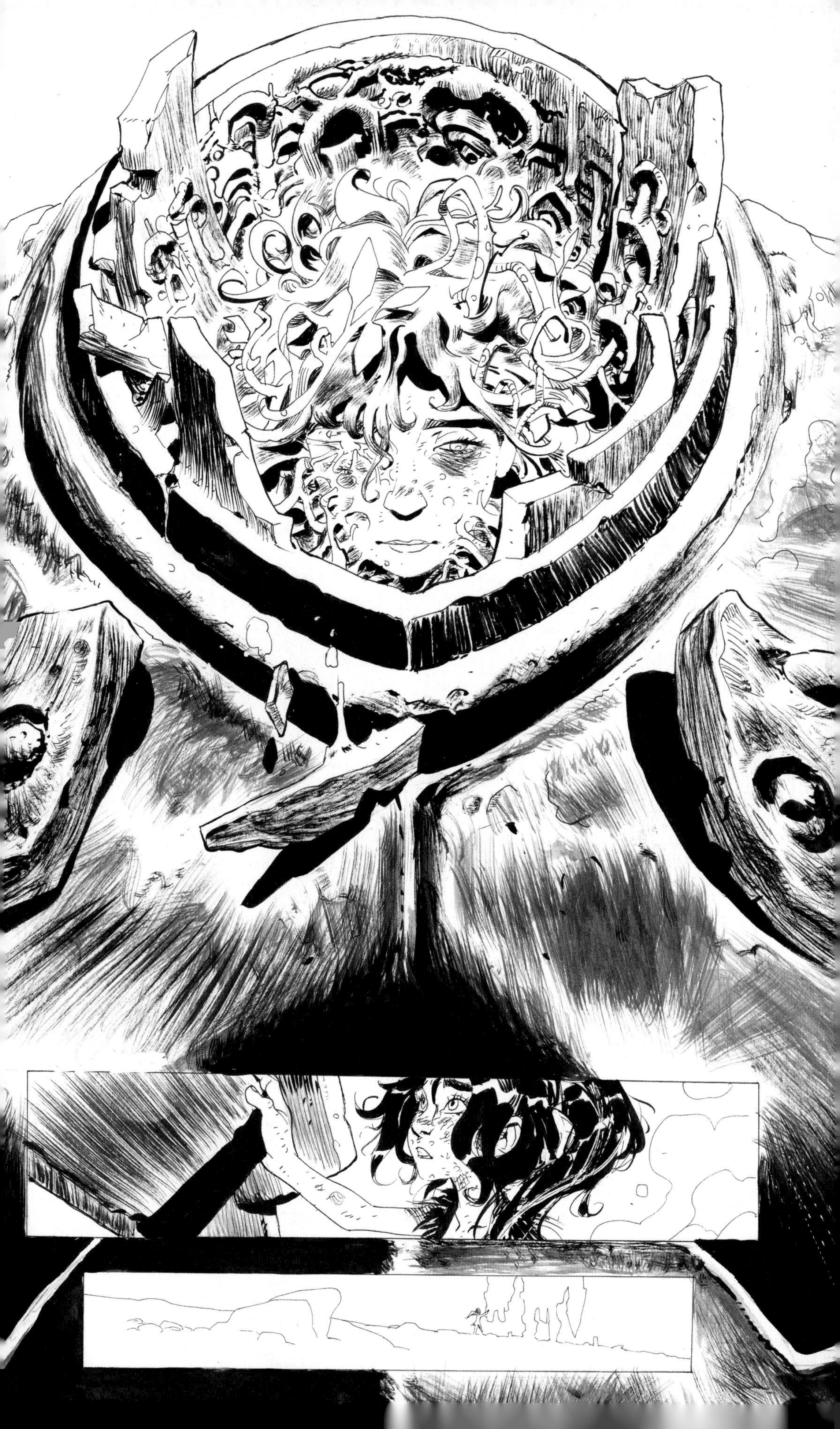

## ISSUE 2, PAGE 3

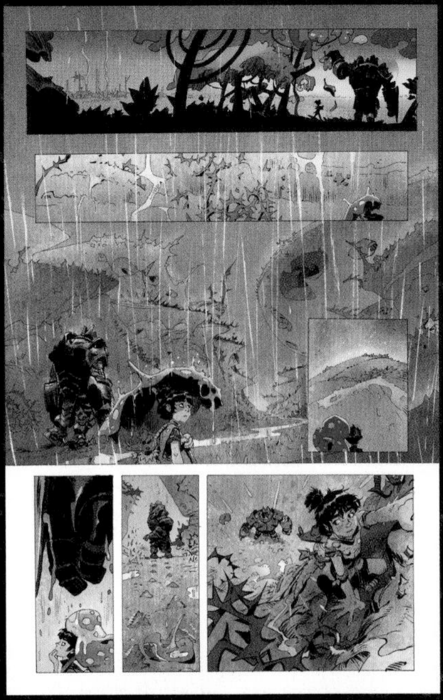

**3.1:** Hours later. It's near dusk, but it's raining so heavily it might as well already be night. The girl and the warrior keep trudging along through the downpour. The warrior not paying the weather any attention; the girl with a big leaf over her head as a makeshift umbrella. A dour scene. They're picking their way along the bottom of a small gorge, with thorn-shrubs here and there. (NB: not vertical cliff-faces on either side, but relatively steep and rocky slopes.)

**3.2:** But now the girl looks sideways and upwards slightly. Looking towards the top of the gorge, there's a GLOW coming from one side. As if there's a FIRE burning up there, on the lip of the cliff, where our heroes can't see it. The cloudy sky underlit by whatever is causing the glow.

**3.3:** Bit wider. The girl, pausing. Thoughtful. Tempted. It's clear she wants to go have a look. The warrior doesn't slow down.

**3.4:** A few steps later, the warrior twists to check on the girl. But: *damn*! She's not there. Not in shot at all.

**3.5:** The girl's scampering up the rocks to see the glow for herself. MB, up to you whether you angle this with the girl in the f/g and the warrior down below, or vice versa, with the warrior in the f/g looking upwards away from us. Note that there are quite a lot of those THORN SHRUBS jutting out of the rock around where the girl's climbing - that'll be important later.

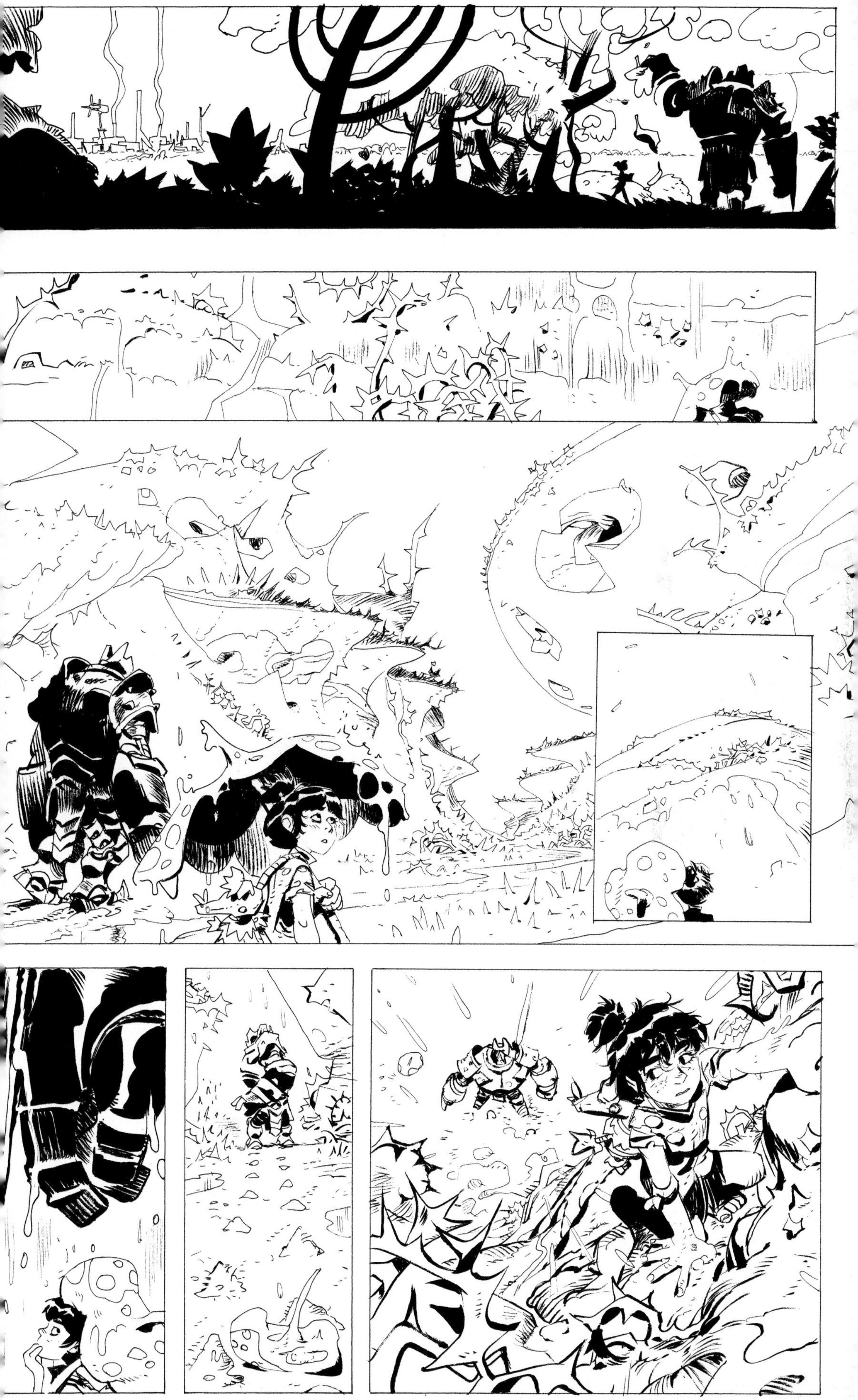

Top 1/3rd of the page is made up of three panels, each being 1/9th of the page. Panel 4 occupies the lower 2/3rds of the page.

**3.1:** Cutaway to THE WARRIOR. Still on the side of the bed in her lavish room. But now slightly tilting her head, frowning, eyes looking up and away, as if she's hearing - or feeling - some strange, distant thing. It's now NIGHT TIME outside her window.

**3.2:** A weird cutaway now. We're close on the STONE MONUMENT which sits underneath the HOLY TREE, which we last saw back in chapter 1. Specifically we're close on the metal ESCUTCHEON hanging from it. The stone around it is CRACKING. A single splintering faultline, as if a really localised quake has broken the stone lengthwise.

**3.3:** Back to the girl. Trying to steady herself, to catch her breath. And yet her attention is being caught by something else. In the close f/g a HAND -- the EMPEROR'S in fact -- is reaching out towards her, palm upwards. A gestural INVITATION TO DANCE...

**3.4:** LARGE. As the EMPEROR leads the girl through the throng towards the dance floor. He's immaculate in a finely cut suit, maybe a cape? All eyes would be on him, if they weren't instead on the girl. Aristocrats arching eyebrows, variously impressed, lusty or jealous. The girl, blushing, totally lost, just letting this bizarre evening happen around her without resisting.

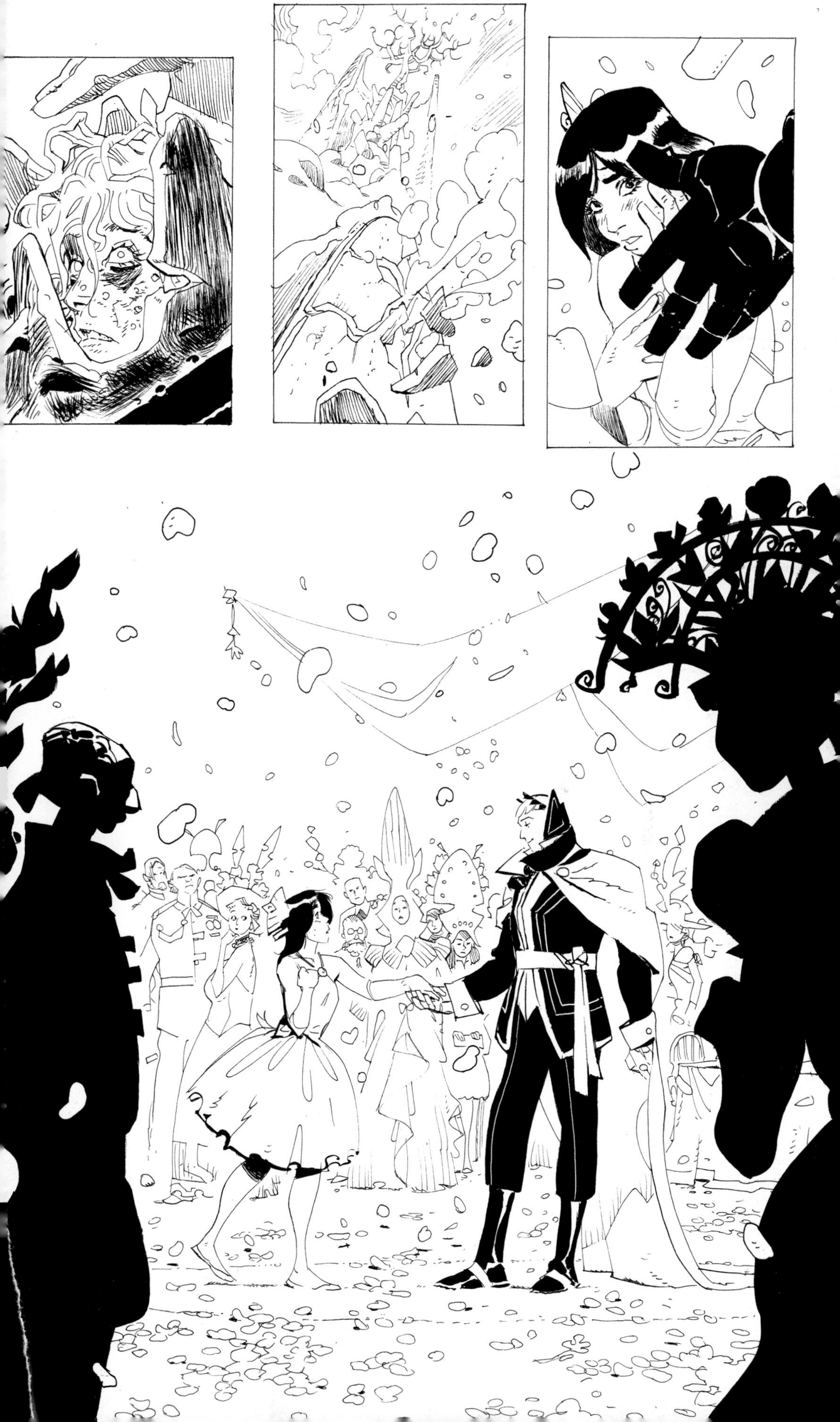

## ISSUE 4, PAGE 10

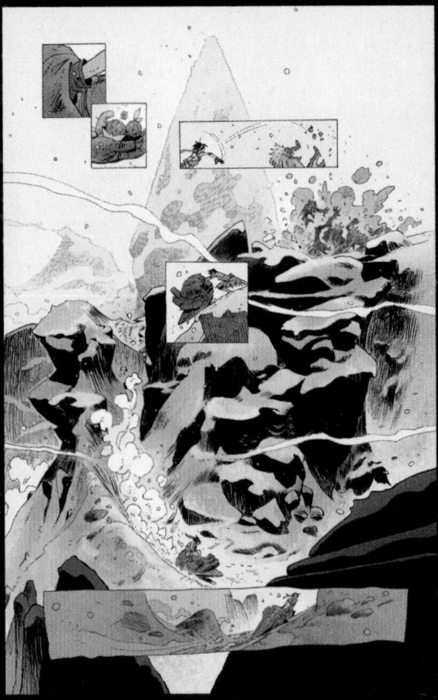

**10.1:** She pulls several old SNACKS from her pockets (or sleeves). The food she took from the ball. She'd forgotten it was even there.

**10.2:** She THROWS the snacks towards the beasts. One or two of them already snapping as they fly past, on instinct. Others sniffing the air.

**10.3:** Wider. The WOLVES in the f/g, FIGHTING with each other over the morsels. In the b/g the girl picking herself up, slinking away.

**10.4:** Wider still. The girl hurries onwards, ever-upwards, colder and colder, leaving the wolves far behind.

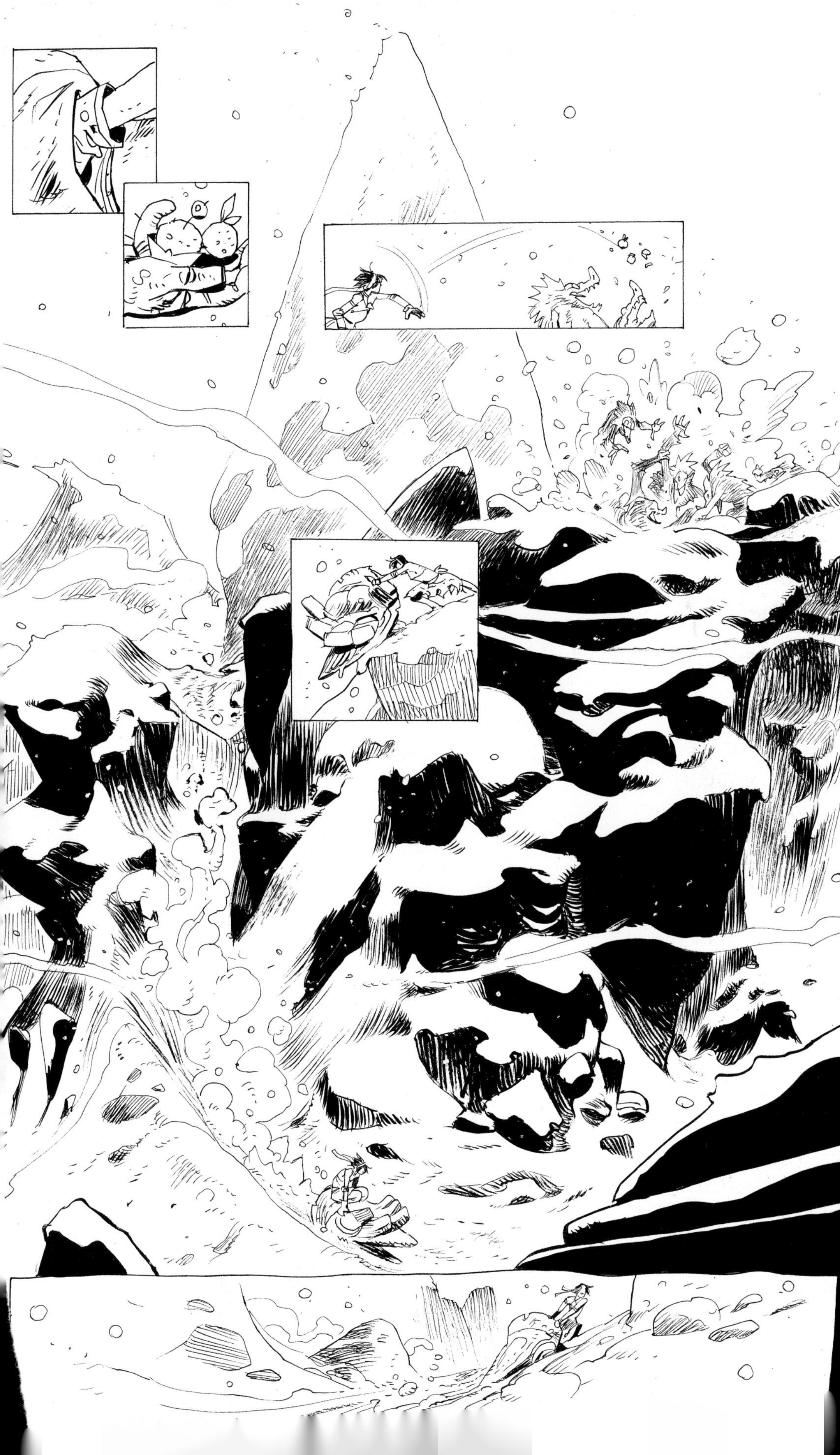

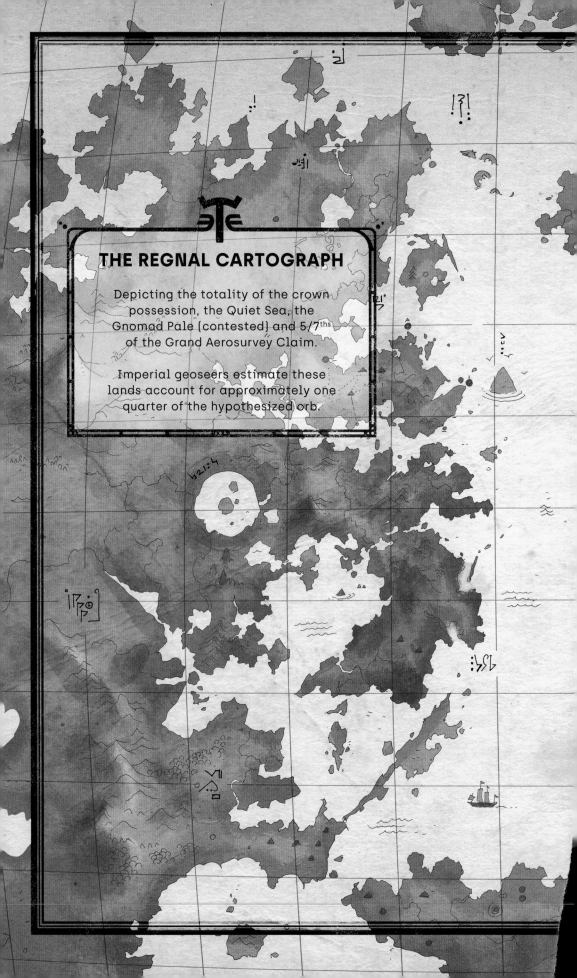

## THE REGNAL CARTOGRAPH

Depicting the totality of the crown possession, the Quiet Sea, the Gnomad Pale (contested) and 5/7ths of the Grand Aerosurvey Claim.

Imperial geoseers estimate these lands account for approximately one quarter of the hypothesized orb.

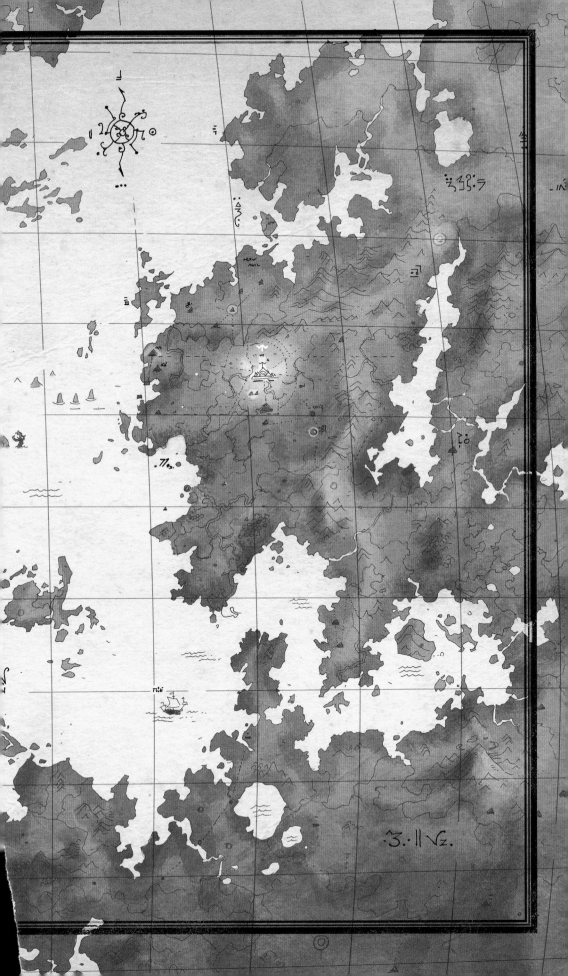

# STEP BY BLOODY STEP

## THE CREATORS

## MATÍAS BERGARA

ART

Born and still residing in Montevideo, Uruguay, Matías Bergara has been illustrating comics for several different publishers since 2008, after leaving a career in literature. Co-creator of *Coda* (2018).

## SIMON SPURRIER

STORY

A novelist, screenwriter and graphic novelist based near London, UK. His comics work ranges from award-winning runs on franchise properties such as *Star Wars* and *X-Men*, to original creator-owned works like *Coda*, *The Spire*, CRY HAVOC and *The Rush*.

He is normally much wordier than this.

## MATHEUS LOPES
### COLOR

Born in Brazil in '91, Matheus Lopes
has worked as a professional
colorist since 2012. It's the only
job he's ever had.

## EMMA PRICE
### DESIGN

A multidisciplinary
graphic designer and
illustrator, Emma has
created logos and comics
for Image Comics, Vertigo,
Best Jackett Press and
Aftershock Comics. When
not designing, she can
be found shivering in the
English sea.

## JIM CAMPBELL
### GLYPHOLOGY

A professional letterer since 2009, Jim
Campbell has been nominated for Ringo,
Tripwire and two Eisner awards. His work
can be found in 2000AD, and in many
fine books from BOOM, ComiXology
Originals, Dark Horse, Image, Oni,
Titan, and Vault. He lives, works, and
occasionally sleeps, in a small English
market town with a nice pub at the end
of the road.

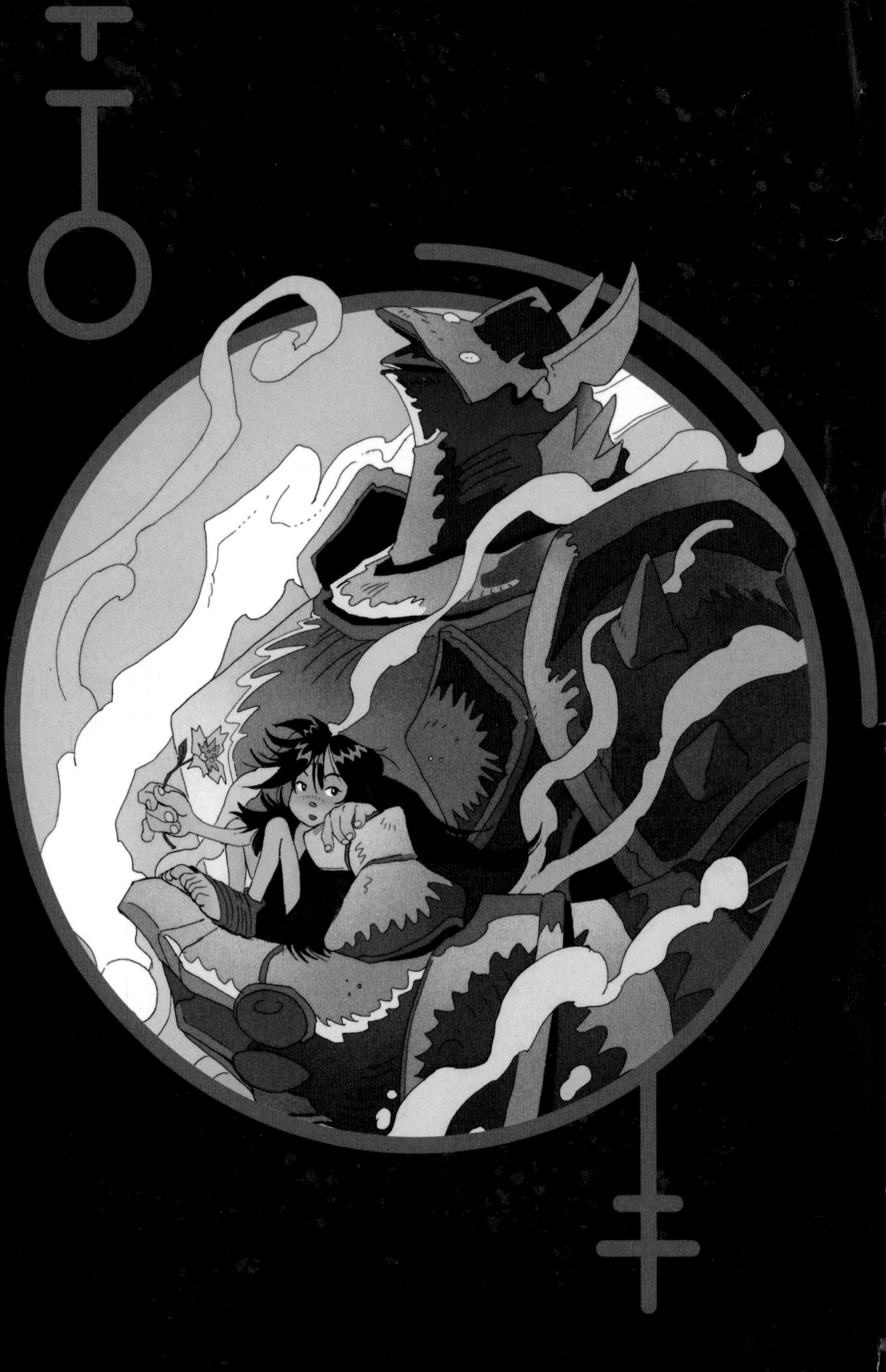

ART Ine Fragueiro